A MINOR FALL

A NOVEL

PRICE AINSWORTH

SELECTBOOKS, INC.
NEW YORK

This edition published by SelectBooks, Inc.

For information address SelectBooks, Inc., New York, New York.

First Edition

ISBN 978-1-59079-409-8

Library of Congress Cataloging-in-Publication Data

Names: Ainsworth, Price, author.
Title: A minor fall / Price Ainsworth.
Description: First edition. | New York : SelectBooks, 2017.
Identifiers: LCCN 2016040713 | ISBN 9781590794098 (hardback)
Subjects: LCSH: Personal injury lawyers--Fiction. | Values--Fiction. |
Deception--Fiction. | Meaning (Psychology)--Fiction. | Houston
(Tex.)--Fiction. | BISAC: FICTION / Legal. | GSAFD: Legal stories.
Classification: LCC PS3601.I58 M56 2017 | DDC 813/.6--dc23 LC record
available at https://lccn.loc.gov/2016040713

Text design by Pauline Neuwirth, Neuwirth & Associates, Inc.

Manufactured in the United States of America

10 9 8 7 6 5 4 3 2 1

For Dad

PART I

WHAT I ALWAYS SAY . . .

And it came to pass in an eveningtide, that David
arose from off his bed, and walked upon the roof of
the King's house: and from the roof, he saw a woman
washing herself; and the woman was very beautiful to
look upon.

—2 Samuel 11:2

1

I LEARNED TO TRY PERSONAL INJURY LAWSUITS BY WATCHING TIM Sullivan try personal injury lawsuits. I borrowed his phrases. I copied his outlines. I plagiarized his closings as if memorizing lines from a poem or a Shakespearean play back in high school. Relying on stock questions and uniform transitions that I had stolen from a leading partner of the Peters & Sullivan Law Firm gave me time to think about what I was going to say or do next.

It didn't take me long to learn that despite the stress associated with travel to unknown venues, unexpected rulings by unfamiliar judges, and unfavorable verdicts from hostile juries, cases would fall into a comfortable pattern at trial. The courtroom, any courtroom, became familiar to me, and I felt at home there. Of course, when the unexpected happened, as it invariably did at trial, I learned to pass it off as inconsequential and to show no emotion in front of the jury other than righteous indignation.

The experienced trial lawyer becomes so adept at this practiced stoicism that he's able to convince himself he can fix whatever has just happened. The underdog psyche is characterized by telling yourself some evidence in your briefcase will rebut a point or the last juror on the back row is still on your side, if only because of your innate charm and charisma. You rationalize. You press on. Sure, when you look back on the trial with the passage of time, you can point to the moment when things started to go south; but during the trial, in the heat of the conflict, you convince yourself that you can still win the case. After the trial, over cocktails with Sullivan, I would explain to him what went wrong and how at the time I thought I could fix it. He would always say, "Davy, do not shit thyself."

While during the trial you might not let yourself accept the fact that some unexpected testimony had just torpedoed the case, there are instances when you know you are about to win. It is a moment of ecstasy and relief. I was on the verge of one of those moments. I could feel it.

It was a Friday morning in late February of 2005. I was twenty-nine years old. This was the third day of trial in the new Harris County civil courts building in Houston, Texas. A jury sat dispassionately in olive-green leather chairs in the jury box. Some jurors rocked back and forth. A mottled green, burgundy-flecked, gold-streaked commercial carpet, darkened by the purple shadows of the long counsel tables and empty pews intended for onlookers, dampened any noise in the room. I sat with my client, Jorge Alvarado, at the plaintiff's table. This, like the rest of the cases I had tried in my short "career," was a civil suit seeking money damages as compensation for an injury. Defense counsel was Gregory Gath, a towering man twenty years my senior who proudly claimed to have gone to law school "back in Philadelphia." He had just passed the witness, Mrs. Andrea Alvarado. The judge was a passive old man named Benjamin Elam. He had thick bifocals and a grey smoker's complexion.

I was not supposed to win this case. Judge Elam knew it. Mr. Gath knew it. Mr. Sullivan knew it when he assigned the case to me for trial. My client, an ironworker, had stepped backwards through a hole in a warehouse roof. He had fallen eighteen feet onto his neck and head. Knocked unconscious, Jorge suffered a brain injury that had kept him from working since the incident.

Damages weren't the problem. In fact, I led off our case with damages testimony.

Jorge's supervisor testified about what a hard worker Jorge was. I played the videotaped deposition of one of Jorge's treating physicians, a psychiatrist. Jorge's testimony had gone pretty well, despite the fact that I thought he might have smoked a little marijuana, perhaps self-medicating, on his way to the courthouse the day before. His wife Andrea's testimony had gone very well. She was a licensed vocational nurse. She had maintained consistent employment, some dozen years before the incident and during the two years since, while managing to care for their two small kids and Jorge. Her description of the changes in Jorge's personality since the fall had been dramatic. Gath, despite his Yankee superiority, had not laid a glove on her.

Liability was the problem. I had sued the general contractor, a large employer in Houston. They had subcontracted the roof construction job to a group of ironworkers. Jorge, who worked for the subcontractor, had cut the hole in the roof a few days earlier so that he and other construction workers could get on the roof of this warehouse project near the shipping channel. The point of the case was that the general contractor bore some responsibility for not marking the hole in the roof and securing it from accidents, a requirement spelled out in black and white in the Occupational Safety and Health Administration (OSHA) code. That code violation probably wouldn't be much help in a case involving the person who put the hole there in the first place. Why did he need a warning about the hole he had made? The nature of Jorge's injury was, however, was such that he was unable to recall cutting the hole, and it was unlikely that any of his fellow ironworkers would offer testimony that would hurt his case. While none of them would lie about who made the hole, they would probably (conveniently) not remember who made the hole, understanding that the next case in which they were called to testify could well be their own.

It was clear to me that Gath intended to win his case by cross-examining my OSHA expert witness, a kindly old man who was pacing the hallway outside the courtroom wishing he could go outside and smoke a cigarette. I had to call the expert to prove up the OSHA regulation; but, if I called the expert, Gath would prove that Jorge had most likely cut the very hole in the roof through which he fell.

I was supposed to lose most of the cases on my docket. I worked for a top-drawer plaintiff's personal injury law firm in downtown Houston. The firm's business thrived on the referral of cases from other lawyers. Usually, a referral lawyer with a good case also had one or two not-so-good cases that he wanted to refer . . . that is, get rid of. This cow-and-a-calf approach to getting business led Sullivan and his seven partners to hire eight young attorneys, including me. The firm assigned an associate to each partner.

Admittedly, I was something of an afterthought, younger than the others, and perhaps more naïve. Still, I wanted what they wanted: the trappings of success, including power, prestige, and possessions. Sullivan and the other partners handled the good cases. The associates handled the others, and from time to time we assisted the partners at trial. Among the associates there was an intense, albeit at that point good-natured, competition to prove ourselves worthy of handling better cases. We were each trying to win a few of these impossible cases, attempting to distinguish ourselves from our peers.

We kept the associates' files in one large file room. In the back of the room, the associates had constructed a small shrine to St. Jude, the patron saint of hopeless causes, complete with a small figurine of the saint purchased at a local religious bookstore and votive candles that those of us on the "St. Jude Squad" threatened to light from time to time but never did. Handwritten on a sheet of letterhead taped to the table where the little figurine sat was the prayer, "St. Jude: Come to our assistance that we may receive the consolation and succor of Heaven in all our needs, trials, and sufferings." Jorge's file sat in that room for a considerable amount of time.

Apparently, I had been contemplating my next move at trial for what must have been a considerable amount of time. I awoke from my daydreaming to hear the judge clearing his throat and saying to me across the valley between the raised bench and the counsel tables, "Mr. Jessie. Mr. Jessie. Please call your next witness." It was a bit of a gamble, but I called the defendant's corporate representative to the stand. Gath had introduced the young man to the jury panel during jury selection. I had flipped through the discovery materials in my file at that time to determine that he was the safety director for the general contractor. His name was Anderson because his daddy owned the company. He had a civil engineering degree from Texas A&M University. He also had attended a Presbyterian seminary.

I had five points to make with the witness. There was plenty of time before the next break, so I saved my best point for last. First, I went through the obtuse language in the OSHA code. Yes, the general contractor had a responsibility to see that such holes in the roof were covered, cordoned off, or protected by a railing put around the roof opening. I glanced at the jury, noting that they weren't particularly impressed. The next three points dealt with specific references to the company's safety manual, which reiterated the OSHA requirements and discussed the fact that the general contractor had an obligation to see that the subcontractors' employees abided by the general contractor's safety directives. Again, there was little interest on the part of the jury, even though one of the references included a "lunchbox safety lecture" that depicted a worker falling backwards through an unguarded hole in a roof.

The fifth point, however, would hit its mark. "Let's see if you can agree with me, Mr. Anderson, and my summary of your testimony thus far. As safety director of Anderson Construction, you would agree, wouldn't you, that Anderson's obligation under OSHA was to cover the hole, cordon it off, or put in a railing around the opening?"

"Yes," he said flatly.

"The failure to cover the hole was a violation of a federal law designed to protect workers like Mr. Alvarado."

"Well, our obligation is principally to our company employees rather than the subcontractor's employees, but, yes, that is a correct statement."

"Thank you. Further, Anderson's failure to cover the hole, cordon it off or put up a railing was a violation of the concepts stated in your own company's safety manual, a manual that you helped prepare."

"That's correct."

"But, Anderson violated a standard much older than any standard of conduct stated in your policy manual, didn't it?"

"I don't understand what it is you're asking," Anderson said, as he shifted his weight in the witness chair and raised his hands with both palms up.

I ignored him. "Anderson violated a standard that predates the OSHA Act, didn't it?"

He hesitated to respond, shrugging his shoulders and shaking his head from side to side indicating that he was not following my question. I doubted that anybody in the courtroom was following my question. I continued with what I thought was just the right amount of righteous indignation. "Anderson violated a standard of conduct older than the laws of the State of Texas, the Constitution of the United States, the Magna Carta, or even the New Testament. Isn't that right?" While he hesitated again, I turned to the jury, and an older woman on the front row had raised one hand and was waving it in front of her as I had seen women do back in Abilene at the Church of Christ when I was growing up. "You violated Deuteronomy, didn't you, Mr. Anderson?"

"I . . . I . . ." he stammered, but I didn't wait for a reply. I pulled a worn Bible out of a briefcase and turned to a Post-it marked page. The Bible was mine. I'd had it since I was a teenager. The briefcase, actually an old catalogue case with the firm name printed on the side, belonged to Sullivan. I had a nice briefcase that my younger brother had given to me when I had graduated from law school in 2002. But I thought it was too shiny and new to carry to trial, so I always pulled one of Sullivan's beat up-old catalogue cases out of Sullivan's closet to take to trial because I thought that it made me look more like a seasoned trial lawyer.

"Deuteronomy is sometimes referred to as "books of the laws" in the Old Testament, isn't it, sir?"

Gath stood up and shouted out, "Objection, Deuteronomy?"

"You know the Bible, the Old Testament, the Ten Commandments, and all that, Mr. Gath—adultery, murder . . . " I interrupted.

"I know what the Ten Commandments are, but what do they have to do with . . ." Gath began asking while attempting to button his suit coat around his ample midsection.

"Your Honor," I interjected, "there is case law in Texas supporting examination of an adverse witness about recognized standards of conduct. It so happens that there is a standard set forth in a Biblical passage. I can tie this up with a few questions."

"Very well, you may proceed, Mr. Jessie," said Judge Elam, with a hint of a smile revealing his yellow-stained teeth.

I turned back to face the witness and waited for his answer.

"That's right," Anderson said.

"And that same book, Deuteronomy, tells us in Chapter 22, Verse 8, that, 'When thou buildest a new house, then thou shalt make a battlement for thy roof, that thou bring not blood upon thine house, if any man fall from thence,' doesn't it?" I asked, looking up from my reading.

"That's what it says," he responded. "Some versions use the word 'parapet.' "

"Anderson Construction was building a roof, correct?" Sullivan always said to the associates, "Hit the witness over the head with a flat rock."

"Correct."

"You know what a battlement or parapet is, don't you?" I asked, nodding my head up and down.

"Yes," he said nodding his head along with me, "it's a protective railing."

"The failure to put a protective railing around the hole in this warehouse roof was a violation of OSHA regulations, your own company's policies, and even the dictates of Deuteronomy. Isn't that right, Mr. Anderson?"

"I guess so," he whispered in a barely audible response.

"Let me check my notes, Your Honor; but I don't think that I have any more questions for this witness," I said, and I grabbed a pen and scrawled a note on my legal pad. The note told my expert witness to leave the courthouse at once to avoid a subpoena from Gath. I folded the note, wrote the expert's name on it, and handed it to Mrs. Alvarado in the front row. I whispered to her to take it to my expert out in the hallway. "No further questions, Your Honor."

The old judge smiled his tobacco-stained smile at me and turned to Gath.

"Your witness, Mr. Gath."

"We'll reserve our questions for our case in chief, Judge," Gath replied in an overly courteous Philadelphia-lawyer tone that couldn't conceal his anger with the witness. The defense still had to put on its case, and both sides had to do their closing arguments, but I was going to win. I knew it, and Gath knew it. The only question was, how much would the jury award? I thought that the woman on the front row wouldn't let the numbers drop too low. I couldn't wait to tell my wife. I couldn't wait to regale the St. Jude Squad about my exploits of the afternoon, but first I had to argue the case, and the jury still had to make its rulings.

Like all beginning lawyers, I thought that the closing argument was the most important part of the case. Usually, it was the most fun part. I had spent several hours the night before putting my thoughts together for my argument, and I had tried to practice my closing that morning while facing the mirror and putting on the red-and-blue striped tie that I intended to wear with my navy blazer and grey slacks.

I was so distracted by my concern about my appearance that I did not accomplish much by way of rehearsal. I was just average looking—average height, average build, average features. I still looked very young, though I was not as thin as I had been in law school, and I had some difficulty buttoning the collar button on the starched white, buttoned-down oxford shirt. In my mind, I always pictured my short hair, parted on the left, as a deeper, richer color than the dull brown that it actually was. Should I get some of that shampoo with henna in it? My eyes, which looked brown from a distance, were really a mottled green and brown when I looked at them closely in the mirror. I thought that I was okay looking, but I wished that I looked older and more distinguished. My skin was fair, more rosy than ruddy. I shaved every day, but I probably could have gotten away with shaving every other day, and my jaw line was almost square.

The problem with my face, and I had never pointed this out to anyone, including my wife Michelle, was that it looked to me like the right side of my jaw was becoming more prominent than my left. Was my face becoming lopsided? Did anybody else have this problem? Maybe that was why all those old paintings of retired judges at the courthouse showed the men leaning unnaturally on a fist at their chin. If the left side of my brain, the logical side, controlled the right side of my body, maybe I was becoming deformed because I was not paying enough attention to the creative right side of my brain. Maybe I should finish that poem I was always starting. Maybe I should dust off a draft of one of those short stories I wrote in college. I kept a copy of one, the best one I thought, at the bottom of my underwear drawer and sometimes would take it out and read it. It seemed syrupy and innocent, but maybe with a few changes . . . I used to think I would be a writer or a poet or something creative.

One of the reasons I had wanted to become a trial lawyer was the storytelling part of the job. The first lines of my unfinished poem weren't bad either, I thought, but so far there were only two lines, and, well, the first line was borrowed (that is, plagiarized). Rather than working on my closing, I stared at myself in the mirror, turned my chin from side to side, and vowed to start chewing my food on the left side only so that I would build up my left jaw line. And I might work on that poem when I got the chance.

The *Alvarado* case was the first time I recognized that jurors usually make up their minds before the closing arguments take place. The arguments just reinforce the jurors' positions and give them ammunition in their deliberations to confront the jurors who disagree with them. Gath's closing argument concentrated on damages. He reminded the jury that the fall did not cause any broken bones. He argued that the fall should be considered minor, not because of the distance the man fell, but because of the minimal objective impact it had on him.

Because I thought I was winning on liability, I also focused my argument on damages. I talked to the jury about the insidious nature of closed head injuries: the personality changes, the loss of memory, the loss of focus and the inability to maintain attention, the frustration with being unable to do the simple tasks that you were able to do before the injury, the embarrassment of not being able to provide for your family, the humiliation of having your spouse care for you like a child, the likelihood of a subsequent accident, and the ever-present fear of having another epileptic seizure in front of your kids. I tried to explain to the jury that while Mr. Alvarado did not have broken bones or bleeding cuts, he was a broken man, and his injured body part, his brain, was responsible for performing the most important functions of life. I did not discuss my theory as to how one could tell by looking at him which side of Jorge's brain was more damaged than the other.

The jury paid attention to what I was saying, but the only part of my argument that elicited a response from the jury was the part I plagiarized from Sullivan. I think he stole it from Scotty Baldwin, a legendary trial lawyer in East Texas who was a generation older than Sullivan. The argument goes something like this:

Ladies and gentlemen: you've been a good jury. You've paid attention to the evidence and I'm sure that you've been diligent in following the court's instructions. Judge Elam has instructed you each evening not to discuss the case with anyone, including your spouse. Now, I'm looking at this question on the verdict form that asks you what amount of money damages should be awarded to Mrs. Alvarado for her loss of "consortium," that is "the mutual right of the husband and wife to that affection, solace, comfort, companionship, society, assistance, sexual relations, emotional support, love, and felicity necessary to a successful marriage." I won't suggest to you what amount of money you ought to put in that blank, but I will tell you that, after you return your verdict, the judge is going to lift the restriction regarding talking to your spouse. You need to put a number in here of which you will be *proud*.

A couple of the jurors grinned, and the lady in the front row laughed.

2

I GOT TO BRENNAN'S ABOUT 7:00 P.M., AFTER THE JURY HAD RETURNED its verdict thirty minutes earlier. Brennan's was about halfway between the courthouse and my home. It was an upscale restaurant with incredible Creole entrees, impeccable service, and intimate tables for dining. It was the setting for the lunch scene in the movie *Terms of Endearment*. It was owned by a member of the family that owns Commander's Palace, Mr. B's Bistro, and other restaurants in New Orleans. We ate there sometimes. But the main reason we went there was to meet in the bar and spill out onto the brick-covered patio (which we referred to as the "brickyard") to smoke cigars, drink scotch, and find out what was going on in the Houston legal community.

I handed the valet the keys to my car, nodded to the tuxedoed maitre'd, and cruised down the short hallway to the bar, stopping only to sample a praline from the platter that always sat on the buffet in the hallway. I was walking on air. I could see two of the associates from my firm in one corner with other lawyers our age, but before I could say anything, Mr. Whiskers, the bartender, shouted, "Davy Jessie, the Duke of Deuteronomy."

Everyone in the bar laughed, and a few even clapped. I don't know how he already knew about the testimony or the verdict, but Mr. Whiskers, so-nicknamed for his resplendent Mr. French-like beard, knew a lot of things. He could tell you the over and under on the Bucks/ Bobcats game. He could take your bet on anything ranging from sporting events to the next day's Dow to the outcome of local trials. He could tell you what every state representative from Harris County liked to drink. The rumor was that Jack Nicholson still called him from time to time.

I stopped at the bar, and he handed me a Famous Grouse on ice. He poured himself a shot, and we clinked our glasses together. "Boy, I'd hate to be your wife tonight," he said, laughing and tucking his thumbs into the armholes of the colorful silk vest that stretched over his round belly. I nodded for him to top off my glass, and after he did, I eased over to my group in the corner.

"Two hundred and fifty thousand dollars on that dog? That case wasn't worth that amount before tort reform." Eli said, as I pulled an unoccupied chair over from a neighboring table.

"That's what I call 'consolation and succor,'" Rod said.

"Compensation and succor," Eli said laughing.

"Compensation that doesn't succor for once," Rod added.

"I argued for more," I said. "They might have given me more, if I'd argued for less. They gave the wife almost as much for consortium as they gave the husband for a closed head injury."

"Don't second-guess it, man. That's a home-fucking-run," Eli replied. He had been hired by the firm two years before I had. He already had a couple of substantial verdicts. That, and because he was assigned to Peters, the senior-most partner in the firm, made Eli the senior member of our group. The other associate from our firm who was at the table was Rod Day. He was probably my best friend in town, and he was smiling from ear to ear, genuinely excited for me.

"Hey, didn't I take the psychiatrist's deposition in that case?" Eli asked, and I nodded. I could tell that Eli was calculating in his head what part of the potential fee would be apportioned to him in his annual "fee column," the report card the partners used to grade the associates' efforts.

Another young lawyer at the table, a grey-suited, prematurely balding young man employed at one of the large defense firms in town, asked, "Where did you ever get that Deuteronomy stuff?"

"Sullivan," Rod said, before I could. He knew I was assigned to Sullivan. "He always says it in speeches against tort reform, claiming that even the Old Testament sanctified the tort system. Still," he said, turning to me and raising his beer glass, "it was pure genius to remember to use it in a fall-from-a-roof case."

"I got lucky. The safety director had been to seminary."

"Have you talked to Michelle?" Rod asked.

"I called her from the car. She's on her way over," I said.

We sat in the bar for about an hour, with different lawyers sitting down and replacing others as they left. Each replacement required a re-telling of that day's trial story. Several people asked about Gath's reaction to the verdict. Most of us figured it served him right. No doubt, he had signed on to the case telling the insurance company for the general contractor that he expected either Peters or Sullivan to try the case. By the time Michelle got there, you'd have thought I'd won *Pennzoil v. Texaco*.

I didn't see her come in, but I felt her put her arm around me, and I stood up to give her a kiss. She was beaming with pride. Red-haired and green-eyed, it was her engaging smile that I had first noticed when her brother Jonathan introduced us the third day of law school in the fall of 1999 in the "Keeton Casino," the lunchroom at The University of Texas School of Law. Michelle's smile was perfect, no doubt the result of expensive, cosmetic dentistry and early orthodontics. Like me, she had worn her navy blazer that day, but she had matched hers with a light wool flannel, black watch skirt and a crisp, light-blue pinpoint oxford. She often wore dark green colors like the hunter-green stripe in the black watch because they set off her hair and made her eyes sparkle. The brass buttons on the blazer shined in the bar light like the gold of the small, tasteful Rolex watch that her parents had given her for law school graduation.

After we sat down, Mr. Whiskers brought over a bottle of champagne and told us that Sullivan had called it in with his congratulations. I wondered even at the time if Sullivan had really ordered the champagne. Sullivan had spent far more time in this bar than I ever would, and I'm sure Mr. Whiskers would have had carte blanche to put the bottle on Sullivan's tab. I always tried to be careful about what I said or did at Brennan's. I don't know if Mr. Whiskers still talked to Jack Nicholson or not, but I know that he talked to Sullivan. After a glass of champagne, Michelle escorted me out of the place. It took us several minutes to get to the front door because Michelle had to stop and talk to several of the patrons on our way out. Whiskers gave her a hug and called her "Sugar." We left my car, and Michelle said she would drive. I realized I had not eaten anything all day. "I'm starving," I said.

"We could stop and eat, if you want. I was thinking we might go home and start working on the next little Clarence Darrow," Michelle said.

I smiled. "I'll just get something at the house."

Michelle hadn't liked law school, and she disliked working for a large, downtown Houston firm even more. She liked the people she worked with well enough. It was the business part of the practice that she didn't like. She wanted to have a child. Though we had never really talked about it, I assumed that the plan was that she would stop working at that point. We had put off getting married until after I had finished a federal clerkship and taken a job. We had put off having a child until our careers were on track. Now did seem like a good time. "Did all the associates in your firm show up tonight?" she asked as we stepped outside onto the red brick steps that went up to the front door at Brennan's. A parking valet pulled up in Michelle's car and I fished a couple of dollars out of the breast pocket of my blazer when he came around and opened the passenger door for me.

"Only Eli and Rod," I said as we fastened our seatbelts and Michelle put the car into drive. "It's Friday night, after all. I'm sure Ozzie (our nickname for Franklin Ozem, III) had something to do. The brickyard really isn't his scene. I don't know where the others were."

"What did Eli say about the case?" she asked. When I told her about the home-fucking-run comment, she kissed me and whispered, "Well, let's run home and fuck." She had the ability (I don't know if it was learned or inherited) to turn a phrase, and it was usually funny, dirty, or sexy or some combination of all three. I will never forget the first time I saw her naked. While the hair on her head was a luxurious, deep red, her pubic hair was a bright, orange-flame color. "Lots of women have Dorito chips," she said, "But how many have nacho cheese flavor? Makes you just want to lick your fingers, doesn't it?" And of course, involuntarily, I put my fingers to my lips.

Michelle's small Lexus sedan pulled away from the curb. "I wonder why Lawyer Sullivan didn't show up this evening?" she asked, as she turned onto Smith Street and eased onto the Southwest Freeway. I hadn't said anything, but that question had crossed my mind as well. I had wanted Sullivan to hear the others toasting my success at trial, but there would be plenty of time on Monday morning to tell the story at the office at least once more.

3

MICHELLE AND I MADE LOVE before we ever got to our bedroom. That was not unusual for us. We probably had more sex on a gold damask sofa that she had back in law school than at any other location. She explained the first time we sat on the couch that the fabric was an acanthus leaf pattern—I didn't recall ever having seen an acanthus plant growing wild in Abilene or Lubbock. We had been with each other long enough to know what the other liked and wanted during sex, and we enjoyed being with each other. I couldn't remember when we had last had sex, so we were obviously overdue.

It might have been the smile she first gave me that first brought us together, but it was something else that kept us together and resulted in our getting married. I loved her almost as much as she loved me. Somehow, she seemed more capable of love. She was always open and honest and somewhat vulnerable. She was passionate, almost to the point of being volatile. If she was happy, you knew it. If she was upset, you knew it. Her wide, pretty, expressive face always gave you a clear indication of what she was thinking—a trait trial lawyers and card players practice to eliminate. She made no pretense of wanting to be a trial lawyer. Her background may have equipped her to appreciate the skills required to be effective at the gamesmanship, but she wasn't about winning or losing.

At fifty, she might struggle with various diets and exercise regimens, but at twenty-nine, Michelle exuded a voluptuous ripeness that was intoxicating and virtually irresistible. We used to laugh at the number of times she could go to the liquor store and come away with what the proprietor called his "pretty-girl discount." I'm sure she never paid for a drink in a bar, and I doubt that she ever received a traffic citation that wasn't reduced to a warning by the time the officer completed the paperwork.

That is not to say that she was flirtatious or acted in any way that would upset other women. She made friends easily. It was because of her warmth. Her outgoing manner, broad smile, and willing embrace drew you in to her. But, from the first time I touched her, I sensed that her skin was slightly warmer to the touch than my skin, or anybody else's, for that matter. If 98.6 degrees Fahrenheit is normal body temperature, Michelle's never dipped below 99 degrees. It made you want to hold her, to caress her, to make love to her. Michelle was the personification of that feeling you get just when the sun goes down on a hot, humid July day in Houston and the fecund air feels rich, fertile, and full of possibilities.

If there were problems in our marriage, and by all outward appearances, there were none, they probably stemmed from our mutual ability to avoid conflicts with each other. I'm sure that is a trait that Michelle learned from her family having to deal with her father. From time to time, Michelle's mother must have wondered what Michelle's father was up to, but she never discussed her concerns directly with her kids. I spent my time, both at the office and at home, trying to convince those around me that I was confident and self-assured. Michelle and I might get irritated with each other occasionally, but we never really argued about anything. I could always tell when she was upset about something, but that doesn't mean that we ever addressed what the underlying cause might have been.

Obviously our family and my work situation were going to be a problem at some point, but we never discussed it. At twenty-nine, Michelle was approaching a decision point where she would have to decide if she was going to choose a partnership track or a mommy track at the firm where she worked. An unspoken animosity festered between the female lawyers in her firm that had chosen one track over the other. I could see the women in the firm attempting to recruit Michelle to each side. I thought that I already knew which option she would pick, but she had not said anything officially or to her employers. It appeared to me that most of the women who picked the mommy track eventually left the firm. I don't know if there just wasn't much call for part-time lawyers or if the requirements of looking after kids made it impossible to work as a lawyer even on a part-time basis. I knew that Michelle wouldn't leave the office until she finished whatever had been assigned to her, and I didn't see how she would be able to balance the need for perfection at work with the need to be at home with kids.

I assumed that, whichever track Michelle ultimately chose, it was incumbent upon me to go to work and make money. She might have been faced with a difficult choice, but I didn't see myself as having any. Watching Tim Sullivan made it clear to me that if I was going to be a successful trial lawyer, there were going to be many occasions when I would not be available for my family, with or without kids.

Most non-lawyers think that lawyers create conflicts. Sullivan always said that a small town will support two lawyers before it will support one. But the truth is that lawyers are hired to resolve disputes, not create them. Perhaps it was a bit ironic that two people in the conflict resolution business chose to avoid conflicts in their personal lives. Our friends, most of whom were colleagues or people Michelle knew from growing up in Houston, saw us as a model couple, and we spent considerable effort in trying to maintain that image. We lived in the right house, drove the right cars, wore the right clothes, and even attended the right church. Lately, the notion that it was time for us to have a baby consumed our marriage. We talked about that a lot, but we never talked about what would happen after that.

I thought that Michelle saw having a baby as an opportunity for her to stop practicing law, at least eventually, and devote herself to raising a child. I guessed that was what she wanted. I knew this is what she thought she was supposed to do. I wanted to have a baby because I thought Michelle wanted to have a baby. I had not figured out how I was going to be available at five o'clock every evening to coach Little League, but I looked forward to doing that, as my father had done. I told myself it would work out, or I would figure out some way to make it work.

Without discussion, we had left the condoms upstairs in the drawer of the nightstand again on the night of the *Alvarado* verdict, just as we had been doing for the last three months on those occasions when our schedules permitted us to have sex.

At the office on Monday, I sat at my desk, returned calls, and read mail until about 10:30. I decided that nobody was going to congratulate me anymore about my win without prompting, so I went to the kitchen, got some coffee, and drifted down to Mr. Peters' office. I knocked and went in. Mr. Peters was not there, but three associates were. They were standing around the antique telescope in Mr. Peters' office, taking turns looking through it. A warm sun glistened against the high-rise window.

"Davy," Eli said, "you've got to check this out." They had focused the telescope on the rooftop swimming pool of the Four Seasons Hotel, twenty floors below. While July and August can be unbearable in Houston, late February can be glorious—warm and bright, with everybody getting a jump on summer activities like golf and sunbathing that much of the country can only imagine while sloshing through frozen bus stops and train stations. The male lawyers in New York had only their dog-eared copies of the *Sports Illustrated* swimsuit issue. We had the real thing.

Several women were around the pool that morning, and more seemed to be coming out and positioning themselves in reclining chairs to face the sun. As I stood back from the telescope awaiting my turn, I looked out across the skyline and wondered how many bankers, lawyers, accountants, and energy traders were doing just what the four of us were doing. Identifying the women by the color of the few small pieces of clothing they were wearing, we rated the women on their desirability. The morning's consensus winner, a dark-haired, already tanned beauty in a revealing, multicolored two-piece, got up and left as a group of new arrivals began taking up the empty chairs. We took that as a sign that it was time for us to start thinking about lunch.

Eight of us had started at the firm within two years of each other. We were colleagues and friends, but there was an acknowledged level of rivalry among us. Each of us knew that the amount of money we brought into the firm constituted our grade, and we competed to see who could get the best cases assigned to him, who could turn the cases the quickest and for the most money, and who could curry the most favor from the partners who ran the firm. The competition was somewhat diluted by the fact that each of us had been paired with a different partner, but I understood that the competition among the associates was a reflection of the more intense competition that was taking place among the partners. Of course, each of these levels of competition resulted in more and more money being brought into the firm, thereby benefiting all of the partners, and, in theory, all of the associates. In the end, it was all about money, and that fact was certainly acknowledged.

Each of the associates except Rod was new to Houston. We had all finished clerkships with federal judges or the Texas Supreme Court or had short stints with prestigious defense firms. We all came from good law schools and middle-class or upper middle-class families that were proud to point to the first lawyer in the family, again with the exception of Rod, whose father was a respected trial lawyer himself. This was the first job that any of us held that actually put some money in our pockets. We were all passably good-looking. Admittedly, Rod was nothing less than handsome, and nobody, to my knowledge, but me had ever noticed my overly developed right jaw line. Having Sullivan's private tailor come by the office to outfit us in handmade suits and sport coats didn't hurt. The practice, despite the state legislature's attempts to "reform" the tort system to protect insurance companies and tortfeasors, was thriving. We saw ourselves as young princes, surveying our realm of Harris County. Life, in all of its abundance, was there for the taking.

We split up for lunch. I don't know where the other guys went. I was meeting my boss at Damian's, an expensive Italian restaurant where Sullivan ate four times a week. He had probably been there since it opened that day, but I knew he would not yet have ordered lunch. He was seated in the bar area with his female paralegal Theresa—Sullivan called her "Riza," and because he did, we all did—and three cronies who were defense lawyers from major firms around town. They were each drinking Sea Breezes.

As soon as Timothy Sullivan walked in the door, the staff at Damian's would shout their hellos, and the bartender would start scurrying around to slice up fresh grapefruits for the juicer. Sullivan didn't always drink Sea Breezes throughout lunch, but it was a good bet that he would start with one. The sweet, pulpy grapefruit juice blended with vodka and cranberry juice in a perfect combination that made for a good appetite and sometimes delirious afternoon. A phone for outgoing calls was discretely placed by Sullivan's table near the bar, and a never-ending stream of lawyers, businessmen, and politicians would drop by the table for a Sea Breeze or two and then blissfully drift off into the bright Houston sunshine.

Over the two years that I had worked for Sullivan, I learned a lot about people while I was sitting in that restaurant bar. Cases were considered, deals were made, arguments were held, and time was frittered away like so many used grapefruit rinds. One time, I remember a shoving match that resulted in one lawyer knocking another into a Jeroboam of red wine that had been displayed on an old Tuscan sideboard. The bottle broke, and what seemed like gallons of red wine flowed down the wall and escaped along the baseboards while several, white-jacketed busboys and waiters hurried to staunch the flow with white napkins. They wrung out the napkins into a grey, plastic tub that a busboy would use to clear a table. The maitre'd rushed over to apologize for placing the bottle in such an obviously precarious position, and he assured Mr. Sullivan that it wouldn't happen again. Peace resumed, and the bartender went back to slicing grapefruits to feed the steady whir of the juicer.

My purpose in coming to Damian's that day was not just to seek attention. Sullivan had left a message with my secretary Eileen telling me to join him regarding a new case we were taking.

As I walked into the bar, Sullivan waved at me and proclaimed to the others seated around the table, "Gentlemen, I believe you know my associate, Eugène de Rastignac?" I shook hands with the defense lawyers, said hello to Sullivan and Riza, and sat down. I heard a smiling Riza whisper to Sullivan, "Rastignac? Does that make you Goriot or Vautrin?" I was disappointed that I could not place the literary reference to the characters in Balzac's novels but was impressed that Riza could. Probably Sullivan had previously referred to someone by the name of Balzac's ambitious social climber in her presence, and in an effort to keep up, Riza had read Balzac's *La Comédie humaine* in its entirety. After a minute or two of pleasantries, the defense lawyers got up and left.

"Are y'all hungry yet?" Sullivan asked; and, without waiting for an answer, ordered us each a Sea Breeze. "We've got someone joining us in a few minutes, so let me tell you what's going on. By the way, good work on that *Alvarado* case."

Tim Sullivan was an almost distinguished looking, grey-headed man of sixty who always wore a coat and colorful tie, unless he was on the golf course. He had broad Irish hands that permitted him to lift a ball out of a deep rough, a ruddy complexion, and a thick waistline that was testament to the fact that he had enjoyed a professional lifetime of too many veal chops and excessive alcohol. While his suits were the expected $600-per-hour lawyer attire (navy or grey, chalk stripes in both, and brown gun check or grey Glen plaid on Fridays), his shirts and ties and suspenders were always outlandish combinations that would appear cartoon-like or foppish (or both) on others, but on him came across as an outgrowth of his flamboyant, winning personality. He was charming without effort, and usually smiling as if he had just heard a joke to which the rest of us were not privy. He could quote the Persian philosopher Omar Khayyám's *The Rubáiyát* at length. He never settled a case at mediation without exclaiming:

> Some for the Glories of This World; and some
> Sigh for the Prophet's Paradise to come;
> Ah, take the Cash, and let the Credit go,
> Nor heed the rumble of a distant Drum!

He could drink and not get drunk. He wore wire-rimmed glasses that he was always losing because he took them off or set them on his head to read. He could make conversation with anybody about anything, and he had the largest working vocabulary of anybody I had ever met.

I will never forget the trip to New York to take depositions where we spent the evenings at the King Cole Bar in the St. Regis Hotel with Sullivan conversing with the parade of humanity that sat down next to him at the bar in sequential fashion. Sullivan loved the art nouveau mural by Maxfield Parrish, and it seemed to me that Sullivan's role at the bar was not too different from King Cole's in the painting—listening to petitioners who came to him for advice. It did not matter who they were, men or women, executives or debutantes. In a few minutes, they knew each other and they told him very personal information. Sitting there quietly observing on my barstool, I almost came to the conclusion that each of the interviewed patrons had come there with the hope of meeting Sullivan and telling him something that they had been needing to tell someone.

During a short lull between bar patrons, Sullivan leaned over to me and whispered, "Human beings have a need to talk to someone. They want to know that somebody else agrees with them and is on their side. All those hours you spent in 'Trial Advocacy' class in law school . . . did anybody ever tell you where the word 'advocacy' comes from? I'm no Latin scholar, but don't you imagine it has something to do with 'adding a voice?' You can learn as much about 'advocating' sitting right here at this bar as you can in all the damn trial advocacy classes combined. You have to be able to talk to people to be able to advocate for them. Conversation can be man-to-man or woman-to-woman, but if it happens to be man to woman, and they are both practicing heterosexuals, then there's an extra spark. Watch," he said as a particularly pretty woman with an expensive haircut sat down next to him and put her small beaded purse on the bar.

He ordered her a glass of wine and tossed off a few trusty lines from Khayyám:

You know, my friends, with what a brave Carouse
I made a Second Marriage in my house;
Divorced old barren Reason from my Bed
And took the Daughter of the Vine to Spouse.

In a few minutes, the woman began telling Sullivan about how messy her recent divorce had been and how nasty her custody fight was going to be.

He could do the same thing when picking a jury.

In many ways, he was like a father to me in my early adulthood. I watched him, learned from him, and wanted to be like him. I found myself repeating phrases he used and mimicking his gestures. I downloaded *The Rubáiyát* off the Internet. Like my real father, he often gave me very good advice. But, unlike my real father, Sullivan was rich. He had all the trappings that wealth brought, and it was the trappings of wealth that I found so alluring. I laughed at him one time during trial, when a concerned tool pusher and his young wife explained to Sullivan in the hallway outside the courtroom that the in-trial settlement offer the defendant had just made was a lot of money to them. They understood that it was not that much to Sullivan, but to them, it was a fortune. I expected Sullivan, whom I thought sincerely cared about his clients, to say something like, "It's your case, and you have to decide what's best for you."

Instead, I was shocked when he told the young couple, "That's right. I'm richer than three feet up a bull's ass, but I didn't get that way making bad decisions on settling lawsuits. Now, get back in that courtroom, and let's get the case to the jury." Of course, the verdict, which was by no means a foregone conclusion, came back for the plaintiffs in an amount substantially greater than the offer.

"Thanks for the champagne. I guess the defendant will appeal," I said.

"Not if Gath can avoid it. I'll bet he doesn't want his name appearing on the reported case. I think you can settle that case, because Gath will get shit in his neck," Sullivan said knowingly. Many of Sullivan's favorite sayings contained the word "shit." "Getting shit in your neck" was how Sullivan described the emotional condition that panicked litigators suffered when they determined that they had better settle a case rather than continue to pursue it.

"Offer to drop the pre-judgment interest, and I predict he'll pay the verdict," Sullivan continued. "I can't see Gath getting involved in a complicated appeal based on legal technicalities. The man doesn't know much law and he isn't curious."

With that said, he moved on to new business. He had accepted the referral of a complex "pollution" case in eastern Kentucky. The case involved over one hundred parcels of property, small farms and rural acreage, with several hundred plaintiffs claiming varying degrees of ownership in the different pieces of property. The plaintiffs asserted that the defendant, Boyd Oil Corporation and its successors, had systematically harvested oil from the Martha Oil Field near Paintsville, Kentucky, in a manner that left "TENORM," technologically enhanced radioactive material, on the plaintiffs' properties. Allegedly, the recovery technique of water-flooding the field had permitted radioactivity contained in subsurface shales to come to the surface. The "technological enhancement" was the water. Wherever the water went, the radiation went.

The case had been filed several years earlier after another group of claimants had successfully sued Boyd on similar claims. The referral lawyers in Kentucky had exhausted their bank accounts prosecuting the case, and they were looking for help—both to try the case, and to defray the expenses.

"A buy-in?" I asked.

"A million dollars to them up-front and we pick up the expenses from this point forward," Sullivan deadpanned. "We'll get sixty-six percent of the forty percent contingency fee."

"A million dollars," I repeated.

"Actually, one-point-two," Sullivan said. He was always referring to millions of dollars as "something-point-something." This had led the associates to refer to settlements or verdicts in our cases as "seven-point-five thousand dollars" or "two-point-three thousand dollars."

Sullivan admitted that it was a huge undertaking. Apparently, he had already discussed it with Peters, the other partners, and the bank. The firm had set up a separate line of credit for the case. It wasn't the kind of case in which we would typically get involved. While there was the risk of personal injury presented by the radiation, the case was framed as an injury to the environment with damages, including the cost of remediation and the decrease in property values.

"Where is Paintsville?" I asked.

"You've heard of Butcher Holler and Loretta Lynn? That's where it is. Look, Davy, here's the deal. We can't all work on this case. It will be a tremendous discovery battle. Every client will have to answer interrogatories and requests for production and then give deposition testimony. Boyd has lawyers in Kentucky, Washington, DC, and Houston. They will paper us to death with motions. We need to assign one lawyer in the firm to be the point person on this. You're that person. We'll shift most of your other cases over to Eli, Rod, and the others. I'll help you. Of course, I'll be there for trial. We all will help you, but you are going to be our radiation lawyer."

In my mind, I was already asking if this assignment was a reward or a curse. Sullivan must have sensed my concern, even though I was trying to look interested in what he was saying. Taking on the referring lawyers' 1.2 million dollars of debt for this case seemed enormous. Could any case have the potential payday that would warrant such an investment?

"I can tell what you're thinking," Sullivan said. "No, you and Eileen are not going to have to handle all of the paperwork. We're going to get you some help. I've asked a contract lawyer who has a lot of experience in putting together computerized client databases to join us for lunch. If you like her, we'll hire her on an hourly basis. I've also talked to an environmental lawyer in Lexington. I think he might be willing to come on board. So, what do you think?"

There really was nothing I could say, other than, "When do we get started?"

"Right now," he said and stood up as a tall, dark-haired woman in a handsome beige suit walked up to our table. She might have been a few years older than I was, but she was one of those women who will be as good-looking at fifty as she was at thirty-five. Beneath the soft-shouldered suit jacket, she wore an ecru silk shell and a small, diamond cross pendant. The suit skirt stopped just above the knee and her stockingless calves were muscular and tanned. She said hello to Tim, and he introduced her to Riza and me. She was Beth Sheehan. Unbeknownst to her, she was the winning contestant at the Four Seasons pool that the St. Jude Squad had watched through the telescope earlier that morning. She sat down, and I noticed that Riza moved her chair a little closer to Sullivan. "Beth, Davy Jessie here is our firm's expert on TENORM pollution," Sullivan said, and winked at me. "He's the lawyer with whom you'll be working most closely in the next few months. Can we get you a Sea Breeze before lunch?"

She extended her right hand across the table to me and said, "Hi Davy. It's nice to meet you." As she leaned across the table, the small cross dangled from her neck, suspended between us, and I fought off the urge to look down her blouse. It wasn't that hard to do because she had these incredible brown eyes, so brown that the pupils and the irises seemed to be all one rich shade of dark chocolate.

But as I shook her hand, I couldn't help thinking about what she looked like in a swimsuit. And of course, I wondered what she looked like without the swimsuit. I don't know if there has ever been an empirical study of the phenomenon, but I have noticed that you can go to a strip club where a woman is only wearing a G-string, and the first thing that pops into your mind is "I wonder what she looks like without that three-inch patch of cloth?"

After a drink, we stood and went into the main dining room. Sullivan and I followed the women. He pulled a chair out for each of them as they sat at the white, cloth-covered table. After Beth sat down, Sullivan leaned over to me and whispered, "Like I always say, she's sitting on the world we all want to conquer." He may not have been a theoretical physicist, but Sullivan understood enough of quantum physics to know that string theory in general, and G-string theory in particular, is an attempt to unify and explain through a single model the theories of all fundamental interactions of nature.

A week later, the four of us were in Peters & Sullivan's corporate jet flying to eastern Kentucky to meet our new clients. Riza and Sullivan sat across from each other, and I sat across from Beth in the plush leather passenger area. To the rear of the plane was a small bench seat with a liquor cabinet and ice compartment below the seat. As we took off, Sullivan had passed out a case summary that the referral lawyers had prepared, as well as bottled Coronas with lime wedges for each of us. It would still be cold in eastern Kentucky, so we all had worn jeans, sweaters, and coats. The coats were stacked in the luggage area in the back of the plane. The hum of the plane, and the ice-cold Coronas, had caused the others to drift off to sleep, including Beth with her closed laptop still resting on her knees.

Beth was probably better looking dressed in just a sweater and jeans than she had been in either a swimsuit or a fashionable business suit. She wore her auburn hair a little longer than that of most female lawyers. Her sweater, while not revealing, outlined her shape nicely. The small diamond cross on a simple gold chain that hung below her neckline was the only accessory that she wore, other than wedding and engagement rings. I had noticed the cross before, and for some reason, I got the impression that it was an item she never took off. The only luggage she had brought was a well-traveled Louis Vuitton duffle and a matching case for her laptop. She had not said much to me during the week and hadn't said much more than hello as we boarded the plane. However, her incredible figure, large brown eyes, and full lips had been the subject of several conversations among the associates that week.

She had certainly gotten our attention. I assumed that the clients we were going to meet at the conference room at the Jennie C. Wiley State Park outside of Salyersville, Kentucky, would be equally impressed.

The park was a series of steep, wooded hillsides, some still covered with patches of snow and ice and which encircled a beautiful, steel-grey lake. It had been dark when we arrived at the facility, and I had not been able to tell much about the place. Sullivan had sent Riza into the lobby to check us in. He always did that. I guess she had instructions about how to do it. Sullivan and I each had our own cabins, and Riza and Beth shared a unit that had separate rooms with a common den area between them. I had gotten up early, showered and dressed, and walked down to the restaurant connected to the lobby for breakfast by myself.

The breakfast included a "country" ham that was shockingly salty but delicious. I stared out the window, thinking about what a pristine setting the park was. Native stone, a dark grey granite, had been used to construct the little conference center, and we appeared to be the only people that had stayed in the dozen or so cabins that night. The morning sky was cloudy and cold, and the grey lake mirrored the clouds.

"Health food nut, I see," Beth commented when she walked over to my table and eyed my plate of ham, eggs, biscuits, and red-eye gravy. She put down her Louis Vuitton duffel and laptop case and sat down across from me. It was one of the first things she had said to me directly.

"You're up early. Couldn't you sleep?" I asked.

"Sure," she said, and asked the waitress for coffee, black. "Were you worried that my suitemate might have kept me up all night?" She smiled.

"No," I said.

"It was as if my suitemate wasn't even there." Her brown eyes flashed as they caught mine. Beth cocked her head to one side and raised her eyebrows as if to ask me a question. She looked down and grinned as she turned her gaze toward the window. I wondered to myself how many thousands of dollars had been spent by the firm so that Riza would officially have a room before spending the night in Sullivan's room, but I didn't say anything. They were an item and everyone knew it, but it didn't do anybody any good to talk about it. I wondered how Sullivan managed to lead what amounted to two lives—one at home, and one at work—but he seemed to thrive on the chaos. At times, it seemed that when confronted with the option of orderly routine or confrontation, he would deliberately choose the course that was certain to create havoc. Maybe he was just a thrill junkie, "jonesing" for some new level of excitement.

I started to change the subject. I should have. But, for some reason, I felt compelled to give Beth a word of caution. "Be careful," I said, "Sullivan hates gossip. And, remember, whatever you say to Riza goes straight to Sullivan." Unwittingly, I had confirmed Beth's suspicions. Now, she wouldn't let the topic drop.

"Looks like a pretty sweet deal. Fly around the country in the boss's private plane, drinking Sea Breezes and Coronas with fresh limes," Beth said.

"Are we talking about Riza now, or me?" I asked.

Beth laughed, and said, "Well, I assume that everyone on the team has a different job description. I presume that you stayed in your room all night."

I nodded and smiled back at her. I thought to myself that Riza and my job duties weren't all that different. But I didn't say anything about that, and I tried to switch the discussion to the morning's activities. We were meeting our clients at the conference center. The referral lawyers would introduce Sullivan, and he would speak about how he saw the case developing from this point. He would have to talk about the amount of work that needed to be done without offending the re-ferral lawyers. He would introduce Riza, Beth, and me, and the four of us would spend the morning helping folks fill out biographical data questionnaires for input into Beth's laptop.

Frankly, it was difficult to believe that the case had gone on this long without that type of work already having been done. But, it wasn't. The case was a mess. It was hard to understand how more than a million dollars could have been spent on the case up to that point, but I guess large sums had been spent on experts and environmental testing. It looked to me like we would need more help. I guess Beth had the same thought, because, as I signed the breakfast check to my room, she asked, "So, Davy, how long before you get your own paralegal?"

"Eileen is a damn good secretary," I said.

"Yeah, I like how she answers your phone, 'Whips, trips, and busted lips.' But she's at the office. What good is her being there going to do us here?" she asked, still smiling.

About halfway through the client work-up, Sullivan and Riza disappeared. He called me from the car and explained that he and Riza were going to take the plane over to Lexington to meet with our new environmental lawyer on the case. Sullivan was going to see what he could do about arranging a press conference to announce his participation in the case. He told me to finish up and have everything packed up by that evening so they could fly back and pick us up for the flight home.

I looked around. Beth and I were seated at a table surrounded by about fifty or sixty people holding stapled forms and pencils. All of the people, young and old, looked grey and tired. They weren't just tired because of the tedium of the morning's activities; there was an air of defeated exhaustion about them. They milled about. They talked to each other very little. Many smoked.

I was impressed by how Beth would take a form from someone in what used to be a line in front of our table and comment on the ambiguity of the form to cover up for the client's lack of proficiency in reading and writing.

To a person, they were likable. In terms of material wealth, they had nothing. Some didn't have running water in their homes. Perhaps most surprising, none of them expected to recover a penny from this lawsuit. It crossed my mind that perhaps the referral lawyers had "promoted" this case without much input from the clients; but the more I talked to the clients, I came to understand that was not the situation. Instead, they lacked avarice.

I had not met people like this before, even growing up in Abilene. About the only thing that seemed to ignite a competitive spark was to discuss University of Kentucky basketball. I thought this a bit ironic, since most of the clients had not finished high school, much less college; and the last time I checked, there was only one player out of twelve on the Kentucky squad that was from Kentucky. Who is to say how or why we develop the allegiances that we do?

Most of the clients wore work clothes. There were some overalls, but mostly blue jeans with Carhartt or Dickies jackets. The only spot of color in the room was Woodrow Carter. I guess because his name had appeared first on the petition, he felt compelled to dress up. He had worn a tan, corduroy sport coat with a white carnation boutonnière. As the last of the group was leaving, I asked Mr. Carter if he would mind running Beth and me out to the airport.

Beth overheard me, and asked, "Are we going home tonight?" She reached down into her laptop bag, and began fishing for something. "I guess I better call my husband and tell him to expect me." She pulled out a cell phone.

Before she could dial, I said, in a tone quiet enough that Mr. Carter couldn't hear us, "I'd hold off on that until we talk to Sullivan. There's always a strong headwind going back to Houston from the southeast. He didn't say anything about it, but I wouldn't be surprised if we stopped over someplace."

"Someplace, like where?" she asked.

"My first guess would be New Orleans," I said.

She looked to see that Mr. Carter couldn't hear us talking, and asked me with her brown eyes flashing again, "Is 'headwind' a euphemism for blow job?"

I laughed out loud, and Mr. Carter heard me and came over. I told him that we were ready to go, and he went to pull his pickup around to the front of the building while we finished packing up. After he had walked off, I said to Beth, "You've been around Sullivan now. Does he impress you as a man that would rather spend the night at the Jennie C. Wiley State Park or the Windsor Court?"

"Is home not an option?" she asked.

It's true that I had left out that option. But I had traveled enough with Mr. Sullivan to know that we were going wherever Mr. Sullivan wanted to go. He used a corporate jet like most people used a car. I knew that I intended to hold off on calling Michelle until we stopped some place for fuel, and I had a better idea of where we were going. At least, that was my intention.

Beth didn't flinch when I threw her duffel and my bag into the back of Woodrow Carter's ancient, green Ford Ranger pickup. She crawled onto the bench seat between us; there was no backseat. She put her hand on Mr. Carter's knee as he shifted the standard transmission into first, and told him, "Thank you for driving us to the airport." Color flushed into his cheeks. He flicked the cigarette he was smoking through the crack in his side window, and it fell harmlessly onto the gravel path as we eased around the lake to the main road.

On our ride to the airport, Mr. Carter explained that Jennie C. Wiley was the wife of a white settler in the late 1700s. She was captured by Indians. Her five children were murdered, and after months of captivity, she escaped and was reunited with her husband. They continued to live in what is now Johnson County, and eventually had five more children. Thousands of their descendants still live in the area. Some were plaintiffs in our case.

We turned off the main road and began driving up an unkempt pavement that wound up one of the steep, rocky little mountains that shadowed the main road. But when we got to the top of the hill, there was no top. Mr. Carter explained how the coal companies had removed the top of the mountain and deposited the removed earth in the valley below. What was left was a barren plateau that sat like a man-made mesa among the craggy hills and mountains that surrounded it on all sides. I wondered to myself why the coal companies picked this particular geographic formation among all of the others for demolition. Was it the only one that held minerals in sufficient commercial quantities to warrant destruction? Was it just a matter of time until the companies leveled the other mountains? And why did the scraping away of the mountaintop stop at this height? Would all the local mountaintops eventually even out all of the valleys until eastern Kentucky looked like wind swept Highway 84 between Roscoe and Lubbock? Dad used to tell me that I should write a novel about my time at Texas Tech and call it "Wuthering Without Heights."

The flattened hill was now suitable for a short, asphalt-paved landing strip in front of a small, private fixed-base operation (FBO) and a monolithic federal prison facility that sat just beyond the end of the runway. A couple of fixed-gear planes were parked outside of a corrugated tin hangar beside the cinder block FBO building. It would probably require a certain level of skill to land the Peters & Sullivan jet between the mountaintops on such a short runway without running into the prison.

Barely visible, a couple of hundred yards away, a line of grey turkeys walked down the hillside away from the prison. An old tom hung back to make sure his hens had safe passage. "There go the turkeys," I said, almost as if I were talking to my dad while we were hunting from a jeep in West Texas.

"Yeah," Mr. Carter said, squinting. He stopped the pickup and watched as the flock disappeared into the grayness of the hillside. I don't think he had noticed them until I pointed them out. "The spring season's not too far off," he said to me. I would imagine that game seasons were about as relevant to him as they were to my grandfather. If you had your shotgun or rifle in the pickup, and you got a chance to put food on the table, you took it. I didn't say anything to him about that, but I think he sensed what I was thinking. Without saying anything to me, he smiled at me. I told him about the time I saw my dad shoot a running turkey at about that distance with a .30-30 from the driver's seat of a Jeep. I was just a kid, but I can remember that shot to this day. I saw the turkey tumble after the shot. I expected that the turkey would be demolished by the bullet, but when we drove over to it, only its head was missing. "Probably luck," I said, "but it was a helluva shot."

Mr. Carter started the pickup and eased back onto the road. "I used to be a fair shot myself," he said. He dropped us off in front of the FBO, and we waved as he drove off. During the course of the day, and principally in the last half hour, I found myself becoming attached to the clients. I wanted to win. I wanted them to win. I felt like they needed me. I sensed that the case couldn't be won, but I was already telling myself that if anybody could win this case, it was Sullivan and me. I'd figure out something. As Sullivan's plane dipped down out of the clouds that seemed to rest like a roof on the mountaintop piers that surrounded us, I wondered if I was already violating his first rule.

The four of us landed in New Orleans about six o'clock that evening. Riza and Tim were pretty looped by the time they picked us up.

It turns out that they had held a press conference and then met the Lexington lawyer at the Wild Turkey distillery outside of Lexington. There was a hospitality room, and they had purchased several bottles of Rare Breed for the ride home. I felt compelled to try and catch up, and I forgot to call Michelle when we stopped to refuel in Memphis. I don't know if Beth remembered to call her husband, or not. I never heard exactly what was said in the press conference, but apparently it went well.

A limousine picked us up in New Orleans. It dropped Sullivan, Beth, and me at the Old Absinthe House at the corner of Bourbon Street and Bienville and took Riza over to the Windsor Court to check in and make sure that our bags went to the correct rooms. The Old Absinthe House has a wormy oak, square bar that seems to be held up by a few slumping patrons on barstools positioned strategically around the square. The place smells like stale beer and vomit, but Sullivan always stops there first when he gets to town. After a few drinks you forget about the smell. We had each finished a drink, Sullivan having ordered something called a "Sazerac" with Michter's rye, when Riza came back with the room keys. Sullivan began a long discussion about where we ought to eat that evening. He suggested an item at each place to con-sider in our vote: the dessert soufflé at Commander's Palace, the gumbo at Mr. B's, and the fresh snapper at Galatoire's.

Experience told me that he would still be sitting in the Old Absinthe House an hour later discussing various restaurants — and I knew that if I was going to break through the bourbon-induced fog that had settled over me, I needed to eat right away. I told Sullivan that I was beat and that I was just going to walk to the hotel and call it a night.

"Come on," he said, "let's have one more, and then make them throw us out of here and we'll go get something to eat. We've got a driver; where do y'all want to go? Don't wimp out on us now, Davy. We're just getting started. None of y'all have cigarettes, do you? Something about this place makes me want to have just one cigarette."

When Sullivan went around the bar to try to buy a single cigarette from the bartender, I took my cue to slip out unnoticed. I knew that

Sullivan would see my leaving as a flaw in my character, but some sense of self-preservation took over, and I had to get out of there. I stepped out of the bar on the Bienville side and saw the parked limo. I walked over and asked the limo driver directions to the Acme Oyster House. I had been to New Orleans several times with Sullivan, but it couldn't hurt to double-check. As I walked back to Bourbon Street, I sensed that the car pulled away from the curb to follow me, but he couldn't turn left on Bourbon Street. Still, as I went into the Acme on Iberville, I thought I saw him coming behind me, and I figured he had made the block at Dauphine. I thought to myself that the best plan for the evening was to get a dozen raw and maybe some bread pudding with some coffee before attempting to call home. I didn't expect that Michelle was going to be too happy to hear from me.

An hour or so later, I was in my room at the Windsor Court. It was sumptuous, full of dark woods, thick rose velvets and plush brocades, and tasteful indirect lighting. I took off my shoes and lay down on top of the bedspread. I picked up the receiver of the phone next to the bed and called the front desk for an early wake-up call. I held the receiver on my chest for a moment and stared at the ceiling. Then, I called Michelle.

She was asleep when I called, and the telephone woke her up. "Hello?" she said, hesitating before she spoke.

"I'm sorry to wake you."

"Yeah. What time is it? Where are you? I tried to call your cell phone all afternoon."

I tried to explain that I had been commandeered to New Orleans, but I just sounded drunk. The more I spoke, the more awake and the more angry Michelle became. After telling me that she was tired of me calling in drunk and not even knowing what state I was in, she asked me when I would be home.

"Tomorrow, I'm sure," I said. To some extent, I was worried that Sullivan might not want to go home the next day if he was out too late tonight, but it was the only answer that would work at the time.

"We'll talk then," Michelle said, and hung up. I put the telephone receiver on its cradle, and fell asleep in my clothes.

I awoke suddenly, and sat straight up when I heard someone pounding on the door to my room. At first, I thought that maybe I had slept through my wake-up call and Sullivan might be trying to get me up to go to Houston. He loved to chastise hungover associates and would always say to them, "You can't stay up with the owls if you can't get up with the eagles."

"Just a minute," I yelled, and looked at the clock on the other side of the bed. It was three o'clock in the morning.

I walked to the door and looked through the peephole. Beth was leaning against the wall on the opposite side of the hall. I opened the door.

"No fair sneaking off like that," she said, and walked past me into my room. She looked at the crumpled bedspread, and then at me, as she walked over and sat down in a plush chair. "Sleeping in your clothes these days?" she asked.

I looked down at myself. My shirttail was half out. At some point, I had apparently taken off my socks. Beth, on the other hand, while obviously inebriated, managed to look pretty much still put together.

"Have you had anything to eat?" I asked.

"I would imagine several cans of mixed nuts," she said.

"How about a cheeseburger?" I asked and flipped through the in-room dining menu on the desk.

"Chivalry lives," she said. I ordered us each a cheeseburger with fries, hoping that the grease might soak up some of the alcohol. Sullivan always called it "Vitamin G."

"I guess this means no Commander's Palace this trip," she said. I told her about the time I had been to Commander's Palace with Sullivan. Of course, Riza was there, and some other lawyers were too. As the waiter took our orders, he told us about the amount of time needed to prepare the soufflés for dessert, and we each had ordered one. By the time we had finished our meals, and the countless bottles of Far Niente chardonnay, nobody wanted dessert. Sullivan paid for the soufflés, but nobody ate them.

"At least you got to eat!" said Beth. I also told her about the time I was in Manhattan with Tim and Riza and we had gone to some place

with great veal chops after drinking all afternoon. Always, before ordering a steak, Tim would say, "You can tell a lot about a person by observing which side of a T-bone he eats first. Does he eat the tenderloin
side first because there is a chance that something might happen to
him before he gets to the tenderloin side if starts with the strip side, or
does he eat the strip side first and save the tenderloin for dessert?"
Then Tim would avoid the dilemma altogether and order the veal chop
at a price considerably more than the T-bone.

When the waiter brought the chops, Tim began complaining that
his was not prepared properly. I realized Sullivan was going to send the
chops back, and I devoured mine before he could get the waiter's attention and explain to him the problem with the preparation. Tim and
Riza started laughing. "Did they eat the veal chops?" Beth asked.

"No. Sullivan sent them back, paid the bill, and they went somewhere else. I went back to the hotel then, also."

"Do you always sneak out?" Beth asked.

We continued to talk, and before long, room service knocked on
the door with our cheeseburgers. The waiter rolled a folding table
into the room and placed it in front of the chair where Beth was
seated. He latched the top into a round table surface position,
smoothed the white tablecloth, and uncovered the plates of food. He
asked me if he could get us anything else, as he handed me the bill. I
signed it, and he left quickly. I pulled a chair over to the table from
the desk.

"Sometimes it's impossible to get away," I said. "Actually, I probably
owe you an apology for tonight. I knew, once I left, that it would be
difficult for you to leave. You know, the bars in this town never close."

"I didn't know I could leave."

"Yeah. Essentially, we're serving as chaperones, I guess. It looks less
questionable if someone who knows Tim walks up, and he's with Riza
and somebody else."

"I genuinely thought they enjoyed my company," she said.

"I'm sure they did."

"I'll bet you've seen some wild things," she said. When I didn't respond, she continued between bites of her cheeseburger. "We left the Old Absinthe House after a few hours and walked to several other places. Then we got in the limo and cruised around the Quarter and the Garden District. I sat across from Riza and Sullivan, who sat on the back seat. As they were drinking wine and talking, I just laid my head back and closed my eyes. I don't think I ever fell asleep, but when I opened my eyes, they were kissing."

Again, I didn't respond. I could picture in my mind the dark limousine as the lights of New Orleans glistened in the windows.

"I barely opened my eyes so that they couldn't tell if I was asleep. After a while, they stopped kissing, and Riza got down on the floorboard in front of Sullivan. I couldn't believe it. She unzipped his pants, and started going down on him right in front of me."

"Do you think I was supposed to participate?" she asked.

Again, I shrugged. "I doubt it. They probably just thought you were asleep," I said, trying to downplay the story.

"At first, I was shocked. But I admit that the more I watched, the more excited I got. I'd never seen people having sex right in front of me. It's much different than watching a movie. Part of me wanted to knock on the limo driver's window and tell him to let me out. Part of me wanted to move over so that I could have a better view."

"What did you do?"

"I just sat there, acting like I was asleep. In a few minutes, Sullivan was finished. He zipped up, and Riza sat back next to him with her head on his shoulder. I 'woke up' when the doorman at the hotel opened the car door. Everyone said goodnight, and I came to your room. I had to tell someone what had just happened."

She was obviously still high. For a moment, I wondered if she had come to my room because she was turned on, but she made no movement to get up from the table, and I didn't either. I felt a sexual tension developing. Maybe it was just because she was so beautiful and had so easily discussed the sex scene she just witnessed. I thought about getting up and walking over to her and kissing her. I resisted the urge but it occurred to me that I would not be able to resist if she made the first move. I also wondered if she could tell what I was thinking. If she could, she didn't let me know.

"Have you told anybody else what you saw?"

Beth's usually large brown eyes now squinted at me. "You think I was being tested, don't you?"

I shrugged.

"You've seen this before, haven't you? I'll bet you've been in the same predicament."

"On Sullivan's plane. Longest flight of my life," I said.

"Did you ever tell anyone?"

"Only you, just now."

"Not even your wife?"

"Especially not my wife. I'm married to Sullivan's daughter, Michelle."

"You're married to Sullivan's daughter?" she asked.

"We met in law school."

"And I thought I was being tested."

"You haven't told anybody. I guess you passed."

"I told you." She said.

"I don't think I count."

Beth smiled. "Maybe not yet." She stood up and walked over to me. She stood next to me for a minute without either of us saying anything. She pulled her hair back behind one ear. This time, I thought that she might kiss me. Part of me wanted her to.

"Thanks for the cheeseburger. I'm going to bed. I can't wait to see if this job gets any weirder tomorrow," she said as she turned and left the room.

I GOT BACK TO MY DESK ABOUT noon the next day. I barely said hello to Eileen and went into my office and closed the door. By one o'clock, I had made my way through the "in" box of both the email and snail mail and called Michelle at her office, but she didn't answer. At five o'clock, a tired-looking Beth knocked and came into my office.

"Have you got a minute?" she asked.

"Sure."

"I just needed a word with my fellow co-conspirator."

"Are we engaged in a conspiracy now?"

"Well, maybe not a conspiracy. My fellow confidant."

"So, you still haven't told anyone about Sullivan? Not even your husband?"

"No, but he wasn't in when I called."

"Neither was my wife. I'm sure she's working up a list of questions to ask me when I get home."

"At least your spouse cares enough to still ask questions. Mine will just wonder what we're going to do about dinner."

"Your situation sounds better than mine."

"Believe me, it's not," she said. I didn't respond. "I almost forgot what I came in to tell you. I just got a call from Riza. She said that Mr. Sullivan has requested our presence at the brickyard at 5:30. I told her I would tell you. By the way, what is the 'brickyard'?"

I explained why we called it the "brickyard." "It's one of Sullivan's favorite spots. I'd say it's about one notch below Damian's on the list of places you're most likely to find him when he's in Houston."

"Where do home and the office come in?"

"Damian's is the office. Brennan's is home. A great number of cases have been settled at Damian's. Did Riza say what the topic of discussion was to be?"

"No, she didn't. I assume it has something to do with radioactive pollution in the oilfields of Kentucky, or I wouldn't have been invited." As she left, she added, "I'll meet you there."

After she left, I called home and left a message on the answering machine that told Michelle I was meeting her dad at Brennan's after work, and that I would see her at home after that. At Brennan's, I learned from Mr. Whiskers that Sullivan had just left. I went back through the bar to the courtyard and found several of the firm's attorneys seated around a table with Riza and Beth and lawyers from other firms. Eli waved me over and asked about how I had been able to secure an assignment with the most beautiful contract lawyer ever hired by the firm. I told him I was full of secrets and ordered a scotch.

"Well, mystery man, suppose you tell us something about this case in Kentucky," Eli quipped.

"I don't know enough about it yet to talk about it," I said.

"Well, you're about to find out more," Riza interjected. "The bad guys filed a motion to strike our expert. Mr. Sullivan wants you to prepare the response. He wants you and Beth to go back out there this weekend."

I nodded my understanding, and thought to myself that I had better tell Michelle about Beth tonight rather than having her find out about Beth from one of the other wives, or from Tim after we had already gone back to Kentucky. I remembered the message I had left at home and became concerned that Michelle might get home, listen to the message, and come to Brennan's. I finished my drink and left, hoping, and at the same time dreading, that I would catch Michelle at home.

I could tell that Michelle was not home when I pulled past the wrought iron gate into the driveway a few minutes later and her car was not in the garage. I worried that she might have already come home and gone to Brennan's, although that seemed unlikely. She would get home soon enough. I let myself in the back door and went upstairs to take off my coat and tie.

I was proud of our house. It was typical of new construction in West University, an "inside the loop" community with good schools and a rapidly progressing gentrification whereby two-story brick or stucco homes that stretched from lot line to lot line steadily replaced fifty-year-old bungalows with porches and yards. Like many big cities, a series of concentric, circular freeways circumscribe Houston. Loop 610 protects the inner sanctum of downtown, the medical center, and a few prestigious neighborhoods like West University and River Oaks, as well as distinct sectors of urban blight. Our house was a painted brick, with all four bedrooms upstairs. The bedroom next to the master was just large enough to function as a nursery and not much else.

While I was too embarrassed to tell my college professor dad what we had paid for the home, I told myself it was a good investment considering the way prices seemed to be escalating all around us. If I could continue making the payments, I expected to sell it someday and move up to River Oaks.

I leased a new car when I took the job at Peters & Sullivan. The house was the only thing of any value that I had ever purchased. Michelle had grown up in River Oaks, and she too had been excited about the house when we bought it; and then, almost immediately, she became concerned that the payments were too high. "People make a home, not granite countertops and antiques," she would say. And I would remind her that the little room next to our bedroom would make a great nursery.

Michelle handled all of the paperwork regarding the purchase. She had some experience in real estate law. I read the documents, but I had no idea which disclosures were forms and which highlighted potential problems. My favorite document was the "geotechnical investigation" designed "to determine the engineering characteristics of the subsurface soils, and to develop recommendations for the proposed 2-Story Residence at 2924 Friar Tuck, in West University Place, Texas." I doubted that my parents' ranch-style home in Abilene was ever the subject of a geotechnical investigation. But their foundation seemed to be fine thirty years later, and they had long since paid it off. I was particularly impressed with the "Site Geology" section of the report, as it seemed to pinpoint, from an archeological standpoint, our position in the evolution of the region:

> The site lies within the Gulf Coast structured province; a huge sedimentary basin containing thousands of feet of sediments. These sediments consist generally of geologically unconsolidated sands, silts and clays, which dip toward the Gulf of Mexico. The sedimentary strata generally thicken down drip, and are occasionally interrupted by growth faults, which also dip toward the Gulf.

As I came back downstairs, I could hear Michelle checking the messages on the phone in the kitchen. The look on her face suggested that somewhere within our structured province a sedimentary shift was taking place . . . no doubt the result of a growth fault in my character.

"So, how is the new contract attorney working out?" Michelle asked.

"Fine, I guess. She hasn't had to do much yet."

"Just fly to Kentucky and back with you, Dad, and his paralegal?"

"Right," I said, then decided to leave out the discussion about New Orleans, if I could avoid it. I don't know why. Keeping secrets had not worked well for me so far.

"What do you know about this woman?"

"She's married. She went to U.T. Law School before we did. She's supposed to be good at maintaining computer databases."

"Is she pretty?"

"I guess. If you like tall brunettes. I'm partial to redheads myself."

Michelle almost smiled. "Listen. I'm your wife. I get to know what state you're in, and where you are going, who is going with you, and when you are coming home."

"I know. I'm sorry. I was with your dad."

"Yeah, I know. I went by the house on my way home to take Mom the list of volunteers for the lunch at church on Sunday. Dad was there. Listen. I've known Tim Sullivan my whole life. The world does not need another Tim Sullivan. I didn't marry Tim Sullivan, or even the next Tim Sullivan. I married you; at least, I thought it was you."

"Is that lunch this Sunday?"

"Don't tell me." Any hint of a smile was gone now.

"I have to go back to Kentucky on Sunday."

"Is she going?"

I tried to explain that I didn't plan the trip, or who was going on it, but Michelle just got more upset the more I tried to explain my lack of control over the situation. As a young lawyer, she understood the need to respond, without question, to a senior partner's seemingly impossible request; and as Sullivan's daughter, she also knew that family and family commitments were too often sacrificed in the interest of career advancement. The conversation ended with Michelle stomping upstairs and me standing alone in the kitchen. The conversations that followed that weekend were little more than perfunctory, and there was certainly no tearful farewell when I left for the airport on Sunday morning.

Because Sullivan was not going, the return trip to Kentucky was on a commercial airline and took the better part of a day. We changed planes in Cincinnati and rented a car in Lexington. Beth pecked at her laptop for most of the plane trip while I slept and caught up on reading professional "magazines" like *The Texas Bar Journal* and *The Texas Supreme Court Digests*. Eileen would collect the materials for me and hand me a folder whenever I flew out of town. Reading the *Bar Journal* meant looking first through the names of attorneys who had been disbarred or disciplined to see if I knew anybody, scanning the memorial death paragraphs, and examining the article titles to see if any pertained to my practice. I usually held my breath as I read the *Digests* hoping, often unsuccessfully, that the Texas Supreme Court had done as little as possible to destroy the plaintiff's personal injury practice that month.

When we got to Lexington, I drove the rental car. I remember the stark contrast between the lush, rolling horse farms around Lexington and the granite crags of eastern Kentucky. Still, the Daniel Boone Parkway was a nice drive, and I enjoyed the silence. It was dark when we checked into the Paintsville Inn.

A depressing mildew smell that emanated from the heated indoor pool on the first floor permeated the box-shaped hotel. Beth and I took our keys from the young woman at the front desk, and we set out with our luggage to find our rooms, which were next door to each other on the third floor. My room had two queen-sized beds with worn, red bedspreads and thin, gold blankets that looked like they had been sliced from a large wheel of polyurethane cheese. I threw my bag in the closet area, designated by the hanging rod, and turned on the television to ESPN. I opened the door from my room to Beth's and knocked on the door that opened to her side. After a moment, I heard her slide the bolt and saw her door open.

"Well, it's not the Windsor Court," she said, smiling. I agreed, and suggested we try to find some place to eat, but she had already called the front desk and determined that the best place in town was a Dairy Queen a few blocks away. We decided to take the car, and she went back into her room to get her purse. I felt like my boss had banished me to Siberia. My wife was so mad at me that she would only speak to me in short, declarative sentences. It was nice to be able to talk to somebody. As we walked past the pool on our way to the lobby, Beth asked me if I had remembered to bring my swimsuit.

4

IT'S FUNNY HOW YOU CAN THINK SOMETHING and how you can *know* something. And I don't mean how you learn something you feel like you should've known all along. I mean there have been times when I suddenly knew things would happen that before I had only assumed would happen. It can work in reverse also. There have been times when I know things will happen that I assumed would never happen. For example, growing up I always thought that Jonathan and I would go to work for Dad's law firm. Even when it became clear in Jonathan's third year of law school that Jonathan was going to do something else, I still convinced myself I was going to go to work for Dad. I thought that Dad would need me to help keep him organized and to keep his cases moving through discovery. I thought I could inform him on developments in the law. I thought that is what he wanted me to do. It wasn't until I saw him interact with Davy at Easter brunch at Brennan's during our second year of law school that I knew that it was Davy who would be going to work for Dad and not me.

We were seated at a large, round table upstairs in the garden room with the white trellises. My mother, Amy, my dad's mother, Zela, and I had been to Tootsie's earlier that week and bought hats to match the spring outfits we intended to wear to brunch. It's not easy to find a hat for sale, much less one that will coordinate with a dress you'd already bought, but Tootsie's on Westheimer was ready for our occasion—or at least for the Kentucky Derby. Mom, Grandmother Zela, and I had a lot of fun trying on the hats in the store, although I admit that I was a little self-conscious when it actually came time to put the hat on and go to brunch. The straw brim on mine was so large that it was difficult to sit in the back seat of Dad's Mercedes with Grandmother on one side and Jonathan between us. You had to sit up very straight so that the back of the hat wasn't crushed against the seat, and you didn't want to lean too far to the middle when Dad turned the car or you might put Jonathan's eye out.

Dad and Jonathan had gone along with the theme, each wearing something that suggested they might have just gotten back from Louisville. Dad wore a blue and white, seersucker Haspel suit with a madras tie, and tan and white wingtip shoes that he called his "spectators." I only saw him wear those shoes on Easter Sunday, but he would wear the suit to church in the summer. I don't think he ever wore that suit to the office. Jonathan wore a double-breasted, navy blazer with tight, white jeans and loafers without socks.

William Drummond, a golfing buddy of Daddy's, and Davy were waiting for us when we went upstairs to the table. Davy had on his usual navy blazer, but he hadn't yet graduated to the grey slacks he would wear almost every work day after law school. He was still in his khaki phase, and, even though he had on a starched white button-down and a Brooks Brothers repp-striped tie, he looked a little wrinkled, and the tie was slightly askew. I'm sure he was nervous. He and I had been dating for awhile and Davy had known Jonathan since college, but Davy hadn't been around my parents very much. I had invited him to come to Houston for Easter brunch and told him that Mom said he was welcome to stay at my parents' house. But Davy opted to stay at a friend's apartment and to meet us at the restaurant. William had come in his own car, and judging by the redness in his cheeks, he might have had a Bloody Mary or two downstairs before the rest of us got there. He was also wearing a navy blazer but with an open-collared polo and ridiculous plaid pants. The men shook hands, and then Dad went around the table and pulled out chairs for each woman in our party. Since Jonathan had not brought a date, other than Grandmother Zela, and William was solo, it was impossible to sit boy–girl, etc. Dad seated us so that I was next to Grandmother. Davy was between Dad and me.

We had barely taken our seats when the milk punch started flowing. Brennan's serves a brandy and milk concoction that tastes like ice cream.

That's the "milk" part. The "punch" part is what it will do to you if you start drinking it at ten thirty in the morning. We each had a glass while we considered the menu. Well, everyone but William had one. When the waiter got to William, he held up one hand and said, "Podzy," which is an affectionate term for "partner" in Houston slang. "If you don't mind, I'd just as soon have another one of those bloodies that Whiskers was making downstairs for me." Mom and Jonathan were already discussing his summer plans, and Grandmother was asking me about what classes I was taking and trying to recall if Dad had done well in those classes. I was trying to be polite and to respond to her questions, but I was also trying to listen to what Dad and Davy were saying to each other. Dad seemed to be absorbed in what he and Davy were discussing.

I couldn't hear all of it, but Davy was telling Dad about being on the U.T. mock trial team and their upcoming competition. I knew the "case" they would try had something to do with slander; an employee was accused of stealing something from a coworker's locker. I understood that Davy and his partner had to be prepared to present either side of the case depending on their assignment in each round. Dad nodded when Davy told him about using *Othello* and Will Rogers' quotes on "reputation" in closing. But what really got Dad's attention was Davy's answer to his question about how in the world people judge these competitions.

"It's all about style and procedure," Davy said frowning and shaking his head. "Did you make the proper objection at the proper time? Did you get a ruling from the judge before you moved on to the next question? Did you lay the proper predicate for admitting the evidence? Easy stuff. When there are two experienced teams, it usually comes down to which team the judges like the best. What they ought to do is go down to the workforce commission, hire three jurors for each round, and ask them to decide the case—not on how well the mock trial lawyer tied his tie, or how confident he sounded in his objections, but on how well he presented the facts of the case."

Jonathan must also have been listening to Dad and Davy because he interjected, "Wouldn't each round then be decided on how fairly the packet of information on the 'case' was drafted? If the facts, as set out in the packet, favor one side, then the coin flip that determines which team will be plaintiff and which team will be defendant will decide the case."

"But isn't that how it is in real cases?" Davy asked, turning to Dad. "Doesn't one side or the other usually have the better side of the facts, and it's up to the lawyers to persuade the jury to see the facts differently . . . in a way the jury might not have without the lawyer's presentation?" He turned back to Jonathan.

I'd seen the two of them argue over stuff like this for hours. If they had been as effective at arguing with other debate teams in college as they were at arguing with each other, they probably would have won some tournaments. "Are we supposed to be learning how to look like we are winning, or are we supposed to be learning how to win?" Davy asked.

Before Jonathan could answer, Dad reached over, straightened Davy's tie, and said, "Both." Jonathan and Davy laughed, and smiling, Dad turned to Mom and asked if we were about ready to order.

I knew the second I saw Dad adjust Davy's tie that it would be Davy, not Jonathan or I, who would eventually go to work for Dad. I can't say what it was about Davy that Dad found appealing. Maybe he saw himself in Davy, a young, bright guy of modest means who thought he wanted to do trial work and assumed that he would be good at it. Maybe he liked Davy's attitude about winning. Maybe he could see that I was falling in love with Davy, and that he might as well try to get along with him.

Another thing happened that day at lunch. Sometime, after the milk punch, or maybe after the turtle soup with a splash of dry sherry, and probably before the pecan-crusted snapper and ice-cold Far Niente chardonnay that Dad had ordered for us, and certainly before the bread pudding with bourbon sauce when Grandmother Zela seemed to doze off (dipping the front brim of her hat into the cup of her chicory-infused coffee), I knew that I was going to marry Davy. He might have *thought* at the time that he was going to marry me. But I *knew* at that point that we would eventually get married.

After lunch, we went downstairs and waited on the valet to bring all of the cars around. Dad decided that he would go out to Marmion with William, and that Jonathan would drive us home. "Marmion" is an exclusive, all-male golf club out north of town near Bush Intercontinental Airport. It is supposed to be nice, but being a female, I've never actually seen it. Dad says that Marmion is not all male by design; it's just that membership was limited to four hundred people and the first four hundred who signed up were all males. His golf club was sort of like his law firm. So far, both were all male. Davy was going to follow us to my parents' house in his car. I hoped he was okay to drive because I was feeling a little bit drunk.

When we got to Mom and Dad's house in River Oaks, a building that expressed a Houston architect's vision of a French chateaux, Mom said that she would take Grandmother home, and Jonathan left in his car without saying where he was going. Mom told him to be careful as she walked around and got into the driver's seat of the Mercedes. Grandmother Zela was asleep in the backseat. They left just as Davy pulled up. What had a few minutes before been a large, family gathering was now a private meeting at a large house. I was worried what Davy would think about the house. It is a little bit over the top, but he didn't say much. Just, "Nice place" or something to that effect.

"Thanks," I said. "Let me show you around."

I took him through the garage and walked past my room and Jonathan's room, without my pointing out either to Davy, to a set of stairs just past the front entry. Davy followed me quietly up the stairs and down a hall to one of the guest rooms. "Where are we going?" Davy finally asked. "Is this your room?"

"No." I replied. "This is one of my favorite rooms in the house. My room has twin trundle beds. Great for sleepovers in high school. But we're not in high school, anymore are we?"

I sat down on the bed in the middle of the room, and Davy walked over to me but he didn't sit down. A bedspread of colored squares of silk cloth covered the bed. The four-inch squares were olive green, burgundy, gold, and purple and in the center of each was an artificial stone of turquoise, ruby, topaz, or amethyst. I ran my open palm across the bedspread. I couldn't remember if Mom had bought the bedspread in Morocco or Taos. Davy stood facing me. "Are we the only ones here?" he whispered.

I nodded and leaned back on my elbows. I took off my hat and "Frisbeed" it onto the floor. "We don't ever have sex in my bed do we?"

"No," he said. "We are usually on that gold couch in your apartment. This is like being in some French hotel."

"La Colombe d'Or," I said, but I could tell that he didn't recognize the reference. I could also tell that he was getting excited. I pulled him toward me and began undoing his belt and khakis. "I think I'm going to have just one more shot of milk punch," I said, and we both laughed. "And then perhaps I can interest you in another bite of snapper."

When we woke up, the afternoon sun was glinting through the broad, plantation shutters, sending geometric patterns across the multicolored bedspread. I balanced my head in my palm with my elbow on a pillow, and brushed Davy's hair out of his face. "You had a good day, didn't you?" I asked.

"That was fun," he said.

"That's not what I meant. You get to do that pretty much every day, don't you? I meant at brunch today. You got along well with Dad, didn't you? I think he was very impressed. And Daddy is not easily impressed."

"I'm sure that he would try to get along with anybody you brought home."

"No. Don't sell yourself short. I think you might have just furthered your legal career today."

Davy just shrugged his shoulders. "I don't imagine it would do me much good if your dad or mom found us naked in one of their guest rooms."

"Okay, okay." I said. "Let's get dressed and put the room back together. But you watch. Today was more important than any old mock trial competition."

I was right, of course. A few weeks later when we were back in Austin, Dad called Jonathan to ask Davy if the two of them would be interested in clerking at the Texas Trial Lawyers Association where Dad was the incoming president. Jonathan declined, but he passed along the request to Davy who jumped at the chance. I suppose Dad called Jonathan instead of me because he didn't want to act like he expected to find Davy at my apartment, but that is where Davy was when Jonathan called.

That summer, Dad probably saw Davy as much as I did because I took a job clerking for a big firm in downtown Houston, and Dad would see Davy every week at TTLA in Austin. Jonathan and I both lived at home that summer since he took a job with a public-interest outfit over in the Heights.

The next time I saw Dad and Davy at the same time was at the Peters & Sullivan firm Christmas party later that year. Frankly, it was a bit unusual for Peters & Sullivan to have a Christmas party where anybody other than the staff was invited, but that year they rented out a room at the River Oaks Country Club and invited families and friends to attend. Even Jonathan went, by himself to be sure, but he did go. I'm not certain that he left on his own. Jonathan seemed to be quite taken with a cute paralegal that might have been a few years older, and I noticed them talking to each other several times during the evening. Daddy spent most of the party talking to friends of his that he had invited from the local legal community, but he did find a moment to corner Davy and me together.

"So what have you two been up to in Austin this semester? You only have one more semester to go. Have we made any plans?" Daddy asked.

I knew that he was fishing for information about whether Davy and I had made any marriage plans. We hadn't, but I couldn't resist the opportunity to play with Dad a little. "As a matter of fact we have."

Daddy's eyes widened and he began looking around the room for Mom. Davy raised his eyebrows at me. Daddy saw Mom, got her attention, and waved for her to come over. As she walked up, Daddy put his arm around Mom's shoulders, and said, "Amy, Michelle and Davy here have some news they want to tell us. Isn't that right Michelle?"

Mom's eyes immediately shot to my barren left ring finger, so I don't think she was as surprised as Dad when I told them that I had decided to take a job with Miller and Shumard, the firm I had worked for the previous summer. It was a well-known firm with many lawyers practicing many different kinds of law, but they mostly represented businesses and handled big commercial real estate matters. I didn't tell Daddy that I had called and accepted the firm's offer before exams that semester so there would be less pressure on me to make high grades. No respectable firm ever rejected a new hire if her grades went down after she had accepted an offer.

Dad nodded his approval and asked Davy what his plans were. "I think that I'm going to take a clerkship with Judge Collins in the Eastern District of Texas," Davy said.

"One year or two?" Daddy asked him.

"I guess just one."

Again, Daddy nodded and began asking Davy all about Judge Collins as the two of them walked over to the open bar.

"I thought you might be about to pass along some other news," mom said to me, smiling.

"That's all for now," I said and laughed. "I don't suppose you know who that woman is that Jonathan has become so taken with?" I asked and indicated without pointing to the pair across the room by themselves.

"I can't say that I do," Mom said. "Judging by her appearance, I would think that she works for you father's firm rather than that outfit where Jonathan works. You should see some of those women. All long, straight, grey hair and no makeup. Your dad calls them 'bunny huggers.' But Jonathan seems to enjoy working there. He says he is going to buy a house over near his office."

"What does Dad think about that?"

"He says, 'What in the world would he want to do that for. I've spent my whole life trying to get out of the Heights, and now Jonathan is trying to move back.'" She said it trying to sound like Daddy. "Of course, I think that is the very reason your brother is doing it. Because he knows that it riles up your father."

I recognized that, to some extent, both Jonathan and I were always trying to get Dad's attention, but Jonathan sure had a different way of going about it than I did. I guess it was already apparent that neither of us was going to be the trial lawyer that Daddy was. Frankly, I didn't have any interest in the courtroom or the lifestyle that seemed to come with that type of practice. I wasn't as good at making speeches as Daddy or Jonathan. Sure, I could turn a phrase on occasion and talk my way out of a traffic ticket. Jonathan said that I had a "potty mouth," but he always laughed at my attempts at double entendre. Jonathan liked the courtroom well enough, but I don't think he liked being compared constantly to Dad so he was trying to find his own way.

When Davy and I did finally marry at the end of his clerkship, Dad used it as an opportunity to invite almost everybody who practiced law in Harris County to come see the fruits of his successful practice. I understood that Daddy's practice was largely based on referrals from other lawyers who could refer their cases to whomever they pleased but were more likely to refer them to an attorney with a successful track record since the referral lawyers were entitled to a share of the contingent fees.

At first, Davy had resisted the extravagant wedding plans, suggesting that he'd like to have Judge Collins perform the ceremony. However, it was decided that we would have the wedding in the church my family had always attended—Daddy informed Davy that Sam Houston himself had once been a member of the congregation—and that the federal judge, along with my brother and Davy's brother, would be attendants. The wedding service took place in the large sanctuary at the First Presbyterian Church in the museum district near the Rice University campus, and the reception was at at The Menil Collection. I think that Daddy was a little worried that somebody might get drunk and fall into a piece of art, but security was tight, and the reception came off without a hitch.

Davy and I spent the night in Houston at La Colombe d'Or, and we flew to Albuquerque, rented a car, and drove up to Santa Fe the next morning. The whole wedding, reception, and honeymoon were something of a blur, but I think Davy will remember the Inn of the Anasazi where we stayed in Santa Fe. He laughs every time I call it the "Anusaucy."

5

WE GOT BACK FROM SANTA FE ON A SUNDAY, and Davy went to work at Peters & Sullivan on Monday. I was, of course, already working at Miller and Shumard. Mostly I read documents, looking for pages that might be privileged and making sure that we didn't turn over to the other side anything that shouldn't be turned over. That, or I spent hours poring over documents that the other side had produced in discovery trying to find some nugget that might be helpful to my firm and its clients in complex business litigation. It was tedious, boring work, and if it hadn't been for some nice people working with me, I don't think that I would have made it through that first year. After that year, Davy and I bought a house, at least a mortgage on a house, in West University. I liked the house, but I didn't see how we were going to pay for it with just Davy's salary as I was already planning my exit strategy from the practice of law.

I enjoyed decorating the house with Mom and Jonathan's help. I think that they enjoyed it too because we went with a different theme from either of their houses. Mom's house was an ornate, French-style home in River Oaks and Jonathan's was an Arts and Crafts revival over in the Heights. After scouring copy after copy of *Southern Accents*, we decided on a Country French motif. I remember thinking that my house was like a provincial little cousin of my Mom's house. I liked the bright colors of Provence and Mom's comment that distressed pine and old oak furniture wouldn't show the wear and tear of having young children sealed the deal. I had already decided that having kids, at least one kid, was what I wanted to do next. Davy seemed fine with the notion, and I even let him think it was his idea that the little bedroom next to ours would be perfect for a nursery.

I didn't tell anybody at work that I was thinking about having a baby, but I didn't have to. There were enough female attorneys at the office that the firm had been through this several times before. There appeared to be a couple of different scenarios. A woman lawyer would get pregnant, have the baby, and not come back to work; or a woman lawyer would get pregnant, have the baby, and hire nannies to raise the child while she tried to work part-time but really worked full-time without securing herself a spot on the partnership track; or a woman would not ever get pregnant and hang on until she made partner. The women attorneys that I had met each seemed to think that their way was the best. The more I worked, the more I thought that any scenario that involved the continued practice of law sounded less and less desirable. I began to fall in love with the idea of having a baby.

The problem, frankly, became getting pregnant. While sex in law school had been spontaneous and frequent, it now had become "occasional." That is to say that it had to be an occasion before we had sex: birthdays, holidays, or a verdict in one of Davy's trials. We even joked about naming the baby after the plaintiff in whatever case had concluded when we marked it with our celebratory conception. It sounded better to me than "Valentine" or "Anne Versary Jessie." We told ourselves that we had been trying for about three months when Davy went to Kentucky for the second time. But we really only had sex two or three times during those three months: a couple of times after trials and one Saturday morning before we both went to work to try and catch up on some things from the previous week.

Most evenings we were just too tired, or one of us, usually Davy, had consumed too much alcohol after work to be very romantic. He would come home, we would have a dinner that I had thawed out, and then he would go to bed and leave me sitting in front of the television downstairs working on my laptop. After I had gone to bed, I sometimes would hear him get up at two or three in the morning when the scotch had worn off and turn on the TV, and I would think about going downstairs and getting him to come back to the bed for sex, but I was just too tired.

I often noticed the next morning that the television was tuned to Cinemax when I turned it on to check the day's weather while I made coffee. I guess that I assumed that he was masturbating while watching soft-core porn on Skinemax, and that assumption probably bothered me some. When we were in law school, we even used to do it together. We would each be reading our assignments at opposite ends of that gold damask couch in my apartment, and I would stop reading and start watching him and my hand would slip inside my shorts, and then he would realize what was happening and start watching me and one thing would lead to another. I'm sure Dad, if he had been there, would have quoted Dante, "That day no farther did we read therein." Now, it was that spontaneity that was missing. I thought it was missing because we were both too wrapped up in work, and my quitting would help.

I didn't tell Davy, but I felt like something was different when we made love after one of his trials. It was some goofy car wreck case with a plaintiff that couldn't control his flatulence in the courtroom. It hadn't taken the jury very long to rule against him, and I hurried home after Davy called me with the results. I caught Davy before he had very much to drink. It wasn't that the sex was different, but I felt differently immediately afterwards. I thought I might be pregnant. I know it sounds silly to think that you might be able to tell immediately after intercourse that you were pregnant. It was probably just that we had decided to stop using protection and my subconscious was telling me that getting pregnant was a distinct possibility. Or maybe I really did know.

Still, I cut out the drinking and went way back on the caffeine for the next few weeks. It was while Davy was in Kentucky on the second trip that I noticed that I wasn't having my period at the usual time. I remember lying in bed a couple of days after my period should have started, debating in my head as to whether getting pregnant at that time was a good thing or a bad thing. If the period didn't come by morning, I decided that I must be pregnant. I tossed and turned all night, waiting to bleed or not to bleed. When I woke up the next morning from what little sleep I had gotten, I knew I was pregnant. I really didn't need a pregnancy test to tell me, but I stopped at a CVS on my way home from work and bought three different test kits. I raced home, ripped open the first package, and did the test without reading the instructions. I took my time on the second and read the entire package insert. I did the third one just for good measure. All three came up positive.

I couldn't wait to tell Davy, but I had to because he was halfway across the country at the time. I wanted to tell Mom and Dad and Grandmother Zela, but it didn't seem right to tell them without Davy knowing. I had to tell somebody. So, I got in my car and drove over to Jonathan's house in the Heights. I knocked on his door, but nobody answered. I waited for a few minutes on his front porch and then called him from my cell phone.

"Where are you?" I asked when he answered. There was a lot of noise in the background. "I'm standing on your front porch and nobody is home. It's after six. I knew you wouldn't be at work."

"No. I left work hours ago. I met some people for drinks at Mandola's on West Grey. Is Davy out of town? Come join us," Jonathan said.

"Yeah, Davy is in Kentucky. Do I know anybody there?"

"Well, it's kind of breaking up. Come on over and have some Oysters Damian with me."

Normally I loved Oysters Damian and Jonathan knew it. All of the Mandola brothers served the dish in their various restaurants in Houston. They shucked the oysters, fried them in a cornmeal batter, and served them on the half shell covered in *pico de gallo*. "I don't know about oysters right now." I asked. "How does the snapper look?"

"It looks like it is coming off the grill about an inch and a half thick, lightly drizzled in garlic butter with lemon wedges. Simple but elegant."

"That's my mantra," I said. "Order me one with the scalloped potatoes and the *ensalada mixta* and I'll be right there."

Ten minutes later I pulled into the parking lot at the River Oaks Shopping Center on West Grey and thought that I saw that cute paralegal from Dad's office pulling out of the parking lot at the other end. I worried for a moment that Dad might be there with Jonathan, and I would have to put off giving him my confidential news until I could get Jonathan alone and sworn to secrecy. But that didn't make any sense because it would have been odd for Jonathan to be having drinks with Dad and his coworkers, and besides, Jonathan would have told me if Dad had been there. I saw Jonathan wave at me from the bar where he was sitting alone as the hostess asked me how many were in my party. I told her that I was meeting someone and walked across the room to Jonathan who stood and gave me a hug.

"Did everyone leave when they heard I was coming?" I asked.

"Sis, I guess that they just had other places to be. How are you doing?"

"Good. I wanted you for myself anyway. Have you ordered?"

"You look good. Yeah, I ordered for both of us. Is it okay if we just sit at the bar?"

"Whatever is faster," I said. "I'm starving."

"Do you want to get some wine or something?"

"No. I don't guess so. Water will do."

"Let's see. You've come by my house to see me. Something you almost never do by the way. You look great. You're starving. And you're not drinking. Something up that I should know about?" Jonathan asked smiling.

"You have to promise not to tell anybody yet."

"I promise. Not tell anybody what?" he asked.

"You've figured it out already. I'm pregnant."

"Congratulations. Am I the first to know?"

"Yes. I wanted to tell Davy first, but he is in Kentucky. Some pollution case he is working on with Dad. You can't tell anybody until I tell Davy."

"Fair enough. But why don't we just call him?" Jonathan asked.

"I don't think this is the kind of news you should get over the phone. I've had to avoid taking his calls at the office because I know that I'll blurt it out if I talk to him. The one time I did talk to him, I had to hurry up and get off the phone before I told him. I'll tell him as soon as he gets home. You just have to keep it a secret for a few days."

Jonathan nodded his agreement, but I could tell that he wondered if something might be wrong that would keep me from picking up the phone and calling Davy right away.

"Have you given any thought to what you are going to do about work?" Jonathan asked.

"Frankly, I've thought of little else. I'm not sure that I'm cut out for this law practice gig. I like the money, but I'd like to try being a stay-at-home mom for awhile."

"You'll be good at that. Any kid would be lucky to have you around full-time. I guess Davy's okay with your quitting work?"

"I guess so. Honestly, I don't know if he has given the idea much thought. He's so caught up in his own practice that I don't think he sees much of what's going on with anybody else."

"Well, you know that it's not an either/or thing. You don't have to work at a big firm like Miller and Shumard. You could go to work at a nonprofit or go to work for yourself or whatever. I know that you might not like the, shall we say, 'unsavoriness' of some of the folks I represent, but there are other options. You know, if you quit when the baby's born, you will have been practicing about the same amount of time that you were in law school. You never know how things will turn out. You might look back and wish that you had kept your hand in the game."

I thought about what he said for a moment before responding. "But that is just it, isn't it? It's just a game. Dad seems to love it. Davy . . . and you seem to also." I included Jonathan in that sentence because I was always careful to let him know that I thought what he did was important even if everyone in my family didn't seem to share that opinion. "But I don't think that I do."

"Well, like I said, I'm sure the kid will benefit from having you around full-time. I'm sure that the only reason you and I are partially sane is because Mom was around full-time for us."

He was right about that of course. Growing up, we had rarely seen Dad. He was always gallivanting around the country promoting himself as a big shot trial lawyer, trying high profile cases, and attending political functions. Every move was calculated to turn the next case into a bigger case than the last. I recognized that Dad's reputation made it somewhat difficult for Jonathan or me to succeed at this profession. We were never going to be as flamboyant, try as I might with my potty mouth comments, or as successful at winning big cases as Dad had been. And yet, we would always be compared to him.

Many of the plaintiff lawyers' kids that we had known growing up were drunks or crazies that seemed to live off their daddies' money. For one thing, it seemed to me that the practice had changed a lot since Dad started. Tort reform had eliminated many causes of action and juries were tainted by the insurance industry's advertising campaign on "lawsuit abuse." There weren't many cases around other than car wrecks and bad slip-and-fall cases that a young lawyer like Davy could try in an effort to bolster his reputation. And when he did win, it seemed like the court of appeals always took away the verdict on some new ruling of law.

But it wasn't just the lack of success by comparison that seemed to affect the offspring of the successful lawyers. They weren't damaged by the inattention of their peers; they were damaged by the inattention of their parents. Jonathan and I had been lucky. We had Mom. And we had each other. I'm sure that one reason Jonathan had gone to work for the public interest firm was so that he would get Dad's attention. And while I was thinking all this, the thought also crossed my mind that maybe that was one reason I had become so enthralled with the idea of becoming pregnant. Maybe I was trying to impress Dad also.

A bartender laid out crisp, white napkins on the bar in front of us as placemats and another brought our food. I took a bite of the snapper before continuing the conversation.

"Let me ask you something Jonathan, and please don't get mad. Why didn't you go to work for Dad when you got out of law school?"

"Well for starters, he never offered me a job. I brought it up one time before graduation, but he cut me off before I even got started. Gave me this speech about how a man's got to make it in this world on his own. Pull himself up by his bootstraps. Blaze his own trail. You know, that sort of thing. It did kind of hurt my feelings. I guess that I always thought that we both would go to work someday at Peters & Sullivan."

"Me too. But I don't think now that I would want to be there. I don't think that I want to practice anywhere," I said.

"I hear you Sis, but I kind of like what I'm doing now. If the truth were told, I probably got this job because of Dad. My boss was a lawyer at Butler Binion before, and I think he lost some big case to Dad way back when. I think he sees it as some kind of dig against Dad that he gets to boss me around now. Whatever. I like the work. The paycheck's not bad. I don't expect that I'll do it forever."

"You ought to be an interior decorator."

"Your house did come out alright, didn't it? I don't know about decorating, but I have been thinking about using some of the trust money some day to buy old houses and fix them up for resale."

"Sounds like a plan. You might give some thought to what we are going to do about this nursery."

"You ought to get some input from Davy on that. Okay, let me ask you a question and you promise not to get mad."

"Promise," I said.

"How do you think Davy is going to react to the baby news?"

"I think that he will be excited. He sees himself as a future Little League all-star coach. Which means, of course, that the little guy will have no interest in baseball."

"If it is a little guy. It might be a little girl," Jonathan said.

"True. I guess that I don't really know how Davy will react to the news. It doesn't seem that we've talked much lately. He has been traveling a lot. He knows that I've been thinking about having a baby. He called me from Kentucky while I was at work, but, like I said, I didn't think that was a good time to tell him."

"Are you worried that Davy will be gone as much as Dad was when we were growing up?"

"It could happen. I see him becoming more and more like Dad every day. It's like Davy worships Dad or something. I guess we all do to some extent. Davy has seemed detached lately. I thought that it had something to do with this Kentucky case. I know that Davy sees it as a big deal."

"I'm not sure that all of Dad's traits are ones that you would want your husband to emulate."

"Why whatever do you mean?" I asked rolling my eyes.

Jonathan just shrugged his shoulders. I could tell that he was thinking carefully about how he might answer my question, and we sat there at the counter for a moment eating our entrees in silence. Probably he was thinking about how we both thought that Dad was always running around on Mom, but we didn't really know anything for certain. Maybe he had information that I didn't and was considering whether or not he should protect me from the news. Or maybe he knew something about Davy that I didn't know. He and Davy were good friends. What if he knew something about Davy and was afraid to tell me? I put my fork down a looked at him for a second trying to read his mind. Finally, I interjected, "Do you know something that I don't know?"

"No," he said. "I know that Peters & Sullivan has hired a good-looking female contract lawyer that is working on that Kentucky case with Dad and Davy. I guess I assumed that if anybody was going to put the moves on her, it would be Dad. I'm not saying that Davy has done anything wrong. I guess I'm just telling you that I'd be careful is all. I know Davy pretty well. I'm sure that there is nothing to worry about," Jonathan said trying to sound reassuring. But the seed had been planted, and I was worried.

"How do you know so much about what is going on at Peters & Sullivan?" I asked.

Jonathan didn't answer.

"Have you talked to Davy?" I asked.

"No," was all Jonathan replied.

"Did you know that she went with Davy on this trip to Kentucky?" I asked.

"Yes," he said.

Suddenly, I was concerned and not just about how Jonathan was getting his information.

6

Jonathan and I finished our meal in relative silence. I ordered a flan for dessert, and he had a cup of coffee. We tried to lighten the conversation by discussing ideas for decorating the baby's room, but both of us were distracted and didn't come up with any firm ideas. After dinner, I left him with the check and went to my car. I turned onto West Grey out of the restaurant parking lot and then took Kirby Drive through River Oaks on my way to West University. I had intended to go home, but I couldn't stop thinking about my conversation with Jonathan, so I decided to drive by my parents' house. I circled the block where their home was located to see whose cars were parked in the driveway in back of the house. I don't know if I had hoped or assumed that Mom would be there by herself, but I was pretty sure that Dad's car was not there.

From the back of the house, I could see over the low finished-stone wall across the courtyard with the giant oak tree to the window of my parents' bedroom. I parked the car at the curb. It was just beginning to turn dark, and I could see that the reading light was on at the chair beside my parents' bed. I nervously checked to see that nobody else was on the street, turned off the car, and got out. I stood at the stone wall and could see that Mom was sitting in her reading chair with a book opened in her lap. It didn't look like Dad was home. I thought about going through the gate to the back door, but instead I just stood there watching my mother read.

In a way, I felt sorry for her. Sure, she was surrounded by luxury—a beautiful home in a wonderful neighborhood. But I knew that she must feel lonely. Enclosed with her antiques and expensive artwork, she sat by herself. Who knew where her husband of thirty-five years was? Probably she didn't. She may have known where he said he was going to be, but that didn't mean that she knew where he was. Her kids, to whom she had devoted so much of her life, were gone trying to make their own lives. She had friends and church and charity endeavors, but none of them were here right now. It was just her alone in a big, quiet house with a comfortable chair and a book. Probably it was some book that she had read before but decided to read again rather than trying to concentrate on some trite sitcom on television.

"That could be me," I thought to myself. I didn't know if Davy and I would ever be able to afford a house in River Oaks, and I didn't know if Davy would ever leave me at home by myself to read a book. I felt as if he had left me at home right then. I understood that sometimes work would take you away, but I wondered what Davy was doing and what Jonathan knew and wasn't saying about him. I had never thought much about my parents as young people. Had they gone through the decisions that we were facing now? Had Mom just decided that it was better to keep quiet about Dad for the sake of her children? Did she regret her decisions that had left her here by herself? At least for twentysomething years, she had her kids' lives to share. That must have been some comfort. Certainly, it had not been boring, had it? She must have enjoyed that to some extent.

If, when, I have this baby, at least I will have him for the next twenty years I thought. Can anybody plan farther into the future than that? Whatever happens with Davy, I will at least have this baby to raise, and I am looking forward to that. I would much rather do that than review countless interrogatory answers in cases that I don't care about anyway. Did Mom ever think that she might have wanted some career other than raising children? If so, she had never let on to me that she did. Sure, Mom and I had tangled over the years, but I admired her. If she could put on a bright face and confront the world on behalf of her kids, then I could, too. There wasn't any hard evidence that Davy had done anything he shouldn't have, and I was probably making more out of the conversation with Jonathan than it deserved. Still, I wished that I hadn't been so short with Davy when he left town the other day.

What was I thinking? Was I trying to drive him away? No. I had just been upset that he was leaving town again and at a time when I needed him to go with me to an event. I wasn't trying to drive him away; I was trying to keep him at home.

As it got darker, the lights in the courtyard came on automatically, illuminating the begonias around the giant oak tree. Somewhere down the street a dog barked, and Mom looked up from her reading. I don't think she saw me standing at the wall, but I eased back to my car and got in. I felt tears running down my cheeks, and I felt alone and scared. When my cell phone rang it took me a moment to locate my purse, and then another second to dig around in it before I found the phone. When I saw on the cell phone screen that Davy was calling, I thought about not taking the call again, but I wanted to hear his voice. I answered before the call went to voicemail, but I didn't want him to hear that I was upset, and I didn't want to tell him about the baby over the phone.

Davy sounded like he was a long way away from me on the phone. He said something about having to be in Lexington because he needed to go to the Kentucky law school library there. He also said that he expected to be home the next day. I felt like I might start crying again, but I didn't want Davy to worry about what was going on with me. He sounded like something might not be going well on the case. That was what I understood to be the reason why he had gone to Lexington and extended his trip.

I was worried when I got off the phone that I might have been too short with Davy in my effort to end the conversation. I don't know why I didn't just let the phone take a message. I don't know why I didn't just let myself cry on the phone with him or why I didn't just tell him about the baby. I'm sure that he could tell that I was upset, but he probably thought it had something to do with his being out of town.

As I hung up the phone and turned onto Kirby Drive to head toward West University, I told myself that I would make everything right when Davy got back to Houston. I'd put on a nice dress. I'd tell him the news, and then we would go to dinner with my parents and Jonathan and tell them the news. I thought that Davy would be excited about the baby, and I knew that my parents would be. After dinner, I'd take him home and make him forget that he had ever been to Kentucky. When I got home, however, the worry swept over me again, and I found myself rifling through his dresser drawers looking for any clue that might suggest Davy had been unfaithful to me. I didn't find anything like that, but buried beneath his folded T-shirts in his underwear drawer I found an old manuscript of a short story that Davy must have written in college. He had never told me anything about it. I didn't know if it was hidden away in the drawer so that I wouldn't find it, but now that I did, I had to read it.

The Traveler

Buses. For reasons I can't really explain, I don't like them very much now. The exhaust fumes have a nauseating, weakening effect. The rides to other colleges can be long and boring. There was a time when I was very young that bus rides offered some enjoyment and the excitement of travel. Now, they are only a means of transporting our college debate team and all our files to tournaments. The freshmen load the cargo area with sample cases full of Malthusian crunches, nuclear wars, melting ice caps, and other generic disadvantages.

I remember the first time I rode on a bus. I must have been about five years old. Mom decorated me in a little cowboy hat and boots and gave the bus driver explicit instructions not to let me off until we arrived at Water Valley, Texas. I was thrilled with my new-found independence. The greasy driver and I stuffed ourselves with the cookies Mom had made, and he talked on and on about the importance of highway safety and driver courtesy. In time we detoured from the interstate and stopped at a one-street town that the highway had forgotten. There stood my grandmother, camera held at her waist, eyes squinting into the sunlight, wrinkling the crow's feet that I have only recently noticed accompanying Dad's smile. I suppose my younger brother, who has their same eyes, will inherit those wrinkles as well. Mama made the bus driver pose while she snapped photographs.

She and Papa ran a little gas-and-grocery store. The store smelled of oiled-wood floors and old-fashioned unsliced bologna. Antique cakes of cheese and little paper ice cream cups sat deliciously in a porcelain refrigerator. The Coke machine was stocked full of root beers that foamed like root beer ought to foam when you drop salted peanuts into the bottle. But I remember the candy counter best of all . . . soft Tootsie Rolls and peppermints big enough to drink Kool-Aid through. Mama would always hide a couple of Zero bars in the freezer when she knew I was coming. I was much older before I noticed the gnawed holes in the meal sacks or the bare wiring. To me, Mama's grocery store was a haven of strawberry push-ups and Bama peanut butter.

Mama and Papa lived there with my great-grandmother. Grandma was in her late eighties. She had her own little room behind the kitchen where she collected scraps of cloth for homemade quilts that she was already too blind to piece together. She cherished my Dad. She would sing little ditties to me about sheep and hogs walking in a pasture and tell me how much I looked like my grandfather. She died in her nineties. An uncle once told me she was registered in Oklahoma as part Indian.

I loved Papa with all of my five-year-old heart, but I don't know if I ever understood him. He was medium height with particularly large shoulders, a weathered tan, a grizzled-gray stubble, and see-through blue eyes. His boots were worn out and his yellowed straw hat was sweat-stained brown around the crown. He would jerk me up in his swarthy hands and rub his knuckles over my flattop while I howled with delight and Mama cringed with overprotectiveness.

In the fall, he would take me out to the ice house to watch him skin a young, whitetail buck. As young as I was, I stood open-mouthed admiring the skill with which Papa would peel away the hide form the fatty carcass with short, quick strokes of his knife. The dripping blood steamed into puddles in the cold wetness of the ice house. When he finished, he would axe the body in half and give the ribs and forelegs to some less fortunate folks that lived down on the river. He usually took the skins and sold them in San Angelo.

I loved him for his oddity. He showed me .30-30 shell casings with bullet holes through the middle and kegs of nails in wax. Someday, he was going to add a room on behind the grocery. And he threw me baseballs endlessly. I would swing my little bat and slap his forkballs skittering down the driveway. With every hit, he would shake with laughter and threaten to fan me with the next three. But the next three would be as slow as the last, and I would send them careening and old Papa would go to fetch them, laughing as he ran bowlegged.

He drank. The trash can behind the house was always full of empty Falstaff beer cans. I remember one hot summer night when I lay in bed and heard him and some others talk drunkenly out on the porch. They talked about rodeos. They all remembered when Papa was trying to hog-tie some calf and his pony got the rope straddled across his belly and was yelling in pain. None of the old cowboys could remember seeing Papa whip out his knife, but before they had realized it, the rope was cut and the calf was free. One of the cronies mentioned that the calf had cost Papa the prize money. It was some time longer before Papa came inside and went to bed. I stayed awake a long time listening to the summer night whistle in through the open window screen.

One summer when I was a few years older, my little brother Charlie went with me to Mama's. Grandma had died and the new highway went even farther around behind Water Valley on its way from Big Spring to San Angelo. Papa took Charlie and me out to the ballpark over in Grape Creek. I guess because we were out-of-towners, we didn't get to play until the late innings of a game that was extended by a tie score that neither team could break. Charlie and I found ourselves in the Water Valley outfield and Carlsbad was at bat with the game still tied. Charlie could not have been over six. The Carlsbad pitcher was probably sixteen. He had a big, bushy head of hair that stuck out in all directions from beneath his baseball cap, and the players on both teams referred to him as "the Lion." Carlsbad and Water Valley were both small towns and anybody without a beard qualified for the kids' teams.

I don't remember much about the game itself. I remember some big kid knocking one over my little brother's head. There was no outfield fence, just an indefinite line beyond which the pasture had not been mowed. Charlie finally got to it, made a stem Christie-like move to pick up the ball, threw it to me as the cut-off man, and I threw the guy out at home. As we jogged in from the last out, some old fellow asked us if we were Gid's grandkids. We nodded yes and he smiled. If Water Valley could score in the bottom half of the inning, they would win. We got two outs fast. Charlie was next up and then it would be my turn.

Charlie's little head was swallowed by his batting helmet. If Mom had been there she would never have let him go to the plate against that muscular teenager. And in all truth, Charlie was scared. But Papa came over and whispered something to him, and Charlie went to the plate.

When Charlie crouched down into his stance, everybody realized what Papa had probably whispered. Charlie's strike zone could not have been over 14 inches. The pitcher threw a couple of balls and then Charlie took one on the arm. I saw tears in his eyes as he jogged to first base with his bottom lip jutted out. The Water Valley players were all yelling at the Lion, claiming that he had plunked Charlie on purpose. I can't say whether he had or not, but his pitch had succeeded in making Charlie and me members of the team. As I came to the plate, I looked around for Papa. He was over on the Carlsbad side with his back to me, talking to some guys in lawn chairs.

The first pitch bounced through a hole in the bottom of the backstop. Before anybody could figure out where the ball was, Charlie was on third, sitting on the base. Their shortstop was complaining that Charlie had not bothered going to second, but the umpire had been busy looking for the ball, and anyway, I think he felt sorry for Charlie's bruised arm.

The shortstop settled down and the game resumed. I heard Mama yell from the pickup. Charlie whined boyhood obscenities at the pitcher from third. But I couldn't hear Papa. I wanted a hit for Papa. The pitch. I just shut my eyes and swung. The ball got by the surprised first baseman and rolled to some little fellow in right field. Charlie slid into home in spite of the fact that the little right fielder was just standing with the ball. The team mobbed Charlie.

I looked around and saw Papa collecting dollar bills from several of the Carlsbad men sitting in their lawn chairs. He came over and picked Charlie up and put him on his shoulders and tapped the bill of my cap. We all climbed into the pickup and went back to Water Valley with Papa grinning, honking the horn on his truck, and waving at everybody.

That night Mom and Dad came down from Abilene and Dad brought a tape recorder. Several aunts came over and Dad got them to sing for the tape. Papa came home late and everyone pretended not to notice the smell of liquor on his breath. Without much persuasion, Papa started to sing too. Before long, the aunts were just taking turns playing the harmonica and guitar around the Formica kitchen table while Papa sang songs the rest of them had forgotten. His voice was weighty with emotion and reminiscence. He sang cowboy songs—one right after another. I can't remember all of the songs, honestly to me they all kind of sounded like the same song, but they included one about saying farewell to Old Joe Clark and another one about not being buried on the prairie. The little kitchen was yellow with the light from the uncovered hanging bulb. Outside in the hot night, the crickets chirped incessantly. I did not want to leave the next morning. Papa said that everybody hated to leave Water Valley, but that they all did.

The next summer found Charlie and me back on the bus and off to visit our grandparents. We had to wait around awhile in the Big Spring station to switch to a bus that would leave the highway far enough to get to Water Valley.

I knew something was wrong when the bus pulled up to Mama's grocery. There was no Mama standing there with her Brownie camera. Instead, Aunt Mary greeted us with the only smile she could muster. As we walked down to the kitchen and stood under the giant pecan tree, Aunt Mary told us that Papa had died a few hours earlier.

I remember how he had thrashed pecans from that old tree with a long cane pole while Charlie stumbled around in the leaves picking up the pecans. The pole was still leaning against the kitchen porch where he had left it. It may be leaning there still.

Maybe I could understand his death when I was twelve better than I can understand it now. There was really nothing left for him to live for. No more roundups, no more rodeos for working cowboys, and while the pastures were full of prickly pear cactus, no ranchers bothered to pile them up to burn as drought feed for their cattle. The river was dry from a man-made reservoir. The best places to hunt were all private leases. Besides, hunting to Papa wasn't a real sport.

One must look one's best for intercollegiate debate. Suit and tie—and polished boots. I tie my tie and see how my blue eyes are shaped like Papa's but aren't the same pale, clear blue as his, bleached by alcohol, the hot West Texas sun, and constant wind. I am sure the boys from SMU will snicker at my boots and drawl. But I'll bet they have never beaten the Carlsbad Bears in extra innings, and if Papa were here, I know whom he would be betting on.

The story wasn't Hemingway, but I thought it was sweet and poignant and innocent. Probably it had been written in college, and more than likely it was autobiographical. Somehow, it made me think of the all the reasons I had fallen for Davy in the first place, and I read it several times before I put it back in the drawer.

7

Apparently, Sunday night wasn't the busiest night at the Paintsville Dairy Queen, but there were a few customers waiting in line at the walk-up window when Beth and I pulled into the parking lot a few minutes after leaving the Paintsville Inn. The customers, each of them smoking, nodded politely at us and tried to avoid staring at Beth as we took our place in line. I had noticed several pretty girls already on my brief trips to Kentucky, but Beth stood out for reasons beyond the fact that she already had a midsummer tan. Beth ordered first, and started by asking the woman at the window what she recommended.

"We're famous for our footlong chili-cheese dogs," was the reply. Beth ordered one, and I ordered two with a side of tater tots, and each of us ordered a Coke.

"Keep your receipts," I told Beth, as we found an empty picnic table outside, away from other diners.

"I don't mean to be antisocial," Beth said, as she looked around, "but I don't know our clients well enough to know if any are here." She glanced around furtively, took the lid off her Coke and poured it on the ground, leaving the ice in the cup. Then she took my drink and did the same thing. In a rather surreptitious fashion, she proceeded to open a bottle of wine while keeping it concealed in her large purse. She filled both our cups, holding the bottle below the table, and handed me mine. I took a long drink.

"Far Niente?" I asked.

"A little taste of home."

"You are a fast learner."

"You'll find it complements the chili."

I tried to eat one of my hot dogs by picking it up, but all I did was make a mess. Beth cut hers into sophisticated bites, washed down with swigs of chardonnay over ice. I decided that her approach was better and for a few minutes we sat cutting up our foot long, chili-cheese dogs as if we were a mirror image. She looked around and commented that this place was not too different from where she grew up in a small town in Pennsylvania. Her dad was a union steelworker; and her mom, whom Beth described as certifiably crazy, was a housewife who had developed an affinity for Prozac in recent years. Beth had gone to Penn State, and she had a friend from college that had gone on to law school at The University of Texas who told her she would like it. In law school, Beth had dated some rich guy.

I told her that Paintsville was different from where I grew up. Not that I grew up in the center of affluence. But in Abilene, things just felt newer and cleaner. Nothing was very old. The subdivisions were new, the houses, though modest by Houston standards, were new, the school buildings were new, the churches, including the Church of Christ that we attended, were new, and you ate inside at the Dairy Queen.

She smiled at this. "Well, the Dairy Queen part is probably similar," I admitted. Every small town in Texas has a Dairy Queen, and it usually functions as a civic center with retired farmers and ranchers meeting for coffee in the morning, school kids getting ice cream after school, and teenagers congregating at night, particularly after football games. I told her that I had this idea that someday I was going to write a short story entitled, "A Clean, Well-Lighted Queen." She told me I should do that. I told her that I had also been working on a poem, but so far, I had only written two lines and that I had plagiarized the first line. She laughed and I refused to recite either line, but I did eventually tell her that I stole the first line from Woody Allen.

"But look around. Sure, this place calls itself a Dairy Queen, but it's different. Nobody here looks happy. It's not that they look unhappy. They just look tired."

"That's how they looked in Pennsylvania," she added.

I asked about how she got from Austin to Houston, and how she met Sullivan. When did she meet her husband? Was he a lawyer also? What kind of work did he do? She told me that after law school, she took a job with an information technology company in Houston that eventually went broke. She didn't know anybody in town, had broken up with the rich "boy," and met her husband through an online dating service. He was extremely good-looking and worked as a sales representative for Merck, the pharmaceutical company. In his free time, he worked out, trying to maintain his high school-athlete physique. He was from a small town that I'd never heard of in Tennessee. We laughed at the fact that most people in Houston are from a small town somewhere. Her husband traveled quite a bit. The president of the failing company for which she had worked put her in touch with Sullivan. I wondered how he knew Sullivan, and I wondered how close she was to the company president or why he would take it upon himself to find her a job. But I didn't ask.

She asked how I had met Michelle. I told her that Jonathan Sullivan and I had debated together at Texas Tech before he had graduated and gone off to law school the year before me. By my third day of law school, Jonathan had introduced me to his sister. I told her that Jonathan, through his dad, had also gotten me a job clerking at the Texas Trial Lawyers Association, a statewide association of personal injury attorneys, the summer after my second year of law school. Tim Sullivan had been the incoming president. "Clerking" at TTLA is where I got to know Mr. Sullivan. About all I did as a law clerk at TTLA was to get Mr. Sullivan to wherever it was that he was supposed to go around Austin with whatever materials he was supposed to have when he got there. Then after that first year, I didn't see him much. I told her that a couple of times during law school I was invited by the Sullivan family to some parties in Houston. Once, during third year, I went to a firm Christmas party at the River Oaks Country Club. Another time, I think it was second year, I went to an Easter brunch with the family at Brennan's. I said, "I remember all of the ladies, including Michelle, wore hats." It was like the Kentucky Derby with milk punch instead of mint juleps. After law school, I had gone off to East Texas to clerk for a federal judge; and Michelle had taken a job with a big firm in Houston. During that year, Michelle and I spent most of our weekends traveling back and forth on Highway 59 to see each other, and toward the end of the clerkship, we decided to get married. "Shortly after that, Tim Sullivan offered me a job." It took about five minutes to tell Beth my complete life history.

"Were you worried about going to work for your future father-in-law?"

I explained that my dad warned against it. He had no problems with my marrying Michelle. Everybody loved Michelle. Dad thought that she looked like Ann Margaret. But what if I wanted to quit the firm, or change jobs, or more? Did I ever think I might want to practice in Abilene? I told Dad that my goal was to make partner at Peters & Sullivan. I knew that there were some who thought I was marrying my way into the firm, but I was confident that I could prove my worth if given the opportunity. If I had to work a little harder than the other associates, I would. I figured I stood to make enough money at Peters & Sullivan that after a while Michelle wouldn't have to work. We could have kids, and Michelle could do whatever she wanted to do. I didn't think I would ever go back to Abilene. Sullivan always said, "I like a chopped beef sandwich and cold beer as much as anybody, but there are folks eating *foie gras* and drinking Montrachet, and we might as well have some for ourselves."

"Your plan seems to be working out."

"So far, I guess."

"Is Michelle still working?"

"For now. We bought a house but the payments and property taxes are killing us. It seems maybe babies aren't too far off. How about you? Any kids in your future?"

"I thought so. Now I don't know." Beth paused and thought to herself for a moment. "We tried for awhile with no results. Then we did the whole in vitro fertilization thing that only resulted in a couple of miscarriages. The process wore us out." She took a drink of her wine. "I'm not sure having kids with Ari is such a good idea at this point. Neither one of us is at home a lot. When he isn't home, I don't really know where he is or what he is doing. We'll see."

"Are we out of wine?"

"Yes, but I have one more bottle back at the hotel."

"Good. It's occurred to me why the Paintsville Dairy Queen is so deserted on a lovely evening in March," I said.

"I guess it has nothing to do with the fact that everyone in town is tired of eating chili-cheese dogs, even if they are world-renowned?"

"Come on. I'll show you."

Back at the room, I'd left the TV on while we were gone. We returned to find that four NCAA men's basketball playoff games had started just as four games had concluded. It was my favorite television event of the year. I liked the first few days of the tournament better than the last. All of the schools that you've never heard of have a chance and play these crazy, exciting games that come down to a wild desperation shot, or a bad call, or a choked free throw. In the end, it was always UCLA, or Indiana, or Michigan State, or Kentucky, or North Carolina, or Duke—or somebody like that who was going to win the tournament. But in the first round it was all about the Richmond Spiders or the Chaminade Silverswords.

"You do like the underdogs, don't you?" Beth said, as I explained why I thought Texas Tech had a real chance to advance even though they played UCLA in the first round and probably Gonzaga in the second. We were standing in front of the TV in my room, and the doors between our rooms were still open.

"I'm going to change clothes and get that last bottle of wine," she said and went into her room and closed the door on her side behind her. I went over to my closet area, took my hanging bag and laid it out across one of the beds. I unzipped the bag and started unpacking my things. I was almost through when she came back in, carrying a bottle of Far Niente and an opener. She was wearing a Penn State T-shirt, gym shorts, and stretched out sweat socks.

"Are the Lions playing?" she asked, as she handed me the wine and opener. I explained that they had not made the tournament, and that CBS was focused on some school called Pacific out of "basketball country in California." As I opened the wine, she unwrapped two of the Styrofoam coffee cups beside the in-room, four-cup coffee maker. I poured us both a glass and took a sip. "This is fun," she said, as she stretched out on the bed that was now covered by my hanging bag, and propped the pillows up so she could watch the game. It was fun. I may have felt somewhat like an outcast, cut off from my family and friends, and saddled with the impossible task of attempting to resurrect the TENORM litigation, but it was fun to hang out with Beth. I enjoyed talking to her. She seemed to enjoy talking to me. We both finished our first glass of wine, and I poured us each another.

"We need ice," I said, and grabbed the small plastic ice bucket emblazoned with the Paintsville Inn crest. I turned the latch on the door to my room so that the door wouldn't close completely as I left. Eventually, I found the ice machine on our floor, but it was not working. I took the stairs down to the second floor, but struck out there as well. I decided to go to the front desk and ask if there was a place I could get some ice. I still had my coffee cup in my hand. The girl at the desk apologized for the fact that the ice machines weren't working, took my bucket, and went back through the office to the kitchen. I told her thanks when she returned with the bucket full, dropped a few ice cubes into my cup, and took the elevator back up to my floor.

When I got back to my room, Beth was asleep on her back, with her empty coffee cup resting between her hands on her stomach. I put the wine in the ice and set it on the dresser by the TV.

I turned the sound down all the way on the television, and as quietly as I could, put away the hanging bag. I gently lifted Beth's coffee cup from between her hands, and placed it on the table between the two beds. As I reached up to turn off the lamp on the table, I stopped to stare at Beth for a second. She was as pretty as any woman I had ever seen. Her long, dark hair fell away from her tan face on the white pillow. With those large brown eyes closed, her high cheekbones became more prominent, and her full lips parted slightly as she slept. Beneath her white Penn State T-shirt, I could almost make out the outline of her dark nipples as her chest rose and fell with each breath. Her hands rested on her flat stomach, and her grey athletic shorts were tight enough to reveal the gentle upward curve of her pubic mound. Her legs were smooth and tan and muscular. She may have been a few years older than me, but I was already beginning to show the signs of dissipation and desk work. Beth was in perfect physical shape.

"She could fuck you in half," I thought to myself, and turned out the light. But not before noticing that sometime during the evening she had taken off her earrings and wedding rings. "Maybe that is just her bedtime routine," I thought. But I noticed the little cross was still in place. I turned out the light, stretched out on the other bed, and finished the wine. I watched in silence as Pacific stunned an overrated Pitt to advance to the next round. Several times during the game, I thought about kissing Beth. I thought to myself that there was no reason for anybody to find out if I did. Isn't that what Sullivan would do? I even thought about getting undressed and getting into bed with her, but I fell asleep during the West Coast game that followed. When I woke up the next morning, Beth had gone to her room and closed her door to mine.

I got up, showered and dressed, and spread the case materials regarding the Defendant Boyd's Motion to Strike Plaintiffs' Experts out on the little table in my room. I had avoided reading the motion the day before on the plane, but I couldn't put off doing the work any longer. I had pretty much read the "Summary of Argument" section when Beth knocked on her door to my room, and I told her to come in.

She was dressed in jeans and a sweater. She really was beautiful. "So, what's the game plan for today, boss?"

"I've got to work on putting together a response to this motion. Honestly, I haven't even read it yet. Aren't you supposed to be getting discovery responses from some of the plaintiffs?"

"Right. I'll need the car. Riza gave me a map before I came. This could take quite a while. I've been looking at where all of these different plaintiffs live. Are you going to be here all day?"

"Yeah, I need to meet with our expert tomorrow, but he's coming here to meet me. I'll spend most of today reading, and I may have to call him a couple of times."

We traded cell phone numbers, and she left through her room, leaving the door to her room open, and leaving me to think off and on throughout the day about Beth and her Penn State T-shirt.

By mid-morning I had finished reading the defendant's motion, and I leaned back in my chair. We were in trouble. The motion, if granted, would exclude our expert's testimony, or restrict it in such a fashion that the plaintiffs wouldn't be able to show to the jury at trial that the above-background levels of radiation on the plaintiffs' properties presented any health risks. At the heart of the motion was the theory that exposure to low levels of radiation had not been scientifically proven to cause health problems. Without our expert's testimony, the plaintiffs' case would be subject to a summary judgment for the defendant because Kentucky law required the plaintiffs to establish a health risk to them in order to make a recovery for damage to their properties. I knew Sullivan was excited about getting to try a case in which the defendant was responsible for contaminating the plaintiffs' properties with radiation; but if the defendant was successful on this motion, a summary judgment motion would follow, would be granted, and a jury would never hear the case.

I had no idea how to respond to the motion, because when our firm had appeared in the case, we were limited to calling the expert hired by the plaintiffs' previous counsel. I read through his resume and compared it to the resumes of the defendant's experts, which were attached with affidavits and case law to the defendant's motion. From a practical experience and work history standpoint, we matched up pretty well. Our expert, Mr. Sterling Walton, had spent most of his adult life supervising the cleanup of radioactive contamination sites, both for the government and private industry. From the standpoint of educational background, the defendant's experts all had PhDs after their names, and Mr. Walton was just that—Mr. Walton.

The affidavits that were attached to the defendant's motion referenced numerous scientific articles which supported the conclusion that exposure to low levels of radiation was not harmful. The articles were also attached. As I understood the articles, from the position of a layman, the assertion was made that exposure to sunshine and microwave ovens and dental x-rays had not been shown to cause any increased risk of disease or injury; therefore, the slight increases in radiation on the plaintiffs' rural properties couldn't be shown to establish an increased risk of disease or injury.

Finally, I read the cases that the defendant had attached to the motion. Most of the cases dealt with the standards for reliability of expert testimony and were from federal courts in neighboring jurisdictions. There were very few cases on point that arose from the Kentucky state court system. The leading case was *Goodyear Tire and Rubber Company v. Thompson*. In that case, the Kentucky Supreme Court held that an injured party's expert testimony was inadmissible to show that the manufacturer of a multipiece rim breached its duty to warn of the dangers associated with changing a tire on a multi-piece rim. The Kentucky court pointed out that the expert did not demonstrate the acceptance of his "reverse installation procedure" in industry or regulatory standards. As the evidentiary "gatekeeper," the trial court must exclude expert testimony not based on "generally accepted" scientific principles or methodology.

When I finished reading the cases, I called Mr. Walton. He lived in Ohio, and he planned to meet me the next day in Paintsville. He seemed like a very nice older man. I discussed the defendant's argument with him briefly, but he didn't seem overly concerned. Apparently, he had heard such arguments before. The conversation with Mr. Walton calmed me down a bit.

That afternoon, I called Eileen to find out what was happening at the office. She had not seen Sullivan or Riza that day. Eileen was busy preparing summaries of the cases on my docket so that they could be distributed to the other associates. She asked if we were going to have any cases to work on except the Kentucky case. Eileen had worked at the firm for a long time before I was hired. She had seen several batches of associates come and go. A sudden reduction of caseload would be the kind of thing that blipped her radar. I didn't tell her about my concern that the Kentucky case was tenuous. I didn't want her to worry. I thought I would figure something out.

After I talked to Eileen, I called Michelle at her office. Our conversation was brief, and her comments seemed terse and hurried. She asked me where Beth was. I asked her how the lunch had gone at church. I didn't tell her that I was worried about the Kentucky case being close to dismissal. I didn't want her to worry either. If I had told her the issues in the case, she would have stayed up all night researching the matter. I wasn't quite sure how, but the Kentucky case had become my problem. I would have to figure out some way to fix it, if it was going to be fixed. As I hung up the phone after talking to Michelle, I had the distinct feeling that I was sitting on an island a million miles from shore. I felt cast off from my family, my home, my practice, and my friends. I was beginning to wonder who my friends were, or if I had any.

I turned on the television and flipped through the channels. Then I shut it off and left the hotel. I walked to the Dairy Queen and ordered a chili-cheese dog, wondering how Beth's day had gone and at the same time wondering if her efforts to complete the plaintiffs' answers to discovery were even necessary.

It was dark when I got back to the hotel. When I got to the room, Beth had already changed into her Penn State T-shirt and grey shorts, and was in my room sitting on the bed where she had fallen asleep the night before. She was watching basketball on TV. She was drinking a beer. When I walked in, she asked, "What is 'UW hyphen M'?"

"University of Wisconsin-Milwaukee, I think. Basketball country, no doubt."

"The beer is on ice in the sink in my room," she said. I followed her direction and then sat down on the bed where she was sitting cross-legged. "Do you think we have enough beer?" she asked. "We have a lot of games scheduled."

I shrugged, but didn't answer.

"Bad day?" she asked as she turned down the volume on the television with the remote control.

"Could be," I said. "The motion looks pretty good to me." Admittedly that statement was not an in-depth discussion of the facts or case law, but it was more than I had said about the motion to either my boss or my wife.

"Did you talk to your expert?"

"Only briefly. He's supposed to be here tomorrow. He thinks he can help. How did your day go?"

She looked at me instead of the basketball game on TV and began telling me about the different homes she had visited that day. She had crisscrossed back and forth over a three-county area, meeting with plaintiffs in their homes. She was trying to fill in the blanks in the discovery answers previously provided by the plaintiffs. The homes were located in various "hollers" in the Martha Oilfield. Some were difficult to get to by car. "But, all in all," she said, "I enjoyed it. The people are all very nice. And they all want to feed you. Because I don't know the area, this job could take a couple of weeks. Houses that look close to each other on a map are separated by the fact that there are no roads between them. I'll weigh 300 pounds before I get back to Houston."

"Your husband won't recognize you."

"Assuming he would anyway."

"Things will get better when you get home."

"Are we talking about my marriage now, or yours?"

I laughed. "Your being here has no doubt caused tension in both of our marriages."

"No. There may be tension in your marriage, but I'm afraid mine may be past that point."

"What happens after the tension stage?" I asked, sincerely curious about what might be in front of me.

"I don't know. You get to a point where you're both going to work and focusing on your jobs. Ari and I have always had jobs that involved a lot of travel. At first, it was fun. I had not traveled very much growing up. The plane rides were exciting. Seeing new towns and places was exciting. Then, when I got home, it was as if we were still dating. We'd go to dinner or clubs and have fun. Or, maybe we would rent dirty movies and stay inside all weekend and act like newlyweds. Over time though, more and more, the weekends were spent recovering from the week; and now it seems like Ari and I are not even home on the same weekend. We were both home last weekend. It didn't go so well."

"No dirty movies?"

"No dirty movies. Oh, we attempted sex. But it didn't work. Honestly, I don't really know why the attempt failed." She paused, obviously thinking about the past weekend with her husband. She told me that, lately, she and her husband were better at fighting than communicating. They seemed to communicate best by yelling at each other. One time a neighbor had even called the police.

"I'm sorry," I said. "I didn't mean to pry. I was asking about the marriage part. Not about the sex part. I guess neither is really any of my business."

"Yeah, I know what you were asking. I don't really know why I told you the sex part. I guess it's just on my mind. Does it make you nervous to know that you are trapped in a secluded hotel room with a sexually frustrated contract lawyer?"

"You make me nervous!"

She threw her head back and laughed. "Why would I make you nervous? You're a successful young trial lawyer with a prestigious, downtown Houston firm. You're married to your boss's daughter, who, by all accounts, is an attractive, successful young lawyer in her own right. I Googled her when we got back from New Orleans."

"Why did you Google Michelle?"

"I don't know. I Google everything. I guess I was surprised to learn that you are married to Sullivan's daughter while knowing as much as you must about Sullivan."

"Have you Googled me?"

"Sure. Pretty boring stuff, but I would summarize my research under the heading 'Budding Career.' Have you Googled me?"

"No. But I did see you in a bikini one time."

She flushed red, but smiled. "When did you see me in a bikini?" she asked touching her right index finger to her pursed lips.

"You were at the Four Seasons pool."

"What were you doing at the Four Seasons pool?" she asked.

"I wasn't there. Several of us were in Peters' office using his telescope."

"His telescope?"

I nodded, and thought for a moment. "What were you doing at the Four Seasons pool?" I asked.

She laughed, and stood up from the bed. "I ought to tell you some wild story, but the truth is that a girlfriend of mine who works at the hotel lets me go there to sunbathe. I was between jobs and thought I was going to a private place. I never imagined people might be watching me through a telescope," she said shaking her head. She put her beer on the nightstand, walked over to me, and stood very close to me. "So, what did you and the guys say about me and my bikini? Of course, you'll never tell me because you are so proud of your ability to keep a secret." She said bouncing her forefinger on her lips again.

"We were complimentary. Honestly, I've had trouble getting the image out of my mind. Especially after I met you at Damian's that day."

"Why are men so caught up in how women look?" she asked. Without answering, I pulled her to me and kissed her on the lips. She didn't pull away and instead put her arms around me and we kissed for several minutes. After a while, she leaned back from me and quietly asked me, "Do you want to do this?"

"We'll probably be accused of doing it, whether we do it or not," I said realizing even as I said it what a weak justification it was for what was about to happen. She stepped back another step, and without a word, removed her T-shirt and shorts. Wearing only her sweat socks and the cross necklace, she walked across the room and turned off the lights. I remember thinking that she was the only woman I had ever seen naked in person who looked like a Victoria's Secret model, but apparently she didn't wear underwear. From the light of the television screen, I watched her walk back across the room, sit on the edge of the bed, and begin unfastening my belt and pants. With her mouth and hands on me, I climaxed.

When I opened my eyes, Beth was smiling up at me. "Take off your clothes," she said. "Now, I need you to do something for me." I took off my clothes and she stretched back onto the bed. I kissed her mouth and neck and breasts, and was working my way down her abdomen when she stopped me. "Let's do that later. That's not what I want for you to do for me now," she said, as she rolled over on top of me and began kissing me. "First, I need you hard. Though surprisingly," she said, as she reached back and stroked me with her right hand, "you're already getting there." I didn't say anything as she continued with the kissing. While I began to return the kisses, she moved to my neck and chest. Her hair and the cross necklace brushed back and forth across my chest, and I could feel myself slipping toward another orgasm. She moved her mouth to my stomach. In a moment, she sat up, straddled me, and put me inside of her.

"What about contraception?" I asked rather clinically. But she just laughed and told me not to worry as she had taken care of that. The only interruption in the smoothness with which she moved was that, as she put me inside of her with her right hand, she grimaced slightly. "I can't believe I'm not wet enough," she said.

"I don't think that's an issue," I said, as I could feel the silky, warm wetness pulling me deeper inside of her.

She slipped her right hand to her mouth and licked her fingers, and returned her hand to her clitoris. "No," she said, "I'm wet enough," and she tilted her head back and closed her eyes. As she stroked herself with her hand, her body rocked up and down on me; and even in the flickering light of the television screen, I could see her breasts, white below her tan line, flush red. As she came, her body rocked harder on top of me.

She paused for a moment, her hands resting on my chest. "Your turn again," she said, and reached up with her right hand and grabbed the headboard of the bed. She bit down on her bottom lip. With the full force of her body, she pressed up and down against me, pulling me inescapably deeper inside of her. Eventually, she collapsed forward on top of me, covering my face with her chest, the little diamond cross falling into my mouth.

We slept in my room. Bucknell upset Kansas, but North Carolina, Duke, Michigan State, and Kentucky all advanced to the next round. We woke up the next morning when Beth's cell phone went off in her room. She got up and took the call in her room. I overheard her exasperated tone but couldn't understand most of what was being said. I could tell that she said something about not being able to get home before midnight if she left at that moment. After a while, I could tell that she was crying. Clearly, she had been crying when she came back into my room. She stood at the door between our rooms, with her arm on the doorway. She was naked, and tears were running down her cheeks.

"I have to go home," she said. "That was Ari."

"Why? What's wrong? Did you tell him about last night?" I asked.

"No. I need to go home. I can't tell you why right now. I'll call you when I can."

I lay in bed and listened to her shower and pack. I told her to take the rental car back to the airport, and that I would catch a ride from Mr. Walton or one of the plaintiffs. Beth was on her cell phone, talking to an airline, when she left. After Beth was gone, I got up and took a shower. I stood with my eyes closed, letting the hot water stream over me. "What am I doing here?" I thought to myself. As I reflected on the events of the previous evening, I felt myself beginning to throw up, and I went down on my knees and vomited into the tub.

PART II

WHAT I NEVER SAID . . .

For thou didst it secretly: but I will do this thing
before all Israel, and before the sun . . .

—2 Samuel 12:12

8

MR. WALTON KNOCKED ON THE DOOR to my hotel room about 10:30 that morning. I had closed the door to Beth's room and tried to make sure that it was not readily apparent that anybody else had been in my room. He introduced himself, and we shook hands. He was a kind-looking, grandfatherly gentleman, who had brought with him a stack of manila folders stuffed with pages that stuck out in all directions.

I gave him a copy of the defendant's motion to strike his testimony, and we sat down at the little table in my room. After he had looked through the motion, he put it down and sighed. I was impressed with how matter-of-factly he reacted to the defendant's attempt to characterize his testimony as slipshod and unscientific. He had been through this process before.

"It's the same thing they tried last time," Mr. Walton said. "They attack the linear no-threshold hypothesis and ridicule the RESRAD computer model." He explained to me that there were two schools of thought among scientists as to whether low-dose exposure to radiation was harmful. The "linear no-threshold" school holds that any exposure increases the risk of injury or disease. As the dosage goes up, the risk goes up. The other school, which included numerous peer-reviewed articles written by the defendant's experts, opined that below a relatively undefined threshold, there was no scientific evidence that exposure to radiation is harmful. They admitted that above the threshold the risk of injury is real; but the low levels of radiation found on the plaintiffs' properties where TENORM had been measured fell far below any scientifically supported threshold.

Mr. Walton described for me the residual radiation computer model, RESRAD, that he had used in drafting his report. As he explained it, a computer program existed whereby future land-use scenarios were projected that would yield identifiable rates of risk from exposure to low levels of radiation. The problem with the computer model was that it relied upon future land-use scenarios, and some had little or no application to eastern Kentucky. The model projected homes being built on the TENORM-impacted sites with grazing livestock in the area and even the possibility of fish farming. When I suggested to Mr. Walton that I doubted any fish farming would ever take place in Butcher Holler, he calmly replied that the example was only one of many future land-use scenarios that were incorporated into the computer model, which essentially used averages from many different alternatives. Wasn't it up to the landowner to decide how he wanted to use his property? Why should the landowner be restricted by Boyd Oil's negligent production methods? And besides, this is the same computer model that the federal government used when it determined that land had been properly cleaned up so that it could be released for unrestricted use under federally mandated guidelines.

I knew very little about radiation and less about computer models for future land-use scenarios. But when he said that the federal government relied upon the computer model, a light went off. "Does the federal government set guidelines for what are acceptable levels of radiation at cleanup sites or for federal workers exposed to radiation?" I asked. "Do they rely upon the linear no-threshold hypothesis in setting these standards?"

"Of course," he replied, and began digging around in his stack of papers until he came up with a couple of documents.

"So, your opinions track the theory relied upon by the federal government and the defendant's experts rely on a controverting theory?"

"I guess you could put it that way."

"Why couldn't we move to strike their experts because their opinions are not based upon a theory generally relied upon in the relevant scientific community?"

"Well, you're the lawyer. Their side of the debate is the subject of numerous articles published by experts in the field. Two of those experts are designated by the defendant—Boyd Oil, in this case. I can tell you that this is about the same point where the earlier group of cases was settled. They filed a motion to strike my testimony. The motion was denied. I don't think the plaintiffs in that case ever filed a motion to strike the defendant's experts. Of course, there has been one major change since that case."

"Don't tell me that the scientific community has adopted the position espoused by the defendant's experts," I said.

"Well, they would say so, but I'm talking about a much more fundamental change. The judge in that case has been replaced. Do you know anything about the new judge?" He asked, sincerely concerned about any information that I might have to offer. "Rumor is that he might be a Boyd man."

"I didn't know there was a new judge," I said. We spent another hour or so going through the stack of documents that Mr. Walton had brought with him. He took his time explaining the importance of each item to me, and it was obvious that the man knew what he was talking about. Jurors would like him if they ever got a chance to see him.

I took some of the items from Mr. Walton's folder to the front desk to have them copied, and I charged the copies to my room. I asked the young woman at the front desk if she knew who the new judge in town was, but she told me she didn't know him because he had grown up in Boyd County, Kentucky, and hadn't been in Paintsville all that long. She made it sound like Boyd County and Johnson County, where Paintsville was located, were separated by a very great distance. I told the girl that I would need to check out of the hotel, and I went back to my room.

Mr. Walton agreed to drive me back to Lexington. I tried to call Michelle at work, but she wasn't there and her secretary didn't know when to expect her back. Then I called Eileen to see if she could find a hotel near the University of Kentucky College of Law. I could tell that the next day or so would be spent alone in the law school library. I couldn't tell if any amount of time spent in the law library would be of benefit, but I did also meet an interesting old doctor who was meeting with our environmental lawyer in Lexington. I had dropped by the law office to say hello and the local lawyer introduced me to Dr. Larry Mock, a pathologist who was working with him on a cancer case. He was a charming man with pure white hair and clear blue eyes. I put his card in the breast pocket of my navy blazer.

I didn't have any luck reaching Michelle on the telephone at home that evening. Of course it was a relief to me not to reach Michelle when I called the house because I knew that talking to her would bring the guilt I felt for the last evening in Paintsville closer to the surface. But I also knew that the longer I avoided talking to her, the harder it would be to package the event in a tidy little compartment to be stored somewhere in the recesses of my memory. The deception would become more and more evident on my face and in my voice. I thought that if I could talk to Michelle, even if I didn't tell her about Beth, it would make it easier to talk to her when I eventually saw her and would prevent my breaking down and confessing information that would only hurt her. I didn't intend to confess anything to Michelle because that would only serve to make me feel better. She hadn't done anything wrong. I had. If I had to live with the guilt of that, I'd just have to learn to cope. It would be my punishment for my crime, and it didn't need to involve punishing Michelle for something she didn't do. My plan was to start now to try to make things as normal as possible . . . to put things back as they were as best I could.

After a few tries, I reached Michelle on her cell phone. I intended to have as normal a conversation as I could muster. Instead, it felt to me like Michelle was upset the moment she picked up the phone, and my telling her that I was going to be out of town another day didn't seem to help things. It felt like there was something that she was trying to say to me but she was too upset to speak about it. She couldn't possibly know about Beth, could she? How would she have found out?

I also didn't have any luck the next day finding any case law that would help us in defending Mr. Walton's testimony.

On Saturday, I flew alone back to Houston through Cincinnati. On the plane, I worked on a draft of the response to Boyd's motion to strike Mr. Walton's testimony, combined with a motion to strike Boyd's experts.

I thought the response and motion were coming together pretty well. My goal was to get a draft together for Eileen to type on Monday. I was distracted by the fact that Beth had not called me since she had left Paintsville in such a rush, and by the fact that Michelle had sounded distant and detached when I finally talked to her. It seemed like she needed to get off the phone. Michelle hadn't even brought up the fact that it had been days since we had actually spoken to each other. It would be nice to have some human contact other than ordering food and answering wake-up calls. Eventually, I put the papers in my briefcase and tried to stretch out and take a nap before I got to Houston. I was nervous and yawning. As I fell asleep, I thought about a couple of alternatives for the next two lines of my poem, but I didn't bother to write them down. I woke up as we began our descent into Houston's Bush Intercontinental Airport.

When I got to the house later that afternoon, Michelle met me at the back door as I came in from the garage. It seemed like it had been a long time since I had seen her. She was dressed up for a Saturday. Her usual Saturday attire was khaki shorts with a brick red, Houston Astros "Craig Biggio" jersey. Years before he had autographed his name across the back. Michelle had worn the jersey so often, though, that the signature had become nearly invisible. Every time we drove by Biggio's house, which was around the corner from us, Michelle threatened to stop and knock on the door to see if he would re-sign the shirt. From what I had heard about the guy, he probably would have. Rumor has it that he passes out signed baseballs in lieu of candy every Halloween. I realized we would have to get the updated autograph another day, though, because Michelle was dressed in a black cocktail dress and wearing the diamond earrings that her mother had given her when Michelle and I got married.

"What's the occasion?" I asked.

"I just wanted to look nice when you got home," she said. She was smiling broadly, and the excited way with which she greeted me made me think that she had something she wanted to tell me. She asked about the case, but I told her very little except to say that it would be difficult to get past the defendant's motion to strike our expert.

Again, I didn't want to tell her so much about the facts that she felt compelled to research the motion. It was not that I didn't trust Michelle's legal research. She was better at research than I was. Her papers in law school were more thorough than mine, and the topic she covered was always more fully explored than any I addressed. The problem with Michelle's research, from a trial lawyer's standpoint, was that she wouldn't consider the memorandum complete until she had arrived at an absolute answer. If the general question, in broad terms, was "Does the law permit this?" Michelle would comb the digests and cases until she came up with a definitive "yes" or "no" answer.

That was fine if you were working for a firm that billed your time by the hour and gave legal advice to its clients based on what the research revealed. To the contrary, if Mr. Sullivan asked me if the law permitted him to do something, the answer was always "yes," and the research would be directed at giving him a road map around whatever legal impediments stood in his way.

We were not paid by the hour; we were paid by the result in a contingency fee practice. We were not looking for the truth; we were looking for persuasion. Of course, the truth is usually the most persuasive arrow in your quiver, but the trick is being able to express it in a manner that resonates with your audience. Sometimes that required massaging the rules of court in order to make the "truth" apparent for the jury.

For example, the general rule is that you are not permitted to ask leading questions of your own witness. Your questions to your witness shouldn't suggest the answers. But Sullivan ignored the rule and always instructed his associates "to ask every question dripping with prejudice." In this context, "prejudice" means "prejudged" or "predetermined"—that is to say that the Sullivan question answers itself in the minds of the jurors without waiting to hear how the witness responds. For example, "Have you stopped cheating on your wife yet?" would be a prejudicial question. When he was at his best, Sullivan would ask a series of questions, each more prejudicial than the last, without waiting for the witness to respond. If he drew an objection to the leading questions, Sullivan would just ask a couple of open-ended ones before slipping back into the leading series. Usually the defense lawyer would stop objecting, probably because he wanted the questioning to be over as soon as possible as much as for any other reason.

I told Michelle about what a beautiful, old town Lexington was and about the wooden-fenced horse farms that were all around the city. She listened with interest, but I could tell that she was waiting for me to finish so that she could tell me what she had been up to while I had been gone. She told me that work had been uneventful, but that I needed to get cleaned up because we were going to dinner at her parents' house.

Michelle couldn't keep a secret for very long, and she was incapable of lying. She had an abiding respect for the truth and could categorize most conflicts as black or white with very little room for shades of grey. She envisioned the law as a steadfast set of rules, and when a situation might arise that had not previously been addressed by the law, then logic and reason would expand the existing principles of the law to cover the new situation. Interestingly, I had met other children of lawyers who seem to have similar notions about the resolute sanctity of the law. In law school I imagined that this mindset had something to do with the fact that the offspring looked up to their parents and their parents' law practice.

As I got older, however, and got out into the world of private practice, I came to see that such a belief system was probably more the result of never having had to want for anything rather than respect for a parent's profession. Michelle loved her father and respected his accomplishments as a trial lawyer, but the truth is that she knew very little about how he spent his time each day. She thought he won cases because the law said he should win. I, and anybody else on the St. Jude Squad, could tell you that often Sullivan won cases despite what the law required. Because Michelle had never been deprived of any material item, she had never, as far as I knew, been in a situation where she might have been tempted to bend the rules to obtain what she wanted.

I knew that Michelle wanted to tell me something, but that she thought she had to wait to tell me. I knew it wouldn't take much prodding on my part to get her to tell me what it was that she was trying to keep secret. For a brief instant, it occurred to me that she might have found out about Beth somehow, but the news, whatever it was, seemed to be causing her to smile uncontrollably. That was not exactly the response one would expect upon learning that a spouse had committed adultery.

When I asked again what the occasion was, Michelle told me that we had to go tell her parents that they were going to be grandparents.

As I realized what she was telling me, I burst into a laugh and we hugged and kissed. I asked her how she knew and when she found out. She told me that she had done an in-home pregnancy test, and when it came out positive, she performed two more tests. When we went upstairs to the bathroom, she opened a drawer beside her sink and there were the positive strips laid out in order. She had called her doctor and made an appointment for the next week. She hadn't told anybody but the doctor's office about the pregnancy, and she wanted to wait until I got home to tell me in person.

"Does this mean our son is going to be named Jorge Alvarado?" I asked. At that point in my life, I actually thought of clients, especially those I went to trial with, as family members. Now they seem more like characters in a play that you have seen multiple times with different actors playing the role each time.

"No," she said. "I think his name will be 'Paul' because he should be named after Paul Thompson." She was referring to the name of a rear-end collision case I had tried a couple of months earlier—and to the facts of the accident—not our method of conception. The case had languished at the office for years, and the plaintiff's deposition had been taken long before I had arrived at the firm.

In civil cases, it is common practice to depose the principle witnesses. A deposition is a procedure whereby attorneys for all parties ask questions of a witness under oath while a court reporter, and sometimes a videographer, records the questions and answers. The deposition transcript, and sometimes the video, can be presented to a jury at trial in lieu of the witness's live testimony. A deposition can be taken to preserve a witness's testimony, to collect information about what the witness saw or heard, or to gather ammunition to cross-examine or impeach the witness if he testifies live at trial. Interestingly, we depose most witnesses in civil cases but rarely do so in criminal cases. Civil cases are about money. Criminal cases are just about life or liberty.

I had been confused when reading the deposition transcript of Paul Thompson as I prepared for the trial because I did not understand why, after every other sentence, the plaintiff said, "Excuse me." Halfway through my opening statement at trial, however, I learned that Paul Thompson had a flatulence problem. During the entire trial, he would pass gas and then blurt out, "Excuse me." There was no evidence that, in reasonable medical probability, the farting proximately resulted from the car wreck. In fact, Mr. Thompson had only received chiropractic care, a healing discipline of debated value. To my knowledge, even the most ardent proponents of chiropractic care do not claim that it can cure flatulence. Of course not having health insurance, Thompson only received chiropractic care until he exhausted his personal injury protection coverage of $2,500.00 paid by the plaintiff's own insurance company without regard to fault.

Still, I thought I was going to win the Thompson case until the very moment the jury returned a defense verdict. In retrospect, I don't think the farting or the minimal medical expenses threw the jury against Paul Thompson, but I admit that his deliberately putting on a nitroglycerin heart patch during my closing argument was a bit excessive. Hopefully, the pregnancy would go better than the case had.

"Paul" would be a fine name, I thought to myself, as I reflected on the converted apostle struck down by a blinding light on the road to Damascus. Paul Jessie had a nice ring to it. And if he ever played shortstop for The University of Texas, the crowd would call him "P. J."

Michelle's excitement was infectious, and I found myself laughing out loud as I stepped into the shower. It wasn't until the hot water hit me that I thought about Beth and the fact that I had not talked to her since she left Paintsville.

As the hot water streamed over my head, I started thinking about what Michelle would do if she found out about Beth. Michelle, I guess because her dad was a plaintiff's lawyer, was accepting of strangers and rarely judgmental of others until she got to know them. However, her concept of right and wrong was concrete and immutable. While we had never discussed what would happen if I cheated on her, it was understood that the relationship would be over and that she would leave at once—or kick me out, whichever would be most expedient. Michelle couldn't stand liars and cheating was just lying raised exponentially. Again, I assumed that this attitude was the result of her being her father's daughter. While I never heard Michelle and her mother discuss Tim Sullivan's philandering, there was always an undercurrent at family gatherings where Michelle and Amy would look at each other with their jaws clenched, Michelle curious about what her father was doing and Amy determined to keep Tim's proclivities from upsetting their daughter.

"Where is your dad?" Amy would say between her teeth.

"I don't know why you continue to put up with that man, Mother. The things he has put you through . . . " Michelle would whisper back to her mother.

Then Tim would burst into the room telling stories and asking questions that drew everyone into the conversation and the undercurrent would be calmed.

I think that Amy liked me, if only because both of her kids liked me, and she would do anything for her kids. The longer I worked at Peters & Sullivan, however, and the more time I spent with Tim, I began to sense an increased level of scrutiny of my actions by Amy—and even an elevated level of distrust. I thought that she was worried I knew something about her husband that she didn't. And of course, I did, but I was not worried that she thought I was capable of the same indiscretions as Tim. Maybe she was worried about it, though. Maybe she saw me trying to emulate Tim, and she knew what risks that entailed. Amy might like me well enough, but if she thought that I was capable of hurting her daughter, she wouldn't hesitate to intervene. I would have to be careful around Amy. I didn't know how much Tim would have discussed Beth with her. Probably he had not said much. But he could have mentioned the fact that the female contract lawyer unexpectedly left Kentucky while I was still there in an effort to deflect attention from whatever he had been doing. As I washed my hair and watched the suds disappear down the drain, it occurred to me that I had been home less than an hour and already I was beginning to suffer alternating bouts of guilt and paranoia that seemed to intensify.

For the first time, I dreaded going to my in-laws' house. I had to relax. There was no chance that Michelle was going to find out about Beth. If I could just get by this one screwup without Michelle finding out, I would never make such a mistake again—and the only way she was going to find out was if I told her. I couldn't let myself do that even if it would relieve the pressure of the guilt that was building up inside me.

Tim and Amy Sullivan lived in a French-style, cream-colored stucco house in River Oaks. Most of the houses in River Oaks are old southern mansions with giant oak trees and towering magnolias in well-manicured yards. Here and there, marble villas and Italianesque mansions have replaced the Georgian and Federal-style brick homes. Sullivan's house was unique because it looked like it belonged in a French vineyard rather than River Oaks. In the backyard was an old oak with a trunk so large that two people could not reach around it; and in the front was a series of towering plane trees that reached as high as the two-story, green-tiled roof.

Stepping inside the house was like stepping into a winery in Burgundy or Bordeaux. Everywhere one looked were fleur-de-lis and acanthus leaf patterns, inlaid furniture with scrolled feet and gilt corners, richly upholstered Bergère chairs with big ottomans, and tufted leather sofas with just the right amount of wear. Large fireplaces with split white oak logs waited in corners of the family room, living room, and master bedroom for the few days of the year when fires could be lit, and Impressionist paintings by various French, Spanish, and Portuguese artists adorned the walls.

The night I got back from Kentucky, we ate in the large dining room at the distressed oak wine-tasting table. When Michelle and I arrived, only Michelle's brother Jonathan and their mom, Amy, were there. Jonathan never brought a date to his parents' house. Jonathan was very good-looking and I knew from college and law school that women enjoyed being around him, but he kept his personal life separate from his family, and me, for that matter. He had black hair that, like his parents, was turning prematurely grey, and he was usually dressed in casual clothes that suggested an outdoorsy, hunting motif. Michelle relied on him for advice that ranged from her career to what to buy for our house. I imagine that it was partly the fact that Jonathan and I were friends that had caused Michelle to take an interest in me. It was obvious to me that keeping a secret from Michelle would necessarily involve keeping a secret from Jonathan.

A place was set for Tim, but he had not yet arrived. While it was not unusual for Tim to be late, I wondered for a moment if his absence was an indication that he didn't want to confront me about Beth with his family around.

We sat around the table in our usual places, and Amy began passing around Chinese food that she had ordered from Dong Ting's, which Jonathan had picked up on his way over. She had put the food into large bone-china serving dishes. Amy used her good china and crystal every day and just put them in the dishwasher. She must have had every serving piece available in the Spode Stafford Flower china pattern. Interestingly, Michelle had almost every serving piece in the Portmeirion Botanic Garden design, which is like a casual cousin of the more ornate Spode. There was a covered vegetable bowl containing steamed dumplings in red chili oil and another one with Birds in a Jade Nest, minced squab sautéed with duck liver and mushrooms spooned onto iceberg lettuce leaves, an oval platter of crispy fried green beans, an open vegetable bowl full of cabbage-wrapped meatballs of pork and crabmeat cooked in a clay pot that Dong Ting called "lion head," a large oval platter of spicy squid with garlic and ginger, and a big bowl of shrimp-fried rice. The conversation amounted to little more than chitchat and nobody asked about the case in Kentucky.

"I almost forgot the wine," Amy said, and she got up to go back into the kitchen. She was taller than Michelle and good-looking in her own right. She had soft grey hair that she kept cut short and refused to dye. I can't remember very many occasions when I saw Amy that she was not wearing a skirt.

Amy hollered back over her shoulder, "Go ahead and start eating. I imagine that Tim will be late." No doubt Amy had made that statement many times in her married life, and Michelle and Jonathan didn't seem concerned about their father's absence. Maybe Tim's habitual tardiness and absence were two of the reasons that Jonathan and Michelle were so close.

When Amy returned with an opened bottle of Wan Fu, she stopped at each place to fill a wine glass. When she got to Michelle's glass, Michelle put her hand over the top of her glass and looked up at her mother. Amy paused and looked knowingly at her daughter.

"You're pregnant," Amy said.

Michelle smiled. "We weren't going to say anything until Dad got here," but before she could finish, her mother was excitedly hugging her.

Jonathan got up from his place, hugged his sister, shook my hand, and told me congratulations. We spent most of the meal discussing funny family names and laughing about what we should name the baby if it was a boy or a girl. After we finished eating, Amy brought out a plate of fortune cookies, and we each selected one. As each person opened a cookie and read the fortune aloud, Jonathan would add the phrase "between the sheets," and we would all laugh. For instance when Michelle read, "You have the ability to excel at untried areas," Jonathan added, "between the sheets," and we all laughed as if we had never played this game before. We got to my cookie last and the fortune in it read, "Do the thing you fear and the death of fear is certain." Rather than continuing the game, Jonathan just looked at me, shook his head, and said while raising his hands palms up, "What have you ever been afraid of?"

I didn't answer.

We were carrying the dishes into the kitchen when Tim came home with his friend William Drummond. They had obviously been playing golf. They wore sport shirts and were sunburned. They had been drinking, but they didn't seem drunk.

It was not strange to see William at the Sullivan's house. He practically lived there. He had been a relief pitcher for the Astros as a young man, but now he seemed to make a living playing golf and betting on sporting events. He was always trying to get me to bet on the Texas Tech Red Raiders or the Texas Longhorns. The line always seemed a bit skewed to me, and the minimum bet was always out of my league. The next time I saw William, he would remind me of the bet he had offered and tell me how much money I had lost by failing to make the bet.

It was William who first recognized that we appeared to be celebrating some event. When he asked what the occasion was, everyone, including Tim, looked at Michelle.

"Dad," she said opening her hands and extending her arms with a flourish of presentment, "you're going to be a granddad."

"That is fantastic!" Sullivan said. "We couldn't be happier." He crossed the room and hugged his daughter who threw her outstretched arms around him. While he was hugging her, Sullivan looked at me, and I remember thinking that his smile seemed to dissipate. There was something about his facial expression that made me think about Beth, and I wondered what he knew.

After dinner, Sullivan, Jonathan, William, and I sat outside drinking scotch under the giant oak tree in the backyard. The circular bed around the tree was planted with begonias that were already beginning to bloom in neat rows of pink, red, and white. The huge oak was illuminated by lights concealed among the begonias and shadows from the trees limbs dappled the veranda of octagonal clay tiles and swayed with the breeze across the cream stucco walls on the back of the house. Jonathan was excited about the baby, and he and William began suggesting names again. William thought that "William" was a perfect name because it gave a boy so many options like "Will," "Bill," or "Willie" depending on his personality. "Well Willie," Jonathan chided him, "What if it's a girl? Did you ever think of that, Podzy?" They eventually wandered off into the house.

Sullivan waited until Jonathan was beyond earshot and said to me under his breath, "That boy may die hungry but he won't die tired." I don't know that Sullivan really thought that Jonathan was lazy. There was a tension, almost a competition, between them. Sullivan may have felt that his son lacked some entrepreneurial spark, but I assumed that Sullivan's comments were meant for me as much as being directed at Jonathan. At some level Sullivan may have been disappointed that he didn't have Jonathan at the firm to teach him the personal injury and trial lawyer business, but he had me. As he turned his attention to me, I could tell by the serious look on his face that we were about to discuss business. At least I hoped that is all we were going to discuss.

Sullivan asked about the defendant's motion to strike the plaintiffs' expert. I told him that I expected to have a draft response to the motion for him to read by Monday. I told him that I liked Mr. Walton, but that I thought the defendant had done a better job than the plaintiffs of securing experts with superior credentials. I also told him about what Mr. Walton had said about the "new" judge on the case. Sullivan was clearly concerned, and I don't think he had known about the judge until I told him. He said he would check out the judge's history. He found it interesting that the referral lawyers had failed to mention that a judge from Boyd County, Kentucky, was sitting on a case that involved the Boyd Oil Company.

As we got up from the ornate wrought-iron table and chairs to go back into the house to freshen our drinks, Sullivan asked why Beth had come back to Houston without finishing her work on the discovery responses. I told him that I didn't know. I wondered if he was asking why Beth had come back, or if he was asking whether I knew why Beth had come back.

"She doesn't seem like the kind of person who would disappear in the middle of a project," Sullivan said.

"I'm guessing it is some kind of personal problem," I said, realizing that my attempt at vagueness would be interpreted as my knowing more than I had let on.

Sullivan just nodded and chewed the ice from his glass. I worried that he might feel compelled to ask Beth about what was going on since he wasn't getting much information from me, but I couldn't think of anything to say that would get him off the topic. I followed him back into the house, and nothing more was said about the case in front of the others.

At the office on Monday there was a steady stream of people coming into my office to discuss the baby news. Michelle and I had discussed not telling anybody about the baby until we were farther along in the pregnancy, but apparently Tim hadn't felt constrained by our wishes in that regard. Beth didn't come by, and I don't think she came in to work that day. I don't know if Michelle got any work done that Monday. She called me at least a half-dozen times from her cell phone as she went from baby store to baby store. There is no telling how many times she called Jonathan that day. I don't remember her buying any furniture at that point because we didn't know the sex of the baby yet. But she was getting ideas for decorating the little nursery next to our bedroom, and she did come home with an armload of books about pregnancy. I would not have to worry about her getting caught up in the research on the Kentucky case any longer. She was researching pregnancy and babies.

Between the well-wishers' visits, Eileen and I worked on our response to the motion. In essence, the response tracked the language in the *Goodyear* case, which I thought suggested that methodologies that form the basis of government regulations are "generally accepted." I talked to Mr. Walton several times that day, working with him on preparing an affidavit establishing that the linear no-threshold theory formed the basis of government regulations for exposure to radiation workers, and that the threshold theory, while debated among scientists, was not relied upon for drafting government safety regulations. I intended to attach the affidavit to the pleading that I was drafting. The response concluded by asking the court to strike the defendant's experts.

Most of the people in the office had left by the time we finished, and it was dark in Sullivan's office when I left a copy in the seat of his desk chair.

I went back to my office and waited for Eileen to pack up her stuff and leave before I tried to call Beth on her cell phone. There was no answer. I thought to myself that maybe she had quit the job, and for all I knew, was out of my life as quickly as she had come into it. I was proud of the response to the motion, and thought we had a good chance of at least defeating the defendant's motion and possibly even getting the defendant's experts struck. Maybe things were getting back on track.

By the time I got home, I had convinced myself that the case was in good shape and that if I kept my mouth shut about Beth, nobody would ever have to know about my indiscretion. I promised myself that if I could get away without anybody knowing about the brief affair, I would never let anything like it happen again. Still, thinking about Beth, I replayed in my mind the events of that evening in the Paintsville Inn.

After dinner, Michelle and I made love.

I woke up during the night and realized that Michelle was not in the bed with me. I slipped on my boxer shorts that I had dropped beside the bed and went into the bathroom to check on her but she was not in there.

When I went into the small room adjacent to our bedroom, Michelle was sitting cross-legged in the middle of the floor. She was wearing panties and her Biggio jersey and reading a magazine. Other magazines were open all around her. On the floor were masking tape outlines of what I presumed would eventually be furniture, either that or the Houston police had just finished marking off a crime scene.

"How do you feel about Beatrix Potter?" Michelle asked not sounding the least bit tired.

"Fine," I said. "What time is it?"

"I don't know. It's late. You fell asleep, but I couldn't sleep. I'm thinking 'Peter Rabbit' if it's a boy and Dorothy from the 'Wizard of

Oz' if it's a girl. What do you think?" She asked looking up at me and holding a couple of magazine pages of pictures for me to consider.

"Can we pick a story without a villain?" I asked. "Mr. McGregor has always scared me and those flying monkeys give me nightmares."

"That settles it," she said resolutely and closed the magazines. "Noah's Ark. It works for either a boy or a girl. I wonder if we could get a baby bed shaped like an ark." She pulled out a pencil and sketchpad from beneath the pile of magazines and began drawing a mural that would go on the wall behind the baby's bed.

I laughed. "I'm going back to bed. Are you coming?"

"In a minute," she said, and I left her planning the nursery.

The next morning, I got up before Michelle and made a pot of coffee. I read the sports page while I waited for the coffee to brew. I poured myself a cup and took it back upstairs to the shower. Our shower in the master bath was a large glass enclosure with a bench seat on one end. I was in the habit of taking a cup of coffee with me into the shower in the morning. I would turn the shower to as hot as I could stand it, and sit on the bench in the steam and drink coffee. It was a good time to sit in solitude and think about cases and about what needed to be done that day. Michelle would always kid me about the length of time I would spend in the shower. She told me she thought I was returning to the womb. The shower was my favorite part of the house, and taking a shower was my favorite part of the day.

That morning, I remember sitting on the bench in the shower with the steam billowing up, drinking my coffee, when the cup slipped in my hand and some of the coffee sloshed onto my lap.

At first, as I looked down at my penis, I thought I might have burned myself. Small blisters had formed on the shaft of my penis. They were very painful to touch. I abandoned the steam, showered quickly, dressed, and left before Michelle awoke.

I was sitting at my desk, staring off into space, when the phone rang that morning. Normally, the phone rang at Eileen's desk, and she would screen the calls and send them into me. If the phone rang at my desk, it was somebody calling me on my private line. Michelle had that number, my parents had that number, and the people in the office used that line.

It was Beth calling. She was in her office. She sounded nervous and distraught. She attempted the usual pleasantries, but I could tell that there was something she was getting around to telling me. I asked her why she hadn't called before and why she had left Paintsville in such a rush.

"Davy," she said in a hushed tone as if she were worried that somebody near her might be trying to listen in on her conversation. "There is something I have to tell you. I have herpes. I got it from my husband, I think. I'm afraid that you may have been exposed." She spoke very softly into the receiver. "I'm so sorry. I never would have done anything to hurt you. I went to the doctor yesterday. I have to take these pills. I just heard that Michelle is pregnant. You have to be careful. I thought that I would be past all of this when I got married."

She continued talking, but I couldn't understand most of what she was saying because she was talking so softly into the phone and because I couldn't focus on what she was saying. Immediately, I felt isolated and disconnected from everyone around me. I didn't tell her what I had found in the shower that morning. I would eventually tell her, but it would be a while before I ever told anyone other than the person who gave it to me.

I sat at my desk and thought for a moment about calling my dad. While it would be nice to hear his voice, I couldn't see how he would have any advice to offer for this particular situation. Surely, nothing like this had ever happened in his life, and I really didn't want him to know what I had done.

Growing up, I had the opportunity to talk to my dad almost every day at breakfast and every evening at dinner. Dad cooked breakfast, and Mom cooked dinner. Invariably, Dad left the college where he taught English and Shakespeare in time to be home by five o'clock, and we would sit down as a family to eat. Usually, the conversation started off with him asking about what happened in school that day, or if I had heard about some event that occurred in the world of sports. Occasionally, there would be a question about how hard a test had been or if I had received a grade back on a paper; but, for the most part, my parents didn't concern themselves with my grades. They knew that I was harder on myself than they would have ever been, and good grades just weren't an issue at our house.

The only scholastic discussions we had were when my dad asked me about what we were reading in English class. My mom had been the one who had taught me to read. We would take a nap every day after lunch before I started school, and she would read to me from picture books. Eventually I would memorize the rhyming lines, and I began to recognize what lines went with the pictures on a certain page. The first book I remember "reading" on my own was *Captain Kitty*. I can't remember now if the first line was "Captain Kitty sailed to sea in a beautiful 'pea-green' boat" or "in a beautiful 'sea-green' boat," but I remember to this day that the last line was "We've been away, but I must say, Home looks good to me!" At age three or at thirty, coming home has an emotional resolution. Mom may have started me reading, but it was Dad who monitored my progress in school.

Dad had read everything, including the books assigned for me to read in elementary and middle school. I think that he thought I would grow up to be a writer or poet. I think he would have been proud of me if I had done that—whether I wrote *Captain Kitty Comes Ashore* or *What if Holden Caulfield Goes to Law School?* When I got to high school, if there was a book assigned that he had not read, he would read my copy at night after I had gone to bed. It was not that he wanted to quiz me about the plot or engage me in a conversation about the themes and symbols of the novel or play so that I might get a better grade in class — sometimes we did discuss the symbols if he thought the author had done something particularly noteworthy. Instead, I think he read the books because he thought that reading developed a student's understanding of the world; and, as a concerned parent, he wanted to be in touch with what it was that the public schools of Abilene were doing to shape my mind. Considering the fact that I can still recall passages of *Captain Kitty*, there may be some validity to that.

He was opposed to censorship in any form. If it was published in a book, I could read it. While there were always annotated copies of *Macbeth* and *Hamlet* lying around the den, there were also copies of the complete works of Dan Jenkins and Peter De Vries. He cautioned me not to be too caught up in trying to determine if any part of a work of fiction was true or "really happened." Sure it is interesting to know what we can of what happened to Mr. Shakespeare while he was alive, but not because we assume his plays are autobiographical. Instead, it is interesting to know about his life to see how the things that happened to him influenced what he wrote. Dad told me that "wondering what happens next" is the highest compliment you can pay a writer of fiction. He carried this philosophy to such an extreme that he would open a modern novel in the middle and read to the end while trying to guess what happened in the beginning.

When Little League started up in the spring, the dinner conversations were cut short because Dad always coached my team or my brother's team. If I didn't make it as a poet, Dad wanted me to be a shortstop and my brother to be a catcher or first baseman. Some years our teams would be better than others. But I don't remember Dad ever raising his voice at the players. His focus was always on telling us what to anticipate doing in any given situation—choke up on the bat if you're behind in the count, never throw behind the runner, move up to the grass with men on base during late innings in a close game. Sure, he wanted to win, and he blamed himself if we lost—he should have changed pitchers earlier in the fourth inning, he never should have sent that runner home on a passed ball, he should have sent the runner to third base in the sixth inning.

Baseball to Dad was like an intricate, theatrical play, with peculiar subtleties and nuances that changed every time a pitch was thrown, not unlike trying to control the outcome of a trial with each question that is asked. He thought boys could learn about life from playing a game or reading a classic work of fiction, but I couldn't recall a game experience or a work of fiction that had prepared me for handling the situation in which I found myself. Previously I had worried about how, as a young lawyer at Peters & Sullivan, I would ever have time to coach my son's Little League games or get home in time for dinner to discuss what had happened at school that day. Now I was wondering if I would even be around to watch my son grow up.

In high school, the occasions when my family would sit down for dinner became less and less frequent. I had a job in a store at the mall, and I usually worked evenings. After I got cut from the baseball team at the end of my sophomore year, I found my way onto the debate team, and my weekends were spent at out-of-town debate tournaments.

Most weekdays though, my dad would still cook breakfast, and he would use that time to catch up with me. In my senior year, the honors English class had a vocabulary test every Friday over words selected from whatever it was that we were reading at the time. We had all week to look up the words and learn the definitions and how to spell them. It became a running joke at my house for me to sit down for breakfast on Friday and ask Dad what each word meant. Then, I would go take the test first period, repeating the definitions that Dad had given me at breakfast. Usually, he would use the word in a sentence so that I could understand what it meant, rather than giving me a definition *per se*. It's easier to learn the meaning of a word in context rather than in the abstract. Sometimes, I forgot what Dad told me, but I don't think he ever missed a word.

When I went away to college at Texas Tech, I called home religiously once a week at first. By the time I completed law school at The University of Texas, I was calling home only to make arrangements at holidays to come home.

Sitting in my office, I wondered what Dad had fixed for breakfast that morning.

I thought about calling Beth back. Suddenly, I had questions to ask that a minute ago I had not contemplated. Where did she go to the doctor? What do the pills do? What does herpes do to your body? Had she told anybody else about the herpes, or about the affair?

Part of me wanted to call Michelle. Lonely and detached, I needed to talk to someone who was a friend. I needed to tell the whole, sordid story. But I couldn't call Michelle. I couldn't tell her about sleeping with Beth. I was too ashamed to tell her that I thought I had herpes. And for the first time, it occurred to me that I might have infected her the previous night. As I stood up from my desk, I could feel the blood rushing to my head and I thought I might faint.

Sweating, I picked up the phonebook from the credenza and rifled through the pages until I found the number and address of the Houston City Health Department, Riverside Clinic on Delano Street. I considered tearing out the page, but I thought better of it and scribbled down the address and phone number. I put on my navy blazer, felt in the pocket for my keys, and left without telling Eileen where I was going.

9

My first stop was at Ninfa's restaurant on Navigation. I circled the building a couple of times to make sure that Sullivan wasn't there. I'd been there many times with him, for a Mexican breakfast of *migas* or *huevos con chorizo* accompanied by a Bloody Mary or two. When I was satisfied that Sullivan was not at the restaurant, I parked my car, went in, and found a secluded table near the bar in the back. A waiter recognized me, and nodded. In a moment, he brought over a menu and a Bloody Mary. I told him I didn't need a menu, but that I would need another Bloody Mary by the time he could get back with one.

The place was almost empty, although even without customers, it had a festive feel. Multicolored cutouts hung like banners from the ceiling, Tejano music blared over the speaker system, and numerous waiters in pastel-colored Guy Ybarra shirts milled about wiping table-tops and putting out place settings in anticipation of the noon rush. The place had long been a Houston institution because of its good food and strong margaritas. I wanted to have a third drink before going to the county STD clinic, but I just couldn't take the chance of seeing somebody I knew in the lunch crowd.

The clinic was between Ninfa's and West University. I parked as far away from the front door of the place as possible. The building was a small, drab, brick building with no windows on the front. After entering through a foyer, I stopped at a frosted-glass sliding window behind which a woman sat typing at a computer terminal. Without looking at me, she handed me a clipboard, and asked, in a tone loud enough for all of those seated in the tile-floored lobby to hear, whether I was there for "STD or TB."

In a voice barely above a whisper, I said, "STD."

"Venereal diseases get the green form," she said as she directed me to fill out the paperwork on the clipboard. I took a seat and noticed that several other people in the lobby were also completing questionnaires on clipboards, while others sat holding laminated cards with numbers on them. A few seats down from me, a couple of pretty teenage girls were whispering to each other and giggling. One of them held a card with the number "8" on it.

I considered giving false information on the form—a fake name and address, a bogus rendition of the recent onset of symptoms—but ultimately wrote in my correct name and used my office address and direct-line phone number. I didn't check the box for married.

As I handed the clipboard with the green form back to the woman behind the frosted-glass window, another woman at different sliding window down the hall called the number of one of the teenage girls. I watched as they both went to the window, and the one holding the card reached into the front pocket of her blue jeans and handed a crumpled ten-dollar bill to the lady. The lady behind my window handed me a laminated card with the number "30" on it.

I returned to my seat and waited for about an hour before the woman at the other window called my number. At this second window, I paid my ten dollars. The lady handed me a receipt and ushered me through a set of double doors to another waiting room. The teenage girls were still there, but they were quiet now, and the one still held her laminated card.

The dusty beige room had metal folding chairs around the walls and a low table in the middle that was littered with out-of-date magazines that people read while waiting so that they could avoid making eye contact with the other people in the room. On one wall was a display of informational brochures on various STDs. After a while, the teenage girl with the laminated card was called down the hall, and in another hour, I was called as well.

I was taken to what looked like a hospital room where a man in rubber gloves and a name tag that read "Dr. Neftali" instructed me to sit down and roll up one shirt sleeve so that he could draw two vials of blood. After he capped and labeled the vials, he escorted me to a tiny room barely large enough for a small desk, a secretarial chair, and a metal folding chair like those in the last waiting room. On the walls were photographs depicting various maladies of the male sex organ. Looking at the photos, I diagnosed myself with herpes before the tired, middle-aged woman came into the room with a folder that I presumed was my file. She sat at the desk.

"The good news Mr. Jessie is that you do not appear to have AIDS." She said in a sterile, emotionless manner. "Of course, you should repeat the test six months from your last possible exposure to confirm that you do not demonstrate antibodies to the virus. Unfortunately, the bad news is that you do have genital herpes. It will be necessary for me to examine you to confirm the diagnosis," she said, still without introducing herself.

I stood and removed my pants and underwear while she slipped on a pair of rubber gloves and some reading glasses. I tried to drop my pants and underwear casually onto the metal chair, but the pants, and whatever dignity I had left, fell to the floor and my change spilled out of the pockets. Coins rolled noisily across the dusty tile floor.

The lady scooted over to me on her secretarial chair and lifted my flaccid penis away from my scrotum so that she could examine the now angry red blisters on the shaft. She then rolled back to her desk, popped off the glove, and made a few notes on my chart. Then, she scribbled her name on a preprinted prescription pad that sat on the desk and handed me the page. "This is for acyclovir. You should take three pills a day for five days, or until the symptoms disappear." She said it in a way that made me think she had memorized the explanation. "This will help dry up those blisters, but it isn't a cure. Different people have different rates of recurrence. Some will have symptoms every month. Some may have them only once or twice a year. Some never experience another outbreak. The virus that causes the outbreak lives in your spinal cord, and this drug only assists your immune system in suppressing the outbreak. You should be very careful about direct skin to skin contact as well as sexual contact during an outbreak, as that is when you are most likely to spread the disease. But, even when there is no outbreak, the disease can be spread through a process called viral shedding. I've given you a prescription for enough pills to cover several outbreaks. I think you'll find over time that the number and severity of the outbreaks will diminish. Do you have any questions?"

In my stunned state, I could only shake my head. As I walked out of the clinic my mind wandered. Was the disease named "herpes" because of something having to do with snakes? I knew that a person who studied snakes was called a "herpetologist." Maybe whoever it was that originally identified the disease thought the scabs that formed where the blisters had been were reminiscent of the scales of a snake. Or maybe a diseased penis reminded him of a snake.

I had never much cared for snakes myself. I can remember walking home from school one day to find my mom in the driveway with a hoe chopping the head off a long kingsnake whose decapitated body continued to flip and curl and try to escape. Several kids my little brother's age who had gotten home before me were standing around watching the spectacle. One of the mothers, whose child was watching, commented to my mom that it was just a harmless kingsnake.

Mom responded, "The only good snake is a dead snake." The memory of my mom wielding that hoe still makes me uneasy, and I have never been able to understand how anybody could be interested in snakes.

Even the fall from grace story in Genesis didn't make much sense to me. Oh, I understood that the phallic serpent represents evil and all that, but would you take an apple or a pomegranate or a quince or whatever from a snake? I can see a snake sneaking up on you and eating your plant of immortality, but I can't see taking food from a snake. Assuming that the devil could take whatever form he wanted when trying to distribute the fruit of the tree of the knowledge of good and evil, it seemed to me like he would have had a better chance of success as a cute little squirrel or maybe a raccoon with those tiny, almost human hands.

The whole "tree of knowledge of good and evil" story has always left me thinking that something, a few paragraphs or maybe a page or two, was missing. I am not referring to the two stories of creation in Genesis or the problem with how many wives Adam had or the sudden appearance of additional cast members about the time that Cain and Abel showed up. I mean that when I read about the tree it always seemed to me that the punch line had been redacted or lost in the transcription process. So, I tried to figure out how to fill in the blanks left in the text. What would be the drawback of having the knowledge of the difference between good and evil? Was Gilgamesh a hero because he killed the Bull of Heaven or because he sought knowledge of the human condition?

Of course, God told Adam not to eat the fruit of the tree, but there must have been a reason that God didn't want him eating the fruit beyond just the parental "because I said so" reason. Could it be that having this knowledge might elevate man to a level that usurped a role that God had relegated to Himself—deciding what is good and what is evil and differentiating between the two? A great deal of human history from before Hammurabi to after Napoleon has been spent trying to define what is legal and good or illegal and evil. Maybe God wanted to be the source of all law, and eating the fruit put man in a position whereby he felt compelled to take over the role as the giver of law.

Could it be that God didn't want man having knowledge of good and evil because He didn't want man to be in a position to criticize the fact that God, though seemingly all-knowing and all-powerful, had permitted evil to slither into the creation picture? If Adam ate the apple, then it would just be a matter of time until Job started shaking his fist at the heavens. Setting aside the idea that God might have a reason for having evil exist in the world—the "it's all about choices" sermon—the notion that man would steadily nag and complain to God once man learned that evil existed—the "what have I done to deserve this" lament—would surely be the kind of outcome God would want to avoid.

Or could it be that, once man had knowledge of good and evil, man would see that he was capable of both. Each of us, no matter how well-intentioned, can violate even the most rudimentary concepts of right and wrong. When we learn that something as simple as a broken promise can give birth to a lie which by our action or inaction can fester into something truly injurious and sinister, we see that we're something less than good, and our opinion of God, if we assume *arguendo* that He put us here, suffers with the realization.

Outside, in the bright light of the beautiful spring day, I noticed the two teenage girls crying in the front seat of their car as I walked across the parking lot to mine.

I drove to an ATM machine and withdrew two hundred dollars. I realized that I had to enter my personal identification number to initiate the transaction, but I left my shades on and tried not to look at the security camera while the machine spit out my money in twenty-dollar bills. I had no idea how much the medication was going to cost, but I wanted to be sure and pay cash for it so that there would be no record of the transaction on a credit card bill. The ATM machine was close to work, and I used it frequently. Michelle wouldn't pay any attention to the amount or time of the withdrawal when the bank statement came through.

Then I drove east toward the ship channel, and away from our home. Eventually, I found a drive-through pharmacy in a part of town where I didn't think anybody would know me. Again, I left my shades on when the pharmacy attendant came to the window and took my prescription slip. I avoided looking directly at the camera in the corner of the pharmacy window and waited in the car while the prescription was filled. When the attendant returned, she asked me if I wanted to put the charge on my insurance, but I told her that I didn't have insurance and paid the bill with cash. Several cars lined up behind me while the pharmacist explained the regimen for taking the pills right away, how to begin taking them again when I anticipated the next outbreak, and how many refills I had remaining on the prescription.

I nervously drummed my fingers on the steering wheel while nodding my understanding of the instructions and glancing at the rear view mirror to see if I knew anyone in the cars behind me. When she finally handed me the stapled sack with the prescription, I screeched the tires as I pulled away from the window.

I opened the sack while driving and put the brown bottle of pills in my pocket. I tore up the label attached to the bag into little pieces so that I could flush them down a toilet.

The next outbreak? I knew there was no cure, but I had not begun to calculate the consequences of the next outbreak. What was I supposed to do? I dug around in my glove compartment and found a bottle of Aleve, and transferred the contents of the two bottles. Then I scraped the label off the bottle that had contained the acyclovir, tore it up into little pieces and stuffed that into my pocket to be flushed later as well.

Was I going to have to repeat this episode every month? Would I ever be able to have sex again? I assumed I wouldn't ever be able to have sex again with Michelle. What about the fact that I had already had sex with her once? Maybe, while she was pregnant, I could avoid having sex with her, but what was I going to do after the baby was born? Would I only be able to have sex with women that had herpes? Beth was the only person I knew with herpes, or who knew that I had been exposed to herpes. Would I have to have secret sex with Beth any time that I felt like I just had to have sex?

I stopped at a gas station and disposed of the label remnants. As I flushed them down the toilet, I realized that I had thrown away my entitlement to a refill, and that someday, after three or four more outbreaks, I would have to return to the clinic.

I drove through Hermann Park and watched the couples with strollers leaving the butterfly museum. I had to talk to somebody. I had to ask somebody the questions that were racing through my head, even if he or she couldn't answer them. I called Beth on her cell phone, and asked her to meet me at the Monarch Bar in the Hotel Zazu, which was the old Warwick Hotel beside Hermann Park.

It was almost lunchtime, but the Monarch Bar was deserted. It billed itself as the "scene to see and be seen," but there were only a few people in the lobby checking out of the hotel. I found a seat in the back and ordered a Corona. I told the waitress I was waiting for someone, but that I didn't expect to order lunch. I wondered as she took my order if she could tell that I was harboring a venereal disease. Could she tell that I had been unfaithful to my wife? Could she tell that I was watching my world crash down around me?

I saw Beth as she walked through the front door, across the lobby, and into the dimly lit, overly decorated bar. Apparently back when "George Bush the First" had been president, the Queen of England or British Prime Minister stayed at the Warwick. I doubt if either would have stayed at someplace called the "Hotel Zazu." In any event, the Monarch moniker was still affixed to the bar. But that could just be because of its proximity to the butterfly museum. Beth was wearing jeans and a sweater with the cross necklace on the outside of the turtleneck. As she sat down across from me at the table where I was sitting, her eyes were red and swollen, but she still looked incredible. The anger, that I had intended to unleash on her, melted away as I watched her sit down.

"It's official," I said, "I've got it."

She looked around to be sure that nobody could hear us before she said, "I was afraid of that. I'm so sorry. I never would have done anything to hurt you. Did you go to the doctor?"

I told her about the dehumanizing experience at the STD clinic. I asked her whether the medication had helped her, and she told me that it had. When a waitress came by I ordered another beer, and Beth ordered coffee with cream. The question about what to do next sat between us for a considerable period of time without either of us addressing it, or even talking. I sipped my beer, and she stirred cream into her coffee cup.

"What's the story with your husband?" I asked, deciding that my anger was better vented against him.

"He and I have barely spoken. He says he doesn't have it. He says I must have gotten it someplace else. I think he's lying to me. I don't know. He could have had it for years and not told me. He could have gotten it last month, for all I know. When I tried to talk to him about it, he just claimed that he had to leave on business and began packing a bag. I screamed at him to stop and talk to me, but he just packed his things and left with me yelling at him.

"I'm thinking of running, too," I said.

"What do you mean?"

"I think I'm going back to Kentucky on the pretense of working on the case. I'm thinking about leaving today. I have to take three pills a day for five days, so I'll probably be back in about a week. Do you know of anything that needs to be done on the case out there? Did you ever finish up that discovery?"

"No, I don't think I will," she said. "There really isn't much that needs to be done in Kentucky, however. I guess I am going to call Riza and tell her the status of everything, and that I am moving because of my husband's work. I don't know what I am going to say. But I think I am not going back to work at Peters & Sullivan any time soon. Another unexplained gap on my resume. It would be hard to say which has been more disappointing between my career and my personal life."

"Something will turn around."

"No," she said, "it's like I am damaged goods now. Nobody will want me. Remember when you were single? Each time you had sex with someone, there was that pang of fear the next day as you asked God to please not let you catch anything or get pregnant? It's like when you get drunk and hungover, and you make a deal with God that if He'll just let you feel better, you'll never get that drunk again, but the after-sex remorse is a bigger deal. I thought I was past all of that."

Nervously, she reached into her purse and fumbled around until she pulled out a crumpled copy of a newspaper page. Beth unfolded it and spread the page out over the table where we were sitting. It was a page out of the personals section of *Free Press Houston*, a weekly newspaper that was usually available in Houston at most coffee shops and diners. The paper generally covered stories about local politics and entertainment, but it always carried an entertaining section of personal ads. The paper would highlight a particularly outrageous ad each week. "Look at this," she said. "This is where I am in my life."

Beth had circled the highlighted ad from that week's paper:

> Have you been recently diagnosed with genital herpes? Are you concerned that your sex life is over? Has your diagnosis left you sexually frustrated? Are you afraid to discuss your diagnosis with potential partners?
>
> I'm 6'1" SWM, H/WP and I've also been diagnosed with genital herpes. Life does go on! We can enjoy sex together and not worry about spreading the disease further! Contact me at Box BW63T.
>
> Photo available.

"Can you believe this?" Beth asked. "Apparently, this guy is preying on women like me, who have recently been diagnosed with herpes. Worse yet, I've actually been thinking about calling him."

"Don't call him," I said. "Who knows if herpes is the only disease he has?"

Beth looked at me, and her eyes widened. In a moment, she put her hand over her face and started to cry. I felt sorry for her, and I felt sorry for me. I could tell that she was farther along than I was in a process of realization of the complications of contracting an incurable venereal disease. I had already started to worry about passing the disease to Michelle, and I had only briefly considered the implications of not ever having sex again.

When Beth showed me the personal ad from the *Free Press Houston*, the thought became more concrete in my mind.

Of course, the thought crossed my mind again that I could have sex with Beth. If we just had sex with each other, nobody else would ever get the disease from either of us. She was beautiful. I honestly believed that she liked me. Maybe she and I could just leave and start a new life somewhere, and not ever tell anybody about the disease.

As attractive as Beth might have been, sex with her was not something in which I had any interest. She must have read my thoughts. She looked at me with her hand over her mouth, and whispered, "You think I am damaged goods also, don't you?"

"No, of course not, not the way you mean it. But do you think God is punishing us for having an affair" I asked.

"Yes, don't you?"

"I haven't let myself think about it yet. I guess part of me does. Part of me says this is a virus that seeks a host where it can replicate and survive, and it doesn't discriminate between moral or immoral hosts."

"Somebody had to put the virus here in the first place," she said.

"We're just feeling guilty."

"And I'm scared," she said. "I'm scared that my husband and I will end up divorced, and I don't have a job, and we have all these debts from his harebrained business schemes. He's a drug rep. We don't have that kind of money. And, nobody will ever want me again. And I'll never have children. And I won't be able to find a job. I never have truly practiced law. I'm a glorified computer operator. I haven't read a case since studying for the bar exam."

"You'll find another job," I said.

"And I'm scared for you, too."

"For me?"

"Yes. I know I don't know you well. Certainly not well enough to have sex with you. But I know how you are about keeping secrets. You're not planning on telling your wife, are you? How are you going to keep it from her? Are you just going to stop having sex with your wife? How long can you keep that up? You can't just move to Kentucky indefinitely."

"No," I said.

"Oh, my God. You've already had sex with her, haven't you? She's pregnant, Davy. You have to tell her. Have you had sex with her during this outbreak?"

"That's not really any of your business, is it?"

"No," she said. "It never should have been any of my business. I'm sorry, Davy. I can't tell you enough how sorry I am, but I can't continue to sit here and talk to you about this right now. I have to go." I would never see her again, and I knew that as she hurriedly crossed the lobby and went out through the front door.

I finished my beer and paid the tab, but before I left, I called Joe Abney, a friend of mine who worked at the Willis & Bonham firm over on the Gulf Freeway. The firm specialized in mass torts, having made fortunes in representing asbestos victims and people who had taken Fen-Phen and other prescription drugs with deleterious side effects. The firm was always testing the litigation waters, to see what the next big mass tort might be. For every Fen-Phen success, there was a breast implant, Accentual, or Baycol disaster. Sometimes the cases panned out; sometimes they didn't. But, always, the cases were huge undertakings requiring a great deal of staff and funding.

I knew that one key to success in the mass tort context was to try to keep the cases in state court and out of the federal courts where the multidistrict litigation panel could scoop up the cases and send them to the federal judge and venue of the panel's choosing. The plaintiffs' attorneys would rather keep the cases in a Houston state court, where the juries were more likely to be favorable to the plaintiff's side and where the judges had to stand for election instead of being appointed for life like federal judges. One way to avoid federal court was to sue an "in-state" defendant, thereby avoiding the federal court's diversity jurisdiction. Federal courts have diversity jurisdiction over suits between parties from different states. However, if one defendant is from the same state as the plaintiff, there is no diversity jurisdiction. I asked my friend Abney if Willis & Bonham was looking at any new litigation against Merck.

"We might be," he said. "Why do you ask? Are you looking to refer cases? That doesn't sound like the Peters & Sullivan I know," he said.

"No," I said. "I just thought you might like to know who their local drug rep is for purposes of avoiding diversity in any filings in the Houston area." I gave him the name of Beth's husband and their home address. By the time I got home from Kentucky five days later, Beth's husband had been sued individually, along with Merck, in 2,500 Vioxx cases in a Harris County state court. His life as a drug manufacturer's representative was finished.

I spent most of my time when I got back from Kentucky sitting in my office with the door closed. I had read everything online that I could stomach about genital herpes, and I had even called a toll-free number at the Centers for Disease Control to ask questions. I searched the Internet for articles about ongoing research for a cure, but nothing looked very promising—at least not in the short-term. The known medications coupled with the body's immune system would kill a portion of the virus during an outbreak but not the virus that lay dormant in the spine. I imagined that it was something like the arcade game in which you bop the varmint on the head when it appears from its hole and wait for the next one to appear. The trick would be getting the entire virus to present itself for destruction at one time, and it didn't appear that anybody was going to solve that problem any time soon.

The blisters on my penis had scabbed over and were still unsightly, but I had avoided being naked around Michelle because sex had been the farthest thing from her mind. Morning sickness had not been restricted to mornings, and she had spent most of her time either at work or in bed.

My caseload had dwindled down to just the Kentucky case against Boyd Oil. While there were multiple plaintiffs involved, there was only one set of operative facts, and there was not much to do on the case at that point except prepare to take the depositions of Boyd's personnel and their experts. If the judge ruled against us on the motion to strike our expert, the depositions would probably not go forward.

Eileen had taken on Beth's job of completing the plaintiffs' discovery responses, and I was merely signing off on them as she completed each set. Our local counsel in Kentucky was planning on presenting the plaintiffs for their individual depositions, assuming that we overcame Boyd's motion on our expert. It seemed like I was just killing time waiting for the next shoe to drop, but I kept my office door closed and tried to look busy. I tried unsuccessfully to remember my ideas for the next few lines of my poem. I scribbled ideas for a short story but I didn't really write a paragraph.

As was his customary practice, Sullivan burst through my office door one morning without knocking. I had situated my computer monitor facing away from the door for just such an occurrence. I clicked the mouse with the cursor on the minimize key, and asked him what was up. He closed the door behind him as he sat down in one of the client chairs and put his feet up on my desk.

"Good work on that expert motion," he said. He tried his best to sound encouraging. "I think we'll be okay."

"I hope so."

"I'm doing some work on checking out the judge. You were right to think there might be a problem." Sullivan looked at his shoes for a moment, evaluating the results of a recent shine. He frowned at a spot and then smiled as he looked back up at me. "How's the baby business at home?"

"Fine, I guess. Michelle has been pretty sick."

"That's what I heard. Serves her right for what she put her mother through." I too had heard the stories about how sick Amy had been for the first three months that she carried Michelle. "But it passes," he said. "Keep a ready supply of saltines and 7UP." Somehow I doubted that he had ever made many runs to the convenience store for crackers and soda. "What do you have scheduled for tomorrow?" Sullivan asked.

"Nothing. I'm just getting ready for Boyd's people and their experts. Assuming we get to go forward."

"Good," he said. "Can you try a rear-end collision tomorrow? The case shouldn't last three days. The plaintiff is the wife of a friend of mine from the River Oaks Country Club. She was rear-ended on Westheimer. Whiplash, physical therapy visits. Routine stuff." Sullivan made it sound like I would be doing him a big favor by agreeing to try the case, but there was really no way I could refuse.

"Sure," I said, happy to have something to think about other than my personal problems. Sullivan got up and opened the door.

"Great," he said. "I appreciate your doing this. I'll send the file around. It should be fairly straightforward, but it may be difficult to use your usual biblical references," he said winking at me. Then, to Eileen, seated at her desk outside my door, he asked, "How are the discovery responses coming? I'm sorry that our contract lawyer fizzled out on us. Eileen, please let Riza know if you need any help on this."

"Honestly, Mr. Sullivan, Beth had finished most of the work. It's just a matter of putting the discovery responses into the correct format. I think I can get it all done on time."

A few minutes later, one of the mailroom clerks showed up in my office with a five-inch folder containing the Jean Henderson file. A quick glance through it suggested that this might be one of those "good experience" as opposed to "good verdict" cases.

As simple as a rear-end collision lawsuit should be to try, the actual trial of such a case is complicated by the many hurdles set up by the law to keep the injured party from being compensated. These hurdles, well known to any second-year, personal injury trial lawyer, sound ridiculous and arcane to litigants experiencing a trial for the first time.

A woman is in an accident through no fault of her own. In Mrs. Henderson's case, she was sitting at a red light on her way to work as a real estate broker at an office on Westheimer. There was a light rain. The driver of the pickup truck that hit her car told the investigating police officer at the scene that he had gotten a call on his cell phone moments before the wreck. He looked down to pick up the phone to see who was calling, and when he looked back up, he had to slam on his brakes in an unsuccessful effort to keep from colliding into Mrs. Henderson's Mercedes-Benz. The defense in the case had taken the position that, immediately before the impact, Mrs. Henderson had veered into the defendant's lane so that she could turn right at the intersection to get to her job.

The reason for the "lane-change" defense was to try to place some fault on the plaintiff. In Texas, a plaintiff like Mrs. Henderson will have her recovery reduced by the amount of fault the jury places on her—as long as her fault is fifty percent or less. If the jury puts more than fifty percent of fault on the plaintiff, even just fifty-one percent, she gets nothing.

The problem is that the jury isn't told the effect of putting fifty-one percent rather than fifty percent of fault on the plaintiff, and the lawyers are precluded from giving the jury this information. The defense lawyer will argue that the plaintiff is fifty-one or fifty-two percent at fault and sound imminently reasonable in making such an argument. If the jury then follows that suggestion, their verdict will bar the plaintiff's recovery, even though the jury may have intended for the plaintiff to recover a percentage of her damages. I knew before the trial started that the defense would set up this hurdle for the plaintiff, but I felt like Mrs. Henderson would be able to get by it.

The police officer gave the pickup driver the ticket at the scene. Most litigants think that fact alone establishes fault. Under Texas law though, the defendant can even pay the ticket; but if he pleads *nolo contendre*—I do not contest—his admission of guilt on the traffic citation is inadmissible in the civil case regarding the personal injuries. The lawyers are precluded from even telling the jury that a ticket was issued. Of course, I was permitted to call the police officer as a witness at trial and ask him about his investigation, but in a city the size of Houston, even with a subpoena, it was hard to get a police officer to show up for a civil trial. It also seemed to me that the police officers were somewhat antagonistic to the party that subpoenaed them since they needed to take time off from their jobs to appear. I got a break during the trial of Mrs. Henderson's case, and the policeman showed up and testified that in his opinion (and over the defendant's objection that the cop was not qualified to render an opinion) the defendant driver's inattention caused the wreck.

Most of Mrs. Henderson's "medical" care was provided by a physical therapist whose office was close to her place of work. The defense would, of course, ridicule the therapists' records, focusing on how short the treatment visits were, how little time the therapist actually saw the patient, how he was not a medical doctor, and how he was not authorized to prescribe medicine for the plaintiff's sore back and neck.

The defense took the position that most of Mrs. Henderson's pain and suffering stemmed from a double mastectomy that she had the previous fall. Our firm had taken the therapist's deposition by video-tape a few months earlier (at a cost almost equivalent to the cost of the plaintiff's medical bill), and I played the video for the jury. After about ten minutes of viewing the videotaped deposition, the jurors' eyes glassed over, but the testimony was necessary to prove that the bills were "reasonable and necessary" so that the jury would be allowed to consider them.

Recently, as a part of its tort reform package, the Texas legislature had passed a law providing that a personal injury victim is only entitled to recover medical bills "paid or incurred." While that phrasing may seem innocuous, the insurance defense bar asserted, and the Texas Supreme Court eventually agreed, that plaintiffs are only entitled to recover the medical expenses that the claimant or her health insurance provider actually paid.

Most litigants are unaware that their health insurance have "side deals" with the healthcare providers whereby charges for care are reduced when they are paid. For instance, Mrs. Henderson had almost $6,500.00 in therapy and emergency room bills, but her Blue Cross/ Blue Shield health insurance had only paid $3,000.00 to cover the charges.

The defense argued that she should only be entitled to $3,000.00 for medical even though she had $6,500.00 worth of procedures. This argument was made to the court, outside the presence of the jury, because the jury wasn't permitted to hear that the plaintiff had health insurance. The jury was also not told that the plaintiff's health insurance company would be entitled to get its $3,000.00 back if Mrs. Henderson made a recovery. In other words, the insurance company charges her a monthly premium for her insurance, takes a risk that it might have to pay for her medical care, negotiates a reduction of those payments with the medical provider, lets Mrs. Henderson bear the burden of hiring a lawyer and pursuing a case against the culpable party, and then recovers from the jury's damage award any amount that the health insurance company has paid for her bills.

The flip side of the law that restricts the jury from learning that the plaintiff has health insurance—which, if known by the jury, would often have the effect of the jury thinking that somehow the plaintiff was making a double recovery—is that the jury is also not permitted to learn that the defendant has automobile liability insurance. Texas required at that time that drivers be covered by a policy with limits of at least $20,000.00. Not everybody complied. The amount was originally set back in 1984 at $15,000.00; it was only increased to $20,000 in 1986, to $25,000.00 in 2008, and most recently to $30,000.00 in 2012. Meanwhile, the costs of medical care have gone up dramatically. While the jury may suspect that the defendant is insured, the lawyers are not permitted to tell jurors that fact, and the suit must be brought against the pickup truck driver rather than his insurance company (even though the insurance company hires his lawyer and is responsible for paying claims against him up to the amount of the policy limits).

The few savvy jurors who understand that insurance is involved, even though it must never be mentioned by the lawyers, often think that by siding with the defendant they will somehow be keeping their own car insurance rates low, a fallacy promulgated by the insurance industry in their tort reform advertising campaign. If a juror really wanted to serve his self-interest and ignore the facts and law, he would always side with the plaintiff because the fact that a plaintiff wins from time to time is the only thing that keeps insurance companies from routinely denying claims, even valid ones.

Unfortunately, most people will eventually have a claim. Hopefully, it will not be a catastrophic claim. Even in my short career, I had already seen the bewildered look on a claimant's face when I tried to explain to him that consistent defense verdicts had emboldened insurance companies to the point where they were refusing to pay a deserving victim just because they felt like juries in our community would never require them to pay.

The books of reported cases are full of instances in which clever plaintiffs' lawyers have attempted to inform the jury that the defendant has insurance without running afoul of the law. Some of my favorite cases are those in which the exasperated plaintiff's lawyer, in his total frustration with the process, says something like, "I'm not allowed to discuss insurance, but you know what is going on here."

I had wanted to try out an idea I had for an argument on how-to-tell-the-jury-the-defendant-has-insurance-without-telling-the-jury-that-the-defendant-has-insurance, and the Henderson case presented the perfect opportunity. Rather than attempting to slice up the defendant on cross-examination, I was nice to him. I ignored his prior incidents and let go the discrepancies between his comments at the scene, in his deposition, and on direct examination at trial.

On closing argument, I told the jury that I liked the defendant. "My Dad drives a pickup truck just like the one the defendant was driving when he crashed into the back of Mrs. Henderson's car. He seems like a pretty good guy. I know Mrs. Henderson has a lot of bills and pain and suffering, and whatnot, but please don't make the defendant pay more than $20,000.00." I went over, stood behind the defense lawyer's chair, gestured toward the lawyer, and concluded with, "He's in good hands up to $20,000.00, but please don't make him pay more than $20,000.00."

I guessed that because he had an argument of his own that he wanted to try out, the defense attorney did not object to my argument that informed the jury about the presence of insurance. Instead, he stood up on his closing and told the jury that the case was really only worth $10,000 and that I was inflating the numbers. He said, "It's just like when your kid comes to you to ask you for twenty dollars to go to the movie and he really only needs ten. He asks you for twenty because he figures that you'll cut it in half."

Admittedly, I thought he had a pretty good argument. Whatever I said in response in my rebuttal would tend to make me look greedy. Fortunately, I had seen Sullivan handle a similar argument in the past using a trick that he had learned from the great Joe Jamail. Closing argument is all about plagiarism. In rebuttal I just said, "In deciding damages in this case, you must decide whether to believe me or a man who would cheat his own son out of ten bucks."

The verdict came back for twenty-point-zero thousand dollars. And for three days I had been able to avoid having any meaningful conversation with Michelle because "I was in trial," a demilitarized zone universally recognized by trial attorneys and their families.

10

AFTER THE *HENDERSON* VERDICT, Michelle had attempted to initiate sex. When I said that I was tired and that my head hurt and that we should wait until we were both up to it, Michelle took it to mean that I didn't find her attractive. I couldn't tell her that I was unable to determine whether the headache I was experiencing was from surviving on coffee alone for the past three days or if the STD was reoccurring. Gritting my teeth in a caffeine-induced clench during trial always gave me a headache, but the prodromal onset of symptoms also included a pain that started above my upper molars and sliced into my frontal lobes.

On Monday, back at the office, the reception was decidedly cool, almost the opposite of the Monday after the *Alvarado* verdict. I had expected this, but it still felt peculiar when it happened. I had seen it with Eli when he had separated himself from the rest of the pack of young associates by virtue of the amount of money he was bringing into the firm. I had won two cases in a row, a feat not incomparable to DiMaggio's hitting streak given the cases the associates were trying. I had been given the assignment of "working up" a significant case. And a partner's daughter and I were about to have a baby.

My fellow associates at the firm, all vying for a limited number of partnership positions, had seen me previously as a friend involved in the same struggle. Now, I was clearly a competitor with an advantage or two, and I perceived that I could expect to receive no assistance from them. After the *Henderson* verdict, it would be a long time before I ever ate lunch with any of the associates again. I was always by myself at lunch, or joining Sullivan and Riza when Sullivan summoned me. The other associates didn't know that the only case I had was about to be thrown out of court, resulting in a loss of more than a million dollars to the firm, or that my personal life portended a similar disaster.

On Tuesday I met Michelle at her obstetrician's office for the twenty-week sonogram. I had read sonogram reports before and had seen the black-and-white photographs, but I had never seen a sonogram performed. While she was still a bit cold and standoffish after the failed attempt to have sex, both Michelle and I were excited about the chance to see the baby. There was a good chance that we might learn the baby's sex. It was also my first chance to meet Michelle's obstetrician, Dr. Nathan.

Michelle signed her name on a clipboard handed to her by a grey-haired woman at a reception desk who smiled at her and called her by name. Each of the ladies working in the office stopped and talked to Michelle as they passed through the lobby assisting patients to and from their examinations. I learned that Michelle's mom had been Dr. Nathan's patient, and that he had in fact delivered Michelle and her brother Jonathan.

The room must have looked like it did in the late fifties—clean tile floors, worn but clean chairs that alternated between avocado green Naugahyde and harvest gold fabric with a cranberry plaid burlap placed here and there for accent. On one wall was a huge cork bulletin board covered with snapshots of newborns. "Happy customers," I thought to myself and smiled.

"What are you grinning at?" Michelle asked, as I studied the photographs. "Do you think that bulletin board should be titled 'Leave It to Beaver'?"

I laughed. "Is your picture up here somewhere?" I asked, teasing her.

"No," the receptionist interjected, "we take down the pictures every year or so. But, I'm sure we have a Polaroid of baby Michelle around here somewhere . . . probably in her mother's file."

In a few minutes, a woman dressed in light green scrubs came through the door to the back and called Michelle's name. We got up and followed her back to a large examination room, where she had Michelle put on a hospital gown over her underwear.

We sat talking about whether it would be a boy or girl, and how we had better get serious about coming up with a name. A different lady came into the room pushing a cart with all kinds of equipment on it.

In a friendly but efficient tone, the woman introduced herself to Michelle as Miriam and asked Michelle to raise her gown up over her abdomen and lie back on the tissue paper-covered examining table. Miriam plugged various wires into the machines around the table and positioned a monitor so that she could see it as she stood alongside Michelle.

As Miriam spread a clear jelly over Michelle's abdomen, she explained how the transducer would send and receive sound waves that would be converted into a black-and-white picture on the screen. She invited me to stand where I could see the monitor better. After several swipes across Michelle's stomach with the transducer wand, an image began appearing on the screen of a squirming infant somewhere inside of Michelle's body.

"Do we want to know the sex?" Miriam asked, as she made notes in a file and began performing a process on the equipment by which she appeared to be taking measurements. The way she asked the question, it was apparent that she already knew the answer. With all of the movement, I couldn't see how Miriam could tell the sex of the child, but with just a brief glance at me, Michelle said, "Of course we want to know. We've got a nursery to decorate."

"Congratulations," Miriam said with an air of anticipation, "you're going to have a little boy. And judging by his size, I would say you're due in about nineteen weeks. Everything looks great. Let me snap a few pictures for Dr. Nathan, and then he should be in to talk to you." She cleaned up Michelle's abdomen and told her to leave on the gown until the doctor had been in to visit with us.

In the past two months, Michelle's body had begun to change significantly. Her breasts were larger, her abdomen clearly showed that she was pregnant; she was even beginning to have some difficulty getting out of comfortable chairs. I had seen her naked getting in and out of the shower, and we had talked about the increasing size of her belly, but until she had that ultrasound, I don't think I truly understood that a separate body was living inside of her.

We had not had sex since I had been to the STD clinic.

Dr. Nathan cleared his throat as he entered the room. He was peering through thick reading glasses at the contents of a manila folder. He put the folder down on the examining table and looked over his glasses at Michelle as he touched her on the shoulder and said hello. Then he extended his hand and introduced himself to me. He had thick, bushy, grey eyebrows, wisps of grey hair coming out in all directions on his predominantly bald head, and the kind of hands that old doctors have after washing them every five minutes for more than forty years.

"So, I see that we're about to have a little boy. That should make his grandfather quite happy," Dr. Nathan said and smiled. "Everything looks good. I estimate that you will deliver around September 15th. We may adjust that somewhat as we go along. How is everything with you, Michelle? Did you get over the morning sickness?" He asked patting Michelle on the shoulder.

"Yes," Michelle said. "I'm feeling much better. In fact, I'm feeling pretty good. I'm hungry all the time. No real cravings or anything. Just hungry. I did have some itching and burning the other day . . . you know . . . vaginally . . . I'd say it lasted a week or so, but everything's fine now."

Dr. Nathan raised his eyebrows quizzically, and then he put his hand on my shoulder. "Why don't you wait outside just a moment, Mr. Jessie, and I'll take a look. I'm sure everything is fine."

I stepped outside of the examining room and walked down the hallway to the lobby. I knew that even if I had given Michelle herpes and she had experienced an outbreak, it seemed unlikely she would present the symptoms at this time. Dr. Nathan couldn't see what wasn't there. Still, as I sat in the lobby waiting on Michelle, I wondered if she might come through the door and ask me how in the world it could be that she had contracted genital herpes. And of course, I worried that both she and our unborn child might have the disease.

A moment ago, I thought I would have until mid-September to develop a response to that question. Now, I thought that the entire issue might explode in the next two minutes. I could feel the blood rushing to my head. Was I light-headed? Could the employees in the office tell that I was in distress?

I rubbed my sweaty palms on my pant legs and tried to take a couple of deep breaths. I could feel myself getting dizzy. The receptionist got up from her desk, walked over to me and put her hand on my forehead. "My, you are hot, Mr. Jessie. Do you feel alright?" she asked.

"I'm fine," I said. "I guess I'm just a little nervous."

"It's a nervous time," she said. "There can be a lot to worry about, especially with your first one."

I nodded.

"You are really sweating. Can I get you a cold drink or something?" She asked in a reassuring voice.

Before I could answer, Michelle came through the door to the lobby. She was beaming. In her hand, she gripped tightly a copy of the sonogram photograph of our baby.

"Look," she said proudly. "Little Pablo's first picture."

Michelle couldn't stop staring at the picture. "I wonder if he'll have red hair like me or plain brown hair like you."

"Burnt sienna." I said.

Michelle ran a hand through my hair as she looked down at me. "Brown." She said, matter-of-factly. "Burnt sienna has more of a reddish tint."

I looked at the picture, which was little more than an X-ray of shadows. I had the thought that it might be the only picture I ever got to see of Paul. I could make out the head and body, and arms and legs, but I couldn't distinguish details like eyes or nose, much less the sex of the child.

The receptionist looked at the photograph with us. "You know," she said, "there are companies now that do three-dimensional sonograms that show greater detail. Some couples have one done as baby's first picture. Dr. Nathan doesn't do them because health insurance doesn't pay for them. I could give you the address and phone number of a facility that does the 3-D version if you'd like."

"Please," Michelle said. "I'd love to have one." I knew it would only be a matter of days before the framed 3-D color version of the sonogram would be on Sullivan's credenza behind his desk at the office. As Michelle and the receptionist walked over to the reception desk to write down the sonogram information for us, I sat in the chair looking at the black-and-white picture that I held in my hands, wondering if there was any way that the baby could have seen us when the transducer was on Michelle's tummy.

When I left the doctor's office, I started back to the office and called Eileen from the car to see if anything was happening. It was already mid-afternoon and I thought that if nothing was going on at the office, I might try to find Sullivan at Damian's or Brennan's. But Eileen told me Sullivan had left that morning to arrange another press conference in Kentucky, and the office was very quiet.

Since I felt like I needed to talk to someone, I changed directions and took a chance that I might catch Jonathan at his house over in the Heights. I don't know why I didn't try to call him before I showed up on his doorstep.

It was probably about two o'clock when I pulled into Jonathan's driveway. He lived in a beautiful "Arts and Crafts" style home in the Heights, an older neighborhood inside Loop 610 just northeast of downtown Houston. There were pockets of the Heights that demonstrated the worst of urban blight, but there were also leafy streets of homes built in the early part of the last century that had been lovingly restored to Victorian or Mission-style works of art. Although there were some crime problems, the yards were expansive and green, and there were large oak trees dressed in Spanish moss. Sullivan, the son of a construction superintendent, had grown up in a house only a few blocks from where his son, Jonathan, now lived.

Jonathan's American Craftsman bungalow was a partial two-story structure with a low-pitched roof and overhanging eaves that rested on exposed rafters. Four-over-one, double-hung windows graced the front of the house, and tapered, square columns supported the extension of the main roof which shaded the large front porch.

I bounced up the steps to the porch and rang the doorbell. After a moment, I decided Jonathan was not at home and turned to go back down the steps and walkway to my car. Before I could get back in the car, Jonathan opened the front door and came outside onto the porch wearing only a sweatshirt and gym shorts. I imagined that he was about to go for a jog.

"Hey, brother-in-law. What are you doing this afternoon?" Jonathan asked in a voice that was genuinely friendly.

"Nothing," I said. "I thought you might want to go over to the Blue Oyster Bar and have a beer."

"That's a good idea," he said, "although I'll have to take a rain check this time. I've got company. But you can come in and have one with us, if you'd like."

I hesitated. In the entire time I'd known Jonathan, I'd never seen him date anyone seriously. The fact that I'd never seen him bring a woman to his parents' house, coupled with the fact that he lived in an immaculate home in the Heights made me question whether my bursting in on him this afternoon was a prudent move on my part. However, in addition to being my wife's brother, Jonathan was my friend. I thought to myself, how much weirder could things get anyway?

"Sure," I said, "if I'm not intruding. Have you got any cold beer?"

"I don't know about beer," he said, "but I just opened a bottle of wine." I followed him up the front steps and through the front door.

We went through a small, Grueby green-tiled entryway into a quarter-sawn oak paneled family room that was perfectly furnished in reproduction Stickley mission oak furniture. In one corner was a spindle-sided Morris chair covered in burgundy leather with a matching ottoman. A heavy, copper-topped coffee table sat on a Frank Lloyd Wright-designed wool rug in front of a Coke-bottle green leather couch.

Riza stood up from the couch as we walked into the room.

"Hi, Davy," she said. She was wearing a plush, cream-colored, terrycloth robe, monogrammed with a dark green "S" on the left breast pocket.

"I thought you two might already know each other," Jonathan said. "I'll get that wine," he shouted, as he disappeared into the kitchen.

Riza obviously enjoyed the stunned look on my face.

"You can pick your chin up," she said, smiling. In one sentence, she had told me not to look so surprised, and to keep my mouth shut. She lowered her voice so that Jonathan couldn't hear her from the kitchen.

"Neither knows," she whispered.

"They won't find out from me," I replied in an equally soft whisper, and then called out to Jonathan, "Can you make mine a scotch?"

"Sure," he called back. "Tough day?"

"I'm going to be a dad," I said.

Both Jonathan and Riza laughed.

11

MICHELLE WAS IN THE KITCHEN cooking when I got home a little while later. I came up behind her as she sliced peeled potatoes into a boiling pot of water. She made wonderful mashed potatoes. I don't know if it was boiling the potatoes in salt water, the spoonful of sour cream, the chunks of butter, the minced garlic, or the grilled green chilies, but the girl could make mashed potatoes.

I kissed her on the neck. She paused for a moment, and then resumed her slicing when I pulled away. "I thought you might fire up the grill and cook those little steaks that are marinating in the refrigerator," she said. I noticed a colander of freshly washed asparagus by the sink.

"What's the occasion?" I asked.

"I just thought we would have a nice, early dinner together at home—as a family," she said. "Go change your clothes and fix yourself a scotch."

I did as I was told and then went out onto the back porch and lit the gas grill. After the grill had heated up, I took a wire brush and cleaned the grill surface. I went back inside and got the steaks, a pair of tongs, and a Famous Grouse on the rocks. I put the steaks on the fire, turned down the heat to medium-high, and closed the cover. I sat down at a small, French bistro table with my scotch in one hand and the tongs in the other. I knew I had to tell Michelle about the herpes—that she had been exposed—that she might already have the disease. I knew that telling her was the right thing to do. From what I had read on the Internet, I understood that there were real risks if a mother delivered a child vaginally while experiencing a herpes outbreak. The child could contract the disease in the birth canal, and because of his undeveloped immune system, he could develop blindness or a brain injury, or even die; not to mention the fact that, if he escaped horrible injury or disfigurement, he would have a chronic condition of herpes.

Apparently, women with herpes delivered children all the time, and the key was for them to tell their obstetricians. If there was concern about an outbreak at the time of delivery, a Caesarean section was performed. With medication like what I had received from the STD clinic and no symptoms of an outbreak, even vaginal deliveries were routinely performed.

The vital concern was that the doctor should know about the possibility of an outbreak at the time she went into labor in order to take the proper precautions. Michelle had to know that I had exposed her to the disease. But I was still too ashamed to tell her. If I told her about the herpes, then I had to tell her about the affair. If I told her about the affair, I knew I would lose her. Of course, I would also be fired. I would probably be fired anyway when the Kentucky case imploded. I didn't really care about the job. As long as I had my bar card and my license to practice law in Texas, I could figure out some way to make a living as a lawyer. I could try a case. There would always be rear-end collisions in which the insurance company refused to compensate the victim.

The truth is that all of the secret keeping and covering up was wearing me out. I wondered how I could lift this weight off me and start over. But, I didn't want to lose Michelle; it was not just because it would be a defeat for our marriage. I couldn't imagine living without her.

I had to tell her about the herpes. I tried to play out the conversation in my mind. How do I begin? Should I go to the ATM machine first? Where will I spend the night tomorrow night? Could I just tell Michelle that I needed some time alone and go back to Abilene? What could I tell my parents? Is there any way I could sit down alone with Dr. Nathan and convince him to deliver the child by C-section without telling Michelle the real reason he was doing it?

I was scared, and I felt like my chest was going to explode. I flipped the steaks and sipped my scotch.

No doctor was going to hide from his patient the fact that she had been exposed to a disease that could harm her unborn child. How could I have let this happen? How could I fix this? I thought to myself, "I have to tell her tonight. I can't go on like this. I can't keep this secret any longer. I have to tell Michelle tonight. She's going to want to make love tonight. All the signs were there. I can't keep exposing her to this without telling her." At least Beth didn't know she had it when she gave it to me. I might not have known I had it when I first exposed Michelle, but I knew I had done something I wasn't supposed to have done; and somewhere in the back of my mind, I knew that there was a risk that I might contract a sexually transmitted disease.

If I had unprotected sex with Michelle now, I would be deliberately deceiving her and putting her at risk. How could I do that to someone I loved? Did I really love Michelle? If I did, why would I have slept with Beth? Was this God's way of punishing me for having sex with Beth? What kind of God would punish people He loved?

That was certainly the kind of God I had learned about growing up in Abilene. He was an authoritarian God, intimately involved in the day-to-day lives of everyone on the planet, and He meted out punishment on a regular basis to those who deserved it. His judgment was swift and certain, and it could come in the form of dropping cattle prices, below-average rainfall, or personal bankruptcies.

The God of Lubbock, where I went to college at Texas Tech, was a more benevolent God than the God of Abilene. In Lubbock, I came to see God as more of a father figure, who, while still setting absolute standards of right and wrong, was the loving father of a prodigal son. He could forgive drinking a little trash can punch at the "Phi Delt" house after a game on Saturday night and maybe a minor dalliance with a "Pi Phi," but only if I knelt before Him on Sunday, and sincerely expressed that, "I am working my way back to you, Babe."

In Austin, where I went to law school at The University of Texas, God was a bearded, long-tenured professor. He kept a grade book, although he didn't take attendance. Some would pass and some would fail, but He was far too busy with the weightier issues of the day to be called upon to address anything other than the most exigent of circumstance (e.g., Black Plague, Hitler, pollution in the Edwards Aquifer, tort reform). Grades were recorded for pop quizzes, midterms, and final exams that tested a person's ability to make choices when given a set of facts, not unlike a stated problem that had been sent down long before.

The God of Houston was more distant. He may not have even lived in Houston. He probably commuted from from Sugar Land, Humble, or Kingwood. He was like some cosmic, professional bowler at the far end of the bowling lane that, at some moment when time began, sent the world hurtling toward a spare or a strike or a gutter that those of us on the globe tried desperately, and in vain, to control. Seeing that we couldn't alter the course of the ball, we focused more and more on ourselves and less and less on the greater good or the direction the ball was rolling.

I don't think that I had ever given much thought to what the devil looked like at any point in my life. I guess that was because I thought evil could take on whatever form it chose. It could look like a serpent in the Garden of Eden, a sneering, bald-headed vice president, or like Jack Nicholson in *The Witches of Eastwick* — or my own reflection in the mirror.

I don't think that I ever doubted that evil existed in the world. I've just always assumed that it moved in and out of people and situations without the constraints of time or physical embodiment. The name "devil" in my mind was just a contraction "de evil" or "of evil." I didn't know what caused evil to persist in the world, but I didn't think it had anything to do with a little red guy with horns and a pitchfork. I understood from my Sunday Bible school classes as a kid that "Satan" was from the old Hebrew word for "adversary." However, I never really understood the whole concept about how God could have a formidable adversary if God was all-knowing and all-powerful. Wouldn't it be like the Globetrotters always playing the Washington Generals?

I had been going over in my mind the question about what to do next since I had left Jonathan's house. I felt the need to talk to someone, not so much for someone to give me the answers to my questions. Instead I needed someone to listen and advise me and be a nonjudgmental friend, somebody who would still care for me even after I had told him or her about how badly I had behaved. The problem was that all of the people in the world to whom I felt like I could talk were somehow involved in the complex web of secrets that were closing in on me. Alone with my questions and thoughts, I felt more and more isolated.

After eight minutes, four per side, I took the steaks off the grill and went back inside. I put the steaks on the dining table in the breakfast room and set the places, while Michelle brought over the mashed potatoes and asparagus. I had to tell her. I had to tell her now. I fixed myself another scotch and sat at the place at the head of the table, where I always sat, except on those occasions when Michelle's parents came over for lunch and Tim sat there.

Michelle and I were both slicing into our steaks when the phone rang. She got up to answer it. After looking at the call screen to be sure that it was not a telemarketer call, she picked up the phone.

"Hello, Dad. Where are you today? We had our first sonogram. You are going to have a grandson . . . In September . . . Yeah, he's here . . . We just sat down to eat an early dinner. Tonight? Can't that wait until tomorrow? No, you tell him. I'll hand him the phone." In the brief conversation her voice had gone from excited to crestfallen.

Sullivan was calling from Kentucky. He had sent the plane back to pick Riza and me up. Michelle began putting the food in plastic containers and putting it away in the refrigerator, while I went upstairs to pack.

12

Riza was already sitting in the plane on the tarmac when I got there. She was listening to her iPod and reading an old copy of the *Robb Report* as I threw my bag in the back and took a seat across the aisle facing her. The pilot came to the back of the plane, shut the door, and told us how long the flight to Lexington would take. It would be pretty late before we would arrive. Both Riza and I nodded, resigned to our confinement on a private jet well-stocked with booze and salted cashews.

A few months earlier, I would have seen this unscheduled trip as an unexpected adventure; now, I felt like I was being taken advantage of, and unnecessarily so. While I was somewhat relieved to have avoided once again the conversation that I knew I must have with Michelle, I felt like the opportunity had been pulled out from under me.

After we were airborne, I went to the bar and made myself a Famous Grouse on the rocks. I figured that I probably wouldn't even see Sullivan that night, but I should avoid getting too drunk, just in case. We would be getting to Kentucky in time for a late dinner, and if he wanted to go out, Sullivan would want me to accompany Riza and him. I told myself that pace was important.

I motioned to Riza to get her attention, and, as she removed her earphones, I asked her if she would like a drink as well. She asked for a beer, and I opened a Corona Light for her. I took a small lime from the wooden bowl that sat on the bar and quartered it on the little cutting board beside the bowl. I wedged a lime slice into the opening of the beer bottle and handed it to Riza like I had seen Sullivan do a hundred times. I returned to my seat and watched as the reflection of the full moon off the plane sped across the ground below.

"How fast do you think we're going?" Riza asked.

"Over four hundred miles per hour," I said.

"Do you know why we have to be in Lexington tonight?"

"No," I said shaking my head. "I was going to ask you the same question. Presumably, there is going to be some meeting on the case tomorrow morning that required we leave tonight, but I'm not sure. Michelle did most of the talking when Tim called."

Riza nodded.

"I apologize for asking. I'm just curious. Where were you when you got the call?" I asked.

"I was still at Jonathan's. I checked my messages, and Tim had left one at my condo. I'm surprised I beat you to the plane. I assumed I would be the one holding us up."

"Does Jonathan know where you are going?"

"Of course." She replied. "He's used to it. That doesn't mean he likes it, but he's used to it."

"I know what you mean," I said.

"Do you think either of them suspects that you are involved with the other one?" I asked. "I'm sorry. It's not really any of my business. I just wondered."

"It's okay," she said. "Honestly, it might be nice to have someone other than a psychologist to talk to about it. I don't know what they suspect. I don't think they suspect anything. Maybe Jonathan thinks there is something going on between me and his dad, what with me always traveling with Tim whenever he goes out of town. I don't think that Tim suspects anything about my seeing Jonathan."

"How long have you been able to keep this up?"

"I started seeing Tim when I first went to work at Peters & Sullivan four years ago. I met Jonathan when he came by himself to a firm Christmas party. Tim and Amy were there.

"Cozy," I said. "Do you think Amy knows anything about it?"

"She must know about my involvement with Tim. I don't see how she couldn't. I'm not so naïve as to think that I'm the first 'other woman' with whom Tim has been involved. I think she tries to pretend that I don't exist, and that if she maintains that pretense long enough,

Tim will come back to his senses and dump me. Maybe she's right. Maybe he will. It will probably be because I screw up some case or something, since I guess I know that it will somehow end badly for me. Frankly, I'm getting a little tired of constantly scheduling my life around Tim's marriage. Maybe that is why I started seeing Jonathan."

"Amy doesn't ever ask me about Tim," I said. "I think that Amy thinks I know more about him than I let on, although she doesn't ask. It's just a feeling I get when I catch her looking at me. Lately I've wondered if she's worried that I might say something to Michelle about Tim. Of course I never would. You don't need to worry about that. I do get the idea that Amy has spent a considerable amount of time and effort shielding Michelle and Jonathan from knowing everything about their father. I also think that Michelle and Jonathan try to protect their mom from knowing everything about her husband. It can all get very confusing and I try to avoid getting caught in the middle."

We sat there without either of us saying anything for a moment.

"Are you in love with either of them . . . or maybe both of them?" I asked.

"Who knows?" she said. "Who knows what love is? Sometimes I think I am in love with one or both of them. Sometimes I'm just so tired of all of the hassle that I don't care if I ever see either one of them again. You know what Sullivan says love is?"

I shook my head. I had never heard that particular Sullivanism. I guess it was one topic that I had never discussed with him. Probably most associates don't discuss the meaning of love with their senior partner.

"Sullivan says that 'love is the white stuff that comes out of a man's penis.' "

I flushed red, and again we sat there without either one saying anything.

"You must have to avoid being around Tim when you're with Jonathan. Doesn't that cause Jonathan some suspicion?" I finally asked.

"Maybe," she said, "but I don't think he has ever let his dates meet his parents. Jonathan probably wants to be sure that the dates like him for him and not some estate in River Oaks. He's also very secretive around his parents. I don't know why. I've told Jonathan that it would be bad for me at work if Tim knew I was dating his son. I'm not sure he accepts that. I guess the relationship with Jonathan just has not gone far enough that it has become a problem yet. Probably, it never will. That is a shame because I really like Jonathan. He is smart and clever like his dad, but his personality is different. It is never all about Jonathan."

"You mean that if you were forced to choose between Tim and Jonathan because Jonathan had invited you to Thanksgiving at the Sullivan house, you would choose Tim?"

"I guess so, at this point. In the long-run, I don't know. In fact, there probably won't be a long-run."

"Why Tim over Jonathan?" I asked.

"You mean because Jonathan is more my age? I don't know. My counselor says I have unresolved issues with my stepdad. Whatever that means. Maybe she's right. I've been involved with Tim longer than Jonathan. I've never been involved with an older man before, much less a married one. Not that Tim's that old. I think he needs me. I give him something that he otherwise would be lacking. I understand the pressure he's under at the law firm. I see it every day. I don't think his family really knows what he goes through. They're used to the fabulous income he brings home, but they don't really know what it takes to maintain that level of success."

"Do you think he'll ever quit practicing law?"

"That is one thing I ask him all the time. Why doesn't he quit, get a divorce, and move with me to Santa Fe or Jackson Hole? Hell, I wouldn't care if we moved to Paintsville. However, I don't think he'll ever do that. What is it about you guys and the thrill of the jury verdict?"

"I don't know," I said. "I haven't had the opportunity to win very often—unless I have been trying a case with Tim. It's horrible to lose. You think the jury dislikes you. You take it personally, even though you tell yourself that you didn't make the facts, you just presented them. And there is the economic aspect. I don't mean that you fall in love with the money. I mean that you are always investing the money from this case into the next one, and the process just feeds on itself. It would be hard to just stop."

"Of course you're in love with the money," she said. "It could be done, though. Just stop taking new cases, or taper off intake. Quit spending money. Just take cases that might be interesting to work on, rather than cases that might make a lot of money but cost a fortune to develop."

"I guess you're right. I know I don't see myself doing this forever."

"I'll bet you do. You're just like Tim. You're a chaos junkie. You may tell yourself that you're in it for the big score—that you'll win some monster case and make a huge fee and retire. Though I doubt that it will work out that way. Instead, you'll just buy a bigger house and more cars, and maybe even a plane like this one. Then the kids will graduate from private schools and attend expensive colleges, and you'll look up and you'll be caught up in the lifestyle unable to let go."

I didn't tell her that there was a real possibility that I could be divorced and out of a job on or before September 15th of this year. She was right about me being a chaos junkie. All trial lawyers, at least all the ones I know, are addicted to adrenaline. The unpredictability of the practice, particularly in the courtroom but also at the office with constant deadlines and tactical maneuvering against the other side, was what made it interesting. The challenge was to control something that was uncontrollable. No two cases were alike. You learned all about a subject, and then promptly forgot it, and went on to the next case and the next subject. While it might be a stressful life, it wasn't boring.

Riza took my momentary pause as a sign to continue. "I'll bet you there isn't even a meeting tomorrow. I'll bet that Tim was just lonely and had a few drinks and sent the plane for us to come join him."

"You mean for you to come join him. I'm just a chaperone," I said.

"Maybe. I know what you are saying, and, believe it or not, I'm really not offended. However, don't kid yourself. Tim enjoys your company too. He sees you as an extension of himself. What is it that Tim always says?" she asked.

"Do not shit thyself," I said.

"Exactly. Do not shit thyself. I am as much a chaperone in this triangle as you are. Have you ever compared your year-end bonus to the other associates?"

"No. Well, I assume it might be a little higher because I brought in a little more money than the other associates."

"Try again, Clarence Darrow. Eli brings in the most money. True, he has been there a little longer, but your bonus is always larger than his. Substantially."

"How do you know all of this?"

"I sleep with the guy who decides what the bonuses are. Remember? Sullivan sees your income as a way of transferring wealth to Michelle at your income tax rate instead of the estate tax rate, and without having it pass through various trusts over which he has no control."

"Although he can't control what I do with the money, can he?" I asked.

"Pretty much, he can. I know you haven't thought about your income in this way. Do you have any idea how much money is coming your way once the baby is born? Tim is just salivating about how he's going to circumvent the Uniform Gift to Minors Act through your working for the firm."

I chewed the ice from my glass and stared out of the window. After a while, Riza put her earphones back on, and we flew along without saying anything more. Eventually the gentle hum of the jet engines and the scotch put me to sleep. I don't know how long I slept. Although it didn't seem long enough for us to have arrived in Kentucky, I woke up as we began our descent into what I assumed was the airport in Lexington. The pilot took off his headset and hollered back to us that there was a change of plans and that we were meeting Sullivan in Memphis. A car would pick us up and take us to the Peabody.

"Too late to see the ducks," I said, and Riza laughed. She waited for the pilot to put his headset back on before saying anything.

"Look," she said, "I didn't mean to upset you. I see both of us in similar situations. I enjoyed getting the chance to talk to you. We haven't really ever talked."

"No," I said. "I'm not upset. I just have a lot on my mind. So, how do you see this ending? You said it will probably end badly for you."

"I've decided that I'm going to try to end up with more money than any paralegal in the history of the American legal system. I may even go to law school. But, I realize that I probably won't get either one of the guys. That's okay. I'm fairly independent. Frankly, I'm getting tired of all the juggling. Someone else will come along. Jackson Hole is crawling with good-looking guys trying to meet a rich, single woman."

"Here's to *foie gras* and Montrachet," I said, raising my empty glass. "You should go to law school. You'd be a better lawyer than I'll ever be. I hope you will consider hiring me someday."

"No Montrachet or law school tonight. I'm sure we'll have to settle for barbecue. What time does the Rendezvous close?"

13

To SOME EXTENT, WE are all creatures of habit. Some of us just have bigger habits than others. In addition to being home by five o'clock every evening, my dad ate lunch at the same place almost every day. Usually he took a book to the student center and went through the cafeteria line. He would order whatever was on special and sit quietly by himself and eat and read whatever novel he was reading that day. Sometimes he would go to the faculty club, but the glad-handing cut into his reading time. He read three novels a week.

Though he taught at a Church of Christ college, he was not a particularly religious person. Mom was the one who saw to it that we went to church on Sunday mornings and which church we attended. I can't remember much about the Sunday school classes I attended other than learning to sign the Lord's Prayer while we sang it. I remember thinking that if God was deaf, why were we singing while we were signing? When I was in high school, I began picking the church we attended based on which one I thought would have the best church-league basketball team.

Dad claimed that what little he knew about the Bible came from reading fiction. To understand the nuance or significance of a biblical reference in one of Shakespeare's plays, Dad would go back and forth between the play and the scripture until he understood the context. "Isn't God's favorite teaching tool the parable?" Dad would ask. "'I have multiplied visions and used similitudes by the ministry of the prophets.' Isn't a parable just an exercise in showing us a moral as applied to a specific situation in a way that we'll remember it? That's what good literature is . . . an attempt to reveal a universal truth that the audience probably already knows in its heart through a story or situation that the audience can relate to and remember. If I tell you not to lie, you might remember, but if I tell you that your nose will grow like Pinocchio's when you lie, then there is a better chance that you will remember what I told you. Never discount the power of a good old-fashioned allegory to get a message across. 'The pilgrim's progress from this world to that which is to come, delivered under similitude of a dream.'"

I do not see Tim very often these days, although I could locate him with a few phone calls if I just knew which direction he was going when he left the office.

If he was going to Dallas near lunchtime, I would guess that he was at the Café Pacific or still at the Polo Shop on his way to the Café Pacific. If he was already there, he was ordering a Ramos Gin Fizz served in the classic style. If he was spending the night, he was at the Mansion on Turtle Creek, both to stay and for dinner. There are other hotels in Dallas as luxurious as the Mansion, but they seem larger and less discrete, and they don't have a bar as dark as the bar at the Mansion gets at night. Also it's a short stumble from the bar to the incredible restaurant.

If he was in San Antonio, he was probably staying at the Fairmount. But, from time to time, he would give other hotels a try—I think because he disliked the large glass window in the bar that looked out onto the street. He would have both lunch and dinner, and breakfast on Sundays, at a little place called El Mirador over on South St. Mary's Street. An entire meal might cost less than an appetizer at the Mansion, but the food at El Mirador is incredible. I've heard that the owners are expanding it. I hope it doesn't lose its charm. If available, Tim would order the lobster taco or the venison tamale; on Sunday mornings, the soups are the way to go.

If he was in Austin, Sullivan was at a round table in the bar of the Four Seasons, and you could ask any of the waitstaff about him by using his first name. If he wasn't there, he was in the Cloak Room, a windowless basement bar equidistant between the Texas Supreme Court, the state capitol, and the TTLA building.

If he was in Los Angeles, he was at the Hotel Bel-Air, or in the Polo Lounge at The Beverly Hills Hotel.

If he was in San Francisco, he was at The Sherman House.

In Chicago he was at Nick's Fishmarket.

If he was in Washington, DC, he was in the Round Robin Bar at The Willard.

In Boston he could be found ordering a bowl of the catch–of–the–day fish soup at the No Name Restaurant out on the pier.

If he was in New York, he was at the St. Regis; and if it was after dark, he was probably in the King Cole. I got the chance to eat with him at so many restaurants in New York that I don't really know where he would be at lunch or dinner. I remember one dinner at Le Cirque before the remodel where we started with a bottle of Cristal and each had a large divot of *foie gras*, but I don't remember much after that. Chances are that you would eventually see him at the oyster bar in Grand Central Station or having a cocktail at the Bull & Bear in the Waldorf. At breakfast, though, he would be crowded into Viand Café, up the street from the St. Regis, with the rest of the people on their way to work. Again, he would be at Viand Café with the hope that the grease from the bacon, fried eggs, and hash browns might soak up the alcohol from the night before. Vitamin "G."

The point is, whatever his staff or family might say about how difficult it could be to find Tim Sullivan, the truth is, you just had to know where to look. If you knew he was going to be in Memphis, then you should ask for him at the Peabody and wait for him to come in for dinner at the Rendezvous, a place famous for its "barbecued" ribs. By Texas standards, it's not really barbecue, a process by which marinated or rubbed meat is smoked on a grill. Because at the Rendezvous, the pork ribs are coated with a dry rub and then baked in an oven.

Practicing law in Texas, I've had the opportunity to eat barbecue at most of the great barbecue venues. I like different items at different places. I like the sausage in Luling at Luling City Market and in Giddings at the City Meat Market. They're also famous for their sausage at the Southside Market in Elgin, but I like the pork steak there and the pork chop at Cooper's in Llano or at Opie's in Spicewood or at either Smitty's or Kreuz's in Lockhart. For brisket, I'd suggest Mueller's in Taylor, or the Ironworks in Austin. I also like House Park Bar-B-Q in Austin just because I like the sign: "You need no teef to eat my beef." For ribs, I'd probably go back to Luling, just because I love the sauce, or to the Country Tavern in Kilgore; but it's hard to beat the ribs, or the sauce for that matter, at some of the bigger "shops" like Rudy's.

If you like ribs, though, you owe it to yourself to see how it's done at the Rendezvous in Memphis. If you have to have sauce, the waiter will get you some, although he will insist that you "Try 'em the right way first."

Riza and I had the driver take us directly to the Rendezvous, and then drop our bags off with the concierge at the Peabody. The concierge would see to it that the proper bags went to the proper rooms.

We found Tim downstairs toward the back of the restaurant beneath a photograph of an old judge in a black robe. The judge was a black man with a grey goatee that exacerbated his "don't bring that shit in here" scowl. Sullivan was sitting at a table with a section of a newspaper, a large pitcher of beer, and three mugs. He waved, and we went over and sat down as he poured each of us a beer. It appeared that he might have been there for quite a while judging by the crumpled stack of newspapers beside his chair.

"How was the flight?" he asked, to no one in particular.

"Great," said Riza. "We had a tailwind all the way."

"Good," Tim said. "I'm starving. I took the liberty of ordering us all ribs." He looked across the room to catch the eye of a person I assumed would be our waiter. The greasy, green-painted, brick-walled room was full of people drinking beer, eating ribs, and talking loudly over red-checkered tablecloths. In the center of the room was a large, oval bar. Most of the basement room walls were covered with memorabilia that ranged from an antique rifle collection to a pair of framed panels of stained glass made of shards of green, burgundy, gold, and purple.

We chitchatted, and in a moment the waiter brought us each a heaping platter of ribs. We all dug in, and after I had finished a couple, asked why we had diverted from Kentucky to Memphis. Tim told us that he had spent the morning in Paintsville and that something worrisome was afoot.

It seems that the judge on our case was considering the appointment of something called a "special master commissioner" under the Kentucky Rules of Civil Procedure. The commissioner would serve as a private judge, compensated by the parties, to make recommendations to the court on discovery and procedural matters. Naïvely, I told Tim that the appointment could be good for the case if it took the decision on the admissibility of the expert witnesses' testimony out of the hands of the judge. Tim said that he thought it was a bad omen. He thought the judge, who had to stand for reelection, was trying to provide himself a buffer for ruling against us.

"The old sonofabitch is trying to camouflage his involvement in the case," Tim said. "From what I can find out," he continued between swigs of beer and dabbing the corners of his mouth with a greasy napkin, "this judge would be inconspicuous in a commode."

If the court threw out our expert on the recommendation of the special master commissioner, the judge could save face in the community. Of course, if we refused to agree to the appointment of a commissioner, the judge would probably punish us for our obstreperous behavior. I thought that for the first time, Sullivan saw the case was going down the tubes.

"Davy, my boy, have I ever told you the First Rule of Grease?" he asked.

I looked at him quizzically, assuming that this rule had something to do with barbecue in general or ribs in particular.

"The First Rule of Grease is . . . Last and Most Wins," Sullivan said. "I'm afraid we may be witnessing a practical application of the First Rule of Grease as it's applied to the appointment of a special master commissioner under the Kentucky Rules of Civil Procedure. I'm not sure we want to get into a bidding war with Boyd Oil. Still, there might be some way to salvage our investment," he said, and winked.

Surprisingly, Sullivan seemed to be in a good mood, and we washed down the ribs with a couple of pitchers of beer. He didn't mention the Kentucky case again, or the appointment of a special master commissioner.

"Have you two ever thought that we ought to break away from the firm of Peters & Sullivan and start our own shop?" Sullivan asked. He didn't wait for Riza or me to respond. "The rest of those guys just don't know anything about having any fun. They're all worried about losing money on cases and not focused on how to turn cases into money. Let me tell you something, Davy. You show me a situation where someone has suffered a wrong, and I'll show you some way to turn it into money. And it doesn't matter where the poor soul that's wronged stands on the social ladder. It's like I always say, 'Money hath no odor.'"

14

Riza passed out room keys in the hotel lobby, and we took the elevator up to our respective floors. My room was on a different floor from each of their rooms. I got off on my floor, and after the elevator door closed, I pressed the down button and took the next elevator back to the lobby. The notion that Sullivan might leave the firm and take me with him was intriguing, even if he didn't know at the time he made the suggestion that it was probably only a matter of days until he let me go.

I felt the sudden urge to run away from all of the complications that seemed to be piling up around me. I thought about seeing if there was a flight home that night so that I could be at my house when Michelle woke up. I would tell her the whole sordid story like I had started to do earlier that evening, and then beg for forgiveness. I thought about calling my parents, but it was already too late to call. They would be in bed, and the sound of the telephone ringing would alarm them.

So I decided to violate Sullivan's First Rule of Holes. According to Sullivan, the First Rule of Holes provides that, "When you find yourself in a hole, quit digging."

Instead of a drink in the lobby bar, I walked past the "duckless" fountain, out the front doors of the hotel, and headed to Beale Street. For some reason, as I walked across the lobby, I thought I saw Beth out of the corner of my eye. At least I sensed that she was there, somewhere in the lobby. Before I went out the door, I even turned around to look at the lobby again, but I didn't see her, and there was no reason that I should have expected to see her there. Still, the thought occurred to me that all the birds had come home to roost.

Even though it was only a weeknight, Beale Street was teeming. Music and people spilled out of the bars and onto the street in a parade that reminded me of 6th Street in Austin. In fact, I wandered into one bar for the sole reason that I could hear a band inside playing a Stevie Ray Vaughan tune. I ordered a beer, and made my way through the cigarette smoke to a table about the same time that the band decided to take a break.

As my eyes adjusted to the dimness of the bar lights, I could see that there were small round tables set up around a dance floor in front of the band. At the tables, groups of men and groups of women were drinking pitchers of beer and smoking and laughing.

The thought crossed my mind that if something happened to me in there, it would be a complete mystery to Michelle as to why I was found alone by the authorities in a blues bar in Memphis, Tennessee. Once again, she had no idea where I was or what I was doing, and I had waited too late to call because I dreaded telling her that I had so little control over my life.

A waitress in blue jeans and a bowling shirt came by and I ordered another beer.

She brought it as the band resumed playing. The band consisted of men twenty years older than me. The guitar player and piano player alternated singing duties. Directly across the dance floor from me, a table of coeds sat waiting, to no avail, for someone to ask them to dance. Each of them was pretty in her own way—a fresh-faced blonde, a brunette with long hair and a short top, and a girl with short, coal-black hair and freckles. The black-haired girl seemed to be staring across the dance floor at me; she also squinted her eyes from time to time in a sleepy, drunken way as she swayed with the music that made me think she probably didn't see me at all.

The blonde and brunette got tired of waiting for somebody to ask them to dance, so they joined the crowd gathering on the floor and began dancing with each other. The way they held each other and swayed their hips in unison suggested that they might have danced together before, and it wasn't very long before two guys swooped in from the crowd and began dancing with them. I smiled, thinking that the two guys had found the blonde and brunette's dancing as erotic as I had. When I focused again on the black-haired girl with freckles, she was smiling at the fact that I was smiling, watching her friends. She picked up her mug and the pitcher of beer from her table, and walked in front of the band over to mine. She set the pitcher on my table and took a seat beside me.

"Enjoying the show?" she asked raising her eyebrows and leaning in to me so that she could be heard over the music. Before I could answer, she said, "We don't get many guys in coats and ties out at this hour. Where are you from?"

"Houston," I said, almost shouting.

"What are you doing here?" she asked and turned her attention back to the band.

"Ribs," I said.

She smiled. She wasn't drunk after all. Maybe she was a little high, I don't know. She just had a cool way of blinking her eyes in a slow, sensuously sleepy way that was probably necessary due to the weight of her beautiful eyelashes. From across the room, she was pretty. Up close, when she leaned in to talk to me over the sound of the band, she was incredible. She had on a simple black T-shirt, tucked into a pair of tight blue jeans, and a pair of flat-heeled, black shoes. She spoke with a southern drawl, modified by her years at Notre Dame. She reminded me of a young Ali MacGraw, with freckles. She also reminded me of Beth. Eventually, we started dancing.

Although I've never been much of a dancer, the floor was crowded enough that the whole group seemed to move together, forcing me closer and closer to the black-haired girl. When the band took another break, she asked me if I was ready to leave. I told her I was staying at the Peabody, and she said she would give me a lift, even though it was only a couple of blocks away.

Outside the club, a valet attendant brought around her red Jeep; and, at the hotel, she gave the keys to the doorman.

The black-haired girl hooked her arm in mine as we went through the doors of the Peabody and walked across the lobby. "Should we get a drink down here?" I asked.

"Sure," she said, "and let's take it to your room. It's too bright in here." She looked up at the ornate, stained-glass ceiling of acanthus-shaped scrolls, floral pinwheels, and Arabic designs of green, burgundy, gold, and purple. She was right. The lobby, with its chairs and tables around the marble fountain, was too open and bright. It was a place to be seen, rather than a place to enjoy an intimate drink. I doubted that Sullivan or Riza would be in the lobby at this hour, but going to my room seemed like the prudent thing to do at the time. I paid cash for a scotch and a beer at the bar, and we took the elevator up to my room.

I realized as I opened the door to the room that I had not been in it before. The room was decorated in yellow and cream English chintz fabrics, with a king size bed and dark wood furniture that included a writing desk and a comfortable seating area with a small couch and two chairs. My unopened hanging bag was leaning against the wall in the corner.

The black-haired girl sat down on the couch and put her beer on the coffee table in front of her. "Been in town long?" she asked, looking at the folded hanging bag. I sat down in the chair across from her and sipped my scotch. I told her that I had met some friends for dinner and then left on my own to go find Beale Street. "So, what did you think of our little effort at nightlife?" she asked.

"It's fun," I said, trying to keep the conversation going. "It's like 6th Street in Austin. Smaller than the French Quarter in New Orleans. How often do you and your friends hit Beale Street?"

She smiled. "You mean, how often do I find myself at the Peabody with a married man with one change of clothes?"

I shrugged. She appeared to have a fairly well-developed cross examination style of her own.

"Not often," she said and took a long swig from her beer. "I'm a law student at the University of Memphis. The Cecil C. Humphreys School of Law," she said with a flourish. "It's just up the street in the old customs house on the riverfront. Most of my time is spent studying in the law library."

I laughed. "I'm a lawyer," I said. "I'm familiar with the routine. You hang out at the library until it closes, trying to read for the next day. Then, somebody says, 'Let's go have a beer,' and the next thing you know, it's two in the morning and you're wondering if you're okay to drive home. What year are you?"

"Third," she said. "I figured you were a lawyer. Brooks Brothers' blazer. Repp-striped tie. It's the same uniform my older brother wears every day. He practices in Charleston. I think he took a job there just so that he could be closer to that store that sells those striped ties and blazer buttons."

"Ben Silver," I said. "I get their catalogue. I've always wanted to go there." I stood up, and took off my coat, then hung it in the closet. I stripped off my tie and looped it around the coat collar. I walked back over to the coffee table, picked up my scotch, and sat next to her on the couch. "What about the married man part?" I asked.

"I thought you looked harmless enough. I thought you might be interesting to talk to. I didn't think I had ever seen you before. I doubt if I will ever see you again. We haven't done anything wrong, yet, have we?" She leaned over and kissed me gently on the lips. I closed my eyes as she leaned into me. When I opened them, her face was close to mine and she was smiling. Her kiss and her full lips reminded me of Beth. I cupped one breast and kissed her again for a long time. When I pulled back, she pursed her lips and sighed. Then she asked me as she looked around the room, "Do you think we need all these lights on?"

"I don't know if I can do this," I said.

"Oh, I think you can," she said, and rested her hand on my lap while looking directly into my eyes.

I stood up. "Believe me; I know I can do this. It's been months since I've had sex. If you touch me again, I may have an orgasm," I said.

"Why haven't you had sex in months?" she asked. "Problems at home?"

"We're pregnant."

"I thought that made women more interested in sex."

"Apparently, we went right past that part after the morning sickness. Now, we're in the 'I'm too uncomfortable to move' stage." I said.

"Well, then, why are you standing up and walking away from me? I promise I'll be gentle," she said teasing me and extending her arms toward me.

I laughed, and she smiled. "Come here," she said and motioned with her hands toward her on the couch.

"I can't," I said. "There's something else."

She reached over and picked up her beer, and pulled her legs up under her on the couch. She took another big swig of the beer and idly played with her hair with one hand. "My first class isn't until eleven o'clock," she said. "We may need to call room service to come restock the minibar." I went over to the little refrigerator and opened another beer for her. I handed it to her, and she took my hand and pulled me to her again. We kissed, with her sitting on the couch and me standing over her. I held her hand as I pulled back and stood up straight after we stopped kissing.

If there is such a thing as love at first sight, there must also be a more primordial first sight connection between people that are attracted to each other. Who knows why a connection like this occurs? Maybe you knew her in a past life. Maybe, there is a recognition between individuals of physical characteristics or mannerisms that suggests qualities we recognize in other people we have loved or found attractive. Maybe there is a subtle recognition of need between the two individuals. Maybe it's pheromones.

There is a point in time when you know you are about to have sex with a person. Maybe it's after you've kissed her. Maybe, before. A thousand things can happen to derail the train that is rolling down the tracks. But sometimes it just rolls along.

I had not been in this situation since I learned that I had herpes. I wanted to avoid telling the dark-haired girl with freckles about the herpes, although it wasn't anything like having to tell Michelle. She could just leave after I told her, and I would never see her again. She couldn't think any less of me, because she didn't know anything about me. I assumed that telling her about the herpes would surely derail the sex train. But I knew I had to tell her.

The idea that I could tell anybody, other than Beth, about the herpes seemed like a positive step to me. If I told her about it, and she stormed out of the hotel without ever speaking to me again, it would still be an experience worth having. I would have told somebody, at least, even if it was somebody I didn't even know.

If she left, I would just rent a SpectraVision adult movie and masturbate my way to sleep. At home, I wouldn't even let myself masturbate because of some admittedly less than scientifically based idea that viral-loaded cells might be shed during masturbation and would lie in wait around the house, in our bed, on our couch, in our shower, seeking to infect my wife and possibly our unborn child.

Of course it crossed my mind that something like this situation had gotten me into this predicament in the first place. How could a one-night stand be the prescription for the guilt complex I suffered as a result of having had an affair from which I contracted a venereal disease? At first blush, it appeared that this behavior would be another violation of Sullivan's First Rule of Holes. I assumed that when the affair and the herpes came to light, my marriage would be over. I didn't think my having sex with the freckled-face girl would ultimately affect my marriage, one way or the other. Like the over 6 feet, single, white male that caught Beth's attention with the ad he had placed in the *Free Press Houston*, I was damaged goods, and I had reconciled myself to the fact that I would be consigned to a diseased subculture, an amorphous leper colony, that shared each other's guilt, as well as their sexual urges.

"I have herpes," I said and let out a long breath while looking at the ceiling.

She started laughing, and then stopped, still smiling.

"I'm sorry to laugh," she said. "Lots of people have herpes. My sister does. She says it's a nuisance. She got it from her no-account husband. Do you have it right now?" she asked, still holding my hand.

"Apparently, you always have it once you get it. It lives in your spine. Sometimes, you have breakouts. I guess that makes me a no-account husband."

"It lives in your spine?" she asked. "Does your wife have it?"

"I don't know. I'm worried that she does. I haven't told her I have it."

"Why did you tell me?" She asked, her voice trailing off as she asked the question as if she were connecting thoughts in her head.

"Because I had to," I said.

"You have to tell her too, don't you?"

"I know. I've been trying to; I just haven't been able to, yet. I'm afraid she'll leave me."

"Oh, so this isn't your first trip to the Peabody, metaphorically speaking?" she asked. Before I could answer, she said, "Are you really just worried that your wife will want a divorce, or are you afraid that she'll see that you are not perfect despite your navy blazer and red-and-blue striped tie?"

"What is it with you and that blazer?" I asked.

"That's it, isn't it? You're as worried about your image with your wife as you are about actually passing along the virus or having to talk about a divorce."

"I guess you are right," I said, and she shook her head.

"You've got to tell her," she said. "When is the baby due?"

"In a few months," I said.

"She has to know before then, for the baby's sake."

"Of course. I know."

"But you are trying to figure out some way to fix this situation, aren't you?" she asked. "I'm afraid you're just going to have to come clean and let the chips fall where they may this time, old boy. People make mistakes. Sometimes they stay married. Sometimes they get divorced. Isn't the baby's health the biggest issue here?" She asked. She didn't seem to expect me to answer.

Part of me wanted to ask her to leave before she found out anything more about me. She already had enough information to blackmail me effectively. I didn't know anything about her. I knew her first name was "Chelsea," but I didn't know her last name. In a way, she knew more about me than my wife did. Probably, the girl knew more about me than I did. Part of me felt a sense of relief for having told someone, even if it wasn't the person I knew I should be telling. And interestingly, she had not recoiled in terror when I told her.

"Relax," she said, again tugging on my hand. "I told you I am not going to hurt you. You told me a secret. I'll tell you one." She pulled me over to the couch, and sat down on her knees. She whispered into my ear as I leaned toward her, "I brought condoms."

Then she stood and pulled the package of condoms from the back pocket of her jeans. She held them out for me to see. She walked over to the bed and placed the condoms on the nightstand with a bit of a dramatic flair. Then she walked to the end of the bed and began taking off her clothes.

I stood motionless as the girl neatly folded her jeans and T-shirt across the foot of the bed and walked silently back to the head of the bed where the nightstand was located. She paused momentarily and peeled off her panties and unhooked her bra. Both fell at her feet beside the bed. She turned to face me for a brief second and smiled. The freckles that gave her face such a youthful appearance extended seductively over her entire body except in those areas that I imagined would be hidden from time to time by a swimsuit. She covered her white breasts with her left arm. She reached up with her right hand and turned out the light.

"I'm going to take a little nap," I heard her say in the darkness. "I left the package on the nightstand if you decide that you are ready. If not, I'll understand." I heard her sigh as she got into bed and drew up the covers.

"Burnt sienna," I thought to myself as I stepped out of my cordovan Alden penny loafers and, without removing my socks, grey slacks, or starched button-down, lay down on the little couch. As I stared up in the darkness at where I assumed the ceiling would be, I remembered the crayon by that name in the box of sixty-four Crayola crayons that I used at College Heights Elementary school back in Abilene.

For some reason, it was one of my favorite colors and I tried to color everything with it until the teacher at the start of my fourth-grade year asked me if burnt sienna was really the correct color for the baseball glove I was drawing to depict what I had done the previous summer.

Admittedly, it wasn't, and since then I had been involuntarily compelled to make a mental note any time that I saw something that is the color of burnt sienna. The wrapper on a Punch Rothschild Rare Corojo cigar is close. The chalky mark that a Tignanello cork leaves on a white tablecloth is closer. And, while I only was permitted a brief glimpse before the freckle-faced girl turned out the light in what at one time had been my room at the Peabody, I would say that her nipples were exactly burnt sienna.

When it seemed to me that the girl's breathing pattern meant that she had gone to sleep, I got up, went over to the writing desk, and turned on the table lamp. I stood motionless for a moment to see if she woke up, and she didn't. As quietly as I could, I opened the desk drawer and took out a sheet of stationery and a pen. I sat at the desk and tried to compose the poem that had been running around in my head the last few days, weeks, months. There were a few lines that I had committed to memory rather than writing them down, but I could only recall bits and pieces of them. Still, they were enough to get my thoughts rolling.

I spent most of the night on it—tearing up drafts, throwing them in the wastebasket, and starting over. When I sat back to admire it early that morning, I knew it wasn't any good. The plagiarized first line was still the only thing that was any good.

The condoms were still unopened on the nightstand, and the black-haired girl was still asleep in the bed the next morning when I went downstairs early because I didn't recall Sullivan saying anything about departure time. I left the keycard to the room on the nightstand by the condoms in case the girl needed to charge anything before she left.

I didn't realize that I had left the unfinished poem on the desk until I let the locked door to the room close behind me and realized that I didn't have a key. I thought about knocking on the door and trying to retrieve the poem and decided not to.

I put my bag with the bellman. I assumed I would drink coffee and read the sports pages until Sullivan and Riza were ready to go. I was surprised to see them seated in the lobby by the fountain as I walked by. They seemed surprised to see me too. Tim was saying something to Riza about having to sell quickly and discretely when I came up from behind them and said good morning. They both said good morning, and Tim changed the subject.

He ordered coffee for me, and refills for him and Riza. "Hey," Sullivan said, "where were you last night? I tried to call you in your room to get you to come see the room they gave me. The 'W.C. Handy Suite.' It was something wasn't it?" He asked Riza. "I think you would've liked it."

"I went for a drink on Beale Street and ended up dancing a little bit. I got up early this morning and began working on a poem," I said.

"Dancing?" Sullivan asked.

"A poem?" Riza asked.

Before I could answer either question, Sullivan waved his hand as if to dismiss the topic and stated without attribution, "Every notary bears within him the debris of a poet." Then Sullivan laughed and shook his head and changed the subject.

He seemed satisfied with my explanation as to where I had been when he had called. He told us how legend has it that in the early Thirties the hotel manager and his friend came back from duck hunting and put their (then legal) live decoys in the Italian travertine marble fountain in the middle of the hotel lobby. In about 1940, a circus trainer named Pembroke trained the ducks to march from their home on the roof of the hotel, into the elevator, and across a rolled-out red carpet to the fountain every morning and back at five o'clock every afternoon.

Tim asked us if we wanted to wait around for the ducks to come down. Riza said that we had both seen the "duck march" on previous trips, and, if we waited around too long, Tim would just use the excuse to stay around another evening and go to the Rendezvous. I nodded my agreement, all the while keeping my eyes on the elevators. I wasn't particularly concerned about the mallards marching across the lobby.

I also kept thinking to myself, "Sell *what* quickly and discretely?"

15

THE NEXT DAY, IN Houston, I called Dr. Nathan's office from my cell phone in the car and made an appointment to see him. The receptionist told me that they didn't usually see husbands at the obstetrician and gynecology offices, but Dr. Nathan would make an exception in my case. She told me to bring my calendar. When I asked if she meant my calendar for September, she told me that Dr. Nathan requested that I bring my calendar for the entire year, including September.

I showed up thirty minutes early for my appointment with Dr. Nathan a few days later. I checked in with the receptionist, and she told me to have a seat. I sat with my legs crossed, taking a self-graded examination in *Cosmopolitan* designed to determine which birth control alternative was right for me.

While the room was by no means full, it presented a wide range of ages of women, spanning a spectrum from younger than Michelle to older than her mother. I wondered to myself why a person would enter this particular specialty of medicine. I could see the fun and excitement of childbirth, but otherwise it seemed to demystify the most mystical of all of God's creations. The male sex organ was, obviously, external and visible to see and study. Phallic symbols permeated art, architecture, and literature, perhaps because males had controlled these fields for centuries, and also probably because the male organ was so obvious, an external display of the sentiment of the person to whom it was attached.

Conversely, the female sex organ was hidden beneath folds, internal, plunging away from sight, mysterious. Practicing obstetrics and gynecology would seem to me to put a speculum where before there was only speculation.

But maybe I was wrong. Perhaps every time one question is answered, another two emerge.

A nurse opened the door to the hallway leading to the examination rooms and called my name. She bit her lip to keep from smiling as I cleared my throat and hurried through the door. "Dr. Nathan is in his office, the last door on your right. He's expecting you, Mr. Jessie. How's Michelle doing?"

"She's fine," I said. "Thank you for asking." I hurried down the hall and went into Dr. Nathan's office. He was seated behind a large desk that looked like it could have been a principal's desk in the Fifties. The desktop was covered with a thick piece of glass that protected pictures of his family, including grandchildren, on various fishing trips and sightseeing vacations. Manila folders sat in boxes on either side of the desk, and he was reading a file while talking into an old-fashioned Dictaphone.

He looked up from his dictation as I walked into the room. He motioned to a seat, closed the file he was reading and put it in the open box on the right-hand side of his desk. He looked over his reading glasses at me. "Hello, Mr. Jessie. How can I help you today?" he asked, trying to initiate a conversation.

I was appreciative of the fact that he didn't make any jokes about my coming to see him. "I need to talk to you."

He didn't say anything, and waited for me to continue.

"I'm worried about Michelle, and I'm worried about the baby," I said. He looked at me intently letting my statement register and waiting for me to continue. When I didn't say more, Dr. Nathan opened a desk drawer with hanging folders, and rifled through the files until he came to what I assumed was Michelle's chart. He placed the file on his desk and looked at me again over his glasses.

"They seemed to be fine last time Michelle came in for her appointment. What is the cause for your worry? I must say, this is a bit unusual to discuss a patient's condition, even with the patient's husband, without the patient present. You, a lawyer of all people, must be sensitive to my concern. But let's see if there is something I can help you with, Mr. Jessie. Having your first child can be troubling for fathers and mothers alike. You're not the first prospective dad to come see me without his spouse present. I've been doing this a long time. Sometimes, I think too long. I don't know how much longer I'm going to be able to continue to do it. Anyway, there isn't much I haven't seen, I'm afraid to say."

"Michelle worships you," I said.

He shrugged. "As you know, I delivered her. Her parents, her mother at least, is more a friend of mine now than a patient."

"What are the chances she'll need a C-section?" I blurted out.

"I guess there is a possibility. There is always a possibility. At this point, the size of the baby does not appear to present a problem." He peered down through the reading portion of his bifocals and turned a few pages in the file before him. He looked up at me and said, "We'll just have to see as we go along. Much can happen between now and mid-September." He took off his glasses, began chewing on an already-chewed earpiece, and closed the file.

"What if we wanted to have a C-section?" I asked.

"Wanted to have a C-section?" He said with the earpiece still in his mouth and looked at some spot on the ceiling above. "Well, it's a surgery that involves risks inherent in any surgery. The recovery time is longer. Future deliveries would sometimes, not always, be restricted to C-sections. It's somewhat surprising, but many first-time parents wonder why we don't always do C-sections. I guess the truth is that the risks of surgery have been minimized in recent years, but it is still surgery." He brought his gaze down from the ceiling and focused on me. Your wife will be going through enough trauma with her first childbirth. Why would you want her to go through surgery, Mr. Jessie?"

"Remember last time we were here?" I asked. Dr. Nathan opened his file again, flipped forward a few pages, and put his glasses back on his nose. He looked up from his file, and waited for me to continue.

When I hesitated, Dr. Nathan asked, "Does this have something to do with Michelle reporting to me on her last visit that she had felt a 'recent vaginal itching and burning that had subsided in a week or ten days'?"

Again, I hesitated.

"Look, Mr. Jessie. I can't help you if you won't talk to me. My real concern is Michelle and the unborn child, but I have a feeling that what you have to tell me could potentially affect the health of both Michelle and the baby. Now, tell me what it is that you obviously have come here to tell me." He demanded in a grandfatherly way, but I could tell that there was a note of exasperation in his voice.

"I'm afraid I may have given Michelle herpes. I'm afraid that it will infect our baby if he's born through a vaginal delivery. I'm afraid he could be born blind, or worse, even die. Please, help me. I've got to do something to protect our son."

Dr. Nathan reached into his desk drawer for a pencil. He made a note on the last page of the chart, and closed the file. He took off his glasses again, put his feet up on the desk, leaned back in his old, Naugahyde-covered swivel chair, rubbed his eyes with the backs of his hands, sighed, and then looked at me trying to control his anger.

"You want me to perform a C-section for the delivery of your son so that you can avoid telling your wife that you have herpes, and that she may have it as well? I'm afraid I can't promise to do that, Mr. Jessie," he said. "You know I won't do that. Frankly, I'm surprised you'd even ask me to consider doing that."

I wasn't sure I had asked Dr. Nathan to consider doing that, at least not in so many words, but he was able to consider bits of conversation that hadn't even been said out loud, almost as if he had heard them before.

He put his feet back down on the floor and leaned over the desk toward me. "What about the increased risk to your wife?" Dr. Nathan asked, his voice elevating almost an octave.

"I guess I hadn't really thought about that," I said leaning back in my chair trying to increase the distance between us. "Won't she have to have a C-section now, if she has herpes?" I asked.

"She could. It depends on whether she has an outbreak at the time of delivery. If not, we just give the mother a dose of medication, probably the same one you took when you first contracted the disease, and proceed with a vaginal delivery.

"Look, the bottom line Mr. Jessie, is, if you don't tell your wife that she has been exposed to herpes, I will. I've already made a notation on her chart that indicates she's a strong candidate for a Cesarean section. I'll make you this promise, Mr. Jessie. I'll promise to consider delivering the baby by C-section, if you promise to tell Michelle prior to delivery that you may have given her herpes."

He picked up the closed file and placed it in the correct slot in the drawer in his desk. It was clear from his tone that he considered the conversation concluded and that there was no room for negotiation.

"Okay," I said dropping my head and talking as much to myself as to him. "I'll tell her. I promise I will tell her." I looked back up at him. "Please, don't let anything happen to her or our baby." My voice cracked, which only increased my level of embarrassment.

"I'm not casting any judgments, Mr. Jessie." He said trying to be reassuring. "That's not my job. My job is to take care of my patients. You're clearly emotionally distraught. You need someone to talk to about this. Someone other than your wife's obstetrician." He paused and waited to see if I would say something.

"Would you like me to give you the names of a good counselor or two? Talking this through with a trained psychologist would probably do you some good," he said authoritatively.

"I know," I said. "I want to talk to Michelle about it, but I just can't. It will hurt her so much. I know she'll never look at me the same way again. Until now, I've been perfect in her eyes. I'll never be that way again."

"No, Mr. Jessie," Dr. Nathan said as he seemed to try to calm down for a moment, "she'll never see you that way again. But people aren't perfect. They're just people. Sometimes they do the wrong thing. They get caught up in situations over which they have no control. And yet they continue to try and control the situation, to fix things that can't be fixed. It's true that I am fond of saying that 'people are the solution to their problems,' but I mean people collectively not individually. It's okay to ask somebody for help. I'll see about doing the C-section, Mr. Jessie, because it's probably the right thing to do, given the circumstances—assuming your wife contracted genital herpes during her pregnancy. However, you must talk to her. She's going to be judgmental. She has every right to be. She's going to blame you, and she may leave you. I don't know. I am constantly amazed by the human capacity for reconciliation and forgiveness. True, she'll never see you the way she used to see you." He rested his elbows on the desk and extended his old, open hands out toward me.

"But was that really you, Mr. Jessie? Wouldn't you rather that she, your wife, knows you as you really are—as a human being, not a stereotype—as a person with human foibles and human failures?

"I don't know you very well, Davy, but I know that you must have some, well, promise as a young trial lawyer, or you wouldn't be in the position in which you find yourself as the husband of a senior partner's daughter. I don't know the woman from whom you have contracted herpes. And while I don't know for certain, I suspect that you have transmitted that disease to your wife and potentially to your unborn child."

He folded his arms across his chest. "I've known Michelle her whole life. I delivered her. I've watched her grow up. I started seeing her as a patient when she became a teenager. I followed her through college. Then I know that she went to law school, probably to please her father as much as anything. And I think things happen for a reason—maybe not the reason we planned, but a reason nevertheless. I assume that one of the reasons Michelle went to law school, unbeknownst to her at the time, was to meet you. If you'll permit an old man a moment, I'll tell you what I think about all of this."

I nodded.

He placed his hands behind his head and continued. "In my life, I have seen patients from all walks of life. Some had money. Some didn't. The most precious things to any of them were their children. I had the privilege of helping them bring those children into the world. There are plenty of other doctors who could have performed the service, I know. Most, but not all, deliveries have gone well.

"It has always been interesting to me how, at that critical moment of delivery, most people react in the same way. They are nervous, then they are scared, then they are caught up in the delivery itself, and then they are relieved and happy and full of a wonder that surpasses my understanding, though I have spent a lifetime observing it. It's like life is reduced for a few moments to a common denominator. I don't know if there is any other profession like it. Maybe it would be the same kind of thing at the end of life, a physician offering palliative care. Maybe it's the same for veterinarians. I would image that the poor sheep farmer or small ranch owner is just as happy to see a lamb or colt born as the prize lamb or race horse owner.

"And I'll tell you something else, Mr. Jessie. If you're going to make it in a profession for any great length of time, you are going to have to find that moment that, while you may not get to see it every day, you get to see it often enough that it makes the day-to-day drudgery worthwhile.

"If it's just about making money, you will never have enough. If it is just about looking right or keeping up some image, I dare say the proverbial moths are nibbling at your favorite suit in the closet right now."

"For you," I asked, "it's watching the beginning of life? I don't think there is much in my profession that will compare to that."

"No." Dr. Nathan responded leaning back in his chair again and putting his hands behind his head. "It's not the birth so much as watching how the birth affects people. For just a moment, you get to see how we are all alike, all capable of good, all full of hope. I know parents leave the hospital and drift off into their lives, but, for a few minutes, they all share the same dream.

"Michelle has always had everything that a girl could want. If you tell her mom I said this, I will tell her that you were dreaming. The truth is I think Michelle has missed out a little bit in the family department. Her dad's a good provider, but he wasn't always around, to put it kindly, when she was growing up. I would say the most important thing in the world for Michelle is having a baby. She wants a family. She's been getting ready her whole life to have a family of her own, and now you have come along and put that in jeopardy.

"Maybe I'll do the C-section, but promise me you will talk to Michelle and tell her about the herpes before you come in for the delivery," he said leaning toward me again and gesturing to the pages of paper that sat in my lap. "You brought your calendar with you. You have about ninety days. I suggest you mark a date now for when you are going to have this conversation. This afternoon would be a good place to start."

"I promise. I will," I said and looked down at the calendar that was in front me. As I looked at it, the dates on the pages seemed to swirl together.

When I left Dr. Nathan's office that day, I intended to tell Michelle.

When I got home, she asked me what I was doing out dancing by myself in Memphis. Apparently her dad had told her mom about not being able to find me that night in Memphis, and her mom had told Michelle. I wondered why I felt compelled to keep Sullivan's secrets safe for him when he didn't feel the need to reciprocate. Maybe he just didn't think that I was capable of similar indiscretions.

"I didn't even know that you were in Tennessee," Michelle said. "Who were you dancing with?"

"I don't know," I said honestly. But I found myself on the defensive, and I didn't tell Michelle that night or the next day about the affair or the herpes. As the weeks crept by, I began to wonder if I ever would.

16

CHELSEA WOKE UP IN THE ROOM at the Peabody as the sun began to shine brightly through the sheer curtains, and she wished that she had exhibited the foresight the previous night to close the opaque blinds when she took off her clothes and went to bed. She closed her eyes and tried to count the number of beers she had consumed the night before. It was difficult to estimate, partly because of the headache that was throbbing in her temples and partly because of the size of the number. Her mouth felt like a small rodent might have nested there overnight, and she reached blindly for the telephone on the nightstand. Eventually, she found the receiver and sat up in bed to find the zero to call the operator.

"Good morning, Mr. Jessie." The voice on the phone answered.

Jessie? Chelsea thought to herself. She didn't remember having heard previously her prospective paramour's last name, and she couldn't help but to play the old game of trying her first name with it to check for matrimonial appropriateness. "Chelsea Jessie" would not have worked at all. Too singsong. Way too many vowels.

"Good morning," Chelsea responded into the phone.

There was a slight hesitation on the other end of the line while the operator tried to conjure up a polite way to recognize the fact that he was not speaking to Mr. Jessie, and that he had no idea whether there was a Mrs. Jessie, and what the likelihood was that this might be her. "How may I help you, Ma'am?" was the selection he chose.

"Do y'all have any of those darlin' little personal grooming kits that you could send up to Mr. Jessie's room?" Chelsea asked, affecting her most pronounced southern drawl. "You know toothpaste, toothbrush, deodorant, razor, that sort of thang?"

"Of course, ma'am. Is there anything else I could get you? A pot of coffee perhaps?"

"Coffee would be nice. Thank you." Chelsea said and hung up the phone. She glanced over at the clock and realized that if she were going to make it to her first class on the subject of secured transactions, she would have to hustle. She laid her head back on the pillow and closed her eyes. Maybe thirty more minutes of sleep would help with the headache. After a moment she realized that she was not going to be able to sleep. Besides, the man was coming with the coffee, and she really needed to go to the bathroom. She flung off the heavy covers. If she got going now, maybe she could still make it to school on time. When she stood up out of bed, however, she quickly abandoned the notion of racing to class. It would not be the first session of secured transactions that she did not attend. She had no interest in practicing law in that area, but it was on the Tennessee bar exam, and she promised herself that she would read the materials during the time that her classmates were actually in class.

Still naked, she walked into the bathroom, used the toilet, and stood at the sink looking at herself in the mirror. She pulled her hair back behind her left ear and leaned into the mirror for a closer inspection. "Freckles all present and accounted for, sir." She said to herself and saluted.

For a moment, she wondered if she had been so drunk that she forgot about having sex the night before. Then she remembered the entire episode with the young lawyer from Texas. She had expected that he would join her in the sumptuous Peabody bed at some point during the night and, despite whatever pangs of guilt he might be experiencing, would succumb to her feminine charms. She could not decide whether to be disappointed or glad that she had not had sex with him, but the more she thought about it, she decided that her feelings were hurt.

She worried for a moment that the beer calories were adding up before confirming that her waist was still small and well-defined. She patted her tummy approvingly, proud that there was no jiggle with the patting. As she looked in the mirror, she cupped her breasts and then turned and looked over her shoulder at her bare behind. She wished that her legs were longer, stood on her tip-toes, and decided they were the right length for her body. Her calves, taut from standing as if she were wearing heels, still showed the muscle she had developed playing high school soccer, and how long ago was that now? "What were you thinking, Mr. Jessie?" She asked aloud.

She started the shower after checking the water at the bathtub faucet several times to make sure that the temperature was right. Again, she stood in front of the mirror and looked at her reflection as the fog of the steam made the reflection disappear. A thought crossed her mind about whether having an orgasm might help stop the aching in her head, and her right hand drifted down to her clitoris.

She had barely closed her eyes when she heard the knock at the door. She assumed it was the man with the coffee since she now remembered that she had heard the young Houston lawyer shower and leave much earlier that morning. She sighed, took the plush, terry cloth robe off the hanger on the back of the bathroom door, put the robe on, and closed the bathroom door as she went across the room to the guestroom door.

The young, white-jacketed waiter averted his eyes from her as he said, 'Good morning," and entered the room with a tray carrying a coffee pot, two cups, and a toiletry bag.

Despite his youth, he had worked at the hotel for several years, and his job had required that from time to time he intrude upon rather intimate settings, although this was not his favorite part of the job. He walked across the room as Chelsea let the door close behind him, glancing at her just long enough to determine that he had not seen this young woman before. That was when the job could get awkward—when you recognized somebody and knew that they were not where they were supposed to be. He walked over to the nightstand, being careful not to step on the woman's underwear that had been dropped beside the bed. He couldn't help noticing there was only one set of folded clothes on the bed. He wondered if there was anyone in the shower. It sounded like just water from the faucet was running, but he thought that this fellow Jessie could have taken his clothes with him into the bathroom.

The waiter started to put the tray down on the nightstand, hesitated when he saw the package of condoms beside the room keycard, and then decided to set the tray on top of the package and card. He turned and handed a ticket folder to Chelsea for her to sign for the room charge.

"He's in the shower, but I'll sign for him." Chelsea said, confirming the waiter's suspicions. She took the folder from the man, noticed that he was blushing, signed the ticket with a scribbled "Jessie," and added fifteen percent to the charge. She saw that a room service gratuity was already included, but she included the tip anyway because she was feeling magnanimous. She considered flirting with the waiter just to see if she could get him to blush again, but thought better of it, and walked to the door and let him out. As the waiter left, Chelsea thought to herself that she was about to find out if Mr. Jessie, or whatever his name was, had checked out of the hotel or if she was still able to charge items to the room.

After showering, dressing, combing her hair, and putting on some mascara, Chelsea left the room after picking up the room key and the package of condoms from beneath the serving tray. She had no real plans for using either, but it seemed like the most prudent course. She was considering having breakfast downstairs, putting it on the room bill, and reading the secured transactions assignment just as she had promised herself. Her first step, however, was to pop into the lobby gift shop and buy a new black T-shirt and some aspirin. She chose a close-fitting shirt with cropped sleeves and a small mallard embroidered on the left chest with the phrase "Meet me at the Peabody." She charged the shirt to the room and then went back upstairs and changed shirts.

"Okay," she thought to herself as she sat down at a table in the spacious, yet crowded, lobby bar. She was intent on ordering a full breakfast and perhaps a Bloody Mary or Mimosa to take the edge off the pounding headache that remained in spite of a dose of aspirin and strong black coffee. A waiter brought over a menu and she decided to go with the bloody. She scanned the menu for the Peabody's version of eggs Benedict, and ordered it when the waiter brought over her drink.

She reached into her large black purse that was more like a tote bag and pulled out her copy of the Nutshell Series volume on secured transactions. The day had begun a bit roughly, but things seemed to be improving. Her idea to charge the breakfast to the room was not done as a vendetta against the jilting Mr. Jessie or because she was unable to pay for it on her own. This was what she would have expected Mr. Jessie to do if he had bothered to wake her up before he left so abruptly. Clearly that must have been what he expected when he left the room keycard on the nightstand.

She sat back in the plush, overstuffed chair and tried to concentrate on the reading. Most law school classes use textbooks that contain reported cases clustered around a theme or the historical development of a rule of law. Sometimes excerpts from a statute (depending on the subject matter) interrupt the cases. Sometimes the cases are separated by a series of, supposedly, thought-provoking questions designed to elicit broader thinking by the reader.

The teaching concept is that by reading the cases and statutes, a law student learns "to think like a lawyer" and to glean a global understanding of whatever it is the cases are trying to accomplish in the development of the law. One could synthesize most classes into a few rules that would easily fit onto a three-inch by five-inch recipe card. "Nutshell," and other similar publications, attempted to summarize the cases in the textbooks and distill the recipe-card information for the busy law student who could not find the time to read the cases in their entirety as a kind of Cliff Notes for law students. The professors, of course, frowned upon the use of these study aids, but Chelsea was not dissimilar to other law students in finding herself relying more and more upon them and she advanced through law school.

The waiter returned in a moment with the eggs and a refill on the Bloody Mary. He set them on the table without interrupting her reading. As he left, a tall, dark-haired woman in a handsome, beige suit stopped at Chelsea's table. She was carrying a Louis Vuitton duffle bag in one hand and a matching laptop case in the other. She had a healthy tan and enormous, brown eyes.

"Excuse me." The woman said. "Would you mind if I sat down with you at your table. There don't appear to be any open tables right now."

"Of course." said Chelsea, opening one outstretched hand to the empty seat across the small table from her. "Help yourself." She was secretly glad to have an excuse to put away the book.

Chelsea noticed, and then wondered why she noticed, when the woman took off her suit coat that she was not wearing a bra under her eggshell colored blouse.

"I can't remember if I read that one or saw the movie." The woman said as she sat down.

"You're a lawyer?" Chelsea asked.

"Sort of." The woman answered. "Certainly not one that knows anything about secured transactions."

"Doesn't it seem like the world is full of lawyers?" Chelsea asked.

"I'm sure there is always room for one more hard-working young attorney. What year are you in?" She asked.

"Third." Chelsea answered.

"Oh, you're through."

"Almost." Chelsea noticed as she exchanged pleasantries with the woman that while she was extremely attractive with large brown eyes, there was also a certain sadness about her. It looked like she might not have slept recently or that she had been through some ordeal that left her upset and vulnerable. Chelsea noticed that while the woman was not wearing a wedding ring, there was a tan line where the ring had been, and then Chelsea wondered to herself why she had bothered to notice that. The woman forced a smile when she spoke, but even though smiling was an effort for the woman, Chelsea noticed that she had beautiful, full lips and that she looked directly into Chelsea's eyes when she spoke to Chelsea.

"I'm afraid that I am too far along to discover that there are too many lawyers already. There doesn't seem to be any turning back now." Chelsea said.

17

To THE CASUAL OBSERVER, it might have seemed financially irrespon-
sible for Beth to check into the luxurious Peabody Hotel when she did.
She was not employed at the time, and her husband had abandoned her
and returned to his parents' home in Milan, Tennessee, a small town in
Gibson County about ninety miles from Memphis. Beth had decided,
however, that the unpleasant nature of her visit to the Volunteer state
required that she splurge to some degree on creature comforts, even if
it meant dipping into her rapidly dwindling savings. The task in front
of her demanded a high thread count.

She flew from Houston to Memphis on Northwestern, rented a car,
and drove from the airport to the hotel. After checking in, she took her
bags to her room and ordered a bottle of chardonnay from room service. The bed was comfortable, and she was surprised the next morning at the amount of sleep she actually got. It was the most sleep she'd
had in weeks.

After dressing in jeans, a white T-shirt, and flats, she called downstairs for the car. She had only brought the T-shirt and a suit because
she really did not anticipate staying long, and she didn't think she
would even need the suit. Sitting in front of the Peabody, she studied
the Hertz map as to how best to get to Milan, and she made sure that
she had her MapQuest information on how to get to her in-laws' house
once she was there. She had not talked to her husband in over a week,
but she knew from talking to Ari's mom that he would be there. She
also pulled out the large envelope with the papers that she need to give
Ari and laid it on the passenger seat.

She had only been to the house a handful of times in the past: once
for a family reunion which was held at the City Park across the street

from the house, once for a high school reunion (go bulldogs!), a Christmas, and a Thanksgiving. Ari had driven from the Memphis airport each of those times. On every visit, Beth had wondered about how the city had come by its name. She had never been to Milan, Italy, but she doubted that it looked very much like this.

She liked Ari's parents well enough. His mom seemed particularly nice. They were the kind of people that are difficult to get to know very well—polite and courteous although somewhat closed off and unemotional. They did not seem particularly proud of their son, but Beth was sure that his mom would blame Beth for their separation.

Because of the flood of lawsuits filed against him and his former employer Merck in Texas, Ari had fled the jurisdiction and was not answering his cell phone. Of course, that was not a reason for not taking Beth's calls.

The marriage was over. They both knew it, but there was the small matter of making it official, and Beth had flown to Tennessee with papers she had drafted to obtain an agreed divorce. Her plan was to meet with Ari, see if there was any hope of reconciliation and, if not, try to get him to sign the papers.

There was not much to divide between them. They had always kept separate checking accounts, a fact that Beth now saw as a harbinger of the marriage's ultimate demise, and Ari had taken with him when he left most of the items that he would want in the divorce: his laptop, cell phone, and the clothes that he wore on a regular basis. Beth would be happy if he took the television, stereo, the rest of his clothes, the Bowflex weight machine that sat in their guest bedroom, and anything else he might have wanted, but she assumed that he would never return to claim them.

When she drove up to the brick house across from the park, she thought about how much it reminded her of the house she had grown up in back in Pennsylvania. It was a modest house with a well-kept yard. Ari's dad was a mail carrier in Milan and had held the job most of his adult life. Ari had been a three-sport varsity athlete in high school, and Beth could imagine the parade of kids, boys and girls, that had come to the house when Ari was in school to hang out with the star athlete. Now the street was quiet. Most of the residents were past their child-rearing years, and as happened in rural Pennsylvania, the younger generation had moved off to seek better paying jobs in bigger cities far from home.

When Beth finally got up the courage to get out of the car and go up the cement walkway to the front door, Ari came outside, letting the screen door slam behind him. She said, "Hello," and opened her arms to hug him, but he held back and did not say anything.

He was wearing only Oakley sunglasses, gym shorts, and running shoes with low cut socks. His brown hair was parted in the middle and feathered back over his ears. His chest and shoulders were muscled, but not too much so, and his abdomen and waist were well defined and would probably look that way for his entire life. She imagined that he was about to go for a jog around the park and perhaps saw the car and came outside when he saw who had gotten out. In any event, it was apparent to Beth that he was not going to invite her to come inside.

That was just as well. She dreaded as much as anything having the conversation she was about to have in front of Ari's mom. She assumed Ari's dad was at work.

"Ari,' she said, "I've been trying to call you. We need to talk."

"I know." He said. "I've been meaning to call you back. Mom said that you might be coming to Tennessee. I should have called you to tell you that it wasn't necessary."

"That's okay. I'm here now." Beth said. Because of his shades, she could not tell if he was looking at her when he spoke. "You aren't ever coming back to Houston, are you?"

"I don't know." He said and shrugged his shoulders. "Probably not anytime soon. I couldn't stand all the process servers coming to the apartment. I nearly hit the last one."

"They will find you here, eventually." Beth said. "You know that you don't really have anything to worry about regarding the lawsuits. As best I can tell, you've just been named in the cases for jurisdictional purposes so that the plaintiffs can keep the cases in state court. You just need to be careful to turn each set of papers over to Merck's lawyers. You understand?"

Ari nodded that he did, but Beth was not sure that he really did understand.

"Listen, forget about the lawsuits for a moment. What about us? What do you want to do about us? Are we just going to let the past few years count for nothing and walk away?"

Ari did not respond.

"You're not coming back. Honestly, I don't feel like I'm going to be invited to come here. I don't know if I would want to do that anyway."

Ari nodded, but again he did not respond. There was an extended moment where neither of them said anything, both shifting their weight from one foot to the other and waiting for the other to say something.

"Ari, do you want to get a divorce?" She asked, finally. "I've drafted some papers. I don't really know anything about this area of law, but I found some forms and I think this will take care of it. Do you want me to leave them with you so that you can look them over and let me know what you want to do?"

He stared out across the park and sighed. Another extended moment passed before he asked, "Do you have the papers with you now?"

Beth turned back down the sidewalk without saying anything and got the packet of papers she had left on the front seat of the car. She went back to where he was standing, halfway between the front door of his parents' home and her rental car. He took the papers out of the envelope Beth handed him, took off his sunglasses, and tried to read the pages as tears welled up in his eyes. Beth thought that she caught him wipe at a tear, although it could have been that he was just adjusting his eyes to the sunlight.

"It's pretty straightforward." Beth said. "Of course, anything you want in the apartment you can have. I don't know how I could get things like the weight machine to you. I'll keep them for awhile if you think of something you want me to do with them."

"Will I have to come back for a hearing or something?" Ari asked, looking up from the pages he was holding. Again, he did not look closely at her and instead kept staring out across the park.

"No." she said. "I don't think so. I just have to file them and then in a few days—they call it a cooling off period—we're . . . the divorce will be final. Is this really what you want to do Ari? We could talk to somebody, maybe a counselor. It might be good for us. It couldn't hurt, at least, to try. I could look for a job here. Maybe get an apartment—we don't have to do anything right now."

"Do I need to sign?" He asked, putting the shades back on and handing Beth the packet of papers.

"Yes." She said. "I'm afraid I didn't bring a pen, though. Why don't you think about it? Sign if you want. Whenever you're ready. Then send the papers back to me at the apartment in Houston."

"No." He said. "Wait here. I'll get a pen." He handed her the stack of papers, turned and bounded up the walk, and went back into the house.

Beth was leaning against the car when he got back with a pen. She handed him the documents opened to the page for his signature. She had not yet signed her name where indicated. He signed the page, turned back to the front page, and handed her the executed documents. He handed her the pen and said, "I guess you still have to sign."

Tears were running down her cheeks. "I guess this is it, then." She said. "Goodbye, Ari."

He nodded and walked around the car to the park on the other side of the street. He took off running, slowly at first, but he picked up speed as he got farther away. His long legs stretching out easily and gracefully. Beth was crying now, and she watched to see if he was ever going to look back, but he didn't. As she got in the car to drive away, she noticed that Ari's mom was standing at the screen door. She did not wave or motion for Beth to come inside.

Beth cried the entire way back to Memphis. When she got to the hotel, it was after one o'clock. She stopped at the front desk to see if she had received any messages, but there were none. She went up to her room and lay down on the bed to try to rest her eyes.

Like most lawyers, her first divorce case had been pro bono for a family member, and like most lawyers who had handled a case like this, she knew that she never wanted to handle another one. Her next meeting was not until six that evening, and she wanted to be rested for it. Maintaining her composure at that meeting might be more difficult than it had been at the morning meeting, and she had not done a very good job at that one.

Around five o'clock, she made herself get out bed, combed her hair, brushed her teeth, and watched a little television until it was almost six. Then she went downstairs and walked the short distance across Union Avenue to the Rendezvous. She saw Tim Sullivan on the floor below street level sitting at a table towards the back. She made her way through the restaurant to his table. He was wearing a grey, chalk stripe suit with a starched white shirt and a purple, polka dot tie. His suit coat was draped over the back of his chair, revealing a pair of purple paisley suspenders. He was drinking a beer and there was an almost full pitcher in front of him. He stood as she approached the table and pulled a chair out for her.

"Thank you for joining me." Sullivan said. "I wasn't sure this would work out when you called the other day, but this is perfect. I'm on my way back to Houston from Kentucky, and Memphis is a good place to take on fuel for the flight home. It's also a great place to stop for dinner. How long are you in town for?"

"Just a couple of days. I had some things that I had to take care of here in Tennessee." Beth said.

"Let me get you a beer." Sullivan said, as a waiter brought over a frosted mug and set it down in front of Beth. Sullivan poured her a beer from the pitcher. "Yeah, that's what you said when you called. Did everything come out like you wanted?"

"I guess." Beth replied.

"Are you hungry?" Sullivan asked.

"I am a little bit." Beth said.

"Good. Let's split an order of ribs." He motioned to the waiter who came directly to the table. After ordering, Sullivan turned back to Beth.

"I'm sorry that you couldn't keep working on the Kentucky case. I hope it is not because of anything that has happened at the office to upset you."

"No." Beth said. "I've just got some family stuff that I need to take care of. I enjoyed working on the case. I'm afraid that there is still a lot that needs to be done. Although the plaintiff profiles are almost complete, the information still has to be formatted properly. I think my notes can be deciphered. I'm sure that Davy's secretary Eileen can figure out what I was doing. But it will take somebody several hours at the computer to convert the profiles into interrogatory answers.

"I'm really sorry to be leaving so abruptly. That is all I called to talk to you about the other day. I just wanted to say goodbye and thank you in person. It wasn't necessary for you to interrupt your trip to meet with me, and I appreciate it. I've left jobs before, but I don't think that I've ever left one where I hadn't completed my assignment. Again, I'm very sorry Mr. Sullivan."

"Don't worry about it. I'm sure we can figure it out. It was nice having you around. I hope that you will include my name on your list of references." Sullivan said. "Do you know what you are going to do next?" He asked as waiter set a large platter of ribs down on the table in front of them and gave each of them a clean plate.

Sullivan waited for Beth to put a few on her plate before taking any for himself. She knew that eating the ribs was going to be messy. There really is no polite, lady-like way to eat a barbecued rib even if it is dry-rubbed in the Memphis style rather than dripping with sauce as they are often served in Texas. She could not remember when she had last eaten, and the first bite confirmed for her how hungry she was.

"These are really good." She said, wiping her greasy fingers on a napkin and dabbing it at the corners of her mouth. She was relieved that Sullivan was being so nice to her, but she was concerned about what might have been Sullivan's purpose in scheduling a meeting with her.

"Let me ask you something." Sullivan said

Beth picked up another rib. She was afraid of the question that she feared Sullivan was about to ask her and she wanted to be chewing when he asked it so that she could think out her answer before responding.

"In your travels around eastern Kentucky, did you ever hear anything about the judge on our case?" Sullivan asked.

"Yes." Beth answered, relieved that it wasn't the question that she feared he was going to ask. "It's my understanding that he went on the bench right before the case was referred to your firm. The common sentiment among the plaintiffs is that he is in Boyd's pocket. Apparently, the company paid out quite a bit on the earlier case, and our folks, your clients, think this judge was appointed by the governor to see that kind of thing doesn't happen again.

"I haven't talked about this with Davy. I had assumed that he would have found out similar information and would have discussed it with you," Beth said, putting down one rib and picking up another.

"I may have Davy overloaded right now. I haven't talked to him much in the last few days. Does he seem a bit disconnected to you right now?" Sullivan asked.

Beth dropped the rib she was bringing to her mouth, leaving a greasy streak down the front of her white T-shirt. "Damn it." She said, taking her napkin and trying to soak up the grease before it made too big of a stain on her shirt. Of course, the napkin itself was already greasy and her cleanup efforts only made the stain larger. She eventually put the napkin down in her lap and sighed. "I think that I'm only making it worse." She said.

"Don't worry about it." Sullivan said. "That's supposed to happen when you eat ribs. They are not really any good unless you get them all over you."

Beth smiled, trying to feel less embarrassed. She waited for Sullivan to say something else, but he did not. He was waiting on her to answer his last question.

When the silence between them became awkward, she could not stand it anymore and answered, "No. I don't know any reason why Davy would be 'disconnected' right now." She took her napkin and brushed lightly at her nose, suddenly fearing that she might have left a small spot of grease there. Sullivan, of course, instantly recognized the gesture for what it was; an indication that she was lying. He called it the "Pinocchio Rule." Touching the nose when answering a question was Body Language 101, and he was too advanced in the study of human reactions to let it go by unnoticed.

He considered pressing the issue and then thought better of it. He had already found out what he wanted to know. There was some connection between Beth and Davy—something intimate enough that when it came to personal issues Beth felt compelled to protect Davy. She had not felt such a compulsion when Sullivan had asked her what Davy knew about the case.

She was a lovely young woman, and in a way he felt sorry for her. He assumed that something had happened between her and Davy, probably something sexual. He really did not blame Davy. She was very good-looking. In a different context, he might have made a pass at her himself. No doubt, she had wondered if he was going to do that very thing when she had called him to do her "exit interview" over the phone and he had suggested that they get together in person. Then when they compared schedules, and he setup their meeting in Memphis, she must have wondered if he had been trying to get her alone somewhere. He intended to allay that fear, but he could not help himself from toying with her just a little bit more.

"Hey," he said, "I have your last paycheck from the contract legal service."

He wiped his hands thoroughly on his napkin and opened a moist towelette package from several that the waiter had left on the table after Beth had dropped the rib. He cleaned his fingers with the towelette also before reaching behind him into the coat he had put on the back of his chair and pulling out an envelope. He handed the check to Beth, but she did not open it.

"I think we put a little extra in there to help tide you over until your next gig. I'd have to ask Riza. She handles this sort of thing. I guess I could have let Riza give you the check. I know she appreciates the work you did on this case. She and Davy are on their way to Memphis right now. I sent the plane over to pick them up. They won't be here for an hour or so, and then we'll need to leave early in the morning. But I'm sure they would both like to see you, and you know, ask you any questions they might have about completing the plaintiffs' profiles."

"No." Beth said. "I mean, I better get back to my errands, although it would be nice to see them." She stood suddenly, almost backing her chair into a waiter that was carrying a tray loaded with empty beer pitchers. "Extra?" She asked herself, "for quitting a job? Was this some kind of a come on?" She knew that she did not want to stay to find out, and she certainly didn't want to be around when Davy and Riza got there. Before leaving, she extended her still greasy hand to Sullivan.

"Mr. Sullivan, thank you for dinner. I've enjoyed working for you and the firm. It is a very interesting place. You've got a fine young lawyer and son-in-law in Davy. I'm sure the two of you will find a way to be successful in the Kentucky case."

"Well thank you, Beth." Sullivan said standing. "I hope everything works out for you as well."

On her walk back to the hotel, Beth wondered if her speech at the end, the one she had been rehearsing in her mind for the last few days, sounded too practiced and stiff, and whether she had only made matters worse for Davy. She should never have agreed to meet Sullivan in person and just left matters the way they were during their phone conversation. Still, it would be nice to have that last paycheck; apparently it was going to be the last one she'd receive for some time. When she got back to the hotel, she asked the concierge to send up a bottle of chardonnay and an opener. Her plan was to try to get some sleep, stay in her room until mid-morning after the Peters & Sullivan team departed, and then to head back to Houston.

As Beth left the Rendezvous, Sullivan caught the waiter's eye, and asked if he could have a fresh set of plates and a new cold mug. He told the waiter that he was expecting others to join him in a while and asked if the waiter could find Sullivan a sports page to read while he waited. The waiter was sure that he could. It was not Damian's, but the Rendezvous served nicely as a satellite office.

18

"WHAT KIND OF LAW DO YOU PRACTICE?" Chelsea asked the dark-haired woman in the beige suit.

"That would be hard to say." She replied. "I don't really have a job right now. The last case that I worked on was an environmental case, but all I did was catalogue information on the various plaintiffs. I've done mostly contract work on multiparty cases."

"Interesting." Chelsea said, trying to sound interested. She did find the striking woman across from her interesting, but any discussion of the law bored Chelsea. "What brings you to Memphis?"

"It's a long story." The woman said.

"I'm skipping class. I've got all day."

"First let me order some of those eggs, and how is the Bloody Mary?"

"The second one was better than the first." Chelsea said.

The handsome woman laughed and ordered the eggs Benedict and a Bloody Mary when the waiter came over. "I don't know where to start. I guess I could summarize my trip by saying that I had to find my estranged husband in Milan to have him execute our divorce papers."

"Too bad he couldn't have been from Milan, Italy."

"This is not so bad." The woman said looking around the lobby of the Peabody. By the way, my name is Beth Sheehan." She said, extending her hand across the table toward Chelsea.

"I'm Chelsea Cagill. Nice to meet you. You're right. This is nice." Chelsea said. "Have you been to Memphis before?"

"Not really. We came through here, I guess, on the way to Milan for Christmas, Thanksgiving—that sort of thing." Beth said, tears welling in her eyes. "I actually brought this suit to wear in case he said that he didn't want to get a divorce, and I thought I might try and line up some job interviews. Honestly, I don't know what I was thinking."

"It's a good-looking suit." Chelsea said. "Maybe you should try to set something up. By all accounts, there are some good law firms here in Memphis. We could go through a legal directory. I'd tell you what I know about the firms. I've probably known somebody that clerked at each one, or I'll know enough to tell you what kind of law they practice."

"No, it's not necessary. There is no reason for me to be near my husband, I mean my ex-husband, now. He made it clear that he wants a clean break. I guess I'll go back to Houston this afternoon."

"Houston, huh?" Chelsea asked. She thought about asking Beth if she knew a lawyer there by the name of "Jessie," but Chelsea was embarrassed that she didn't know his first name, and besides, what are the odds that Beth would have ever heard of him? She had never much cared for the "do you know" game because once you figured out that your new acquaintance did know somebody you used to know, what were you supposed to do with that information? She was more interested in trying to figure out what was going on with the handsome woman in the expensive suit than she was in finding out if they had friends in common.

Beth nodded. Thinking of her return to Houston, she felt the tears coming again, just as the waiter brought her food and drink. She took a long gulp from the drink and sat back in the chair staring at the ornate ceiling. "I'm sorry." She said. "I really just meant to join you at your table. You were nice to let me sit down. I didn't mean to unload my personal life on you."

"It's okay." Chelsea said. "I'd much rather talk to you than read for some class that I'm not going to anyway."

Beth tried to eat her eggs, but she achieved little more than just rearranging the eggs, ham, and English muffins on her plate.

"I've not really had the best of luck myself with men lately." Chelsea said trying to sound sympathetic.

Beth raised her eyebrows but did not say anything until she took another long drink from the Bloody Mary. "You mean you didn't just come here for a nice breakfast and a quiet place to study?"

"No." Chelsea grinned. "It's just how things ended up. I actually threw myself at some guy last evening who completely spurned my affections." Chelsea said, again slipping into her best southern drawl. "What is it with men? Why can't they accept a good thing when it's standing right in front of them? They're all such little boys."

They both shrugged their shoulders, and Beth smiled and wiped away a tear. "I know what you mean. I think that I'm through with them altogether. I've just got to get back to Houston and find myself a job, hopefully in an office with as few men as possible."

"Yeah," Chelsea said, "but you look like you could use a day or two off before you go back. Why don't we go do something fun today? Take your mind off your troubles. Help me forget my guilt over skipping class. What time is your flight?"

"I can change my flight, but I don't think that I'm up for a pub crawl down Beale Street."

"No. You need something really touristy. You say that you've never spent any time in Memphis? I'll bet you've never been to Graceland. You won't believe it. It's like what they say about Las Vegas: it's everything right and wrong about America at the same time. It's a study in what would happen to a person of humble beginnings that has the misfortune of being incredibly good-looking and talented. He gets rich and people start calling him the 'King,' and then he gets fat, buys a bunch of Cadillacs, starts wearing rhinestone leisure suits, and puts green shag carpet on his ceilings. But it always makes me smile. Let's go. You'll get a kick out of it."

"Graceland? Really?" Beth asked.

"Yeah. Let's take the jeep over to Graceland. Of course, you can't go dressed like that. If you're going to wear a suit, it has to have bell-bottomed pants and be made out of polyester and not some expensive wool crepe. Maybe in a leopard print."

Beth laughed. The idea of spending the morning with the energetic, freckled face girl was appealing. "But this is all I brought." She said. "I've got a pair of jeans, but I got barbecue all over my T-shirt."

"Actually that would be perfect. But we can get you another T-shirt." Chelsea pointed to the mallard on her left chest. "Allow me to introduce you to my tailor."

"I don't have any place to change." Beth said. "I've already checked out and turned in my key."

"I haven't." Chelsea said. "You take my key and I'll meet you in room 426. I'll put our breakfast on the room, get you a T-shirt, and bring it up. I'm thinking the cocoa-colored one would go with your eyes. You go up and get your jeans on, and I'll be right there." She asked the waiter for a check for the two of them, signed the bill, and went to the gift shop while Beth waited for the elevator.

Beth found the room and went inside. She recognized the yellow chintz fabric that had been on the bed in her room, but this room was larger than hers. The bed was unmade, but the room guest had only used one side. She wandered around the room for a moment, but there were not any clues about who Chelsea was or who might have been her guest there the previous evening. Then she saw a sheet of Peabody stationery on the writing desk with a pen lying on top of the page. She walked over to the desk and started reading the page, being careful not to move the paper. She did not want her new friend Chelsea to think that she was a snoop. Beth noticed that several pages of crumpled stationery were in the waste basket. Someone, in what looked to be a man's handwriting, had started scrawling a poem that didn't appear to have been finished. Beth could not help but read it.

Prufrock's Reprise

I'm an anhedonic hedonist.
I'm sometimes laid, but rarely kissed,

Slow to anger but always pissed
About this pebble in my shoe.

In Prufrock's rolled pants (or tastefully cuffed)
And navy blazer, loafers buffed,
Answer docket calls, "Ready enough"
So often that it might be true.

Hung by a red and blue striped tie,
Little wonder it is that I
Would be so reluctant to try
To press a meaningful question.

And yet I'm in the question business,
Asking witnesses to assess
The convergent risks, hazard a guess
Or meet righteous indignation.

Over trashcan punch back in school
"What's your major?" the ice-pick tool
Trying to be worldly and cool
While focused on lips not answers.

Now over cocktails "What do you do?"
Responses rehearsed, sound almost new,
Categorized by pulpit and pew.
Proper steps, conversing dancers.

Morning chapel before classes start
For my bright, young boy, and my heart
Sinks as the kids' voices impart
The Lord's Prayer in a plaintive strain.

Their clean, quick little hands dance along
In sign language with their sweet song;
Is God deaf from the din of wrongs
Cried out by those with fear and pain?

I worry that I am his model.
If I question, he will as well.
Without faith, is he doomed to hell
On earth as it is in heaven?

For my boy I want just perfection,
Secured by my law profession,
But scarred by my unasked question.
Another skill learned at seven.

I do not dream of mermaids singing.
Their own brown seaweed curls preening,
Sitting on rocks, water teeming
With danger for the unaware.

My dreams instead are of a tweed field.
Dog searching for quail it will yield.
I'm amazed not at the game creeled
But at how he knows why he's there.

The quail burst forth on drum-beating wings
My thoughts return to other things,
Of cabbages and dethroned kings.
Unasked question, unsaid prayer.

There was something familiar to Beth about the handwriting and the depressing tone of the unfinished poem. Maybe it was supposed to be a song. Maybe Chelsea had picked up a frustrated Country and

Western singer on his way to Nashville who was just pretending to be a lawyer. If it was a song, it needed a chorus. She started to pick up the page and study it more closely, but thought better of it, and began changing her clothes.

She put her duffle bag on the bed, unzipped it, and pulled out her jeans and flats. She took off her dress heels and put them in the bottom of the bag. She stripped off the suit pants and jacket and folded them neatly into the bag. She was glad that she had come up to the room to change because she had not worn any underwear. She had not worn panties because she did not like how panties left a line on the suit pants. She had not worn a bra because she did like how prospective male employers tried not to look at her chest in interviews but were unable to keep from doing so. She did not have any interviews set up, although if she had scheduled any, she imagined that they would have been mainly with male lawyers. That was changing. Her law school class had been about fifty percent female, and now there are many schools with more women than men. Still, it was more likely than not that a law job interview would be with a male lawyer.

She pulled on the Levi's 501 blue jeans that she had taken out of the bag and buttoned all but the top button. She intended to tuck the T-shirt in when it got there. She left on the silk, ecru shell, not only because she had not worn a bra, but since it would cover the fact that she had not completely buttoned the jeans. She sat down on the corner of the bed and fidgeted nervously with the little cross on the gold chain around her neck until there was a knock at the door.

Beth went to the door and let Chelsea in. She was carrying a paper sack from which she pulled a chocolate-colored T-shirt. She said, "I forgot to ask you your size. I hope this fits. If not, we can exchange it downstairs."

Beth took the T-shirt, examined the label, and noticed that the logo on the front was identical to the one on Chelsea's shirt. "I bet it will work. I love it. Thanks. We'll be twins at Graceland." Beth said. "Hey. Are you the poet or was that the work of your would-be lover?"

"I don't know what you're talking about." Chelsea said raising her eyebrows.

"The poem or song or whatever it is on the writing desk. Is that yours?" Beth asked.

Chelsea walked over to the desk and picked up the sheet of paper. "This is the first time I've seen this. I guess I was in a fog when I left the room this morning." Chelsea studied the page and read the poem while Beth looked over her shoulder.

"So you picked up a poet last night?" Beth asked while Chelsea continued to read.

"Well, that's debatable. He doesn't seem to be much of a poet. He said he was a lawyer." Chelsea said.

Beth put her hand on Chelsea's shoulder. It felt good to touch someone and she let her hand linger there a moment. She gave some thought to hugging Chelsea's shoulders but did not. "A lawyer poet. They're the worst kind," Beth said.

She left Chelsea standing at the writing desk and went into the bathroom to put on the new shirt. Chelsea read the poem again, folded it like a business letter, and dropped it into Beth's unzipped duffle bag on the bed.

Beth stood in front of the mirror in the bathroom and grimaced when she saw her eyes in the reflection. She grabbed a tissue from the silver box and dabbed at the corners of each eye. She threw away the tissue and pulled the shell off over her head. As she dropped it to the floor, she realized that Chelsea was standing next to her. Chelsea put her left arm around Beth's waist and they stood looking at each other's eyes in the mirror for an awkward moment in which neither of them said a word.

Then Chelsea leaned to Beth and kissed her right breast on the untanned triangle above the nipple. Beth was startled by the forwardness of Chelsea's actions and by the soft warmness of Chelsea's lips pressing against Beth's chest. It seemed like it had been a long time since she had felt the warmth of a human kiss, and Beth found her hands going to the back of Chelsea's head of coal black hair. Surprised by the cool, silkiness of Chelsea's hair, Beth closed her eyes and held Chelsea's head as Chelsea moved her mouth down the breast to the nipple. Chelsea's soft tongue darted back and forth over the nipple, and she caressed Beth's other breast with her right hand.

Beth opened her eyes when the kissing stopped. Chelsea was looking into her eyes and smiling.

"Men." Chelsea said. She kissed Beth on the lips, and, after a moment, Chelsea's right hand drifted down to Beth's button-front jeans. "Looks like you missed a button." Chelsea said and began unbuttoning the remaining buttons on the 501s.

"Wait." said Beth pulling away from Chelsea's kiss and from the hand at her jeans. "There is something I have to tell you."

"Let me guess," said Chelsea, "you have herpes."

"How in the world would you know that?" Beth asked.

"Doesn't every lawyer?" asked Chelsea, and she began kissing Beth again.

The two women were not on a tight schedule, but they were a little bit later getting to Graceland than they had anticipated that morning at breakfast.

19

ONE WEEKDAY MORNING IN early August, I arrived at the Peters & Sullivan office at the usual time, said hello to the receptionist, got myself a cup of coffee in the kitchen, and wandered to my desk. My secretary Eileen was already sitting at her desk, typing. She didn't look away from her computer screen to tell me that there was a notice of hearing in the Kentucky case that she had put on my chair. The notice was simple enough. The hearing on the countervailing motions to strike the expert witnesses of both parties would be heard by the Special Master Commissioner on Tuesday, September 15, 2005, at nine o'clock, in the offices of Boyd Oil Company, Inc.'s attorneys in Lexington, Kentucky.

I stood there reading and re-reading the notice while sipping my coffee. I wondered how accurate sonograms were at predicting the delivery date of a child.

Sullivan would want to leave for Kentucky on the Saturday (if not the Friday) before the hearing on Tuesday. We would probably come back that Tuesday, but even so, there was going to be a three- or four-day gap immediately preceding the birth of our child when I was unlikely to be home or even in our state. I put the coffee cup on my desk, asked Eileen if she had put the hearing on the calendar (of course, she had), and I took the notice around the hall to Sullivan's office. He wasn't in, so I asked his secretary to let him and Riza both know about the hearing, and for them to let me know about who would be attending on our behalf. I went back to my desk and drank my coffee.

The hearing was less than thirty days away. There was probably no chance that we were going to win. After the commissioner ruled and the court "adopted" his recommendation, it would only be a matter of time until the case was dismissed on summary judgment, and I would be blamed for losing one of the most expensive cases in the history of the firm.

There are several points in a civil case when it can be tossed out of court. Immediately after filing there is a procedure in federal court and many state courts to have the case dismissed for failing to state a claim upon which relief could be granted. After some discovery has been completed, the party that has been sued (the defendant) will often file a motion for summary judgment, asserting that there are no genuine issues of material fact upon which reasonable minds could differ. Frequently, this motion will follow other motions designed to limit the evidence available to the complaining party (the plaintiff) to prove his case. For example, if Boyd was successful in getting the plaintiffs' expert Mr. Walton struck, the plaintiffs would then not be able to prove a requisite element of their case—that the pollution on their properties presented a health risk. If Walton's testimony was excluded, a summary judgment motion intended to dispose of the entire case would follow.

I also expected that at roughly the same point in time, my wife would learn of my infidelities and boot me out of the house. Today, I was a well-dressed, promising young lawyer with a prestigious, downtown Houston law firm. I had a beautiful wife, a lovely home, and eagerly anticipated the birth of my first son. Only I knew that in less than a month I would likely be sitting in my parents' home in Abilene, out of a job, facing a divorce, and unable to see my child.

Again, the thought crossed my mind to call my dad and see if he had any suggestion about how to fix this situation. But I knew he wouldn't have any specific advice regarding the lawsuit, and I imagined that his recommendation regarding Michelle was to follow Dr. Nathan's admonition. Still, it might be nice just to hear his voice, and it would certainly be good to get the weight of this overwhelming secret off my chest. It had been some relief to talk to the black-haired, freckled-face girl in Tennessee. It had been stressful at the time, but ultimately some relief when I talked to Dr. Nathan. But a confession to Dad wouldn't be telling Michelle, as I knew I must do; and telling Dad would just get him involved in the problems that were all of my making.

I wondered what Mom and Dad would be doing on this morning before he went to work. They both would have read the paper by now to see if there were any good garage sales in the area. They both enjoyed rummaging through garage sales and flea markets looking for treasures to complete their collections. Mom would buy quilts and Depression glass. Dad would buy old books. Mom and I always gave him a hard time about how many copies of *Hamlet* one man could own.

He also collected what he called "lone wolf" prints. You've probably seen versions of the vintage painting called *Lone Wolf* by the famous Polish painter Alfred Wierusz Kowaski but not paid much attention to them. They have little value beyond their old frames, but it was interesting to compare the prints when Dad hung them on a wall in his study at home.

Each is a little different, although each depicts scene of a winter evening with a little house in the background. There is always a light in the window and usually a hint of smoke from the chimney. On a snowy hilltop above the house, a lone wolf stands watching the house. The wolf and the house look a little different in each print, according to the rendering of the scene by different artists and various lithographs of the original oil painting. As a kid I assumed that the theme of the scenes was the proverbial wolf at the door—no matter how comfortable the home might appear, a wolf lurked nearby in the darkness.

One Christmas morning, as he unwrapped a lone wolf print that I had found at an antique store in Lubbock while I was in college, I asked Dad why he collected the pictures. He pulled the wrapping paper away from the frame and studied the print like he had never seen it before. He said, "I've always wondered about the wolf. Does he long for the warmth of the house? Does he resent civilization encroaching on his territory? Why is he by himself?"

I clicked on my computer and googled dove hunting. Several ads popped up for dove hunting trips to exotic locals like Argentina and Columbia. I considered calling Dad and suggesting a trip.

Before I could call home, I heard the phone ring at Eileen's desk, and she told me on the speakerphone that Mrs. Henderson was looking for me.

That afternoon, I found myself in the living room of Mrs. Jean Henderson's home on River Oaks Boulevard. Going into the house reminded me of going into a bank in Abilene. The building was about the same size, but the grounds at the Henderson home were far more extensive and green. The azaleas were long since out of bloom, but the Asian jasmine that covered the fluted, square columns along the front of the house gave off the heavy sweet scent of summer in Houston.

I was greeted at the door by a gracious woman who worked for the Hendersons. She escorted me to a room partitioned into several conversational seating areas by groups of silk-covered chairs and couches. She brought me a cup and saucer and poured me a cup of coffee, which I placed on the antique nesting table beside me.

In a moment, Mrs. Henderson appeared, wearing a flowing caftan and a matching scarf on her head. She looked good except for appearing exhausted, and she hugged me before she sat down on the couch across from me. Her husband appeared from somewhere in the back of the house. He was whistling and issuing commands to a well-groomed Scottie that followed at his heels. I stood to shake Dr. Henderson's hand.

"It's nice to meet you, Mr. Jessie." Dr. Henderson said with an air of formality. "Jean has told me a great deal about you. All very good, I might add. We appreciated very much your helping her with that car wreck business."

"I enjoyed working on the case," I said.

"I thought the insurance company would never pay that claim," Dr. Henderson said. "I suppose that is one area of our practices that is somewhat similar. Both of us probably spend a great deal of our time trying to get insurance companies to do what they had promised to do in the first place."

"I suppose you're right," I said. "Still, if the insurance companies did what they were supposed to do, I probably wouldn't have a job."

They both laughed.

"Davy," Mrs. Henderson said, "I'm afraid I may need your help again."

"How can I help?" I asked, and she proceeded to tell me about, of all things, a potential medical malpractice claim that she might pursue. It seems that in 2003 she had been diagnosed with breast cancer. A lumpectomy was performed, and she underwent chemotherapy and radiation therapy. Sometime in 2004, she noticed a thickening at the site of the lumpectomy scar and went to see her oncologist. He was concerned and ordered a biopsy that was read by the pathology group for the clinic where he worked. The path report had indicated that the tissue was cancerous.

"Well," Mrs. Henderson said, "having been diagnosed with breast cancer twice in the span of about a year, James and I decided to handle this situation aggressively. I had a double mastectomy . . ." her voice trailed off. It was obviously something that still caused her emotional difficulty. "Remember, this came up during the car wreck trial."

"The problem," Dr. Henderson interjected, "is that when the breast tissue from the mastectomy was analyzed by pathologists, there was no cancer found in the tissue . . . not even in the supposedly diseased breast."

"Could the biopsy have removed all of the malignancy?" I asked naïvely.

"Not likely," Dr. Henderson said. "I asked the oncologist to have fresh cuts of the biopsy tissue sent to the University of Texas MD Anderson Cancer Center for re-examination. I wish to hell I had done that before Jean's surgery."

He handed me the padded mailer that contained pathology slides and a folded copy of the report from MD Anderson. I unfolded the copy of the report. While I was unable to read the slides myself, the pathologist at MD Anderson in his report identified the suspect cells as being the result of changes in tissue that occur from radiation procedures rather than from a malignancy. Without even being told the patient had undergone radiation therapy, the after-the-fact pathologist had correctly diagnosed the condition, a diagnosis that would have prevented Mrs. Henderson from losing both breasts.

"I've been going round and round with Dr. Valdez, the pathologist who originally misread the slides. I've been trying to get him to cover the costs of the surgery and the MD Anderson review." Dr. Henderson said. "I don't see why my health insurance should have to pay for this when it wasn't necessary. But Valdez and his group have quit returning my calls."

"This is potentially a serious case, Dr. Henderson," I said, stuffing the report back in the envelope.

"I'm sorry you've been through this, Mrs. Henderson. You know from having been in the car wreck case, that the case probably won't be settled without filing suit and preparing for trial. We'll have to hire a pathologist to review the slides again and write a report. I know that may seem silly to you in light of the MD Anderson report, but under the current medical malpractice statute we'll need a report that identifies the pathologist's negligence as well as what injury his negligence has caused. We'll probably also need an oncologist to discuss the likelihood of the recurrence of the disease, as well as your response to being told that the cancer had reappeared.

"Ten years ago, this would have been a multimillion dollar case. Now, with tort reform, there are limits of $250,000.00 on pain, suffering, and mental anguish damages. There will be significant costs to prosecute the case—hiring the experts, taking depositions, and so forth. My firm would, of course, front those costs. If you are successful, however, the costs are deducted from any recovery you make. All I am saying is that, despite the significance of your injury, after the cap on damages is applied and fees and expenses are deducted from your recovery, you will probably receive far less than what we would agree is adequate compensation for your claim."

"I appreciate your candor, Mr. Jessie," Dr. Henderson said. "You may not believe this, but I actually was one of the few physicians that opposed the constitutional amendment permitting the legislature to cap non-economic damages in medical malpractice cases.

"I'm an orthopedic surgeon. I treat people injured in accidents every day. If the legislature caps damages in medical malpractice cases today, what is there to keep them from capping damages in car wreck or workplace cases tomorrow? To me the whole idea of setting a limit on what a recovery might be before hearing the evidence in a particular case seems antithetical to justice. Why should a physician get a legislated break on the pain and suffering he causes while a truck driver has to buy enough insurance to foot the whole bill? Hopefully, enough people will learn about how the insurance lobby manipulated the law and we can get it changed, but that's a conversation for another day.

"The bottom line is that I don't care what it costs to prepare this case, and I am even willing to front the costs and still pay you your contingency fee if it will encourage you to get involved in this case. I know that you will need to get those slides to yet another expert to review them. I don't expect the MD Anderson pathologist will write a damning report that uses the word 'negligence,' much less testify against another pathologist here in town. It may be difficult to find any pathologist that will testify against Dr. Valdez and his group. They are pretty well known in this community. They are pretty well known everywhere, for the matter.

"I encourage you to find the best. I want this pathologist Dr. Valdez sued. I don't care how respected his group might be. They could have resolved this for just the cost of the medical care, but they won't even talk to me about it. I want a jury to hear what he did so that maybe he won't make the same mistake again," Dr. Henderson said, rising from the couch where he had been seated next to his wife and snapping his fingers to get the Scottie's attention. The alert little dog followed his owner's every movement. Dr. Henderson clearly was angry, but he didn't want me to think that he couldn't control his anger.

"And another thing," he continued while trying to appear calm, "I want you working on this case, and not that blowhard Sullivan. I asked him to handle Jean's car wreck case, and he assured me that he would. Instead, Sullivan must have decided that you were better qualified to handle that case, so I assume that you are more qualified than he to handle this case." Dr. Henderson smiled.

I stood up from the chair, shook hands with them and thanked them for their confidence in me. I assured them I would begin work on their case immediately. I didn't tell them that, in a few weeks, it would probably be the only case I had.

"We're not in any hurry, Mr. Jessie. You take whatever time is necessary," Dr. Henderson said.

"You know, I should tell you," I said, "that there is a possibility I could be changing firms sometime in the near future. Nothing definite."

"As far as I'm concerned, the case goes with you, Davy," Mrs. Henderson said, looking to her husband as he nodded his agreement. "I don't know what all the legalities of that are, but this is your case," she said.

A few days later, Eileen rang my extension to tell me that Sullivan wanted me to meet him at Damian's for lunch. He was at his usual table in the bar when I got there. Riza sat next to him. They were looking at her laptop computer screen when I walked over and sat down. Without my ordering, a starched waiter brought me a perfect Sea Breeze. I had heard the juicer whirring behind the bar when I walked into the room. Riza closed the laptop and put it aside.

"Hey, Davy. Glad you could join us. How are things at home?" Sullivan asked.

"Fine," I said, "we're just a couple of weeks away, I guess."

"Right," he said. "It's a shame the commissioner has scheduled that hearing on the admissibility of the experts on Michelle's due date. Have the doctors said anything about the baby coming early?"

I wondered if he was looking for some reason to postpone the hearing. "No," I said.

"Good," he said. "I've been thinking about this hearing, and I think you should be the one to argue the matter. After all, you wrote the response. Damn fine work, too."

"I would love to argue it," I said, "but I am worried about whether or not Michelle will understand my being gone at that time."

"Don't you worry about Michelle," Tim said. "I'll talk to her. This is a big case. This is a big responsibility for you. I'm sure you can handle it. I'll send Riza out to help you, if she can. You know what I always say: 'Illegitimi non carborundum.'"

Sullivanisms were usually, but not always, delivered in English. Fortunately for those of us whose education had been something other than classic, the Latin was usually followed by an English translation.

"Don't let the bastards grind you down." Sullivan said.

"Thanks," I said.

"Don't you think you should go out there a couple of days early to meet with our expert and get him ready for his testimony?" Sullivan asked.

"Where does he live?" asked Riza.

"In Ohio, but I'm sure he'd meet me again in Lexington," I said. "Are you sure you don't want to be there for this hearing, Tim? It's the first time we'll have appeared before this special master commissioner."

"I'm confident you can handle it," Tim said. "I'll check with Peters to make sure you can take the plane over and back. That should shorten the time for you to get back, if Michelle goes into labor. Don't worry. Her mom and I will be here, and her brother Jonathan is also available."

I watched to see if there was any change of Riza's expression when Tim mentioned Jonathan's availability. Nothing was noticeable. "Yeah," I said. "Jonathan has even been with Michelle to a couple of the Lamaze classes that I missed."

"Have you got time for lunch?" Tim asked.

"No, thank you," I said. "I guess I better start getting ready for the hearing. I'll take a rain check." The truth is I had to start thinking about how I was going to tell Michelle that I had to be halfway across the country at the time she was scheduled to deliver our baby.

Eileen looked up as I walked by her desk towards my office when I got back. "How was lunch?" She asked, probably surprised at my lack of inebriation.

"Fine, I guess. I didn't stay to eat. Mr. Sullivan wants me to handle the hearing in Kentucky."

"Did y'all talk about your new case?" she asked with the hint of a suggestive smile.

Immediately, I was worried that she had heard something about the new *Henderson* case. I wondered if Mrs. Henderson or Dr. Henderson had called and Eileen had heard enough in taking a message to figure out that they were talking to me about a new case.

"New case?" I asked, trying to see what she knew.

"Yeah. Did Mr. Sullivan not mention it? What do you guys do at lunch? It looks like you are going to be the firm's breast lawyer."

"Breast lawyer?" I asked, now convinced that both Eileen and Sullivan knew about my signing up the new *Henderson* case. Immediately I felt guilty about keeping the information about a new case from Sullivan. Of course, he was bound to find out about it, and he would wonder why I had tried to conceal the fact that the Hendersons had called me.

Eileen looked through a stack of paper on the corner of her desk and removed a manila folder containing a few pages and a disk in a plastic case. "I can't believe Mr. Sullivan didn't tell you about this. You are not going to believe the video. Be sure to tell your wife that you are working on a new case if you take it home to watch it."

I didn't know what was on the disk, but I didn't see how it could have anything to do with Mrs. Henderson. Relieved, I smiled back at her and asked Eileen, "What is it?"

"Did you know there are video cameras in hospital rooms these days? I sure didn't. I don't guess they are in all of the rooms. Anyway, this young, I would say attractive woman is in the hospital having her tonsils out. She is in a recovery area. You know, one of those rooms that is divided into multiple recovery areas by curtains that make a wall around individual patients? The woman is by herself. Maybe her mom had gone to get coffee or something. The young woman is out of it from the surgery. Then a doctor, also young, and I'm guessing he is the surgeon, comes in to check on her. He looks at her chart for a moment, and then walks over to the bed, reaches behind her, unties her gown, and begins to fondle her breasts."

"He does what?" I asked.

"Yeah, he fondles her, but that's not all. Get this. The doctor then leans over and kisses one breast. Then it looks like he hears something. He quickly pulls the woman's gown and sheet up and is reading his file when a female nurse comes into the room."

"This is all on video? How did we get this?" I asked.

"Apparently the nurse notices that the patient's gown is undone after the doctor leaves the area and thinks something is fishy. So she goes to her friend who is one of the people who monitors the video cameras and gets her to make her a copy of the footage. She gives it to the patient's mom when the patient is released from the hospital the next day."

"And it's all on video? I can't believe it," I said, and took the disk out of the case and handed it to Eileen. She inserted the disk into the computer tower beneath her desk and I stepped around where the two of us could see her monitor.

There it was, just as Eileen had described it. The black and white video was grainy and a little bit jumpy, but you could definitely see a handsome young male doctor undo the patient's gown, fondle her breasts for several seconds, kiss one breast before hurriedly covering her up, and start reading the chart as a nurse pulls a curtain back and comes into the area.

The camera must have been positioned on the ceiling and was aimed at several patients in beds cordoned off by curtains that hung on frames below the level of the ceiling. Some of the beds were too far away from the camera to see much about what was going there. But the bed where our potential new client was resting was almost directly below the camera. I assumed that few patients emerging from the effects of anesthesia would notice the camera, but wouldn't a surgeon know it was there?

"Mr. Sullivan's office sent the file over earlier. You are supposed to meet with the woman and her mother first thing tomorrow morning."

I nodded. "I can see the case against the doctor, but it is an intentional act. That has got to be outside of his malpractice insurance coverage. I wonder if he has any money. He doesn't look very old."

Eileen removed the disk from the computer tower and put it back in the plastic case. "You can't tell me that somebody doesn't have to pay for this," she said, holding it up before putting it back into the file and handing the file to me.

I nodded. "There has to be something I can do with these facts." I said and took the file into my office. I put the file on my desk and sat in my chair. I looked through the phone messages and started to return calls, but I put the phone down and pulled up Google on my computer.

I tried several different searches and was surprised by the number of items that came up when I looked for hospital security cameras. Several companies advertised systems that would assist hospitals in monitoring gang activity in emergency rooms, record drug distribution, prevent medical errors, and chronicle patient and doctor visits, among other benefits. Most seemed to be monitored by hospital staff at some central location, and while some indicated that the live video was not recorded out of concern for patient privacy, others discussed using the video for defense in litigation or for teaching purposes.

I looked through the file and found the doctor's name and ran a Google search on him. He was a general surgeon who had gone to good schools (including the Baylor College of Medicine in Houston), but he couldn't have been very long out of residency. He wouldn't have much money, if any, and he wouldn't have any by the time we took a judgment against him. More likely than not, he just had a pile of medical school debt. I couldn't tell if he was married. Still, I'd send the notice of representation letter to his office rather than his home.

I got up from my desk and walked to the door to my office. I explained to Eileen that I was going to close the door and watch the video a few times on my computer, and to let me know before anybody (like Mr. Sullivan) came into my office. She laughed and made some crack about keeping the lights on and no soft music, but she never looked up from her typing.

At my desk, I watched the video over and over. Although something about it struck me as not quite right, I couldn't put my finger on it. The fondling was not rough or aggressive and did not appear to be hurried.

The kissing, actually two kisses—one above the nipple followed by a light, quick kiss of the nipple was almost intimate and not the kind of thing that would make one think of rape or molestation.

Before the nurse pulled back the curtain on the area around the bed, you could see her come into view of the camera and the doctor responding hurriedly to her presence. He picked up the chart, flipped through it, handed it to the nurse, and closed the curtain behind him as he left. Before I left for the day, I put the disk back in its sleeve and dropped it back into the file.

Whatever thoughts I had about combining a conversation in which I told Michelle that I had to be in Kentucky on September 15th with a conversation about how I might have given her a venereal disease, evaporated that evening as I tried to explain why I would need to be out of town. She exploded. I mean, she exploded in that way she had of completely shutting me out as she banged dishes around in the sink and then slammed doors in the laundry room before stomping up the stairs to perform some other menial task. The message was clear enough. She was doing what she could to make this place a home and us a family, and I was abandoning her when she needed me most.

I couldn't tell her about the herpes right then. I'm not sure she could have heard me anyway over the clanging of the pots and pans or the slamming of doors.

I understood that there was never going to be a good time to have the discussion. I knew that it had to be done, whatever the circumstance. I had rehearsed it in my mind a thousand times.

In early versions of the speech, I had tried to blame someone or something else for my contracting the disease. In later versions, I omitted the particulars of who and how and when, expecting those questions to be answered in rapid-fire succession after the basic admission was made. Somehow, I had to include that I still loved her, because I did, that I was sorry, because I was, and that I would do anything to try and make it up to her for the rest of our lives, because I would if given the chance. I thought at one point about giving her the statistics: one in four American adults between the ages of 19 and 50 have the disease. But what did that mean? That other people had fucked up as badly as I had? That was the whole point. In Michelle's eyes, I had been special, unique, and capable of anything. Now, I was just a member of a statistically significant set of circumstances that no one wants to be a part of.

I silently mouthed the words, "I have herpes," when I knew she wasn't looking. When she was asleep, or when she was in the shower and I passed by, or when she was singing in church, I would tell her silently. Then panic would strike. I would worry that the lady by the pulpit who performed the sermon simultaneously in sign language for the television broadcast had read my lips. Had the television camera focused on me as it panned the congregation? Which camera had the red light illuminated? How different do my lips look when I say, "I have herpes" as compared to "Holy, Holy, Holy?"

The words themselves wanted to come out, and by forming the unspoken words with my lips, perhaps I was bleeding off a bit of the blockage that kept them pressed down inside of me.

I knew, of course, how I would eventually tell her. Just by a simple and straightforward statement, and then I'd stand back and see what happened next and deal with it as it. Maybe I mouthed the words so that she might catch me. I know I wanted to tell her. I just couldn't— not yet, anyway.

Instead, I told her about the new cases. With a drink in my hand, I followed her around the house as she did her chores. She rolled her eyes as I told her about the case in the recovery room and nodded as I told her about the new *Henderson* case. She stopped with a load of dirty laundry on the stairs, looking across the foyer at me.

"Have you told Dad or Eileen, or anybody other than me about this new *Henderson* case?" she asked.

"No," I said. I didn't tell her that I had already mentioned the fact to Mrs. Henderson that I might be going to another firm.

"Don't," she said.

"You want me to keep secret from your dad, my boss, the fact that a new case, a potentially good case, even despite the tort reform limits, came into the firm through me? It's the first time I've brought a good case into the firm."

"As practiced as you and the rest of the bunch at Peters & Sullivan are at keeping secrets, maintaining client confidences, holding your poker faces, or whatever you want to call this, it shouldn't be too difficult for you to keep quiet about a new case for at least a little while.

"If you leave, you can't take the recovery room case. It didn't come in to you. But the *Henderson* case came to you, even if you were at the firm when it did. Has it ever crossed your mind that, if you quit the firm, you might need that case to live on for the next few years while you wait on getting another one?"

"Quitting the firm?" I asked. I wasn't sure that Michelle was right about the *Henderson* case belonging to me if I quit the firm, but she was right about the fact that Mrs. Henderson would want me to keep it.

"Yes, quitting the firm. They can't make you go to Kentucky when your wife is having a baby in Houston. You can just quit. Walk away. Go work with Jonathan or somebody else. Why do you think Jonathan isn't up there in the first place?"

"I can't quit. What about your dad?" I asked.

"You are not my dad. It's just a job."

It wasn't just a job. It was my life. But I didn't say that to Michelle. I just stood there, dumbly silent, while she stared at me over an armload of dirty clothes. In retrospect, I could have told her then that I had herpes, because for an instant we were actually having an adult conversation. But I didn't. I just stood there until she sighed and disappeared into the laundry room.

The next morning I showered and dressed early before Michelle got up. I was sitting in his small office at Peters & Sullivan when the bookkeeper, Tom Marston, walked into the room. I wanted to see him before many others got to the office that day and before my new client meeting.

"Good morning," he said, as he took off his navy blue suit coat and hung it on a hanger on the back of the door. Compared to the grand lawyer offices, with their secretarial stations, ample size, and decorative furnishings, Tom's office seemed like an afterthought. It was neat and orderly, but the desk, obviously a hand-me-down, filled up the room and there was only room for his desk and chair, and another chair in which I was sitting.

His office reminded me of the back office at the car dealership where, after looking at the shiny cars in the elegant showroom, you are ushered to sign the paperwork and hand over the down payment. Not unlike the auto dealer's finance manager, Tom's job included explaining the settlement breakdown to the client and distributing the settlement checks after fees and expenses had been deducted.

"Good morning," I replied. I realized how infrequently I had ever talked to Tom and how I had never discussed anything of importance with him. "I need to talk to you for a moment, if I may."

"Of course, Davy. I work for you. Follow me down to the kitchen for a cup of coffee first." He motioned to the door and picked up the stained coffee cup from his desk. As we walked down the hall, I realized that we were about the only people at the office. A few secretaries and paralegals were milling around, but no lawyers had shown up yet.

Tom rinsed out his coffee cup in the sink, set it aside, and started making coffee in the four carafes that to me always just appeared to be full.

"I don't know how this got to be my job," he said. "In the old days, I used to get to work early, and Peters and Sullivan would be sitting in the kitchen over in the offices in the old Houston Bar building, drinking coffee and laughing about whatever dog case it was they were each going to try that day. Gradually, they quit coming in for coffee in the mornings, and I guess it fell to me to get the first pots going. We go through a lot more coffee than we used to," he said and smiled. When the first pot had finished brewing, he poured each of us a cup, and we walked back to his office.

"Now, what is it that you needed to discuss with me?" he asked, sitting at his desk.

"I'd like to ask you about my bonus." I said.

"Sounds like a fellow that's about to have a new baby," he said, smiling again. "Honestly, Davy, I don't really know what the end-of-the-year bonuses will be. It's too early. Peters and Sullivan together decide that issue, usually in late December. They sit down and go over each employee's performance. I usually make the recommendations for the staff, but they decide about the attorneys." He didn't seem nervous discussing a money issue with me.

"No," I said, "I'm not asking if I can get a bonus early. I was wondering how my previous bonuses compared to the bonuses paid to the other associates."

"You know I can't discuss that with any specifics," he said. "If you really want to know the numbers, I'm sure Sullivan will tell you. He probably doesn't remember them exactly, but he could request them from me and I would pass them along. What is it that you're concerned about?"

"Well, it's not that I have been slighted in any way. I guess it's the opposite of that. Have my bonuses been larger than the other associates? Can you tell me that?" I asked.

"I don't know if I'm supposed to, but I would say, yes, substantially larger," Tom replied.

"Substantially? Is that because I've brought in more money to the firm than the other associates?"

"You've done well, Davy," he said. "No, I wouldn't say that you've consistently brought in more money than the other associates. You've had your share of successes. You're probably close to second place among the associates. Maybe third or fourth. It's difficult to compare and assess. I know you spend a great deal of time with Mr. Sullivan, helping him on his cases."

"Why is my bonus so much larger than that of the other associates?" I asked.

"You'd have to ask Mr. Sullivan that, I'm afraid, Davy."

I thanked him for the information and the coffee, and walked to the doorway of his office. Before leaving, I turned to him and asked, "You do the recommendations for the bonuses for the staff?"

"Yes," he said.

"Can you tell me how Theresa's bonuses compare to the bonuses for the other paralegals?"

"No," he said, "Not because I don't think it's the kind of thing we should be discussing. I honestly don't know. Theresa works for a separate corporation . . . some screwball name like 'Paralegals Parami.' I know we've paid that company a great deal of money over the years. Recently, I know that Sullivan even made the company a rather substantial loan out of his capital account. You know, Davy, if you're worried about money with the new baby coming, I'm sure we could do something about an advance. I'd just need to check with the partners."

"Thanks," I said. "I think we'll be okay. I don't know if Michelle will ever go back to work after the baby is born, but we'll be okay. Nice having coffee with you, Mr. Marston."

"You too, Davy. Come by anytime."

"Hey, Mr. Marston, are any other paralegals around here employed by Paralegals Parami?" I asked.

"No, not right now. There have been others over the years. The only other person I remember working for them recently was that female contract lawyer . . . the real good-looking one with the dark hair. She was here such a short time, I can't remember her name."

Promptly at 8:30, Eileen let me know that Tamara Davis and her mother were there to see me. Both were nicely dressed in conservative, inexpensive pantsuits and they were polite to Eileen when she brought them coffee. Tamara let her mother do most of the talking as I went through the "new case sign up" packet with them. Mr. and Mrs. Davis lived in Sugarland, and Tamara had an apartment off Westheimer near the Beltway.

After getting down the basic biographical data (Tamara's dad was a civil engineer, her mother was a stay-at-home mom, and Tamara, age 24, worked at a Montessori school as an assistant), we discussed the more pertinent facts of the case. Tamara had always had problems with tonsillitis, sometimes brought on by allergy bouts, and one time after getting mononucleosis during her freshman year in college at the University of Houston. When her tonsils became inflamed this year, and she was covered by health insurance through her work, she decided to see about having them out. She asked her internist to recommend a surgeon, and her doctor suggested a couple of groups.

Tamara called them and an appointment was made with Dr. Jeff Ammons, the youngest surgeon in the group and the most readily available for an appointment.

Tamara met the surgeon in his office the day before the scheduled surgery, and Mrs. Davis went with her the day of the surgery to Methodist hospital. Everything seemed to go fine. The doctor came out of the operating room and told Mrs. Davis that Tamara had done well and that the tonsillectomy was routine. He expected Tamara to spend the night in the hospital and then go home to the Davis' house the next morning.

Mrs. Davis was shown the way back to the recovery area and stayed with her daughter who was still quite sedated after the surgery. Mrs. Davis left the bedside a few times—to go to the bathroom, to get coffee, and to go to the cafeteria for lunch. That afternoon, Tamara was moved to a regular room, and Mrs. Davis left the hospital about ten o'clock that evening after Tamara had gone to sleep. She went back to the hospital the next morning, but it was almost noon before Tamara was released to go home. Dr. Ammons had already been by to see Tamara before Mrs. Davis got to the hospital.

It was not until they were packing up Tamara's things to go to the car when something unusual happened. Then a nurse, which Mrs. Davis recognized from the recovery unit the day before, knocked on the door to Tamara's room and let herself in. The nurse seemed nervous and hurried. Neither Tamara nor her mom remembered the lady introducing herself to them. She asked how Tamara was doing and said that she was glad Tamara was doing well. Before turning to leave; however, the nurse produce a disk in a plastic cover from the front pocket of her smock and handed it to Tamara.

"Listen," she said, "I know I shouldn't be doing this. I guess I could get in some kind of trouble, but I think you should see this. I had a friend in the surveillance monitoring room download it for me. Look at it when you get home." Then she left, but not before Mrs. Davis made a mental note of the name on the nurse's nametag that was "Jonas."

When they got home to the Davis' house, Tamara went to her old room, put on a gown, and got into bed. It wasn't until that night that they put the disk into a computer and sat down with Mr. Davis to watch what they assumed was going to be a video of Tamara's tonsillectomy. Shocked and upset by what they saw on the video, Mr. Davis wanted to call Dr. Ammons immediately, but Mrs. Davis calmed him down. Of course, none of them knew that there was a security camera in the recovery room, but they assumed that there wasn't a camera in the private room in which Tamara had spent the night. Would the doctor have come to that room during the night? Tamara didn't think so, and she remembered being wakened every few hours by the nurses that came in to check vitals and meds.

Mrs. Davis thought they should call a lawyer, but they didn't know a lawyer. Mr. Davis asked his boss about lawyers the next day at work and got Tim Sullivan's name as a lawyer who had deposed Mr. Davis' boss in a case a few years ago involving the collapse of a crane.

"So that is how we got here Mr. Jessie." Mrs. Davis said. "We thought we were meeting with Tim Sullivan this morning, but basically we just need some advice as to what to do next. Does Tamara have a case?"

I explained the problem with trying to collect from the doctor and told them that I had some ideas about how we might be able to make the hospital responsible for his actions. I kept to myself the concerns I had about what the damages in this case might be (Tamara was sexually assaulted, but not raped, and she was not conscious of the event when it occurred. Still, a jury, just like the Davis family, might get really mad when it saw the video).

I had Tamara sign a contingency fee contract and authorizations for me to obtain her medical records. I explained that I would be writing notice of representation letters to the doctor and the hospital, and that I would send Tamara copies. I walked them to the elevator, and, as they got on, I asked if either of them knew personally any of the folks that worked at the hospital. Mrs. Davis answered for both of them when she said, "We don't know any of those people, and we don't want to know any of them." The elevator doors closed, and I went back to my desk.

I asked Eileen to make two copies of the video, and I spent most of the rest of the day working on my letters to Doctor Ammons and Methodist Hospital. The letter to the doctor was straight forward, about three sentences. I represent Tamara Davis, a former patient of yours. Enclosed is a video of you molesting her. Have your lawyer call me.

The letter to the hospital was much longer and went on and on about why an institution would have surveillance cameras and nobody monitoring them in a fashion whereby they could respond quickly in a crisis. Obviously, the cameras were there to protect the hospital and not the patients. I made sure the letter was full of righteous indignation and dripping with prejudice.

20

THE FOLLOWING DAY, I met Eli and Rod for lunch at the Ragin' Cajun on Richmond. It seemed like we had not been to lunch together in a long time, and I had forgotten how much fun they were. We dissected the Astros and their playoff chances and made our predictions for another dismal Texans season. We each ate a dozen raw oysters, a cup of gumbo, and a softshell crab po-boy. On television sets in the corners of the room, SportsCenter continued to show the previous night's highlights.

They regaled me with stories of a case they were preparing to take to trial the next month; and, though they wouldn't jinx it by saying so, it sounded to me like they were going to win it. The case had come into the firm as a referral to Peters, and Eli had done most of the work on it. He had asked Rod to try it with him because of the number of witnesses involved, and because Rod was the best among the associates at briefing the thorny legal issues that the case was bound to present.

I was jealous of the fun they were having working together on the case. Nobody expected them to win. That's why Peters had given Eli the case. Eli had been careful not to tell Peters how well the depositions had gone out of fear that Peters would take back the case. It involved a man named Fulshear who was shot in his home by the Houston police.

Apparently there had been a disturbance at the house between Fulshear's daughter and an old boyfriend. Mr. Fulshear had called the cops. Because of an error in the police dispatch, the police were sent to the home under the impression that an armed assailant was at the house. Some time had passed before the police arrived, and the family had gone to bed. When Mr. Fulshear later heard something in his front yard, he got a handgun out of his nightstand and went to the front door expecting to confront the boyfriend. When he opened the door, the cops saw the gun and opened fire. One bullet had left Mr. Fulshear paralyzed. I thought about what Sullivan always said about the Houston police, "You are never as close to death as when you've been stopped by the Houston cops."

"Where are the entry wounds?" I asked.

Eli and Rod smiled at each other and looked around the restaurant to be sure that nobody was listening. "There are multiple entry wounds." Eli said. "One of them, probably the last one, is through the bottom of our guy's left foot."

"They shot him while he was on the ground?" I asked.

"Face down in his own home." Rod said.

I knew it would be difficult to win the case. There are myriad hurdles in any civil rights cause of action including trying to hold a verdict in the conservative Fifth Circuit on appeal. But the facts were compelling, and I could understand why Eli and Rod were reluctant to tell Peters how well the case was developing.

We had all ordered bread puddings before they got around to asking me how the Kentucky case was going. I told them that I was certain that we were going to lose it. First, our expert would be struck. Then, a summary judgment would be granted. Sullivan was not even going to attend the hearing on the motion to strike the expert.

"Why did he ever get the firm involved in that one?" Eli asked.

"I don't know," I said. "I just can't figure it out. It's as if he has had nothing to do with the case ever since he assigned me to work on it."

"If the cases were winners, they wouldn't give them to us to handle. We all know that," Rod said.

"I guess you're right, but I thought this was going to be something different," I said. "I thought this was going to be one of those cases that I would help Sullivan work up, and then he would do all of the important stuff at trial. Maybe I would present a plaintiff or two on direct examination or cross-examine a few corporate employees. Unfortuantely, now I don't think we'll ever get to that point."

"I just don't understand why Sullivan would invest so much of the firm's money in this case," Eli said. "I even read an article about it the other day in the *Wall Street Journal*. The article made it sound like the big publicly traded oil companies like Boyd and Exxon and others were watching the case pretty closely to see if there were going to be other radiation contamination cases. There must be other regions in the country where radiation comes to the surface along with the oil when you inject water downhole into the system. What do you call it again?" he asked.

"The plaintiffs call it TENORM, and the defendants call it NORM," I said. "Technologically Enhanced Naturally Occurring Radioactive Material. The plaintiffs focus on the 'technologically enhanced.' The defendants focus on the 'naturally occurring.'"

"Maybe, Sullivan thinks TENORM will be the next asbestos or Fen-Phen," Rod said. "A lot of asbestos cases were thrown out of court before the *Borel v. Fiberboard* case over in Beaumont."

"Spindletop," Eli said.

"Maybe," I said, "but the way this has worked out, if I lose it, or when I lose it, I won't have many other cases at the firm to fall back on."

"There will always be other cases. Maybe they will give you half of mine," Eli said.

"Maybe they will give you all of mine," Rod said.

"Do you ever think about quitting?" I asked realizing that I was initiating a conversation that might be viewed by some as bordering on betrayal or treason.

"I didn't used to," Eli said without hesitation. "But, I'm not sure I can do this forever. I guess I'd like to make partner here someday, if only because I think it would look good on my resume. Sometimes though, I think I'd like to start my own firm. Where would I get cases, though? Advertise? I don't think my wife wants to see me on billboards or on the Fox Channel telling people to call 1-800-WE-B-HURT."

"Surely some of the referral lawyers that send cases to Peters & Sullivan would send us cases. They know we're the lawyers working up the cases for settlement or trial," I said.

"Yeah, but they know that Peters and Sullivan are the names on the judicial campaign contribution checks," Eli responded. "And they know that both Peters and Sullivan have the financial wherewithal to finance a case. Where else could you go to find a firm that will step in and cover a million-dollar tab like the firm did on your Kentucky case?"

"Maybe there is still some way to work this out to your advantage," Rod said. "So what if you lose it? If TENORM is the next asbestos, you'll be one of the few young lawyers in the country that knows anything about it."

"Yeah, man," Eli said, "you could be the Walter Umphrey of oilfield radiation pollution."

"I wish I had never heard of TENORM," I said.

They continued to try and boost my spirits as we ate. While it might mean that I advanced ahead of them in the partnership race if I somehow resurrected the *Carter* case, they offered positive suggestions on how to handle the direct examination of my expert, as well as cross-examination of the defendant's experts. They understood I was in a fight, and they were my friends. They were there to help me if I would just let them. I always enjoyed those lunches with the associates at Peters & Sullivan. And I always learned something from having the opportunity to bounce ideas around with them.

For instance, it had not occurred to me until lunch that day that Boyd was a publicly traded company.

Days crept by. I spent most of my time in my office, with the door closed. Ostensibly, I was preparing for the expert witness hearing in Kentucky. I did talk to Mr. Walton a few times on the telephone. I scribbled ideas for a short story about dove hunting in Argentina. I kept the handwritten pages in the breast pocket of my blazer.

I also called Mr. Whiskers at Brennan's to get information about betting on the outcome of a local trial. I wanted to know if you had to put the money up front or if you could wait until the verdict came in. He told me that he thought I was good for it, and I bet money I didn't have on Eli and Rod to win the *Fulshear* case. I told myself that I could take cash advances on my credit cards if I had to, but I knew there probably wasn't that much credit left on them. In reality, I was trying to come up with a plan for an acceptable departure from the firm, one that wouldn't appear to potential referral lawyers that I had been fired for losing a big case or cheating on my wife. I knew I was going to need some seed money if I went out on my own.

I did get an interesting call one day from an insurance adjustor for the company covering Methodist Hospital.

The adjustor informed me that there was no court that would hold the hospital liable for Dr. Ammons' actions, but, out of an abundance of caution, he wanted to see if my client Tamara Davis and I would be willing to participate in a pre-suit mediation. I told him that we would be willing to mediate with the mediator of the hospital's choosing, but it seemed to me that we could save the cost of the mediation by the hospital offering its liability caps.

Remember, the legislature had capped intangible damages in a medical malpractice case at just $250,000, and the Texas Supreme Court had made it pretty clear that anything having to do with a doctor or a hospital was a medical malpractice case within the definitions provided by the statute. I didn't think that sexual assault by a doctor on a patient should come under the purview of the statute, but I had read enough of the cases to think that the court would decide that the case against the hospital qualified for the protection of the statute and the limitation on damages. There was no way to assess what the damages were without doing an expensive focus group study intended to see what a potential jury might award, so I just asked for the max. After a slight pause, the adjustor told me that he would get back to me.

Michelle's belly continued to grow, and with each passing day, I struggled with how I would tell her about the herpes.

I assumed that she would kick me out of the house when I told her. I assumed that her first call would be to her mother, who would immediately call Sullivan. I assumed I would have a broken marriage, no place to live, no job, and no money within minutes of my revealing the facts to Michelle.

Of course, I had to tell her. My putting it off only made matters worse. I was risking her health, as well as that of our unborn child. I felt some relief because I didn't think that Dr. Nathan would let the child be delivered vaginally, and he would thereby significantly reduce the health risk to the child. But the C-section delivery would be fraught with its own risks.

I needed to talk to someone about my predicament. The only psychologists I knew had been expert witnesses in cases I had tried with Sullivan. I worried that they would call him, or that maybe they had some ethical duty to call Michelle when there was a potential risk to Michelle's health and the health of her baby. And, I didn't have any confidence in the advice they might give me. The psychologists I knew had not made very good witnesses during trial: their opinions had been expressed more like multiple-choice answers rather than concrete diagnoses. I thought that I needed somebody to tell me what to do, and how to do it, rather than asking me how it all made me feel. I felt like crap. I felt like I was looking through the large end of a megaphone, and the hole of light at the other end was growing smaller and smaller.

I thought about talking to Eli or Rod. It would be too much to ask, though, that they not mention anything to their wives, and their wives would call Michelle immediately.

I even thought about trying to talk to Sullivan. He was the only person in the world I knew who regularly dealt with such ridiculous circumstances. He was going to find out everything, eventually. It was not as if he had never had an affair. He already knew that the Kentucky case was headed down the tubes, and he didn't even seem that upset about it. He just kept holding press conferences about the progress of the case and not really doing anything on the case. But if I told Sullivan, I then risked his telling Michelle before I did. If I was ever going to have a chance of reconciling with Michelle, I had to be the one who told her.

Talking to Riza would be just like talking to Sullivan.

I could call Beth, if I could find her. She would at least listen to me without being judgmental. I wondered how her situation had worked out. Was she still married? Did she have a job? Where was she living? Beth would insist that I tell Michelle at once. It was the right thing to do. Whenever I got around to talking to Michelle, however, she would want to know when the last time was that I had been in contact with Beth. It seemed best to put whatever time and distance I could between us—not to pretend that the affair had not happened, or that I had not contracted a sexually transmitted disease, but so that I could honestly say to Michelle that there was no longer anything between Beth and me except having the same virus.

I considered calling Jonathan. He might even feel that his dad was to blame in part for the situation in which I found myself, but ultimately, he would have to tell his sister Michelle what was happening. Telling Jonathan also risked Michelle finding out from someone else.

One afternoon in early September, having pondered the situation for hours that day and for days before that, I called my dad. I knew he would be in his office while he was between classes. At 1:05 p.m., he taught Freshman English for fifty minutes. At 3:05, he taught an upper-level Shakespeare course. I expected that, as was his habit after lunch, he would be sitting at his cluttered desk reviewing note cards he had prepared years ago for his Shakespeare lecture, or perhaps grading papers that had been turned in from an earlier class.

He seemed happy to hear from me. I rarely called him during the day, and when I did, it was usually just to confirm family trips or get-togethers. I could tell he thought that I might be calling to tell him that Michelle had gone into labor a few days early.

"No," I said, "the doctor tells us that everything is on schedule. I think Michelle wishes we could hurry up and have this baby. She's pretty miserable right now."

"Yeah," he said, "I remember how that works. Well, what's going on, then?"

"I need to talk to you, Dad," I said. "I need to talk to somebody, and honestly, I don't know whom."

"You can always talk to me. How can I help?"

"I've got a problem, Dad. A big problem." I paused, nervously searching for what to say next. "At least, I've made it a big problem. I want to tell you about it, but I just don't know where to start."

He could sense that I was wavering on telling him anything about what was going on with me. "What is it, Davy? You didn't wreck that little BMW convertible that I like so much, did you?" He always said that he wanted to buy my BMW when I got tired of it, although we both knew that he would never admit that he could afford it. The irony, of course, was that he could afford the car after a lifetime of saving while I could not afford it, but thought that I had to have it because I somehow deserved it.

"No," I said, "nothing like that. Dad, I just don't know if I can talk to you about this. It's really bad. You're not going to believe how badly I've messed things up. You and Mom are going to be very disappointed in me. You've always given me everything I've ever needed. I don't know where else to turn. My life is about to become completely unraveled."

"I'll bet it's not as bad as you think it is," he said reassuringly. "Tell me what's up."

My voice started to crack. I couldn't help it. "I'm going to lose Michelle," I said. "I'm going to lose my job. I don't know where I'm going to live. I won't have any money to live on." I wondered if Eileen could hear me on the other side of the closed door to my office.

"Davy, slow down. I can't understand what you are saying. What do you mean: you are going to lose Michelle? You can always find another job. You're not going to starve. What do you mean you're going to lose Michelle? Is she okay?" he asked.

"She's fine. I guess. I know I asked you to listen, Dad. I'm suddenly not sure I can talk to you about this right now."

"It is not long until dove season opens. Why don't you come up here on September first? I know it won't be like that time we went to Argentina after you finished at Tech, but I'll bet we can find a limit or two of birds. We could talk then. And you know, your mom and I are coming down there as soon as Michelle goes into labor."

"Yeah. That trip to Argentina was perfect. I wish we were back there right now. We have to go again some time, Dad. I don't imagine that I will make it to dove hunting this year. I'll just see you when the baby comes," I said. "I'm sorry to worry you, Dad. Everything will be okay."

"I don't know what to tell you, Davy. I am worried, but I'm sure you've made more out of this than there is. You've always just tried to handle things on your own, and never would let anybody help you. If you need our help, you only have to ask for it."

He paused, but I didn't respond.

"Davy, having a baby can be stressful on the best marriage. Has something happened between you and Michelle? Are you worried about the delivery process? Does your call have something to do with work? I was concerned when you went to work for that firm . . . that there could be problems with you being married to your boss's daughter. I can't help you unless you tell me what's bothering you."

"I know, Dad," I said.

"You and Michelle can always come live in Abilene. I don't know what the personal injury practice is like here, but there would be built-in babysitting."

"I don't think that's going to happen, Dad."

"Keep it on your list of options. It looks to me like as long as you have a law license, you're never really unemployed. Maybe you could even take a little time and put together a short story or two, or maybe something longer."

"That's true about the employment," I said, ignoring the comment about writing fiction. "Of course, you've got to have cases to work on. And, you've got to have some money to work the cases up. Typically, the plaintiff's attorney fronts the expenses. And the attorney eats them if he or she loses."

"So you'd want to be careful about which cases you took at first. If you were going off on your own, you'd want to avoid anything too risky, it seems to me. But you know better than I do. You're the lawyer, after all," he said, trying hard to avoid sounding condescending after giving me advice.

"Yes, though I've never actually ventured my own money. The truth is that I don't have any money, Dad."

"Where do those two salaries go?" he asked.

"Most of it goes to the house. My car is leased. Our debts, including my student loans, pretty much eat up everything we bring home. Whatever happens, I doubt that Michelle is going to want to continue working after the baby is born."

"What do you mean by 'whatever happens?'" he asked.

Again, I didn't respond.

"Davy, I don't really know what it is we're talking about because you won't tell me. It does seem to me that if you're living on borrowed money and leases, it's really just a matter of time until you have to rein in your lifestyle and make a concerted effort to eliminate the debt so you can build something for yourself and your family."

I nodded, but I didn't say anything.

"If you made partner at that firm someday, who would benefit the most, you, or the name partners? While you haven't asked for my advice, I must admit it looks kind of like a grey-suited pyramid scheme to me."

"You sound like a liberal college professor," I said.

He laughed. "I wouldn't call this a liberal college."

"The experience is good," I said. "I've gotten to try some cases. Most guys my age are still just drafting motions or reviewing documents to see if they are privileged."

"I suspect that's true," he said. "But you don't want to look up in five years and still be helping to clear out the firm's meritless cases under the guise of gaining experience."

"I guess so," I said.

"Davy, it's unlike you to call for help or advice. Your mother would say it's unlike you to call at all. It sounds to me like you might be having problems at home or at work, or maybe both. Apparently, you're not going to tell me any specifics right now. But I can tell you this. It's okay to be vulnerable. It's okay to be broken. Sometimes it takes having the façade lowered so that we can see what it is that was important to us in the first place. The theology guys around here give long lectures about the necessity for a vessel to be broken in order to let anything inside."

"I need to go, Dad." I said, cutting him off. I was familiar with the idea. What was the line from the Cohen song about things having to be cracked to let the light in? Now the thought occurred to me that the vessel lecture assumed that whatever force broke the seal didn't destroy the vessel entirely. What if the force obliterated the object? And what exactly was it that was being permitted to enter?

My mind wandered to the herpes literature I had read that suggested that having had the herpes sores on the sex organ, one would always be more susceptible to contracting AIDS. The virus could more easily enter the broken vesicle than it could the intact skin. I started to ask Dad a question, but I just sat there silently on the phone.

"Yeah," he said after a long pause. He was frustrated, but he tried his best to sound reassuring. "Be careful driving my convertible."

21

THE NIGHT BEFORE I left for Kentucky to attend the hearing regarding the experts, I spent a considerable amount of time laying out my clothes for the trip. The effort was largely ceremonial, because I inevitably would wear a navy blazer, grey slacks, a starched white shirt, and some form of a red-and-blue striped tie. While I laid the clothes out on my side of the bed and compared the tie options, Michelle got ready for bed and crawled in on her side.

I don't know if anybody will ever read this. I seriously doubt that if anybody ever does read it that they would be inclined to accept marital advice from me. Nevertheless, I would recommend that when you get married you buy the smallest bed in which you can both sleep comfortably. We, of course, bought the biggest king-size bed available, even though before we were married we would often fall asleep curled up in each other's arms on that worn-out gold couch Michelle had in the den of her apartment. Now, when Michelle was on her edge of the bed and I was on mine, I wouldn't have been able to hug her even if I had Yao Ming's arms.

"Have you come up with any new arguments?" Michelle asked, genuinely concerned, but masking her anger that I was even going to the hearing with our baby due any day.

"No. Well, I may have a trick or two up my sleeve. The defendant's lawyer will cross-examine our expert, and then we'll reverse the process and I will cross-examine their expert witnesses. Maybe I can get away with just cross-examining one of Boyd's witnesses. I've got a few things for one of their witnesses. Most of the arguments are already set out in the briefs. I hope the commissioner has bothered to read them."

"How do you feel about your chances?" Michelle asked.

I told her that I thought it was a foregone conclusion that we would lose, that our expert would be struck, and that a summary judgment motion would follow shortly. I assumed that was why her dad was sending me to argue the motion rather than doing it himself. She pointed out that Riza was also going, and I responded that I thought Riza's attendance was merely to provide Sullivan a report on my performance.

"You'll be fine," Michelle said, in a way that indicated that she loved me, whether I won or lost the motion, the way your dad told you to be careful when he gave you the keys to his car for a date when you were sixteen.

"Will you be okay?" I asked.

"I hope so," she said trying not to sound worried.

"We get to Lexington about noon tomorrow. I have a meeting on another case, the new *Henderson* case, tomorrow afternoon, and the hearing will be the next morning. It will probably last a couple of hours, and then I'll fly back that afternoon."

"At least Dad is sending the plane." She said.

"Yeah. I'll be back as fast as I can."

"Mom's here," she said. "And Jonathan, I'll be okay."

"Would you ever forgive me if I missed the birth of our child?"

"I want you here," she said.

"I want to be here."

"Do you?" she asked. "You've been pretty distant the past few weeks. It seems like we never talk about anything. It seems like there is something you want to tell me, but won't. We haven't really even decided on a name for the little guy."

I recognized the opportunity to disclose what was really bothering me. She was calmly asking me to explain what was going on with me. I would be leaving town in a few hours. However painful the discussion might be, I had a built-in exit ramp. Michelle was lying there in our bed, miserable with discomfort from her pregnancy. She didn't deserve my deceitfulness or infidelities or secretiveness. She deserved an honest, frank discussion about what was going on with me and our marriage.

"Just talk to me," she said.

I paused from my packing and looked at her lying there under the covers, both vulnerable because of her condition and vibrant with the role that would be hers for the next few days. I was nothing like the person she thought she married: confident, secure, and honest. If I was ever going to tell her about the affair, and the herpes, I had to do it now. What if something happened on the trip? What if she had the baby tomorrow? Dr. Nathan would be there, but I would have failed again to live up to my promise to him to tell Michelle the truth.

"We're married," she said. "What is there that could be going on with you that you couldn't talk to me about?"

I had practiced the speech a thousand times in my head. I knew what had to be said, and I knew how I was going to say it. I had considered leading off with the story of the affair, waiting for a reaction, and then continuing with, "There's more."

"More?" she would ask, and then I would tell her about the virus and my concern that she might be infected, and I'd conclude with my discussion with Dr. Nathan, presented as a heroic effort on my part to try and make things right. But that scenario risked the conversation being cut off before I ever told her about the venereal disease. She might leave, lock herself in the bathroom, or insist that I leave.

The better presentation, it appeared to me, would be to start out with the admission that I had herpes. "Establish primacy," is what the instructors always said back in trial advocacy class. The medical condition was, of course, at this point the most important fact. We could discuss the details of the affair at some hopefully much later date.

I could tell her now, and she could talk to Dr. Nathan tomorrow. They could work out the details of the delivery in a way that would be the least risky to her and the baby. Probably I would be in Kentucky when the baby was born, and it would be a month or two before I was allowed to hold him.

Telling her now would clear up so many questions that Michelle must have asked herself in the last few months about what I was keeping from her—why I seemed so closed-off and distant—and why we never had sex anymore. In a way, telling her might be almost as much a relief for her as for me.

Either way, telling about the affair first or the herpes, I knew the moment at hand presented a clear opportunity to begin the inevitable discussion. I just couldn't let myself start.

"I thought we decided on 'Paul,'" I said.

Michelle sighed. "Right," she said, and rolled over to her edge of the bed to face away from me. "But he has to have a middle name."

I finished packing my overnight bag and put it by the door to the bedroom. I turned out the bedroom light at the door, walked across the room, and got into bed on my side. We lay there, facing away from each other, without either of us saying anything.

I had been surprised to learn that Riza had left the night before on a commercial flight to Lexington, but her absence from Sullivan's plane had made it easier for me to take the rental car to Dr. Mock's office without having to make up reasons for my needing to go there. I was carrying the tissue slides in the *Henderson* case for Dr. Mock to review. I had already mailed him the pertinent records, including the MD Anderson path report performed after the mastectomy. I wanted to hand deliver the slides.

The time alone on the plane allowed me to start working on a short story idea that had been churning around in my brain for the last few months. While I didn't know how the story would end, I knew how it started, and I wrote out the first part on the flight to Lexington without anybody looking over my shoulder. It may not have been any good, but I thought it was better than the poem.

My cell phone started ringing as I went up the steps to the hospital where Dr. Mock worked. Worried that it might be Michelle calling about the baby, I fumbled through my brief case and almost dropped the Henderson slides in the process. I was not entirely relieved to see that it was Eileen on the caller ID. Michelle could have called Eileen and asked her to find me, but when I answered I found out that the Methodist Hospital adjustor had called, and Eileen wanted me to call him back. I jotted down his phone number and told Eileen that I would call him back when I got to my hotel. I didn't tell her where I was.

Dr. Mock and I met in a tiled conference room in a hospital in Lexington. His secretary took me to the room and brought me a cup of coffee. In a few minutes, Dr. Mock appeared in a white coat with a manila folder under his left arm. I presumed the file contained the records I had sent. He smoothed his white hair back, and extended his hand. He had a warm smile and pale blue eyes.

"Mr. Jessie," he said, "so nice to see you. Tell me, how is everything in Houston?" Dr. Mock spoke with just the hint of an Austrian accent. He explained to me that he had done a residency with the legendary Dr. Debakey in Houston before focusing on pathology. Though it had been entirely fortuitous that I had met him that day in a law office in Lexington, Dr. Mock was preeminent in his field. I knew his report in the *Henderson* case, if favorable, would go a long way toward settling the case. And, if the case didn't settle, he would be a terrific witness. He had told me on the phone when I first consulted him about working on the case that he looked forward to coming to Houston and calling upon old friends.

As we sat at the veneer table, he said, still smiling, "I guess I won't be coming to Houston anytime soon."

"What do you mean?" I asked, concerned for a moment that his report might be harmful to the case.

"This is going to be an easy one, Mr. Jessie. I'll bet the pathologist just blew it. I know he saw the slides, and I have not had a chance to myself. However, I bet that the cellular changes he observed and diagnosed as cancerous are instead the result of the radiation therapy Mrs. Henderson previously underwent for her cancerous tumor. That is, of course, the conclusion of the pathologist at the University of Texas MD Anderson Cancer Center when he looked at the slides after the double mastectomy and determined that she did not have a recurrence of breast cancer, but I think my report will be worded in a fashion that will be better understood by a lay person. You will never get to the deposition stage, I'm afraid," he said.

"Well, that would be good news for the case. I've brought the slides with me for you to see." I said and handed the mailer containing the slides to Dr. Mock.

"And, in a sense, good news for Mrs. Henderson," he said opening the envelope that I had handed him and taking out slides. "I expect that she didn't have a recurrence of the disease. Unfortunately, for her, she probably did undergo a completely unnecessary procedure.

"I always have a hesitance about testifying against a fellow physician, but mistakes are mistakes. It doesn't appear from his original report that the pathologist, Dr. Valdez, bothered to consult with the oncologist that sent him the tissue for review prior to his examining the slides. Dr. Valdez probably just saw that the tissue was from a local oncologist and presumed he was looking for cancer. Dr. Valdez saw cellular changes on the slides, didn't bother to learn that the patient had undergone radiation, and mistakenly diagnosed cancer. Of course, if the pathologist had questions about what he was looking for, he should have consulted with a member of his group or perhaps another group altogether.

"I'm very sorry that Mrs. Henderson has been through all of this. After I look at the slides, I should have the report prepared this evening or tomorrow, and I will over-night it to you. Should I send it to the address on the cover letter that accompanies these slides?"

"No," I said. "Let me give you another address. This one is in Abilene, Texas."

I gave him my parents' address. He shook my hand and stood up from the table.

"I don't mean to interfere in business that is not mine, Mr. Jessie." Dr. Mock said as he walked to the door. "But you look a little tired today. Was your flight okay?"

"The flight was fine." I said. "I may be a little tired. I probably just need to get something to eat."

Dr. Mock, with the envelope and file under one arm, put his hands in the pockets of his white coat and smiled. "I remember those early days myself. Late nights. No time to eat. Trying to impress superiors. Don't forget to set aside a little time for yourself. If you don't, I'm afraid you'll be putting your own health at risk. And it will hit you when you least expect it. Again, I don't mean to interfere. Experience can be a rather unforgiving instructor, I've learned." He said still smiling.

I nodded and Dr. Mock left the room. The door closed behind him, and I took out my cell phone to call the Methodist Hospital adjustor back in Houston. I looked around to see if there were any cameras watching me.

After introductions and some brief chitchat about the weather in Houston being unseasonably hot, Houston doesn't really have seasons so maybe "unseasonably" was not the right word, the adjustor said, "Well, okay Mr. Jessie. We are going to settle this case for the $250,000 you demanded. I will have our lawyer draw up the settlement documents. We will not be seeking a release for Dr. Ammons. We will let him float his own boat on this one."

"I wonder what will happen to Dr. Ammons." I asked.

"I don't know. I don't imagine he will have privileges here anymore, and I guess that will mean that his surgical group lets him go. He's fortunate that with a medical license and some surgery experience, he can probably just move away. We both know that if you sue him for sexual assault, an intentional tort not covered by his malpractice policy, he will just declare personal bankruptcy, and you will never get a dime out of him. If you don't sue him, nothing will ever show up on his record when he applies for malpractice coverage. I expect that he will get off without a mark, and the hospital will be left holding the bag. Oh well. Dr. Ammons will be somebody else's problem now. I can tell you that the hospital let the woman go who was supposed to be monitoring the cameras in the security room. Her name was Abby something or other."

I thanked the adjustor and hung up the phone. Before calling Eileen to get 'Tamara Davis' phone number, I thought to myself that for the cost of postage on two letters and a few cell phone minutes, I had just made the firm $83,000. I don't know what I expected when I told Tamara the news. Usually clients express their appreciation and sometimes they even cry when told their cases have settled. But Tamara's reaction was just matter of fact. It seemed that she was also doing the math in her head.

Despite the fact that I was worn out, I didn't sleep very much again that night. I thought about the hearing and when that became too much, I opened a couple of the little scotch bottles from the mini-bar and tried to write a few sentences in the short story. Apparently writing fiction was not going to be a very good stress reliever. If you are a passionate perfectionist who is reluctant to ask for help in your personal life or law practice, you are probably going to demonstrate the same qualities in your literary efforts. As I wrote a sentence, I would be excited and interested in what I was going to write next. Then as soon as I put down the pen, it all seemed like so much drivel, and I wondered what was going on in my head when I wrote the silly sentence.

It didn't take very long to determine the next morning at the hearing on the experts what was going on in the Special Master Commissioner's head. We didn't follow the order of witnesses that would have been followed at a trial because the hearing was just on the competing motions to strike each side's experts. Having filed their motion first, Boyd's lawyers went first and called my expert, Mr. Walton. Then I had the opportunity to "rehabilitate" the witness. The process would be reversed when the commissioner considered my motion to strike Boyd's experts.

I had barely completed my questioning of Mr. Walton regarding his background and qualifications when the commissioner intervened with his own line of questioning, largely based on leading questions that depicted the risk to human health from radiation contamination of the plaintiffs' properties as speculative at best. While practically summarizing the points that defense counsel had attempted to make with Mr. Walton, the commissioner focused his questions on the fact that nobody had actually developed a disease that Mr. Walton could attribute to the radiation. Instead he was concerning himself with what might happen in the future.

Mr. Walton's opinions had been based in part on the computer model relied on by federal government agencies that estimated the cumulative effects of residual radiation, a so-called RESRAD model. This model in particular incorporates various future land-use scenarios (like different types of farming and home-building) that had never been attempted in eastern Kentucky; and the commissioner used that fact to attempt to ridicule the projected results, even though I thought Mr. Walton did a fair job of suggesting that it should be the landowners who determine how their land will eventually be used, not the oil company that channeled enough radioactive pollution onto the properties to limit future uses. In essence it was the same discussion Mr. Walton had with me back in March at the Paintsville Inn.

The hearing was held in a conference room at the Lexington law firm representing Boyd. Most of the plaintiffs were unable to make the trip over to Lexington for the hearing, and those that did, including Mr. Carter, found it difficult to find a seat in the room.

The reason seating was so limited was not because the room was too small. The room was enormous. Instead, it was packed with men and women in blue and grey suits. Each person tapped away at his or her respective laptop computers throughout the hearing, and frequently one would leave the room with a cell phone in hand. I knew all of these people could not be working for Boyd, even though Boyd certainly had plenty of lawyers there. Maybe they were lawyers from other firms representing other oil companies. None of them introduced themselves to me, and I definitely got the impression that they saw me as an enemy.

I sat at the conference table next to Riza, who also had her laptop open, but she didn't seem to be taking notes. The screen was situated so that it was difficult for me to see it, and I wondered if she was instant-messaging to Sullivan and reporting how poorly the hearing was going for us.

The Special Master Commissioner, seated directly across from me at the oval table, turned his attention to me as he tapped the eraser-end of a pencil on a legal pad. "Mr. Jessie, I suppose I should offer you the opportunity to call a witness on your motion. Who'd you like to start with? I'd like to complete the testimony today."

"I call Dr. Thomas, your Honor. I anticipate that Dr. Thomas' opinions will embrace the opinions of the other experts designated by the Boyd Oil Company on the issues regarding the harmful effects of low dosages of radiation. Perhaps, if I'm permitted to go into some detail with Dr. Thomas, I can avoid having to examine the other witness."

"Well, let's see how things develop. By the way we can dispense with the 'honor' designation. I'm just plain old 'Mr. Abbott.' I'm proud to serve at Judge Hurst's designation, but (as you know) I'm not appointed by the governor nor elected by the good people of this commonwealth to serve. I just make recommendations. His Honor will issue the order. Very well. Enough of the formalities. Let's swear in Dr. Thomas."

Without the necessity of an introduction, Mr. Abbott turned to Dr. Thomas, who was seated at the far end of the conference table, and asked the witness to raise his hand and take the oath. A court reporter, seated near the witness, pecked away at her stenographic recorder.

I started with the money. It wasn't so much that I thought that the commissioner would decide that the witness was so biased that the witness' testimony would be tainted, but I did think it was important to make a record of the extent of the affiliation between the witness and Boyd. In fact, I had called Dr. Thomas instead of one of the other experts because Thomas had actually profited quite handsomely from his association with Boyd and the Martha Oil Field.

In addition to his witness fees for the review of records and testing data generated on the plaintiffs' properties, he was a partner in a company that had done significant work in developing reclamation protocols for Boyd. The State of Kentucky had issued orders regarding cleanup of the Martha Oil Field and Thomas's company had earned substantial fees in assisting Boyd in complying with those orders. There was nothing untoward about the money that was made, but it was a lot of money, and I thought it showed a connection between the witness and the party that certainly went above and beyond any connection between the plaintiffs and the expert we had hired.

I probably spent too long on the money, largely because I didn't have anything to work with as far as the man's credentials. And any attack I made on his credentials would serve to undercut my own witness who didn't have the advanced degrees or publications that Thomas had.

Similarly, there was not much ore to be mined in comparing the analysis of the data collected and reviewed by both parties. Though most of the million dollars my firm had spent had gone towards reimbursing the plaintiffs' previous attorneys for the costs of soil and water sampling and analysis, the work had been done on the cheap as most of it had been done by people that had garnered their experience working in the field rather than studying in the classroom. The defendant had probably spent ten times that amount doing roughly the same (albeit more detailed) work.

I did get the witness to say that he had carefully reviewed the reports and credentials of the other experts designated by Boyd. They represented various disciplines of study, but on the principle issue of whether low doses of radiation can cause deleterious health effects, they were all in agreement. And their consensus was a resounding "No." Believe it or not, there are many peer-reviewed articles that support that position. In fact, there are well-written articles that have been published in respected journals that suggest that low doses of radiation might even be good for you.

I handed copies of the expert's report to him and the commissioner. I avoided any discussion of the text of the report and went to the bibliography. Somewhat to my surprise, I saw the commissioner flip through the pages to the back of the report and follow along.

I worked my way through a few of the articles. While Dr. Thomas had cited the studies in his report, it had been a while since he had read them, and he was not as familiar with the underlying data as he should have been (or as he no doubt would be if he testified at trial sometime in the future). It was not that I knew anything more about the health effects of radiation than Dr. Thomas—far from it. I didn't know a fraction of what Dr. Thomas knew about radiation. But it has been my experience that where there are two schools of thought about a concept and an equal number of articles have been published on each side of the issue, there will be an article that is critical of the literature on the other side. And the Internet is a wonderful thing.

It took about an hour. Although I didn't address each of the articles referenced in Dr. Thomas's report, I don't think any fair-minded person would have decided that it was a foregone conclusion that there was a threshold below which exposure to radiation was not harmful. I was assuming, of course, that we were dealing with a fair-minded person.

I ended this portion of the examination by asking the witness if he agreed with a passage from a pamphlet entitled *Evaluation of Guidelines for Exposure to Technologically Enhanced Naturally Occurring Radioactive Materials* published by a committee on the evaluation of EPA guidelines put together by the National Research Council's Board on Radiation Effects Research Commission on Life Sciences. It took longer to identify the source than it did to ask the question, but the discussion touched on what I thought was the central issue at hand—do governmental guidelines incorporate the linear no-threshold approach?

"Dr. Thomas, please confirm that the committee in this 1999 document concludes the following:

> '[a]t the present time, there is considerable debate over the validity of the linear no-threshold dose-response hypothesis for low levels of exposure. It remains as an assumption used in developing all radiation guidelines, including those for TENORM, in spite of the current debate over the validity of this hypothesis . . .'

"Yes, I agree that was the committee's conclusion."

"So whichever side of the debate is ultimately determined to be the right side, current government guidelines for exposure to low levels of radiation continue to follow the linear no-threshold approach—the approach espoused here by the plaintiffs' expert?"

"I guess that's true to some extent."

"Dr. Thomas," I continued, "we've been through many of the articles you cited in your report, but maybe the most important authority is the one you didn't cite."

"I don't know what you mean." He said. "I think my research of the published material was thorough."

I could tell by his answer that he knew where I was going. I also thought that I detected a note of surprise in Dr. Thomas' last answer. "Well, let's look at endnote 27 in your report." I said. "It refers to something called the BEIR V report, doesn't it?"

"Yes." he said.

"What is that?" I asked.

"BEIR is an acronym that stands for the 'Biological Effects of Ionizing Radiation.' It's a report from the National Research Council prepared to advise the US Government on the relationship between exposure to ionizing radiation and human health. The BEIR V report was published in 1990." Dr. Thomas said, trying to sound official.

"BEIR VI came out in 1999, didn't it?" I asked.

"Yes, but it dealt with the health effects of exposure to Radon." He said.

"But that's not the end of the story, is it?"

"Well, there is the BEIR VII-Phase 1 report." He said.

"That was published in 1998, wasn't it?" I asked.

"Yes." He said.

"And the Phase 1 report concluded that it was appropriate and feasible to conduct a BIER VII-Phase 2 study didn't it? That study would be the definitive study to assess the health risks from exposure to low levels of ionizing radiation wouldn't it?" I asked.

"Yes." he said.

"I don't see in your report where you mention that you reviewed the results of the BEIR VII-Phase 2 study in preparing your report, Dr. Thomas." I said, pretending to be searching his report in an effort to find the missing citation.

"It isn't published, yet. So I didn't include it." He said.

"But that's not what I asked you Dr. Thomas. Did you review the BEIR VII-Phase 2 study before you prepared your report?"

"I'm sure I would have reviewed a preliminary draft of the Phase 2 report, but it hasn't been officially published, yet." He said.

"In fact you were one of the persons chosen for their 'diverse perspective and technical expertise' to review the report in draft form, weren't you?" I asked, reading from a copy of the Phase 2 report.

"Yes, . . . I was. How did you get that? You're not supposed to have a copy of that." He said, obviously a little perturbed.

"Now, Dr. Thomas. You've testified enough for Boyd, haven't you, to know that it's the lawyer that gets to ask the questions?" I asked.

"It's my understanding that the final draft of the document wouldn't be made public until sometime next year, in 2006." He said.

"Here is a copy of what I'm reading from." I said, passing a copy to him, Boyd's counsel, and the Commissioner. "I didn't say this was a final draft. But it does look like the one you reviewed prior to the time that you prepared your report in this case, doesn't it?"

"Yes." He said, hesitantly.

"In fact, we see your handwritten notes from time to in time in the margin, don't we?" I asked.

He nodded.

Before opposing counsel and the commissioner could read too far into the document, I began a long question, speech actually, full of righteous indignation and dripping with prejudice, which had been pieced together from the document. "Doctor, you would agree with me, wouldn't you, that the primary objective of this study [was] to develop the best possible risk estimate for exposure to low-dosage, low linear energy transfer radiation in human subjects?"

"Yes." He said.

"And the NRC determined that 'in the fifteen years since the publication of the previous BEIR report . . . much new information has become available on the health effects of ionizing radiation' including 'substantial new information on radiation-induced cancer . . . from the

Hiroshima and Nagasaki survivors, . . . progress . . . in areas of science that relates to the estimation of genetic (hereditary) effects of radiation . . ., [and] advances in cell and molecular biology. . . .'"

"That's true." He said, waiting for me to continue.

As I continued reading from my scripted questions, I observed the defense counsel and commissioner thumbing feverishly through their copies of the documents. "The BEIR VII committee concludes, doesn't it, 'that current scientific evidence is consistent with the hypothesis that there is a linear dose-response relationship between exposure to ionizing radiation and the development of radiation-induced solid cancers in humans [and it's] unlikely that a threshold exists for the induction of cancers'? In other words, any exposure to radiation causes an increased risk of cancer, right?"

"Where are you reading from?" the witness asked, looking at his lawyers.

"I'm on page 10, reading from the conclusion. The bottom line is Dr. Thomas, that the preeminent study in this field, a study that is intended to guide government and industry in developing guidelines for human exposure to ionizing radiation, has rejected the position taken by you and the Boyd experts to the extent that you have asserted there is a threshold of safe exposure to radiation. Isn't that so?"

"We object, your honor." The defense lawyer interrupted before Dr. Thomas answered.

"You don't have to call him 'your honor,'" I said.

"We object, Mr. Abbott." The defense lawyer corrected himself.

"What's your objection?" Mr. Abbott asked.

"This isn't a published document. And it says on page 10 that the draft manuscript is to remain confidential," the Boyd attorney said.

"So as 'to protect the deliberative processes' of the NRC." I said, reading from the conclusion of the sentence he had read. "I don't see how what we do here today will have any effect on the National Research Council's deliberative process.

"The point, Mr. Abbott, isn't whether this document has been published. The point is that it's part of the materials that the witness reviewed in deriving his opinions in this area, though he saw fit to omit it from the itemized list of things he said he had reviewed. Furthermore, it will be published, perhaps not with every jot and tittle that appears in the copy you have in your hand, but the conclusion will be the same. If I can borrow your phrase, 'the good people of this commonwealth' shouldn't be required to live under an outdated scientific paradigm simply because the Defendant Boyd Oil was successful in scheduling this hearing now as opposed to four months from now." I said, pounding my fist with righteous indignation on the conference table.

I looked over at Riza who had a concerned look on her face. At the time I thought she was worried that the commissioner might exclude my questions from the BEIR VII-Phase 2 report, so I added, "If you exclude this evidence you will put the trial court, and any appellate court that might someday review his decision, in the ridiculous position of having to pretend that this report doesn't exist when we all know, Dr. Thomas included, that the consensus of scientific opinion is contrary to the position he has stated, because the report will most certainly be published before any higher court gets around to ruling on this issue."

Mr. Abbott looked befuddled as he continued to leaf through the document, pausing form time to time to look up at opposing counsel. The huge conference room was completely silent. The blue and grey suited crowd had stopped clattering on its laptops. Riza sat with her lips pressed tightly together. The only movement in the room was from Mr. Walton who sat a few chairs to my right. He smiled as he shook his head from side to side, anticipating the ruling that was about to come.

"Well," Mr. Abbott finally said. "If it's not published, I don't see how I can allow it." A general sigh emanated from the crowd. It reminded me of the sound a home crowd makes when its star point guard misses a crucial free throw late in the game with the score tied. I thought Riza looked strangely relieved.

"Do you have anything else with this witness, Mr. Jessie?" The Commissioner asked, but he didn't look up from the papers in front of him.

Because the Commissioner had taken the air out of what I had intended to be my big finish, I fell back on a conclusion that I had used a few times in car wreck cases.

"Do you recall, Dr. Thomas, whether it was the Paul Newman character or the Elizabeth Taylor character in *Cat on a Hot Tin Roof* that tells Burl Ives, 'I smell mendacity in the air Big Daddy'?"

I guess that, because he had never tried a car wreck case, the defense lawyer forgot that he could object. Maybe he was curious to see what I would do next. Or maybe he knew that it didn't matter what I did next.

"No." Dr. Thomas said. "I don't recall."

"But you do smell it, don't you?" I asked. "Do you smell mendacity in the air?"

"I . . . I don't know what I smell." He said.

I turned to the Commissioner and said, "I think I'm about through. Let me check with my assistant and see if there is anything I left out."

I leaned over to Riza and put my arm across the back of her chair. As I whispered into her ear a question about whether there was anything else she thought we should cover, I studied her computer screen. It was not an instant-messaging page. Instead, it seemed to be some type of page that depicted the current pricing of various oil company stocks. Boyd's stock price was at the top of the page.

"Davy," she said already trying to console me over the expected loss, "you've done all you can do. You did a fine job. It doesn't matter if you prove that the Martha Oil Field is comparable to Hiroshima or Nagasaki. He's going to rule how he's going to rule. Don't beat yourself up over this. Some motions are just not meant to be won. But I've got to ask. How did you ever get your hands on that unpublished report?" She asked.

"Mr. Walton told me that the industry has been expecting it for some time. He thought that a draft copy might have gone to Thomas, and Walton suggested that I hire someone to go through the trash can outside Thomas' house periodically. I told Walton to hire somebody and sent him a check, but I think the old man might have done the search himself, judging by that smile on his face." I said.

Riza looked over at Mr. Walton. "What is it that Sullivan always says?" She asked.

"He's grinning like a cat eating shit out of a hairbrush." I whispered. "Do you think the record is ready for our appeal after a summary judgment?"

"Yes," she said.

"We have nothing further Mr. Commissioner." I said.

When the defense lawyer indicated that he had no questions for the witness, probably to avoid having me get another crack at him, the commissioner invited us to give our closing remarks.

I gave my closing argument without referring to my notes. I had been working on it for months, and however Quixotic the effort, I thought it went well.

I talked about how the presence of radioactivity on the land, whether or not the court decided that it presented a health risk, meant that the future use of the land would be restricted. Who would buy property that he knew was contaminated with radiation even if it was only contaminated a little bit? I reminded the commissioner that these properties were all that the plaintiffs had, and that the properties had been passed down from generation to generation going back to the time of Jenny C. Wiley. More importantly, it was all future generations would have. I concluded with the quote I had seen on a bumper sticker. I had intended to save the quote for trial, but I figured that I had better go ahead and use it. The quote is sometimes attributed to David Brower, the founder of the Sierra Club, and sometimes attributed to Chief Seattle. "We do not inherit the earth from our ancestors; we borrow it from our children."

Like Sullivan always says, "Just because it's on a bumper sticker doesn't mean it's not true."

Then his friend William would blow cigarette smoke skyward and respond, "Means it is true, Podzy."

The Boyd lawyer essentially read his argument from a yellow legal pad.

I think even the Boyd lawyers were surprised when the commissioner ruled from the bench after the conclusion of the arguments, rather than taking the matter under advisement. Clearly the commissioner appeared to be reading from a prepared text that was so detailed that I doubted at the time it could have been put together during the testimony or arguments presented that day. He struck Mr. Walton's testimony, and refused to strike Boyd's witnesses.

The folks in the blue and grey suits rushed out into the hallway, and it was difficult to hear over them as they shouted into their cell phones.

Mr. Carter came over to me and told me that he thought I did a good job. "That feller," he said, indicating the commissioner, "thinks that you could put TENORM on ice-cream and eat it." I smiled and shook his hand.

"Don't let the bastards grind you down Mr. Carter." I said.

He nodded, but before he left for the elevator, he made a point of telling me not to take the ruling too hard.

"You kinda look like you might be the one caught in the grinder." He said.

In a few minutes, the conference room was empty. Only Riza and I were still sitting at the enormous table, and she continued to watch her computer monitor. My luggage was downstairs in the rental car, but she had brought her hanging bag inside and placed it in the corner.

"I have to get back," I said, cramming the materials from the table in front of me into the briefcase that my brother had given me and fastening the latch. I stood and gestured toward the door indicating that I would wait for her.

"I know. You need to hurry. You go ahead. I'll catch a cab and fly back later on a commercial flight. I need to do some things here before I go, and I don't want to slow you down." she said.

"There can't be much left to do here." I said. Everybody was gone. Even Mr. Carter had left. "You can call Tim from the car on the way to the airport." I was curious about what she was going to tell him had happened.

"You go, and I'll see you later. I'll see if there is anything Tim wants me to do while I'm still here. Good luck with the baby." She said in a very business-like fashion as she was reaching into her purse to find her cell phone. I assumed at the time that she was going to call Sullivan to let him know what had just happened, and I assumed that everyone in Houston would know long before I arrived.

I grabbed my briefcase and raced to the elevator. I considered stopping on the way to the airport and getting a hamburger or some fast food to go, I was jittery and almost weak with hunger, but I didn't want to waste the time.

I thought about how Sullivan (really Riza) usually called ahead to the pilot and had him arrange for there to be sandwiches on board when we got there. I reconciled myself to the fact that there were usually chips and salted nuts in the compartment where the liquor was kept. Scotch and cashews didn't sound all that bad. It would be a repeat of the dinner I had the night before in my room. I had stayed up all night, periodically watching SportCenter, looking over my notes for the hearing, and writing a few lines for the short story that I had folded in half and crammed back into the breast pocket of my blazer. I hung the jacket in the bathroom so that my shower the next morning might steam out a few wrinkles from my travels.

Usually, after losing a motion or a trial, I would play the courtroom scene over and over in my mind, trying to determine if there was something I could have done differently to affect the outcome. Typically, as a young lawyer, the "what if" questions I would ask myself were about *not* doing something next time. What if I had not called that witness? What if I had stopped asking questions two questions earlier? What if I had limited the amount of money I requested?

But on the way to the airport, and even on the flight home, the only thing that went through my mind (besides the fact that Michelle told me on the cell phone that she was fine) was that Riza had been watching oil stock prices rather than taking notes at the hearing (well, that and the fact that when I got home, I would have to tell my pregnant wife that I was an adulterer who had given her a venereal disease).

I tried to divert my attention by looking through the folder of *Bar Journals* and *Supreme Court Digests* that Eileen had sent along for the trip. Apparently I had fallen a bit behind on my reading because there were several copies of each in the folder. I looked at the *Journals* first, generally just checking out the disciplinary rulings and deaths, until I got to the most recent edition which included the publication of short stories and poems submitted by lawyers to a contest the *Journal* held every year. I remember wondering if other professions (dentists, oncologists, etc.) were so jaded by their practices that they felt the need to encourage fiction writing.

Frankly, the short story winners were very good even though the stories were all about practicing law. The first place poem was okay, but second place was marginal. The shock came when I saw the third place poem: *Prufrock's Reprise*. There in black and white for all the world to see was my poem. Of course, the world wouldn't know that it was my poem because the author was listed as "Anonymous." I knew that I hadn't submitted it. I couldn't believe that the black-haired, freckled-face girl in Memphis had, but I thought she was the only person that might have seen it. However, as I looked more closely at the poem, I saw that a stanza had been added, like a chorus after the fourth and tenth stanzas that I had written:

Remember the clean, well-lighted Queen,
Kids' ice cream socials and teenage scene,
Grizzled old men drinking their coffee
Discussing weather, ballets Joffrey?

I had only told Beth about my Dairy Queen story. She must have been the person who modified the poem and sent it to the *Journal*. But how would she have gotten the poem? And if she did, why did she submit it? Why did she include the chorus? Did she just think the poem needed it (wasn't there a chorus of sorts in *Prufrock*)? Was she asking me to contact her, or was she saying goodbye?

Reading the poem made me think about the handwritten short story in my breast pocket. I pulled it out and tried to finish it. I made a few changes, added a few sentences, got frustrated, folded it back up, and put it back in my blazer.

In a few hours, the plane landed at the Raytheon Fixed Base Operation next to Hobby Airport in Houston, and I walked as fast as I could across the tarmac carrying my briefcase and hanging bag. The cell phone rang. It was Michelle. She didn't sound upset, but she did sound anxious.

"Davy," she said, "something's happening. Thank God you're back. I just went to the bathroom, and this bloody looking stone came out. The book calls it a 'plug' or 'bloody show.' I think we're having a baby. Where are you?" She asked excitedly.

"I'm at Raytheon by Hobby. I can be at our house in less than fifteen minutes. Do you want me to come get you, or do you want me to meet you and Jonathan at Methodist Hospital?" I asked.

"Come get me," she said, and I thought I could hear a sense of relief in her voice now that she knew that I was back in Houston. I could tell that she was reading from a checklist that she had prepared in advance for this situation. "I'll call Dr. Nathan's office, and let them know that we're on the way to the hospital. Then I'll call Mom and Jonathan. After that, I'll call the Hundred Acre Wood Preschool."

It was well known in certain circles (a euphemism for "inside Loop 610") in Houston that a student was unlikely to get into St. John's for kindergarten if he hadn't attended the Hundred Acre Wood Preschool. If you didn't go to St. John's, Harvard was a long shot.

The trouble was that the preschool had an unlisted phone number and address. Most prospective students were registered at birth. Neither Jonathan nor Michelle had attended the exclusive preschool, and Sullivan saw this as a generational failing that Michelle intended to rectify. After considerable effort to secure the address and telephone number from another female attorney in her firm, Michelle had made several trips by the ivy covered gate in front of the unmarked entrance to observe young, blonde women in their tennis dresses escorting toddlers through to a life of privilege and prestige.

"Sorry again about your hearing." Michelle said to me.

For a few seconds, I couldn't remember what hearing she was talking about.

As I approached my car in the FBO parking lot, I looked across the airport towards the skyline of downtown Houston. Even carrying only the briefcase and the light overnight bag, I was beginning to sweat so much that I had to stop, put the bags down, and loosen my tie and collar. In reality, there were three skylines: downtown, the Galleria, and the medical center. My house was close to downtown. Tonight would be spent in the medical center.

The late afternoon sun shone brightly on the stair-stepped glass buildings in the distance. Though it was mid-September, summer wouldn't give way to fall for another month in Houston. It was still miserably hot, and I could feel the sweat soaking through my jacket as I walked to the car. I finished taking off my tie when I got to the car.

From this distance and perspective, Houston was a gleaming, beautiful city, a testament to the newly minted wealth of an economy based on energy and commerce. I could make out the building where the law firm was, and I imagined that I could tell which office was mine. Many times, I had sat in that office and watched planes circle downtown as they began their approach into Hobby Airport. Often I had wondered where they were coming from and whom they were bringing to Houston. New arrivals, no doubt intrigued by the glimmer of the giant, new city, were excited by the prospect of wealth and opportunity, and oblivious to the fact that between the airport and downtown, lay the slums of the Fifth Ward.

Briefly, I thought about getting in my car and driving straight to Abilene. I could call Jonathan and ask him to pick up Michelle. In a few hours she would safely give birth to our child, and I would be well on my way out of the heat and humidity of Southeast Texas, and making my way toward the dry air of the wind-swept hills around Abilene. Fall wouldn't have arrived there either, but the evenings would already be cooler. Dad would have a lead on a good place to go dove hunting. In a few hours I could be sitting around a stock tank, drinking beer, and waiting for the dove to come flying in for a drink of water before roosting in the mesquite trees around the tank. I could just run away and avoid forever the painful conversation that I had now put off for so long. Or I could just leave the car at the airport and catch the next flight to Argentina. That way even my parents wouldn't be involved in my escape.

I threw my bags in the trunk of my car and raced up I-45 to the Southwest Freeway, and took the Kirby exit to West University. Before I turned into the neighborhood, I called Eileen to see if anything was happening at the office and to let her know that I would be taking Michelle to the hospital.

Eileen asked me about the hearing and about the *Davis* case. I told her about the commissioner's ruling at the *Carter* hearing, and that the *Davis* case had settled. "There is something weird about that *Davis* case." I said.

"What do you mean?" Eileen asked. "Back before you were a lawyer, we used to settle cases like that all the time. You are not feeling guilty about the fee, are you? One of the reasons the insurance company is settling is because they know you are willing to take the case to court if you have to."

I thought to myself that the company was more concerned about Sullivan taking the case to court than me, but I didn't say that. I was worried about the fee a little bit. On one hand, I was worried that it might be seen as excessive. On the other hand, I wished that the case had not been settled until after I left the firm and that I might have some claim to at least a portion of the fee.

"No, that's not it. I don't know what it is. I can't put my finger on it. I've looked at that video one hundred times, and there is something that just doesn't seem right." I said.

"Well, I'll look at it again, even though you know the insurance company looked at it more than we did."

"When you look at it Eileen, pay attention to the amount of time between the fondling and the kissing." I said. "It is like the doctor is making sure that whoever is watching the monitor would have had time to come stop him. I know that is good for our case, but it doesn't seem quite, I don't know, natural."

"A doctor is molesting his patient while she is knocked out on anesthesia. Nothing natural about that." Eileen said.

"Don't get me wrong." I said. "We're taking the hospital's money. Just do me a favor and look at it again when you get a chance."

Michelle was standing in the driveway outside of the wrought iron gate when I pulled up to the house. Her overnight bag and a box that contained an infant car seat were beside her. There was a blue bow on the top of the box. She held a new, very small video camera in her left hand. She was nicely dressed, and I noticed from a distance that her hair was fixed and that she had put on makeup. I put the car in park, got out, and opened her door. I took her bag and the box with the car seat and put them in the back seat. Michelle was crying uncontrollably as she got into the car. Tears had smudged her mascara, giving her raccoon eyes. She clutched a wadded-up Kleenex in her right hand.

"What's the matter?" I asked. A thought flashed through my head that Michelle had learned about the herpes, perhaps from a guilt-ridden Beth, or maybe Dr. Nathan had called, having given up on me living up to my promise to him, or (even worse) Michelle had experienced an outbreak of the disease.

Between sobs, I managed to hear that Michelle had called Dr. Nathan's office to tell him that she thought she was going into labor. The receptionist put her through to a nurse who explained that Dr. Nathan had suffered a stroke that morning. He was going to survive, but his optic nerve had been badly damaged. Arrangements had been made for another obstetrician to take over his patients on an emergency basis. Her name was Dr. Godsman. She would meet us in the delivery room at Methodist Hospital once Michelle was admitted to the hospital. "I don't know her," Michelle cried. "What if she's not a good doctor? She doesn't know anything about me or our baby. We don't even know if she has had a chance to see my chart."

I tried to tell Michelle that everything would be okay, but I'm sure that my own concerns made my assurances sound hollow and superficial. I backed out of the drive, and we left for the hospital with my reminding Michelle to put on her seatbelt and telling her to calm down and that everything would be fine.

PART III

ALL IS SAID . . .

. . . for I the Lord thy God am a jealous God, visiting the iniquity of the fathers upon the children . . .

—Exodus 20:5

22

THE AIRY, ATRIUM LOBBY of the Dunn Tower in the Methodist Hospital in Houston is as plush as the lobby of the Four Seasons Hotel in Houston, but the hospital is much larger than the hotel. Even during oil busts and economic downturns, there is constant growth and expansion in the Texas Medical Center, and the Methodist Hospital is one of the crown jewels in the sprawling complex. As I recall when we were there, the hospital had three buildings (Fondren, Dunn, and Main) on one side of Fannin Street and two (Scurlock and Smith) on the other.

From the Fannin Street doors of the Dunn Tower lobby, the room is the size of a Little League stadium. To the right, where the first base dugout would be, was a long, curved, blood-colored granite reception desk. At first base was a large fountain. In the center of the fountain was a statue of a naked man playing a lyre with his left hand and riding a dolphin. The man's right hand was held high in the air like a bucking bronc rider in a rodeo. I imagined that it once held a spear. In right-centerfield was a Starbucks, and café tables were clustered in right field. In left center, there was a statue of Jesus with a woman kneeling before him and an inscription from Matthew about healing the sick. At third base was a grand piano with a pianist that played requests. At shortstop, against a two-story support column, a bronze bust of Dr. DeBakey in scrubs peered down god-like over folded arms. Along the left field wall, stained glass windows divided the Wiess Memorial Chapel from the lobby. Thick carpet and gleaming marble floors provided pathways from the reception desk to elevator banks. Second-story glass walkways provided access between towers and parking garages. Quick-stepping valet attendants parked and returned cars, but unlike the Four Seasons, they rejected gratuities.

A round female attendant in a striped smock at the reception counter asked Michelle to sit in a wheelchair and wheeled her away to the elevators while I filled out the paperwork on a clipboard that another woman in a striped smock at the counter gave to me. Michelle had stopped crying, although she was still clutching the Kleenex and was obviously upset.

I sat on one of the leather-covered barstools next to the reception counter to complete the necessary paperwork. I assume it was because of the way my hand was shaking when I attempted to complete the forms that prompted the somewhat overly friendly receptionist to ask me if this was our first baby. Weakly, I circled the correct items on the form, checked the proper boxes regarding past medical history, filled out the biographical and insurance information, and indicated the reason for our visit.

As I nodded in response to the woman's question, I didn't speak to her. I could tell that she was speaking to me, trying in vain to make conversation, but I couldn't make out exactly what she was saying.

I didn't feel well. It was as if the room was closing in around me. I could tell that other people were around me, yet I could only make them out as shadowy shapes. I tried to focus on the lady in the striped smock who had handed me the clipboard, and then I looked back at the forms. The words on the pages were beginning to swim together, and I couldn't seem to get the pen that I had been provided and my insurance card to stay clamped under the clip at the top of the board. Still talking, the woman extended her hand toward me as I passed her back the clipboard, but I dropped it short of her hand as I tried to give it to her. It crashed on the granite countertop between us and the noise echoed across the vast lobby. I could feel the other people in the lobby looking at us the same way everybody in a restaurant looks at the waiter who drops a tray of dishes.

"It's going to be okay," she said. She spoke in a calming, soothing voice. She picked up the clipboard and thumbed through the pages checking to see that I had completed the appropriate sections. "People have babies here every day. Have you been up to the maternity floor before?"

"Yes," I managed to say, "during Lamaze classes. We toured the unit. It's in this building, isn't it?" My mouth was suddenly very dry—almost like the cottonmouth you get from running wind sprints after baseball practice. I looked across the room at the elevator bank. Nothing triggered my memory as far as having been in this room before. I wondered if there was a water fountain nearby.

I could remember bits and pieces of the building tour. It had been at the end of one of the few Lamaze classes that I had been able to attend. A dozen or so women in varying stages of pregnancy and their husbands, boyfriends, and significant others strolled through the beautiful hospital admiring the state-of-the-art facility. Jonathan had accompanied his sister on those occasions when I was out of town.

The highlight of the building tour had been the scene in front of the newborns' window. On the far side of the glass, sleeping infants wrapped tightly in pink or blue blankets squinted at happy grandparents and extended families that laughed and pointed at the window. You could almost feel the warmth on the visitors' side of the glass that came from the lights being used to ward off any jaundice on the babies' side of the window. Our tour guide had pointed out where the neonatal intensive care unit was as well as where surgical deliveries took place, but I couldn't at that point remember where those rooms were located in relation to the general maternity rooms. I remember being a little nervous in one of the elevators into which, being deep enough to transport a patient on a gurney, the entire Lamaze group had managed to cram. It wasn't so much claustrophobia as fear that one of the ladies might go into labor at any minute that caused me to be nervous.

"Maternity is on the sixth floor of this building, the Dunn Tower. Your wife is going to be in room 624," the receptionist said. "Take a deep breath Mr. Jessie. I'm sure everything is going to be okay." She smiled at me when she spoke and continued to sort through and stamp the various pages of paper that were in front of her, but there was a look of concern on her face.

I nodded that I understood, but when I opened my mouth to speak nothing would come out.

"Are you feeling okay, Mr. Jessie? You look very pale." She said looking up from her papers long enough to assess my condition. She handed me back my insurance card and I fumbled with my wallet as I tried to place it into the little slot between my credit cards.

I put my wallet back into my hip pocket and stood up from the stool on which I was seated at the reception counter. As I stepped away, I could feel my head spinning and knew that I was falling forward. I don't know if I passed out before or after I fell into the reception desk, striking my forehead on the edge of the granite. I don't remember the emergency medical personnel putting me on a gurney and taking me to the emergency room located in the adjacent tower called the Main Building.

I don't know how long I was out. It must have been some time. I had been dreaming my baseball dream. In my baseball dream, which I have been having since the time I played Little League at age eleven, the stadium lights behind the outfield form a cone that stretches from home plate to the outfield. I am playing shortstop and I am playing deep, almost to the outfield grass. Because they're at the far end of the cone in my dream, I can't make out the batter at home plate or the catcher and umpire or the people in the stands behind home or my dad who is in the dugout along the third base line, but I know that they're there.

The runner on third base breaks toward home at the crack of the bat because there are two outs. I move instinctively to my right, but I do not yet see the ball as it comes out of the cone formed by the backstop and the foul lines and the lights behind me. I hear the bat and I feel the crowd in the darkness behind where I know that home plate is suspended as the energy level rises with the contact of the hit. My dad doesn't say anything, but he steps to the screen that protects the dugout. He has hit me a thousand, maybe ten thousand, ground balls at short, and I hear his silent admonition to move to the ball, to play it in front of my body, to play it, and don't let it play me.

I can't really see him, although I can tell that the batter has thrown his bat behind him and started to run to first base. He's fast and running well and I can feel his speed as he strides down the line. I pick up a view of the ball as it comes out of a high, chopping bounce in the infield. The ball is taking too long to come down out of the bounce as I drift back toward the hole behind third base. I feel the runner on third reaching toward home. I will never get him out before he scores. The catcher, like a distant figure seen through the wrong end of a telescope, rips off his mask and blocks the plate shouting at me to throw it home. I know that by the time the ball comes down it will be too late for me to get the runner at home. Still, because there are already two outs, if I can get the runner at first base, I can avoid the run scoring. My only play is at first base.

The ball grows larger as it topspins out of the darkness toward me. I can make out the spin and even the seams on the ball as it falls out of the night sky. I position my body to make the throw as soon as the ball hits my glove, but the ball is taking too long to come down, and I know I'll never make the throw in time. Still, if the runner stumbles, or maybe if I put a little extra on the throw, there is a chance that I might throw him out at first. I turn my body almost parallel to the third base line. I'll catch the ball at my right shoulder and throw it to first in one motion if it will just come down. I stand there in the hole behind third waiting for the spinning ball to land in my glove over my right shoulder.

As I woke up, I felt a young emergency room physician patting me on my right shoulder. I was in a sterile hospital room with the attendant stitching together the laceration in my forehead. I couldn't see exactly what he was doing, and I couldn't feel the needle piercing my skin. Somehow I had the impression that he was sewing my forehead.

I was still groggy, and it took a moment for me to become aware of the fact that I was lying on my back with the young doctor pulling the stitches through and tying them off. He held the last stitch with a pair of forceps in his right hand, and he patted my right shoulder again with his left hand. He paused from his work to catch my eyes with his before resuming the completion of his sewing.

"Easy there," he said trying to get me to relax. "You took quite a spill. I'm just about to finish closing a two-inch tear in your forehead. You're going to have a little scar, but most of it will be above your hairline." He turned his attention away from my eyes and focused on his stitches. Then he gently turned my head from side to side to admire his handiwork and nodded approvingly.

I started to sit up.

"Don't get up, yet," the doctor said, with an air of authority. He didn't appear to be any older than I was.

"I have to go to the maternity floor," I said, trying to push myself up on my elbows before collapsing back down on the upholstered table.

"Yeah, I know," the doctor said. "Your wife is doing fine, and we'll have you up there in just a minute. She called down here to check on you. I told her that you were going to need a few stitches. I'm wondering if I should have used a few more. I put one long loop on the underside to try and minimize the scarring. Now I'm second-guessing myself about whether one or two more in the surface layer of your skin might have been better."

"I'm sure it'll be fine," I said. "How long have I been here?" I asked trying to remember what had happened at the reception desk. My head was beginning to throb with pain, and I had the urge to scratch at the stitches with my hand. I could remember being at the reception desk and thinking that I was beginning to fall forward, but I couldn't remember anything after that. As I lay back, I found myself scanning the ceiling involuntarily for video cameras. There was one on the ceiling in the hallway outside the room.

"You've got to keep your hands away from those stitches," he said, gently taking my hand and placing it at my side. "It's probably been an hour or so since you fell. In addition to talking to her, I've gotten a couple of reports on your wife from her doctor. Your wife is fine and resting in her room. Apparently her delivery is progressing according to the book. You might be surprised, but this kind of thing happens fairly often. New fathers pass out all the time. Usually, it's the first sight of blood in the delivery room that causes the dad to faint. In your case, I wonder, when was the last time you ate?"

"I don't know," I said. when I tried to think back to my last meal, I couldn't remember it. "I'm sure I haven't had anything substantial in several days." I thought to myself that I had probably been surviving on coffee and scotch with very little sleep. "I really do have to go to my wife's room now," I said. "I'm worried about her, and I need to talk to her about something."

"Let me finish this up, and I'll get an orderly to take you up in a wheelchair, if you'll promise to come back later and let me look at how this is holding. It's a rather jagged tear. I'll give you some written instructions for wound care at that time," the doctor said. He placed the instruments that he had been using on a rolling tray, peeled off the latex gloves he was wearing, and threw them in a trash can in the corner of the room. An attendant came into the room as the doctor released the trashcan lid with his foot. The doctor paused before going out of the room and looked at me.

"I promise," I said to both of them. "But where am I?"

They both laughed, and the young doctor told the attendant how to get to the maternity ward.

"One more thing, doctor, if you don't mind my asking."

"Sure, what is it?"

"What are cameras like that one for?" I asked pointing at the camera on the ceiling outside the room.

"Oh that," he said. "I don't really know. To tell you the truth, I forget that it is even there. I'm not sure it even works . . . I think it is like one of those dummy cameras in department stores that are meant to deter shoplifting. You know, we get all kinds of activity in an emergency room."

I sat in the wheelchair on the elevator with my blazer draped over my lap. The wheelchair attendant took me from the Main Building through a series of hallways over to the Dunn Tower, stopped at the elevator control panel, and pressed the button for the sixth floor.

The Methodist Hospital buildings on this side of the street did not have thirteen floors, but the two buildings on the other side of the street each had more than twenty. Taking depositions before in those buildings, it had struck me as odd that neither had a thirteenth floor. Certainly there was no thirteenth floor in the bank tower where the law firm's offices were located. I can't remember ever seeing a thirteenth floor in a hotel. At the Peabody, the thirteenth floor was labeled "S" — I guess for "skyway" or maybe for "where ducks Sleep." However, it seemed to me that a building constructed with religious donations and that was dedicated to the performance of the healing arts of medical science could avoid leaning on superstition. Maybe whatever company made the elevator control panels just didn't make one with a thirteenth floor option. Or maybe the Methodists were covering all of their bases. Quietly, almost imperceptibly, the Muzak piped into the elevator played an instrumental version of The Beatles' *In My Life*. I hummed along with the tune interrupted only by the gentle "bing" of the elevator as we whisked by floors.

As the elevator moved upwards, I thought about how, despite our enhanced understanding of the physical world, we continued to think about heaven and hell as if we lived in a cheap, low-rise apartment complex. Hell was located in the basement parking garage, we lived on the ground floor because it was easier to move your stuff in and out of the apartment, and God lived on the next floor up, which had a better view. Sure, we can rationally explain that at the earth's core is molten magma and beyond the atmosphere is an ever-expanding universe of galaxies, but I defy anyone to find a picture of Jesus praying when He's not looking up as if the angels in the apartment above Him had just dropped something heavy on their floor/His ceiling that landed with a thud.

It didn't matter whether the painting of Jesus hung in a museum or was for sale at the flea market on Interstate 20 in Abilene. If He's praying, He's looking up to see if a response is forthcoming. Looking up while you pray is akin to checking the number of bars on your cell phone to see if you are in a good service area. Conversely, has there ever been a radio broadcast of a Church of Christ sermon in which some hapless sinner isn't being thrown down a bottomless stairwell into the damnation of a dimly lit, un-airconditioned—sometimes referred to as a fiery pit—basement garage?

At some point during the elevator ride, my cell phone rang. I found it in my pocket, saw the call was from the office, and observed the scowl on the wheelchair attendant's face as I said, "Hello?" He obviously didn't understand why a young lawyer with a head injury on his way to see his wife who was in labor would bother to take a call from the office. Probably only a young lawyer would understand that.

"Davy, you were right. There is something funny about this Davis video."

"Eileen, what are you still doing at the office?" I asked. "Hang on a second. I'm getting off an elevator."

When the doors opened on the maternity floor, I asked the attendant pushing the wheelchair if I could walk to Michelle's room and tried to explain to him that I had to take this call. He agreed and pressed a button to ride the elevator back down, and I walked slowly away from the wheelchair and elevator, trying to appear as calm and casual as I could, until the doors closed behind me. "What are you talking about?" I said to Eileen.

"I had a couple of the law clerks figure out how to hook a laptop up to the big screen TV in the large conference room. We've been watching the video over and over for the last hour or so."

I tried to picture the scene in the conference room and hoped that Mr. Peters wasn't there to see it. Of course, Sullivan wasn't there. Surely he must be either at the hospital or on his way with Michelle's mom. "There is something about the timing, isn't there?"

"No, well there is that. It is like the doctor is deliberately trying to get caught, or at least seen by the camera. But that is not why I called," Eileen said and paused for effect. "She smiles."

"What?" I asked.

"Yeah, Tamara Davis smiles. You can't clearly see her face when the doctor leans over to kiss her because his body blocks her face from the camera. But when he stands up straight and pulls the gown and covers up over her, Tamara's expression has changed. She has just the slightest Mona Lisa smile."

I had not noticed the change in expression myself even though I had looked at the video many times. But I could picture in my mind what Eileen was describing. I knew she was right. "Would she smile even if she was doped up on anesthesia?"

"Maybe, but I think there is something else going on."

"I better call Tamara. Can you give me her phone number?" I stopped at a nurses' station and asked to borrow a pen. I wrote down on my hand the phone number that Eileen gave me, hung up the phone, and then sprinted down the gleaming tiled hall.

When I got to room 624, the door was closed. Fortunately the name "Michelle Jessie" was written on a small grease board pinned to the wall beside the door. I leaned my ear against the door, trying to listen to what was going on in the room. It sounded like a television was playing, and in a few seconds I figured out that Michelle was probably watching a "Shrek" DVD. One of the lawyers' wives from Peters & Sullivan had given her a boxed set of the two Shrek movies, along with his-and-her stuffed green ogres, at Michelle's baby shower a few months ago. Michelle had probably packed the two DVDs in her bag to take to the hospital so that our baby could listen to the movies while waiting to be born.

We had both watched the movies since receiving the gift, but we had not watched them together. Michelle had seen them by herself on a rainy Saturday at our house while I was flying around the country on Sullivan's private jet. I had watched the movies on successive nights when I woke up at about three and went downstairs to watch television. We both agreed that the first movie was the best, except we wished the cat had been introduced in the original. There was already talk of a third movie in the series. It would probably be *Shrek vs. Rocky* or *Shrek Meets Darth Vader*. After all, it was the author of Ecclesiastes that told us that "There is no new thing under the sun."

As I listened at the door, I could tell by the theme song playing in the background that Shrek was wandering in the wilderness on his way back to his swamp:

I heard there was a secret chord
That David played, and it pleased the Lord,
But you don't really care for music, do you?
It goes like this: the fourth, the fifth
The minor fall, the major lift.
The baffled king composing hallelujah.

I remember wondering at the time that I first saw the movie what the hell that song had to do with anything in the film.

On the other side of the door, my wife was watching a child's fairy-tale about loving somebody for who they are on the inside, rather than how they appear on the outside, while some young man with a lilting voice was singing the words of the raspy Leonard Cohen tune and changing them all around and adding verses that I didn't remember.

In a moment, I would go through that door and shatter Michelle's fairytale. If I didn't go through the door, it would probably be shattered anyway, since she would find out about it without me telling her, and I thought that was almost as bad as anything I had done to that point. She would never be able to love the inside of me again. I was a keeper of secrets that, when revealed, would make me far more repulsive than any animated, green ogre because in my mind those secrets didn't make me more like anybody else. The princess in "Shrek" hides the fact that she turns into an ogre at night, but how is that going to be a turnoff for a fellow ogre? What I had done at night, or at least under the cover of darkness, would be completely foreign and incomprehensible to Michelle. I had to tell her now, if not for her sake, then for my sake, and, of course, for the baby's sake.

I knew that I should have told her earlier.

With my arms stretched across to the framing on each side of the door, I lightly banged my head against it. I heard Michelle say from the other side, "Come in." I paused, took a deep breath, and let out a long sigh. The door seemed extremely heavy as I pushed it open.

As I went into Michelle's room, I saw that she was in bed and wearing a hospital gown. There was an IV bag hanging on a metal stand beside the bed and a monitor with orange waves on the screen was positioned to one side. In one corner of the room was an upholstered wingback chair. Michelle's bag and the little video camera were resting in the chair.

Her mother was seated at the head of the bed watching the movie with Michelle. They were staring at the television mounted on the wall. Both were smiling and seemed glad to see me. I could tell that Michelle was worried, but I assumed that had something to do with either my head wound or the fact that her regular doctor wouldn't be delivering the baby. So far she didn't know that there really was something that should be causing her concern.

The orange waves on the monitor began to change and I could tell that Michelle was gripping her mother's hand more tightly. Michelle squeezed her eyes closed and then relaxed them open as the waves returned to their uniform pattern on the screen. Michelle's mom looked at her watch.

"That was a pretty good one, wasn't it?" Amy asked trying to sound upbeat and lighthearted. "I don't imagine it will be very long now before they give you the epidural. Are you better, now? That was a bigger one."

Michelle nodded and rested a moment before focusing on me. She blew three or four quick breaths like she was blowing out the candles on an invisible birthday cake. "I thought they were going to stitch you up," she said to me, also straining to sound upbeat.

"They did," I said and raised my hand to my forehead. The skin was numb, but my head was throbbing with pain. Warm blood was oozing out of the stitched laceration and dribbling down toward my face. I took a tissue from a box on a bureau in the room and blotted the blood.

"I have to talk to you," I said. Michelle and her mom both could tell from the tone of my voice that I had something serious to say. The forced smiles disappeared from their faces and they looked at me, waiting for me to say what it was I had to say.

"What about your head?" Michelle asked when I didn't begin. She pointed the remote control at the television and clicked off the power. "Can it wait until you have your head looked at again?"

"I'll go back down to the emergency room in a minute," I said. "I have to talk to you now." I looked at Amy, who took her hand away from Michelle's hand and stepped away from the bed. "Please, Amy. I'll just be a minute."

Amy looked at me in a piercing, cynical way, trying to surmise what I was about to say. Her look said that now was not the time, and this was not the place to begin any in-depth philosophical discussion. She didn't know what I was going to say, but Amy sensed that she needed to protect her child even as Michelle was about to deliver her a grand-child. Amy smoothed her skirt as she stood up from the bed and walked across the room. She hesitated at the door behind me. I didn't begin until I heard the heavy door close behind her.

"I have herpes," I blurted out and fell across the bed, talking into the mattress. It felt like I was across the room watching myself con-fess to my wife what had happened. In all the times I had practiced making this speech, I had never envisioned making it in Michelle's hospital bed while we waited for our son to be delivered. "I'm sorry. I'm afraid I may have given it to you. I'm worried that the baby will get it, if he's delivered vaginally. It may already be too late. Please, have the doctor do a C-section." I began to cry. With the back of my hands, I wiped away the tears that were streaming down my face. I tried to focus on Michelle's eyes as she processed the information, but I couldn't look at her.

"What are you saying?" Michelle asked. She seemed to be measuring her words as she asked me question after question. "What do you mean, you have herpes? Are you sure? What is it? Why didn't you tell me? Where did you get it? When did you get it? How long have you known? Why do I have to have a C-section? I don't have it, do I? What about the baby?" She was sitting up in bed, glaring at me. "What about our baby, Davy?"

Before I could answer any of the questions, the orange waves on the monitor began to change again by dipping higher and lower, and Michelle gripped her face in pain with the contraction. We both watched the monitor. As the contraction subsided, Michelle took a series of deliberate breaths again through her pursed lips, her hands still clenching the bed sheet on either side of her.

"I know that I owe you answers to all of your questions. I will answer them. But right now I need you to call the doctor. Please call the doctor," I said anxiously. "I'm sorry. Please, hurry." Michelle reached up to a button on a call device that had been looped around the headboard of the bed. She held the button down, continued with her controlled breathing, and stared at me waiting for the answers to the questions she had asked me.

In a moment, a female nurse came through the door. I was still lying across the foot of the bed but I had rolled over on to my back. Blood and tears were running down my face. The nurse started toward Michelle, and then stopped when she saw me. "What's wrong?" she asked. "Are you okay?" she asked, looking at me as I struggled to sit up.

"No," I said too loudly. "We need the delivery doctor now," I said trying not to shout. She stepped toward me as if there was something wrong with me and she was going to examine me. "I'm fine but we need to talk to the delivery doctor immediately," I said.

The nurse turned on her heels and left the room.

"Where did you get it?" Michelle asked. She didn't wait for an answer. "How long have you known?" Again, she didn't wait for me to respond. "What can it do to the baby?"

Before I could answer the last question, a young woman in scrubs that I took to be Dr. Godsman burst into the room. "What can what do to the baby?" the woman demanded. She walked quickly to the side of the bed.

"Tell her," Michelle said sternly to me. "Tell her all of it, Davy, and don't leave anything out."

"I have genital herpes, doctor. I've never told Michelle before now. I'm worried that I may have infected her and the child. Is it still possible to do a C-section? Is it possible to see if Michelle and the baby are okay?"

The doctor's eyes widened and then narrowed. In three quick steps, she moved to Michelle. I stood and stepped away from the bed as the doctor raised the sheet from the foot of the bed. "You're only at about three centimeters, and the baby's head has not crowned." Dr. Godsman said as if she were going over the options in her head as she spoke. "I can't really tell one way or the other at this point if you have herpes, or if you're having an outbreak now. I also can't be sure that the baby isn't infected already. But, if you're experiencing an outbreak, your baby could become infected, especially if he moves farther down the birth canal. I'll order a medication that we would've used as a preventative measure," she said shaking her head, "but I doubt that'll do much good now. This kind of infection, contracted at birth, could be very dangerous for an infant. Complications include blindness, retardation, even death. Given the risks and the lack of information we have, I'd recommend that we proceed with a Cesarean section."

She walked quickly over to the monitor and looked at a strip of paper coming from the machine. "Your contractions are coming closer together now. We can be in the operating room and deliver the child in less than twenty minutes."

I walked to the side of the bed. "I'm sorry, Michelle," I said. She took my hand, and we both started to cry. For a moment I couldn't say anything. I was trying to think of what to say next. "I've tried to tell you for the last six months, but I just wouldn't let myself. My guilt, my shame, my fear, all of it just kept me from telling you."

Michelle didn't say anything, and squeezed my hand very hard. She began to shake her head from side to side and I thought that she might start screaming.

"Excuse me, Mr. Jessie," the doctor said. "I know you two must talk. You can do that in an hour or so. Right now, I need to get your wife to the operating room and deliver your baby." The doctor had her hands on my shoulders and looked into my eyes as she spoke. She was directing me out of the room.

Suddenly the room was filled with nurses in scrubs busily hurrying around the room. In a synchronized, almost choreographed fashion, they transferred Michelle to a smaller bed and rolled her out the door and off to an operating room. Amy came back into the room where I was and Tim was with her. Before the doctor and I reached the door, the doctor turned to me and held my chin so that she could observe my forehead.

"You need to have that head re-stitched," she said. "Why don't you run back down to the emergency room and come back after the doctor has added a stitch or two?" Dr. Godsman turned to the Sullivans. "Grandparents, I presume?" She said, trying to force a smile.

"Parents of the bride," Tim managed to say as he tucked his thumbs into the lapels of his sport coat and bounced up on his toes. He was beaming with pride and wanted the doctor to understand that this was his show.

The doctor faced Tim directly while speaking to both Amy and him. The smile disappeared from his face as the doctor spoke. "I'm sure you are familiar with a C-section procedure. I think it's necessary in this instance because of certain complications. I pray that all will go well and you can see your grandson and your daughter in a little while. The operating room is on this floor. You can wait for us here, or in the waiting area down the hall. I will find you after the procedure." With that, Dr. Godsman was gone as quickly as she had arrived.

I was following her out the door when Tim caught me by the arm. He glared at me.

"What is going on?" he asked. I could see the anger rising in his face. "What is wrong with Michelle? Has something happened to the baby? Tell me what's happening?" he demanded.

I met his stare and tried to say in as even a tone as possible, "Michelle is going to have a C-section in order to protect the baby. I've got to go get this cut stitched up again. I'll be back here in a minute." Tim let go of my arm and looked questioningly at his wife. I walked out of the room and down the hall to the elevator.

As the door to the room closed behind me, I heard Tim shout in my direction, "Protect the baby from what?" The words trailed off as the heavy door closed behind me, but it was clear that Sullivan's voice was full of righteous indignation.

23

WHEN I GOT TO THE EMERGENCY ROOM back in the Main Building, Jonathan was already there waiting for me. I wondered how he knew to meet me there. Probably he had been upstairs, was told where I went, and had taken a more direct route to the emergency room than I, lost in my thoughts as I blindly shuffled through the corridors of the hospital. After completing some paperwork intended to have the young physician who had already attempted to stitch my head try his hand again, I was led to a room and told to lie down on a bed.

I closed my eyes and tried to start my baseball dream. In my conscious mind, I was trying to insert rational thoughts into my dream so that if I did fall asleep maybe, for once, the dream would come out all right. I would still be waiting for the ball to come down out of the night sky, though I was thinking that maybe I could catch the ball with my throwing hand and shave a few milliseconds off to get the runner going to first. Jonathan, who had followed me into the private room, was smiling with his hand on my shoulder when I opened my eyes, unable to sleep. It was nice of him to be there, but I wondered if I closed my eyes would he go away, if all of this would go away, and I could go to sleep and get back to my baseball game. It was as futile to try to sleep as it would have been to project a favorable outcome into my dream.

"Man, you look like shit," Jonathan said after waiting a reasonable amount of time for me to begin the conversation.

As a debate team, Jonathan and I had not been a particularly formidable duo, but I think we were respectable. Texas Tech, at the time, was not seen as one of the national powerhouses of collegiate debate. Still, by the time Jonathan was a senior and I was a junior, we won our share of rounds against the likes of the Baylor Bears and the Houston Cougars. More importantly, we got to be friends and could count on each other to stand up and take a turn at the podium even when we knew that we sometimes had very little to say to contradict the other side's case. We thought of ourselves as having been in the trenches together.

I liked Jonathan. I liked how after the first day in the first tournament we debated together, rather than getting upset that we had just lost four consecutive rounds, he just said, "Let's go drink a bunch of beer and see if we can see Jesus." He was his own person, and he didn't mind being on the side of the underdog. If Michelle went to law school to please her father, Jonathan had gone so that he could be independent of his father. And what else are you going to do with a major in political science and a minor in debate from Tech?

In law school, Jonathan and I thought of ourselves as two people among a very small minority who saw the law as a means of equalizing opportunity rather than as a tool for protecting wealth. We were friends. We tried to be honest with each other. Of course the best thing to come of the friendship, to me, was Jonathan's introduction of me to his sister. Now my dishonesty with her had cost me—how much I could not yet say—I only knew it had cost me. In any event, it would serve no purpose to try to pretend that everything was all right with Jonathan. To whatever extent I trusted and relied on him, Michelle trusted and relied on him more, and I assumed that it was Jonathan she would have talked to right before surgery.

"I feel like shit. I wish I could just go to sleep," I said. "I wonder if they would give me a sedative. Has Michelle had the baby yet?" Even without a sedative, I felt groggy and like I was slurring my words when I tried to speak. I had lost all track of time.

The young doctor came in followed by a nurse with a rolling tray of instruments. The doctor clucked his tongue and examined my head. He put on a pair of latex gloves and went to work to repair the open wound. "Let's see if we can get this closed this time," he said.

I tried to lay as still as possible and neither Jonathan nor I said anything. When he finished, the doctor asked Jonathan to take me back to the maternity ward.

Jonathan nodded to the doctor and nurse as they left. "The baby should be along any minute now," he said. "They sent me down to come get you. Why don't you stay in the wheelchair this trip?" There was a wheelchair positioned by the end of the bed. He lifted my left arm over his shoulder and helped me as I swung out of the bed and stumbled into the chair.

"I've messed things up pretty badly, Jonathan," I said as I slumped down into the chair.

"Sounds like," he said. "For somebody who has never had a problem in his life, you've managed to jump to the front of the line." While he was trying to be lighthearted, I could tell that he was genuinely concerned about what was happening. It was obvious that he had talked to Michelle or her mom.

"Did you talk to Michelle? Did she tell you about the affair? Did she tell you about the herpes?" I asked.

"Well, she asked me about it. I only got to see her a second before they took her in for the C-section. I told her I didn't know anything about it. I don't. I really don't know where you got it. But listen Davy, I know Michelle loves you. I don't know if she'll ever get over this, but once upon a time she did love you. She's going to need you to grow up and be there for her tonight. You owe her at least that much," he said, trying to sound encouraging while helping me to get comfortable in the wheelchair.

"I don't think it's going to matter whether she ever loved me," I said. "I don't think there is ever going to be any getting over this."

I asked if everybody knew, and he told me that his parents didn't know yet what was happening. They just knew that there was some complication that necessitated a C-section. He said he expected that Michelle would tell her mom after the surgery when the doctors knew more about any problems there might be. Michelle would avoid giving her mom something else to worry about, something other than the C-section, if she could. After the delivery though, we both knew that Michelle would tell her mom everything.

My parents had not arrived at the hospital yet. Jonathan had called them after Michelle called him before I picked her up to take her to the hospital. They were on their way from Abilene. Jonathan had talked to them again in the car and had given them directions to the medical center. Jonathan told me that Rod Day and his wife were both at the hospital, and Jonathan had asked them to wait for my parents in the lobby. Jonathan told me that he had caught Rod on his cell phone celebrating the victory in the *Fulshear* case at Brennan's. Jonathan had told my parents about the C-section the last time he spoke to them, but he had not told them the reason for the surgery. He thought they would be getting to the hospital very soon.

I reached my hand to the crusty stitches on my forehead as I sat up. I fought back the need to vomit as Jonathan spun the wheelchair around and wheeled it toward the door.

"Are you okay?" he asked and paused to bend over and look at me face to face to determine to his own satisfaction whether I was telling the truth.

I nodded, and Jonathan began pushing me down the series of hallways to the Dunn Tower elevator. He pressed the button on the wall to call the elevator, put his hands on his hips, and let out a long sigh.

"Listen," I said. "I'm sorry I have to do this. I've got to make a call. It's for work."

"Work?" Jonathan asked. "Why would you be worried about work right now?"

"I don't know," I said. "But I am. It will only take a minute." I pulled out my cell phone and dialed the number I had written on my hand.

"I don't think this is a good idea. You are in no condition to be making calls right now," he said.

While the phone was ringing, Jonathan said, "Look, there is something I have to talk to you about also." The elevator door opened, but we let it close without getting on and Jonathan pressed the button for another one. I started to hang up the phone to find out what it was that Jonathan wanted to talk about when Tamara Davis answered the phone.

"Tamara, this is Davy. I'm sorry to bother you, but I need to ask you something."

"Is there something wrong? Am I still going to get my settlement?" she asked, her voice immediately full of concern.

"Well, I don't know. Tamara, when I asked you the other day if you knew anybody at the hospital, your mother answered and said no. But you didn't answer."

There was silence on the other end of the phone. I looked up at Jonathan who was tapping one foot on the floor.

"So let me ask you this time. Not your mother. Did you know anybody at the hospital?"

It is difficult to say with any accuracy what transpired next in the conversation. Essentially, Tamara started crying and saying something about how she knew this wouldn't work but that her boyfriend Jeff—Dr. Ammons—had put her up to it and that he had all these bills from medical school and college, and they were just trying to get a fresh start out from under all of that debt. I tried to get her to stop crying and managed to tell her that I would have to call her back when I figured out what to do next. Another elevator door opened, Jonathan kept telling me that we had to go, and finally she calmed down enough that I could hang up and Jonathan wheeled me on to the elevator.

We had gone only a floor or two when Jonathan said, "That didn't seem to go so well. I told you that you were in no condition to be making calls."

"No," I said, "I still don't have it resolved either. I probably never will. I seem to have a knack for making all the women around me cry." I thought he might be fishing for an explanation, but I wasn't going to tell anybody that I didn't have to tell about Tamara Davis. It turns out that wasn't what he wanted to talk to me about.

"I hate to ask you, man, but what happened in Kentucky?" he asked without looking directly at me.

"I lost the motion," I said. "The judge struck our expert and refused to strike the defendant's experts."

"Yeah, I know that," he said watching the row of lights above the elevator. "Dad told me that just now in the hallway outside the surgical delivery room. They're all speculating about whether you're having a nervous breakdown or something because you lost the hearing. I didn't tell them about the affair or the herpes, and, like I said, I was the only one in the room when Michelle tried to tell me what was going on. Mom and Dad think your behavior has something to do with the hearing in Kentucky."

"Screw the hearing. Screw Kentucky," I said.

"I agree with that. I'm not asking about what happened at the hearing. I mean, what happened to Riza?" Jonathan asked. He looked back down at me in the chair. "I know you have a few issues to deal with right now, and I assure you that I'm not trying to insert myself into this drama. But I just had to find out, and I don't know anybody else to ask."

"What do you mean? I don't know anything about something happening to Riza." I said.

"She didn't come home," Jonathan said. A muffled bong signaled the arrival of the elevator to our floor. The doors opened.

"She's probably just working on some other case," I said, guessing. Jonathan pushed the wheelchair out of the elevator. "She was going to take a commercial flight," I said. "Maybe your dad sent her to work on something else after she left Kentucky. I'm sure that she'll be home tonight or in the next day or so." I tried to remember if she had said anything about having to go somewhere else after the hearing. I couldn't think of anything, but I wasn't thinking all that clearly.

"I don't think so," Jonathan said. He sounded genuinely concerned. "I went by her condo and it's for sale. I don't think she's coming home. She must have told a listing agent to sell the house the day before she left for Kentucky. She doesn't answer her cell phone. It's like she's disappeared." The elevator doors closed behind us and Jonathan pushed the wheelchair down the hall of the sixth floor of the Dunn Tower. Neither of us said anything else. Both of us were thinking about where Riza could have gone.

When we turned the corner in the hallway, Tim Sullivan was standing in front of us. I noticed for the first time that he was wearing an olive plaid sport coat with olive slacks and a purple tie that perfectly matched a thread in the coat. In his left hand, he held a bottle of Far Niente chardonnay. He motioned back toward the elevator with his right hand and attempted a smile.

"Gentlemen," he said.

I nodded, and Jonathan said, "Hi, Dad," as he started to push the wheelchair past his father.

"Why don't you let me take over?" Sullivan asked and stepped behind the wheelchair.

"Really, I'm fine to walk," I said.

Jonathan looked down at me, and shook his head. "He's all yours," he said to his dad and walked down the hall to where Michelle's mother was pacing the floor. I saw her stop pacing long enough to give Jonathan a hug when he walked up to her. Tim pulled the chair back around the corner, pressed the call button for the elevator, wheeled me into the elevator when it opened, and pressed the "door close" button on the panel.

"I'm fine, really," I said. "I'd just as soon walk."

"Oh, ride," Sullivan said while reading the options on the elevator control panel. "I think I know where we're going. There is a chapel downstairs in this building where we can find some privacy."

Sullivan pressed the button for the first floor, where I assumed the chapel would be located. I sighed, anticipating the cross-examination that I knew would be coming. I wondered if Sullivan was going to start the examination there in the elevator, or if he would wait until we got to the chapel.

My mind began to wander across the various trials I had attended with Sullivan, and I thought about the cross-examinations I had seen him do. Each was a work of art. In most trials there would be one or two key witnesses. With each of these witnesses, Sullivan had a "short" version or a "long" version of the questioning.

The short version was for those occasions when the opponent passed his witness with only a few minutes remaining before lunch or five o'clock, thinking that the jury would leave the courthouse with the impression that the opponent desired, or when the opponent had spent a particularly long time with the witness and the jury looked completely bored. Sullivan would fire off a zinger before the judge could adjourn or opposing counsel could return to his chair. In my mind, I could hear him asking the witness, "Sir, considering preparation time, first-class travel, conferring with Elihu Root—*gesture toward defense counsel*—at the Palm over porterhouses and pinot noir, two nights at the Ritz, and your considerable time today, it only cost the defendant thirty-eight thousand dollars for you to come entertain us this afternoon. I'm excluding, of course, what the other half of this Laurel and Hardy review—*another gesture toward defense counsel*—might have cost."

The longer version was an orchestrated, if not rehearsed, event. Sullivan never wrote out his questions, preferring to stack the documents he was going to use in the order he wanted to present them, and relying on a rough outline of the topics he intended to cover. After seeing Sullivan do the long version a few times, I began to notice that more than the penetrating nature of his questions or the juxtaposition of the documents with the testimony, his tone of voice was the dramatic force in the examination. He would begin in a normal voice and increase his volume with each question in a furious crescendo. The most salient point, however, would come when Sullivan would pause, after almost shouting at the witness, and then, in little more than a whisper and with the court room so quiet that you could hear the witness breathing, Sullivan would ask the question that he really wanted to ask.

When I first went to work for Peters & Sullivan, I just carried luggage when I went with Sullivan to trial. I would be responsible for making sure everything was in the file and that the witnesses were lined up and had what they needed to be prepared. Sullivan required that I sit at counsel table with him and take notes throughout the trial. After a while, I took very few notes because I found that I performed better if I kept my head up and watched what was going on in the courtroom, rather than trying to write down everything the witness said.

As a "baby" lawyer, notes were important. At the end of the trial day, Tim, Riza, our next witness, and I would sit in a bar or a hotel room drinking scotch, Far Niente chardonnay, or Coronas with lime wedges, and go over the notes from the day. Sometimes, Tim might jot down something on a pad. Usually he would just listen and add to what Riza and I had failed to write down.

There were times I thought that the recital of our notes from the day was intended to summarize for Tim what the actual testimony had been, as filtered through a listener. Did we get the point that Tim was trying to make with the witness? Riza and I served as Tim's mock jury. He could tell what points he needed to beef up by finding out what we heard. There were other times that I thought Tim had me read my notes out loud just so he could be sure that I was following and learning the techniques he had used.

Once during trial Sullivan was cross-examining a witness. I remember Sullivan standing next to the witness, showing him a document. Sullivan stopped his chain of questions, and, still on the record, shouted across the courtroom for me to "be sure and write this down in my notes, because it was going to be a very important point." The defense counsel objected to Sullivan's highlighting the testimony, but Sullivan just explained to the judge how important it was for a young lawyer to learn to take good notes. The judge nodded knowingly, no doubt cognizant of the fact that the defense counsel's objection had further highlighted the testimony and told Sullivan to "move along" without actually ruling on the objection. I at least tried to look like I was writing down everything that the witness said in response to the question that followed. I did look up from my legal pad long enough to notice that most of the jurors had moved forward to the edge of their seats to see what Sullivan's next question was going to be.

As I got a little more experienced, I got to put on a few witnesses. In time, we divided the trial responsibilities. Sullivan would take the witnesses he wanted, and I would get the rest. He would pick the jury, and I would get to do the opening statement. Truthfully, by the time Sullivan finished picking the jury, everybody knew what the case was about and what the evidence was going to be, so an opening statement was almost superfluous. We would divide the closing argument, but Sullivan always got the last speech.

It was interesting to me to watch Sullivan get ready for trial. As I got more experienced, I would be the lawyer who would have taken most of the depositions in preparation for trial. That is not to say I did most of the work. Often, I would be presenting a plaintiff for deposition or taking the other side's expert's deposition. Sullivan would take the important depos. Deposing the other side's expert is really the easiest job—what are your credentials, what have you read, what were you paid, what are your opinions? The hard part is having the self-control and willpower not to try to cross-examine the expert before trial. Because I had done much of the legwork before trial, I would have a good idea of what the issues in the case were going to be, whom I thought would be the key witnesses, and what I thought would be the important documents.

Invariably, the weekend before trial, Sullivan would sit down with the file and pull a few documents and identify a few items that were "hot." Riza and I would make sure that there were multiple copies of the thin file of documents that Sullivan put together as "his" file, because frequently he would leave it in the hotel bar or on the bumper of the car or wherever.

The documents he selected for his hot documents file wouldn't necessarily be the ones that would jump out at you as being essential to the case. More than once, I remember him sitting at a hotel desk or sprawled across a hotel bed with paper cluttering the floor and stacked on the desk, the television, and the bathroom counter, when he would jump up and shout, "Here it is! Hoisted upon his own 'pittard.'"

Of course, whenever he said things like that, I would scurry off to find a laptop and Google the phrase. I assumed that a "pittard" was some type of sharp object and that somebody was being sacrificed upon his own sword or spear. With a little effort, I would learn that the *Hamlet* reference was to a small bomb, but the effect was the same—somebody was being done in by his own weapon or device. In fact, the correct quotation appeared to be "hoist (not 'hoisted') with (not 'upon') his own petard (not 'pittard.')" But Sullivan was not above attempting to improve upon Shakespeare or at least bend the bard's lines to his own suiting. Then, I'd try to memorize other lines from the same act and scene so that the next time Sullivan used the phrase, I could follow up with a quote of my own. This practice of mimicry had resulted in extended periods of time in which I would use words like "unctuous" or phrases like "a modicum of perspicacity."

Sullivan would carefully file his eureka documents in a thin, redrope folder marked "Tim's hot docs," and smile. Often, I'd read what he had selected and wonder what the pages had to do with proving our case. Inevitably though, he would use the documents to tell a story about which the jury already knew the ending, but nevertheless was anxious to have Sullivan reveal to them.

In one trial, we were alleging the down-moving escalator in a large, downtown Houston bank was defective because it didn't have "side safety plates" between the edge of the moving steps and the fixed side-walls of the escalator. Apparently, several times each year on escalators around the country, young children will have their tennis shoes caught in the space, and the force of the moving step would traumatically crush and even amputate children's toes.

Our client, Scott Aldridge, was a handsome four-year-old boy whose father was holding his hand as they went to the father's office one Saturday morning before the bank opened. Scotty's tennis shoe got caught between the moving escalator step and the stationary wall, severing several of the little boy's toes. Incredibly, there was a memo, discovered in previous litigation involving the same escalator manufacturer, in which a regional vice-president wrote to the home office in Switzerland about product liability law in the United States.

Evidently, the escalator manufacturer had been considering the purchase of the side-safety-plate technology, which reduced the gap at the edge of the step, as a safety device for incorporation into the design of their product. In order to prove design defect in the case, we had to show that the design without the side safety plates was defective and unreasonably dangerous, as well as whether a safer alternative design existed that, in reasonable probability, would have prevented or significantly reduced the risk of injury. The memorandum asked, "Is a down-moving escalator without side safety plates unreasonably dangerous as designed?" A discussion of the law in various states followed. The employee who had received the memo had written in ink beside the question, "Probably so."

I was surprised that Sullivan didn't put that memo in his "hot docs" file. I remember asking him if he was sure he didn't want it. "No," he said, "you use it. I've got the one I want." He showed me an innocuous looking e-mail that discussed a dinner meeting of company executives in Geneva.

Of course, when I used the admission-of-defect document at trial, the defense counsel was ready with stock explanations as to why the memo—which I thought was an admission of fault—was really an observance of the need for an alternative safety device, thick-bristled brushes, that the manufacturer eventually determined should be placed along the escalator sidewall in lieu of side safety plates because the brushes were more effective at keeping young children from putting their feet on the edge of the step. However, Sullivan was able to use the document he selected to show that at the very moment that Mr. Aldridge helplessly watched the mangling of his young son's right foot, the president of the escalator company was enjoying a bottle of Montrachet and eating fondue.

I thought my half of the closing argument in the escalator case had gone pretty well. I had used the often-quoted passage from Ezekiel 22:30 where God searches for a man among the Israelites ". . . who would build up the wall and stand before me in the gap . . ." I had remembered Church of Christ preachers talking about filling in the gaps in society's safety net through charitable contributions to help the poor, and I asked the jury, through its verdict, to stand in the gap between the escalator wall and the escalator steps to prevent other kids from being injured in the future. I did think that Sullivan one-upped me in his half of the closing argument. He argued that requiring the escalator manufacturer to fill in the space between the escalator steps and the escalator wall was akin to taking a position on the Alamo wall against Santa Anna's murderous hordes looking for a breach in the integrity of the Texans' defenses.

It's a close call, but generally speaking, I think Alamo references are superior to Old Testament quotes in the hierarchy of effective jury arguments in Texas.

Sullivan didn't say a word as the hospital elevator descended five floors. When the doors opened, he pushed the wheelchair out. "We just have to cross the lobby, and the chapel is on this floor over there behind the piano," he said, and began whistling as we went across the spacious lobby, through a small vestibule, past a pair of heavy oak doors, and into the long, hushed, Wiess Memorial Chapel.

24

ONE WALL OF THE softly lit chapel was made of carved, oak panels, and the opposite wall held a series of four stained-glass windows that let in light from the lobby. The ornate pieces of glass reflected geometric patterns of color across the cool terrazzo floor that was carpeted down the center aisle. Oak pews faced a pulpit from both sides of the aisle. In the center of the pulpit was a stained-glass window with a figure of Christ, and beneath the window was a bronze plaque with the quote, "These things I have spoken unto you that in me ye might have peace. In the world ye shall have tribulation: but be of good cheer; I have overcome the world."

I continued to sit in the wheelchair while Sullivan pushed me to about the middle of the chapel. He walked around in front of me and sat down next to me on one of the pews. He looked over his right shoulder at the stained-glass window and asked, "Namesake?" I looked up at the window of olive green, burgundy red, golden-yellow, and blue-almost-purple stained glass, and I recognized for the first time that the image depicted was of David holding a harp and unfolded scrolls of paper with writing that might be psalms, or stories, or laws. Beside him was a lamb, beneath him was a rock, and the bottom panel in the window was of a royal lion with a sun behind him.

From his right coat pocket, Sullivan produced a Laguiole corkscrew. From his left coat pocket, he produced several Dixie cups. He kept two Dixie cups, and returned the others to his pocket.

Most of the lawyers that I have met have a specific drink that they always order, without regard to the meal they're having, the time of day, or the season of the year. Sullivan was different. Other than the first Sea Breeze or two that the staff at Damian's greeted him with when he came through the door, Sullivan would actually spend a moment contemplating what the perfect choice of wine or spirits might be for a particular occasion. He might even engage the waiter in a discussion in which it seemed that the waiter's opinion held great sway. To the uninitiated, this hesitation before ordering might at first seem to reveal a level of inexperience when ordering alcohol. When Sullivan finally got around to ordering, I always wished that I had waited to see what he was getting before I had reflexively said "scotch" to the waiter.

He never ordered a Bloody Mary, Mimosa, or Bellini after eleven o'clock in the morning. Bourbons and scotches were reserved for the fall and winter months to accompany steaks served medium rare, and gin and tonics and vodka sodas were favored in spring and summer with Cobb salads or pecan-crusted snapper or blackened redfish topped with lump crabmeat. He might order a beer with barbecue or a dozen raw or an oyster po-boy, but the beer would have to be ice cold, and, if it got warm before he finished it, he would get a fresh one. Every now and then he would request a Martini straight up with olives, but only if the bar had Monopolowa vodka. He explained that one can't distinguish between vodkas. However, vodka was supposed to be made from potatoes, and Monopolowa was the only potato vodka readily available in the States.

More often than not though, Sullivan ordered wine. He was not what I would call a wine snob. He could of course afford anything on the wine list, but he might not order the most expensive bottle if it didn't fit his mood or complement the dish he was ordering.

He never ate at a Chinese food restaurant unless it served Wan Fu. He judged all Italian food restaurants by whether or not they had Tignanello available. Even if they did and he was ordering pasta with cream sauce, he would probably just order an inexpensive bottle of Frascati, but only if it could be brought to the table in a bucket of ice.

Remember when your grandmother would have ladies from the church over for Bible study, and she would serve different salads like ham salad and chicken salad and potato salad? Mine also made something that she called a pear salad. She put a big leaf of iceberg lettuce on a salad plate and then opened a can of halved pears. She put a pear half on each plate and filled the hollowed cavity in the middle with a large dollop of Miracle Whip. Then she would let me drink the juice out of the pear can. That is pretty much what Frascati tastes like. Maybe Frascati isn't quite as sugary sweet, but it almost tastes like pear-flavored water, and it's delicious with a large bowl of pasta with Alfredo or vodka sauce.

Sullivan liked champagne ahead of cocktails before a meal. He liked Montrachet with cheese after a meal. He ordered obscure California chardonnays as if he was searching for the best buy, constantly comparing them to Au Bon Climat, Cakebread, or Marcassin as his yardsticks.

Of the many bottles of wine I had consumed with Sullivan, Far Niente chardonnay was my favorite, and I often told him so. He liked it well enough—he said that he thought it compared favorably among the California chardonnays—but preferred the big Tuscan reds like Tignanello that were kept stockpiled for him at Damian's, and he considered it heresy to drink chardonnay when offered Montrachet. I liked Far Niente's intricate, art nouveau parchment label. I liked the spicy, oak flavor of the wine, and the full, roundness of the flavor as it rolled back over my tongue. Because Sullivan preferred it served very cold, I preferred it served cold. After a few glasses, the velvety wine seemed to manifest itself by turning my hands into soft cotton balls at the ends of my arms.

To tell the truth, what I liked most about the wine was its name. I had read on the back of a bottle that "Far Niente" was an Italian phrase meaning "without a care," but not having studied Italian, I was certain the phrase meant more than that. According to the label, the phrase was carved into a stone on the front of the winery built in approximately 1885, which sat in disrepair from the time of Prohibition until 1979 when new owners took over.

Admittedly, I had spent long hours with Sullivan, drinking Far Niente as if we had nothing to worry about; but even in the early days of my working for him, I thought that "Far Niente" meant something else, something darker, more ominous. For some reason, the phrase reminded me of the Lord's Prayer speech from somewhere in Heming-

way—I can't remember if it was said by the old waiter in the short story
A Clean, Well-Lighted Place or by Jake Barnes in the novel *The Sun Also
Rises*: "Our *nada* who art in *nada, nada* be Thy name."

Probably the waiter had said it, biding his time while the old cus-
tomer finished drinking before they closed up the bar and sent the
man home and out into the darkness. Or maybe Jake had said it when
he slipped into the cathedral near the Hotel Montoya and off the hot
streets of Pamplona. No, I think Jake's prayer was a rambling prayer for
bullfighters and Lady Brett Ashley's prayer in the San Fermin Cathedral later in the book never got started. I can't remember now who said
the prayer, but I used to know things like that back in college, which
was not all that long ago. I'll bet my dad could tell you that.

"Niente" had to mean "*nada*" or "nothing." I assumed "far" trans-
lated directly from Italian to English, referred to distance. Thus, a "far
niente" was a "distant nothing," a black hole in the heavens where one
expected there to have been a moral authority. "Far Niente" is the vint-
ner's recognition of a godless universe. Why would we have any cares if
we knew there was no God? We could act in our own self-interest without fear of punishment or retribution, because beyond our knowable,
observable existence, there was only a distant nothing, a "far niente."

I never told anyone my translation of "far niente." For a long time, I
intended to look it up in an Italian/English dictionary. I never discussed with Sullivan his understanding of the phrase.

In my mind, a "far niente" expressed a thought I had already had,
but had not articulated, perhaps because I didn't want it to be true.
Maybe there was nothing beyond the present. Maybe we're just here
and then we're not. Maybe over the horizon of the here and now, there
is only nothing, *nada, niente.* Why not celebrate that isolating, otherwise depressing recognition by drinking good wine in such quantities
that you lose the hopelessness of the thought and enjoy the endorphin
rush of the present? Eventually, the wine takes hold, and the *far niente*
doesn't seem so distant or empty, just an accepted proposition; and,
with nothing beyond today, you begin to seek enjoyment now rather
than sacrificing for any non-existent future. Or as old Khayyám put it,

Yesterday This Day's Madness did prepare;
To-morrow's Silence, Triumph, or Despair:
Drink! for you know not whence you came, nor why:
Drink! for you know not why you go, nor where.

When I did get around to looking up the phrase, I was pleased with myself to learn that "niente" did translate as "nothing," and not necessarily as "nothing to worry about," just "nothing." "Far" was apparently from the verb "fare," which means "to have" or "to make." "Fare" is defined a lot like "hacer," if my high school Spanish serves me. As best I can tell, "to have" and "to make" can't be accomplished with the same word in English, in which one can have something without making anything. Growing up in Texas, I frequently heard the salutation, "*Como tio?*" After a year of high school Spanish, I assumed that one was being greeted "like an uncle," but thinking about it now, the phrase is probably a contraction for "*Como te haido,*" or how have you been making it.

I don't know if the anonymous stonemason in Northern California just dropped the "e" on "fare" because he got tired of chiseling, or if he didn't allot enough space, or if he was engaged in an early evolution of the art of text messaging. Maybe it's a contraction or a participle form of the word. Or, maybe, the man was the artisan son of immigrant parents, and he grew up hearing the phrase; and like me, he sensed a distant nothingness when he did.

My sketchy understanding of the Romance languages notwithstanding, I was at a point where the *far niente* didn't seem all that far away at the moment, and I could feel the engulfing blackness of it settling all around me. As I watched Tim set the Dixie cups beside each other between us on the pew, it felt as if I was watching him through a microscope.

In an elaborate, and decidedly practiced fashion, Sullivan opened the wine and poured us each a glass. As he handed me a cup, I thought about the fact that I had, in just the short time I had known and worked for Tim Sullivan, consumed thousands of drinks with the man. I also imagined that this would probably be the last.

"I think you'll like that," he said admiring the label on the green bottle. "It's your favorite, isn't it? Be of good cheer," he said and nodded toward the plaque at the front of the room.

"Yes. I'm sure I will," I said.

"Listen," I said. "There is something I have to tell you about a case."

"A case? Don't we need to talk about my daughter right now?"

"Yeah, the *Tamara Davis* case. She is the tonsillectomy lady on the hospital security camera video."

"Right," Sullivan said. "I heard about your settlement. Great result. I know the facts are kind of shocking, but who wouldn't take a quarter of a million dollars to let some good-looking young doctor kiss her chest while she was asleep?" He held up his cup. "Congratulations."

"Thanks," I said. "It's not that simple. I didn't know it when I sent the demand letter or when the adjustor offered the money, but I think the case is a fraud. Tamara and her doctor, um . . . boyfriend, staged the whole thing. My guess is he knew the person in the monitoring room also . . . maybe they are related or something."

"And how did you figure this out?"

"I thought there was something wrong on the video, and Eileen pinned it down. Ms. Davis smiles after the kiss. So I confronted Ms. Davis on the phone just now. She pretty much admitted everything. Do you take the money? Do you withdraw? Do you tell the adjustor before he sends the check and release?"

"What do you think we ought to do?" Sullivan asked.

"Not *we*. You. I'm sending the file back to you. It is your case. The case came in to you and I just signed it up. When I saw the video, I thought there was a chance at a quick fee. What is the old saying about something that looks too good to be true? I'll do you a memo about what all has transpired."

We both took a sip of our wine.

"Hold off on the memo," he said, and I nodded. That is what I thought he would say. I also knew that there was no way he would tell the adjustor, unless of course Sullivan could use the goodwill to his benefit on another case. He might not sign the settlement documents.

Probably some other young lawyer would get called in to sign those while Sullivan sat drinking Sea Breezes at Damian's.

We sat sipping our wine for another moment, waiting for the other one to say something first, to start the cross-examination that we both knew was coming. There was only one way I knew to avoid it. Even then I knew that I couldn't avoid it entirely, but I could put it off a little while longer. With apologies to the gravel-voiced poet priest Leonard Cohen for the slight change in wording, "all I ever learned from 'law' was how to shoot at someone who outdrew you."

"Are you moving to Jackson Hole, also?" I asked.

"How do you know about Jackson Hole?" he asked. He seemed taken aback by the directness of my question.

"I'm guessing that's where Riza is now," I said. Tim didn't respond. I pressed on. "I'm guessing that you are finally about to sever your ties with Mr. Peters and the other partners in the firm and become the sole shareholder in your own firm."

"You know I've been thinking about doing that for some time . . . starting my own firm . . . having a few associates whom I like," he said, regaining his composure.

"Yes, I know," I said. "I always thought that I'd like to be one of those associates. This is good," I said, handing him my cup for a refill. He filled both of our cups.

"It is good," he said, "though not as cold as I would prefer."

"I always wondered why you were waiting before branching off. I guess I assumed that you were waiting for a big fee to come in so that you would have a cushion as you made the transition. I thought maybe the Kentucky case might be the ticket."

"Admittedly, I had hoped as much," he said.

"That's why it baffled me when you didn't seem at all upset when I told you about how badly the case was going. I told you months ago that the defendant was going to get our expert struck, and you seemed to just shrug it off. We were putting all of that money into the case. It didn't hit me until I was downstairs having my head stitched. The money going into that case was the firm's money," I said.

Tim smiled, and sipped the chardonnay while I continued. "At first, I thought that maybe the firm needed to show a loss for tax purposes or something, but nobody needs that big of a loss. Then it occurred to me that by investing the firm's money, only a percentage of which is yours, into a case and publicizing the firm's involvement, you were creating an expectation that the defendant was about to suffer a major loss."

Again, Tim didn't say anything. He crossed and uncrossed his legs. I noticed that his British tan loafers were polished to a high gleam. His shoes always matched his belt, that is if he wore a belt instead of braces, which always matched his watchband. He alternated watches not watchbands. Sullivan referred to this principle of haberdashery as a "leather agreement." He smiled, waiting for me to continue.

I put my cup down on the pew. "Of course, you and I knew the case was a loser, but nobody else did. The fix was in. Boyd even got its own judge to preside over it. My fellow associates were jealous of me getting to work on the case. When I told them it was a loser, nobody believed me. They all thought that I stood to make partner because I was hand-picked to work up the TENORM case. I was handpicked, alright."

Tim refilled his glass, and offered to refill mine, but I put my hand over the cup and shook my head.

"Of course, even I, the hard-charging, dim-witted soldier noticed that all of the big oil executives raced to their cell phones when the special master commissioner, whatever that is, issued his rulings. No doubt their stock surged on the news." I paused, waiting for him to tell me what I already knew.

"What about the plaintiffs? What about Woodrow Carter? I thought we might be able to help him and his family. Now they're stuck on a plot of earth that has little value and no use. What chance do they have?" I asked. "On top of it all, I feel like I let them down."

"You and I both know that we didn't put the radiation on their property. It has been there a long time, and they have been there even longer. The property, absent the mineral rights, was worthless before the radiation was brought to the surface. And, best I can tell, nobody has ever been injured because of the radiation on their property. Is there something you are intending to ask me?" he said in an even-toned voice, and raised his eyebrows.

"You had purchased stock in Boyd, hadn't you?" I asked. "Well, maybe not you directly. Maybe, the money came through a certain paralegal company. Paralegals Parami. But, it was your stock that sky-rocketed today after the hearing, wasn't it? I don't know how much you made, but it must have been a lot. More than a lot. Certainly, it was enough for a paralegal to retire to Jackson Hole. And it was enough for a senior attorney to start a new firm comfortably, without having to worry about income while making the transition."

"But that's not really what you are intending to ask me, is it?" he said, almost as if he were still coaching me on how to perform an effective cross-examination.

"No," I said. "Did you know about Beth? Did you know about—I can't even say the word in front of you—did you know about the herpes? Did you know I would get sick and infect my wife, your daughter?"

"No, of course not," he said. He looked stunned. "I wanted Beth to keep an eye on you and let me know how the case—as you say, my investment—was coming, but I never knew anything about the disease. I'm only finding out now what I suspected for the first time a few minutes ago. You got herpes from Beth? I don't understand why you didn't just tell somebody. Why didn't you tell Michelle before today? Why didn't you tell me before now? Why did you wait until the very minute the baby was being born?"

I knew that I wouldn't be able to escape entirely Sullivan's cross-examination just because I had taken the offensive. He was waiting for me to finish. He was still gathering information. It was a technique I had seen him use often when taking depositions. Though no doubt the opposing counsel had coached his witness not to proffer information and to answer only the questions asked and nothing more, Sullivan would ask an open-ended question and then act as though he was trying to write down the witness's answer on a legal pad.

When the witness stopped talking, Sullivan would look up from his pad, hold his pen as if he were about to continue writing, and raise one eyebrow as if asking, "Is that all?" at which point the witness would take off talking again, in essence answering a question that had never been asked but that had been weighing on his mind.

"I don't know," I said, exhausted. "I kept thinking that I could figure out some way to fix the mess. My keeping quiet just kept making things worse. I didn't want Michelle to see me as a fuckup. I wanted her to see me like she sees you . . . perfect, unflappable, successful. I kept waiting for the perfect time to tell her, rather than just telling her. There is no perfect time to tell your wife you had an affair and you got herpes. You can look for the right opening, but there isn't going to be one."

Tim smiled at me again, not in a condescending or pejorative way. It was in the way of a colleague who was aware of the ridiculousness of the situation. He shook his head from side to side and said, "The expense of spirit in a waste of shame . . ." His voice trailed off as he observed that I didn't recognize the reference. Still, I could tell that behind his now forced smile he was seething with anger, and it was just a matter of seconds until he would reach his boiling point. "You know what I always say about timing?" he asked.

"No," I said, and shook my head as I sighed. I really wasn't in the mood for yet another Sullivanism.

"It's the key to a successful rain dance."

I smiled and shook my head again upon recognizing that in the world of the *far niente*, successful rain dances are contingent upon chance rather than the mercy of a benevolent god.

"I know you have questions, and I will try to answer them," I said. "Can you please just tell me one thing? Was Beth at the Peabody the last time we were there?"

He shrugged his shoulders. "She met me at the Rendezvous before you and Riza got to town. I don't know where she stayed on that trip."

I might not have any evidence of motivation, yet I was a step closer toward establishing means and opportunity for my coauthor.

Then he started. I knew it was coming. I thought I was ready and learned I wasn't. "I guess buying stock in a company or two that you think are about to receive a windfall through litigation is a lot like betting on the outcome of a case that your firm is trying," Sullivan said, not waiting for a response. "Were the ceilings in your office not high enough?" Sullivan asked, with just a hint of righteous indignation in his voice.

For a brief instant, I started to answer.

"Were the bonuses not big enough for you to buy whatever house or car you wanted?" he continued uninterrupted. "Did you grow weary of flying around the country in a private jet, staying at the best hotels, and eating at the best restaurants? Did the tailors fail to alter the three-button suits properly? Did you think that you had done something to earn all of this? What have you done . . . try a couple of cases, cover a few hearings, take notes at my trials? What do you think the average lawyer is paid for that kind of work? Didn't you understand that the only way you could ever earn all of this, if ever, was over an extended period of time? Do you think there is any future for you with my firm? Was there something else you wanted from me? I didn't just let you into my practice; I let you into my home; I let you into my family. I gave you my daughter."

He paused and I realized that he was practically shouting. The walls in the little chapel were still reverberating, when Sullivan asked in a whisper, "This is how you repay me? I know that we sent you to go try some dog cases, but do you think anybody else your age is getting that kind of experience? That experience was a gift. Certainly nobody was giving me at your age the kinds of gifts you have been given. Can you imagine what I could have accomplished in my lifetime if I had received at your age the advantages that you have received?" Sullivan paused again, while the angry red blood that had flooded his face didn't recede.

As he prepared to launch another fusillade of rapid-fire leading questions, each dripping with prejudice, and to which there could be no response, it occurred to me that in a way, Sullivan was jealous of me. Whereas I had been envious of him and his lifestyle and his success, he was jealous of me. Maybe he was verbalizing that he was jealous of the opportunities that I had, in his eyes, squandered, but what he really was saying was that he was jealous of my youth. Of course, youth was nothing that I had earned and nothing that I could have given to him as repayment for the opportunities he had given to me. Ironically, after this night, I would never think of myself as young again.

At that moment, there was a knock on the chapel doors, and Jonathan stuck his head through them. He looked haggard and was out of breath. "I've been looking all over the hospital for this place. A nurse just came out of the operating room and told us the doctor would be out in a minute. You both better come now."

We left the wine and the wheelchair, and hurried to the doors of the chapel.

Outside, after we crossed the lobby, I paused and turned to face Jonathan and Tim, who were following behind me. We were the only people around.

"Jonathan," I said, "Riza is in Jackson Hole." I watched as Tim processed what I had just said, and then he looked at his son. The color drained from Tim's face. Neither of them said anything. They just stood there looking at each other waiting for the other one to speak. As I turned to get on the elevator by myself, I whispered under my breath, "Hoist with his own petard." To Tim, I mumbled loud enough that he might have heard me: "O, 'tis most sweet, When in one line two crafts directly meet." I held the elevator door and nodded at Jonathan to get in. We left Tim standing on the first floor of the Dunn Tower.

"Jonathan," I said. "I'm sorry that I didn't tell you sooner about Riza. I should have. I don't know why I have been so hell-bent on trying to keep secrets. I shouldn't have been keeping secrets from you or my wife. The truth is that the two of you are worth more to me than anything. You can be pissed-off at me if you want, but if you want Riza you had better figure out how to get to Jackson Hole before your dad does." As I talked, the anger and frustration in his face eased. He didn't say a word to me during our short elevator ride. I assumed that at some point he decided to put aside thinking about Riza because he was focused on his sister.

We got to the waiting area where Michelle's mom was standing about the same time that Dr. Godsman came through a pair of doors just past the waiting area. Other families, at least the members of other families who weren't permitted in the operating rooms, were clustered in groups of chairs around the waiting room, and it was impossible to talk without being overheard by all who were in the room. Everyone in the waiting room looked up as Dr. Godsman came into the room.

The doctor nodded to nobody in particular, and then said to me, "There are complications. Serious complications. I am concerned that your son may have contracted a virus in the birth canal. We're running some tests. We'll know more shortly. In an adult, the virus would present manageable problems, but in an infant . . . his immune system isn't fully developed yet . . . he's being followed by a pediatrician who specializes in infectious diseases. We have a small neonatal intensive care unit here on this floor, on the other side of the building," the doctor said, pointing. "We can, of course, move the child quickly to the Texas Children's Hospital. I'll talk to the other doctors, though I doubt that we'll do that now. Honestly, I am concerned that he wouldn't survive the transfer."

Amy burst into tears. Dr. Godsman put her hand on Amy's shoulder, and said to me, "Your wife is doing well physically. She has asked to see her mother. Mrs. Sullivan," she asked, turning to Amy, "would you like to go back with me now?"

Amy nodded, and the two of them disappeared behind the double doors. Tim walked up. We just stood there looking at each other without saying anything. After a moment, I left him there and walked back down the hallway by myself and took the elevator down to the first floor to the Wiess Memorial Chapel that we had left a few minutes ago.

Alone inside the chapel, I picked up the used Dixie cups and threw them in the trash. I put the cork in the bottle of wine and put it in the trash also. I pushed the wheelchair outside the double doors.

I sat down on a wooden pew in the back of the chapel and tried to pray to God that my child's life would be spared. I noticed for the first time that the piano music from the lobby could be heard in the chapel.

I didn't know what the doctor had meant by the word "complications." I could only tell by her grave composure that the worst was possible, maybe even probable. I tried looking up toward heaven, but all I could think about was that cardiology or nephrology or some other specialty was probably on the floor above me.

On a desk at the back of the chapel, printed brochures suggested prayers for Jewish, Christian, or Islamic faiths. I read them over, wondering what doctrinal nuances there were in the different prayers that categorized them into different religions. They all sounded good to me. That is not to say that I am one of those people that say things like, "Although I'm not religious, I am very spiritual," whatever that means. I really think such statements mean that the speaker has never investigated his own faith sufficiently enough to determine what, if anything, he believes. Saying "I'm spiritual" is the same thing as saying "I'm thirsty, but I don't know what I'm thirsty for."

I didn't reject the preprinted prayers because they were the wrong denomination, I rejected the prayers because they were preprinted. Similarly, I rejected the slips of paper on the desk at the back of the chapel to be filled out for "prayer requests" and dropped into a container that looked like a suggestion box. This prayer, whatever it was going to be, had to be my prayer.

I found myself drifting in thought and beginning the prayer over and over, but not finishing and never really getting to the part where I asked that the baby and Michelle be protected or where I asked for forgiveness for what I had done or the pain I had caused or the sins I had committed. I knew what I was supposed to say. If I had heard it once back in Sunday school, I had heard it fifty-one times. I should ask God for His tender mercies and for Him to wash away my sins and iniquities. I should implore Him to take away my guilt and promise Him to praise His righteousness. I should show Him that I was broken and that I was contrite and welcome Him into my heart.

Instead, I just kept saying, "God, please don't punish my child for what I have done. He hasn't done anything wrong. I have. Please, don't let him suffer. Please, don't let Michelle suffer. If this baby is injured or infected, or dies, it will kill Michelle. She doesn't deserve this, just like the baby doesn't deserve this."

Even as I tried to begin the prayer over and over, I felt as though I was trying to negotiate with God. If He would spare the baby and protect Michelle, I alone would suffer the consequences, and that seemed fair because I was the one who had behaved in a manner that deserved punishment. How could a loving god let a baby be born blind or retarded, or die within hours of being born, through no fault of his own? An infant isn't capable of fault. Shouldn't he deserve the greatest protection, rather than being the medium through which punishment would be meted out? Michelle's innocence was as great as the child's. What was her sin, other than trusting her husband? Why should she suffer the loss of her first child? I doubted, whether or not the child lived, that we would remain married; I knew that if the child died, there was no way things would ever be "normal" again . . . like it was when we were first married. That was over. Killed by me. Why I killed it, I don't know. I don't think I meant to, but I must have. I did it.

I kept asking myself and God why this was happening. Was it the result of some fatal flaw in my character—a toxic combination of lust, pride, procrastination, avarice, envy, immoderation, and wrath that exceeded any safe-level threshold? Was it the unfortunate consequence of a series of capricious events, or the affirmative effort of a punishing God determined to rectify past wrongs? It seemed to me to be the result of fear—fear of being alone and isolated, and fear of not being capable of being the person that my wife thought I was. Maybe fear is the cause of evil. Fear begets guilt begets shame begets bad decisions begets guilt.

Through my adultery and the compounding of the sin by my silence, I had destroyed my marriage, wrecked my wife, and injured my child. And yet, here I was, sitting on this bench by myself in some far corner of a sprawling hospital complex, asking God how He could let this happen. I wanted to shake my fist at Him, and tell Him that He was not holding up His end of the deal.

I did think about those examples in the Bible where God's greatest punishment, or call to sacrifice, seemed to be taking someone's first-born child. Moses and Passover. Abraham and Isaac. Even Jesus. But to me, up to this point, those had just been Bible stories. Just like Jesus had told parables to help us understand the moral of his teachings, the Bible stories were like Aesop's Fables to me. Similitudes. A real, loving god would never actually take a child as punishment for the child's father, would He?

Then it would occur to me that if at a point as low as this in my life I was choosing to argue with God, it must mean that somewhere, somehow, I still believed that He existed; and that if He could be persuaded that the situation was deserving of His intervention, He would step in and make things right. And then, I would try to begin my prayer again.

I don't know how long I sat there, a broken person, rocking back and forth on that bench, looking up at the ceiling and then down at the floor, alternately demanding and pleading for help. It could have been seven minutes or seven hours. I don't think it would have mattered if I had stayed seven days in that quiet, long room with the piano playing outside the stained-glass windows because I didn't seem to be able to get the prayer started much less finished. I wanted help, but I didn't know how to ask for it.

My reverie was interrupted by a knock at the doors. This time it wasn't Jonathan who peeked inside. It was my dad, and I knew that my mother was standing behind him.

I went out into the vestibule. I could tell they had both been crying, and I assumed that they had been there for awhile. Mom kept lifting her eyeglasses and dabbing at her eyes with a crumpled tissue. The artificial lighting in the chapel had caused me to lose track of what time of day it was. I glanced toward the area outside the chapel and next to the lobby and could tell from the light in the atrium that the sun was about to come up.

"Davy," Dad said, "Your Mom and I didn't want to disturb you, but the doctors came out of the neonatal intensive care unit just a minute ago. It doesn't look like your son Paul is going to make it. We thought you might want to see him, maybe talk to him, before anything happens. Come on, follow me." He took off walking quickly, with one arm around my mom, who hadn't spoken and had barely looked at me, and the other arm clutching a wrinkled, legal-sized FedEx envelope. We got on the elevator to go back up to the maternity floor.

After the elevator ride, we got off on the maternity floor and I followed my parents around the building to another hallway. There, in front of a large glass window that began at waist level and extended to the height of the ten-foot ceiling, stood Tim, Amy, and Jonathan Sullivan. Behind them stood Tim's friend William, wearing plaid golf pants and no shoes, Rod Day and his wife, both still in their suits from work, and my parents. All were transfixed by what was happening on the other side of the glass.

Four tiny babies, each seeming much smaller and more frail than the babies I had remembered seeing in the infant room during the Lamaze tour of the hospital, lay in their respective plastic tubs under intense white lights. All sorts of lines and cords were coming and going from each tub. Several men and women in scrubs, with coverings over their shoes and hair, and wearing rubber gloves, moved around the room attending to the infants.

None of the people on our side of the glass spoke. All of them, Tim included, looked like their life had been drained away; as though a crack had developed in the vessel that contained each person and their lives had gushed out onto the floor and then escaped along the seams in the tile and baseboard.

I don't know how long the group of them had been standing there when my parents had left to come get me, but it must have been quite some time. They were completely helpless to assist with what was happening on the other side of the glass. It was the kind of helplessness that made you wonder what, if anything, you could control on this side of the glass as well.

My dad caught my eye, and he nodded toward the infant that was in the tub the farthest to our left. The child's eyes were closed, and he had a thatch of burnt sienna hair on the top of his head. He gripped his little fists in convulsive jabs, trying to get comfortable in the blankets in the tub. On the end of the tub facing us was a sticker with the name "Jessie" scrawled in black ink. Several of the cords coming from his tub ran to monitors that flashed nearby, but I couldn't see what it was that was being monitored. One attendant stood at the head of his little acrylic bed and did not leave to assist the other babies. That attendant, his face covered by a mask, his hands covered in latex gloves, kept looking back and forth from the baby to one particular monitor.

About the time that I tried again to begin my futile prayer, I felt a tap on my elbow. It was the doctor who had delivered my son.

"Mr. Jessie," Dr. Godsman said somberly. It looked to me like she was still wearing the scrubs that she must have had on during the C-section. "It's been a while since the delivery. There has been no change for the better since his birth. I'm sorry, there has been a steady decline."

"Is there anything you can do?" I asked.

"The doctors have done all they can," she said, and I saw Amy start to lay her head on Tim's shoulder. Without watching, I could tell that each of the couples had put their arms around their mate. "What I'd like to do is take the baby off all of the life-support equipment he's on, and take him and you to Michelle's room. I don't know how long the three of you would have together. Maybe, an hour. Maybe, less. I've talked to Michelle, and she has given her consent. Though it's not absolutely necessary, I thought it appropriate to ask you as well."

"I'll do whatever Michelle wants to do," I said.

The doctor tapped once on the glass to get the attention of the male attendant standing next to Paul. He must have said something, as several of the other attendants came over to the baby and began moving around the plastic bassinet.

The doctor took me by the elbow and directed me behind a pair of double doors at the end of the hall. I could still hear Amy and my mother crying behind us as we went through the doors and marched slowly down the otherwise quiet hallway.

After a few steps, Dr. Godsman stopped and faced me. "I'm going to take you to Michelle's room and the nurse will bring in the baby. It may be helpful for you to know Mr. Jessie that the hospital provides support for families that lose a baby in childbirth. Maybe we haven't seen this exact set of circumstances before, but experience has taught us some perspective that I'd like to share with you. If the family gets a little time with the child, however brief, they will look back on that time later and it helps them with the grieving process. I know you've had a long night Mr. Jessie, but imagine the night that Michelle has been through. We don't need you upsetting her more, if that's possible. She'll probably still be a little woozy from the anesthesia, but I can guarantee you that she and you both will remember everything that happens in the next few minutes and everything that is said and how it is said."

Dr. Godsman took my arm by the elbow again and resumed leading me down the hallway. It almost felt like I was leaning on her as we walked along. We stopped in front of a closed door that I assumed would lead to Michelle's room. There was a plastic and metal chair placed by the door.

"What should I say?" I asked, looking at the closed door and then at her. I could see the male nurse walking toward us down the hall. He was carrying the baby in his arms.

"Quit worrying about what you ought to say and say what you feel," she said softly and patted me on the chest. I took off my blazer and laid it across the back of the chair by the door.

Dr. Godsman turned toward the nurse and left me there by myself standing. I wanted to stop the doctor and tell her that I didn't feel anything—just numb and empty and alone.

25

YOU NEVER THOUGHT YOU would find yourself in a situation like this. You tell yourself that nobody ever thought that you would end up in a situation like this. You always said you enjoyed the fact that the practice of obstetrics involves constant challenges and that no two days are ever alike. There was nothing routine about this job, and you enjoyed that. Or you thought you did before tonight. You think about the coincidences that have to occur for someone to end up practicing one area of medicine instead of another. About the only area of medicine you had no interest in practicing when you started medical school was psychiatry—too unfathomable, too difficult to know if you were achieving desired results.

Sure, back in medical school your fellow students questioned you about why you wanted to specialize in obstetrics and gynecology because of the high malpractice insurance rates and the weird hours. You laughed them off and told them that you wanted to deliver babies. That always shut them up. It seemed like such a noble calling. Nobody ever asked the follow up question: why do you want to deliver babies? Most of your friends who thought they wanted to be brain surgeons or do heart transplants or stem cell research when they started medical school were now on their way to lucrative careers as plastic surgeons or rheumatologists. They followed the money, but not you. You set your goal and stuck to it.

Of course, your parents knew the real reason that you wanted to become an obstetrician, but even they never talked to you about it. Your parents, what made you think about them at this hour? Maybe part of you wants to call your dad, the psychiatrist, and talk to him. What good would that do? What good had it done to talk to him the one time you needed any real advice? The time for going to him for reasoned advice had come and gone. Conversations with him now were just exchanges of pleasantries.

You could call your husband. It would be nice just to hear his voice. It was early, but he would understand. You look back over your shoulder toward the room where you left the young man and his wife and newborn child. You point to your cell phone to let the male nurse you are walking with that you need to make a call and step into an empty room and close the door behind you.

Your husband will be sleeping and you imagine him sprawled across the bed in his boxers and that Trinity University Football T-shirt. How lucky were you to even meet this guy? What were the odds? He grew up in Dallas, went to college in San Antonio, and then attended medical school in Galveston. You grew up in Los Angeles and went to undergrad and med school at UCLA. But you both happened to do residencies in Houston, his at the prestigious Texas Institute for Rehabilitation and Research. Life has its coincidences. What were the odds of our meeting each other?

His practice was so different from yours. As a physiatrist, a physical medicine and rehabilitation physician, your husband's job was more like that of a construction superintendent. He spent all his time overseeing workers sawing and hammering and gluing and nailing things back together. He could usually schedule when these repairs were going to take place. Sure, he had to take a call from time to time, but there were no late-night deliveries. Even in emergencies, he was usually able to get the patient stabilized and pieced back together so that more extensive work could be scheduled for later when a more thorough plan was developed. Casts and slings, exercise and strengthening, and time to heal were not the kind of tools that obstetricians utilize.

As you dial the numbers and the phone begins to ring, you imagine him scrambling to find his cell phone on the nightstand and staring at the caller ID to see who would be calling at this hour. Eventually he answers, his voice raspy with sleep. "Hello?"

"Hey, Sorry to wake you."

"That's okay. I'm sure the Jaybird will be up in a minute anyway." You imagine that he is looking at the clock beside the bed. "What's going on?" he asks.

The two of you have a four-year old boy named "Jay" that your husband insists on calling "Jaybird." You tell others that the nickname stuck because the little boy has beautiful blue eyes, but you know that your husband compared the boy's colic shrieks as an infant to that of a blue jay and the child was stuck with the name. You both agree that the boy is the most handsome, intelligent child in the world. You think he might cure cancer. Your husband is convinced the boy will someday quarterback the Cowboys.

"Nothing." You lie. "I just needed to hear your voice." You did, and, remarkably, it is helping. The dark numbness that a moment ago seemed about to descend around you, lifts noticeably. But it is still there.

"Is it really that bad?" he asks. You can tell that he is more awake now.

"It's bad." You say, and you proceed to tell him about the emergency C-section you performed earlier, and the fact that the baby you delivered is unlikely to survive. He doesn't ask you about the whys and wherefores, not right away. His concern at that point is you. God you love this man. You don't really understand his fascination with sports in general or football in particular, but you know that he cares about you. And of course, he gave you the Jaybird.

"What could go so wrong that you would be calling at this hour? Are you going to be okay?" he asks. That is part of why you love him. He can tell when something is going on with you and you don't have to spell it out for him.

"You are human. You can't save every baby. You've lost babies before. Not many, I know, but you can deal with this. Do you want to tell me what happened?"

You don't want to, and probably shouldn't from a strictly ethical standpoint, but you do tell him about what happened. The other babies you lost were expected. The pregnancies had been complicated. The fetuses had shown signs of distress prior to delivery. You even had a chance to prepare the families for a bad result, encouraging them not to let this event prevent them from trying again in the future when they were ready.

You start with when you got the call from Dr. Nathan's office about how one of his patients was going into labor the previous evening. You learned that Dr. Nathan, the man who had mentored you through your residency, the man whom you most wanted to emulate in your practice, the man you loved as much as any man except maybe your husband, had suffered a blinding stroke and was not doing well. The patient had gotten to the hospital before her chart had arrived at your office, and you met her there with her husband. Everything appeared to be going well until the husband unloaded the bombshell about the herpes and then the baby was so far down the birth canal that the C-section itself was risky—but you had performed it, and the mother was doing well, but not the baby. Herpes. How could herpes be responsible for killing a baby in this day and age? The things people do to each other. And apparently it all had to do with keeping secrets. The husband had not told his wife until she was in labor that he had herpes and that she might have the disease as well. Why did people continue to try to keep secrets from each other? What good ever came from that?

"I guess we all have our secrets," your husband says, not in a critical way, and you know what he is saying. You think back to that day in your father's study. You were a senior in high school with good grades and a ridiculously high SAT, which even today you thought might be the result of some testing anomaly, and you had been accepted to UCLA already. Then you had become bored or maybe you were trying to get your father's attention by dating some guy that you knew your dad would never say anything about, but wouldn't approve of. You were just sitting there with your mom and dad, and neither of them were saying anything. Your dad just stroked his bearded chin until you came to the conclusion on your own.

"Do you have any idea what time you will be home?" Your husband asks. You don't; you're just waiting around for the inevitable, and you tell him that. He understands and yawns. "I think I may take the Jaybird over to Rice this afternoon. They are playing Tulane at one. He likes watching the guy in the owl suit."

You tell him that sounds like a good idea and that you'll probably just come home in a little while and try to get some sleep. You tell him again that you are sorry for waking him, and he says that it is okay and to call back if you need to. When you hang up, you feel better and you drop the cell phone back into the front pocket of your white coat. You look around the empty room where you have been standing and wonder to yourself what events will take place there over the remainder of the day.

26

As the door to the empty hospital room closes behind you, you think back to when you left the sterile, lifeless room at the little clinic in Pasadena, a few miles from your parents' home. That room is a little box in your memory that you keep inside the larger box, the clinic, that you keep inside a still larger box, your distant past—and you try not to open them, but sometimes they just fall open no matter how tightly you try to keep them shut. Your mom had wheeled you out in a wheelchair that the clinic had provided.

Neither of you said anything on the trip down the hall away from the room after the procedure that seemed to be over before you were even aware that it had started, or when she stopped at the reception desk and left you to go bring the car around, or on the ride home, or even as she held your arm as the two of you went in the back door of your childhood home. You just went to your room, slipped on a loose-fitting gown that any young girl might wear, crawled into your bed and tried to go to sleep.

Convinced that you would never be able to fall asleep, you were surprised when you woke up to see your dad sitting at the small desk in your room. He was reading a book, and you watched him turn several pages before he noticed that you were awake. You closed your eyes and hoped that he had not seen that you were awake.

"Hey," he said. "You've been asleep quite a while. Are you okay?" He asked, gently shaking one of your feet beneath the covers.

You nodded.

"Your mom made some dinner. Are you hungry? I could bring it to you."

You shook your head.

"I'll leave you alone." he said. "Call me if you need me." He stood slowly like it was difficult for him to stand because of some undiagnosed arthritic condition, but you both knew that he was searching for something to say that he couldn't say. He turned off the desk lamp and closed the door behind him when he left the room. You felt a sense of relief that he was gone—that the conversation had only been superficial, that the procedure was over, that you were no longer pregnant. Then you felt guilty for feeling the relief.

You lay there in your bed watching as evening settled on the Henry Link white wicker furniture that your mom had painstakingly collected to decorate your room. The twilight that peeked through the white plantation shutters on your window blended with the peach-colored, Laura Ashley floral comforter that you pulled up tight around your chin. Your mom had tried so hard to give the room a feminine feel; you had always been her little girl. Now you didn't feel feminine, you certainly didn't feel like a little girl, and the Jacobean white room just felt desolate and cold.

Even at the time you wondered what would have happened if your dad and you had talked at that point, and you continued to wonder that to this day. You didn't want to talk to him then and not much after that. He might have been a psychiatrist, but he wasn't your psychiatrist. He was just your dad. What could he have said that would have really helped? In retrospect, it seems like you just floated through the end of the high school year and the summer that followed, out of the white wicker room and into the shabby, institutional setting of the dorm room with the blocky wooden furniture and dingy tile floors at your first year in college, without saying anything.

It would be hard to determine at what point you swam up from the darkness, devoid of conversation beyond the compulsory "how are you?" and "can I get you anything?" that settled over what used to be a little girl's bedroom that evening, but fortunately, you continued to do well in school. Scholastic success had always come easily for you, and sometime along about your third year you decided to apply to medical school.

Your dad, the doctor, of course thought that was a grand idea and he told you he was proud of you, but you continued to see your parents less and less. Now, they lead separate lives on the other side of the country from you and your little family of two physicians and a blue-eyed boy. You wondered what they might be doing and tried to recreate your parents' daily routines, and you realized that you don't know much about their routines over those last few years. You had started to notice that your dad repeated stories, even during short telephone calls, and when you did see your parents he seemed to read the same section of the newspaper over and over, well before your mom decided to sell the house and move to a campus setting that offered different levels of care ranging from apartments to assisted living to Alzheimer's care to hospice.

You think to yourself that maybe you should call them later in the day. What if Jaybird grew up and never called you? It is hard to imagine a time when he won't need you or your husband just to get through a day—to feed him, to bathe him, to entertain him, and to help him learn. But that day will come you guess. He will grow up and go off to college and meet someone. That's what you hope for him, isn't it? Independence? He will probably stop calling home about the same time that your parents stop recognizing you. That will be your independence. Hopefully, your husband will still be there. You think to yourself that all living is assisted living, even if you reject it at the time.

It was in the first few weeks of medical school when you began to enjoy yourself again, maybe for the first time. The classes were challenging, the professors were interesting, and you became intrigued with the intricacies of the workings of the human body. Of course, you related all the materials and lectures to your own body, imagining yourself with whatever maladies and deformities you happened to be studying at the time, considering the known side effects of the prescribed remedies and weighing the risks versus the benefits if you really were diagnosed with a disease or condition and had to take the cure.

There was so much to learn, so much to memorize, and so much to read. You poured yourself into it, and you were good at it, especially the memorization part. But you were concerned that rote recitation would have little application when you actually had to assist real people. By the time you graduated, you were near the top of your class and had your pick of residency opportunities around the country. You chose Houston because you liked the program and without any regard for where you thought you might someday want to live. As it turned out, Houston was the best thing that could have happened to you for two reasons: you met your husband, and you met Dr. Nathan.

In many ways, Dr. Nathan became a third parent to you. You trusted him and it was easy to talk to him. Of course, he had made a good living in his life, but he didn't seem to care about the money. All he cared about was his patients, and he wasn't all that concerned about the volume of patients that he had. He was the one that made the transition from memorization to real-world application for you. Of course, at his age, he had seen everything, and he was willing to let you make your own mistakes and introduce new modalities. He was also always there to rein you in if you ventured too far afield.

As an adjunct professor, he spoke to your group a few times at grand rounds, and eventually you got the opportunity to shadow him at his office and at the hospital when he did deliveries. You bonded with him as a mentor and tried to do things like he did or as you imagined he would do. You called him all the time, and he was patient with you.

You had hoped that he might ask you to join his practice when you completed your residency, but he told you that he was just going to close his office if and when he ever retired. However, you reached an arrangement with him where you would cover for each other if one of you was sick or on vacation. Dr. Nathan encouraged you to go in with some younger doctors who would be more aggressive in trying to obtain patients and make fees. He had been right to give you that advice and your practice was doing well, even if you didn't enjoy so much the administrative side of things and you certainly didn't like the once a year "partnership" meetings where you divvied up profits and set goals for the next year.

You were upset the evening before when Dr. Nathan's office called and asked you to cover a delivery for him because of his stroke. You promised yourself that after you got home, and had a nap, you would call his wife so that you would be fresh and upbeat when you talked to her. From what little you had heard, it sounded bad, and you wondered if he would recover. You decide to call your office on the off chance that somebody would be there who might have heard more news about how Dr. Nathan was doing. You lean against the wall and dial the number on the speed dial. You are surprised when somebody answers.

"Trudy?" You ask. "What are you doing there this early on a Saturday morning?" You knew that if anybody was going to be there it would probably be Trudy. She was the best nurse in the group and worked harder than any of the doctors ever worked.

"I had some stuff to finish up from yesterday and I didn't want it to wait until Monday," she says.

"Has there been any more news about Dr. Nathan?"

"No. Nothing else. We did get the chart in on Dr. Nathan's patient that had the baby last night. How did that go?"

"Not well," you say. "I had to do an emergent C-section and it doesn't look like the baby is going to make it. The family is with the baby now."

"Oh God," Trudy says and you can hear her flipping through the chart while she is talking to you.

"I don't guess that there is anything in there that suggested the woman might be a candidate for a C-section, is there?" you ask, confident that there is not. You feel your heart start to race as Trudy is silent on the other end of the line. You feel like you do whenever a police car pulls you over for speeding. Only this is worse. Much worse. Your stomach rises up in your chest and your breathing quickens. The confidence then completely disappears. "Trudy, did I lose you?"

"No, I'm here. I'm sorry. I was just trying to read this note from one of the last office visits. It is difficult to make out. It's written in Dr. Nathan's handwriting and it looks like he had a discussion with the father. There is something about likely needing to do a C-section, but it is difficult to read. I guess that it's a good thing that you did one," Trudy says.

"I guess," you say, and think to ask her to read the entire entry to you because you are suddenly worried about getting sued—then you feel a sense of panic sweep over you. Wasn't everyone in that family a lawyer? But you think better of asking Trudy to read the entry to you, and you tell her goodbye. The chart says what it says and you never got a chance to read it for yourself before you were called in. You had told yourself some time ago that you weren't ever going to treat patients from the standpoint of worrying that you might get sued. That was Dr. Nathan's philosophy—no unnecessary tests or defensive practices. Just treat the patient and try to help her.

As you drop the phone back into your coat pocket, you wonder what it was that would have prompted Dr. Nathan to scribble the note in the chart. If only you had gotten a chance to see the chart before the patient showed up at the hospital. With all of the hi-tech gadgetry around, it seemed like there would be some means of instantly trans-mitting a patient's records to the doctor that had the responsibility for seeing a patient at any given point in time. Despite medical break-throughs and technological advances, too much of your job was still dependent upon chance and circumstance, and was reactive based on the most likely event and probable outcomes. While this specific situ-ation would probably never present itself again, you'd make sure that next time somebody in your office would see the chart before you saw the patient in the hospital, even if you had to send Trudy over to the other doctor's office to read the file.

"We are the solution to our problems," Dr. Nathan would have said—hopefully would say.

You thought about calling your husband again to tell him that you thought you might get sued. Instead you walk to the nurses' station and pour yourself a cup of coffee. He would just tell you not to worry about that and just plan for what you are going to have to do next. You know that you won't have to wait long. Waiting is all you can do right then.

27

WHILE SITTING AT THE nurses' station, you begin to contemplate the fact that it will be incumbent upon you to fill out the death certificate on the Jessie child. That's something you don't have to do often. You tell yourself that you're in the life business not the death business. You usually fill out birth certificates not death certificates. You're not even certain what information needs to go on the form. You think about getting the pediatric infectious disease guy to do it, but it looks like he has already gone home. You ask one of the nurses to pull you a form and you get yourself another cup of coffee. The coffee is not very good and you used to not even like coffee, but the warmth of it is comforting, and now you drink it all the time. You sip the coffee and stare at the form. It reminds you of a tax return.

The biographical information at the top of the page will be easy enough to ascertain. It's the middle section, listed as "Paragraph 33. Cause of Death," that has you concerned. The paragraph divides into two parts. In Part 1, the form tells you to "Enter the chain of events—diseases, injuries, or complications—that directly caused the death. Do not enter terminal events such as cardiac arrest, respiratory arrest, or ventricular fibrillation without showing the etiology." Then there are a series of blank lines ("a." through "d.") with words between the lines that read "due to" or "as a consequence of."

Beside the first blank line ("a."), the form tells you to list the "IMMEDIATE CAUSE (Final disease or condition resulting in death)." You assume that the words "respiratory arrest" will eventually go there. Then the other blank lines follow with the words "due to" or "as a consequence of" between them. You wonder what you should put there. How far down the chain of events are you supposed to go?

The form instructs you in the margin that as you fill in the blanks "Sequentially list conditions, if any, leading to the cause listed on line 'a.' Enter the UNDERLYING CAUSE (disease or injury that initiated the events resulting in death) LAST." You think about "(a) respiratory arrest; due to or as a consequence of (b) herpes viral infection; due to or as a consequence of (c) parental transmission; due to or as a consequence of lack of communication; due to or as a consequence of (d) shame and guilt." Should lack of communication come before shame and guilt? Should you handwrite in two more lines and add "(e) sexual transgression; due to or as a consequence of (f) isolation and loneliness"? Should "isolation" and "loneliness" each get a separate line?

In Part 2 of section 33, the form tells you to "Enter OTHER SIGNIFICANT CONDITIONS CONTRIBUTING TO DEATH BUT NOT RESULTING IN THE UNDERLYING CAUSE GIVEN IN PART 1." Obviously, that is where you discuss things like "loss of faith," "inadequate role models," "nihilism," "narcissism," and "inappropriate alcohol consumption."

After you finish the second cup of coffee and part of a third, you see the nurse assigned to the Jessie child signal to you with a slight raise of his head that it is time to go back to Michelle Jessie's room. You drop the incomplete form into the chart and place the folder under your arm. Sunlight is beginning to shine through the outside windows, but you can't help feeling a sense of gathering darkness as you start walking back down the hall. The male nurse pauses at the desk to look at some paperwork before following behind you.

Earlier you had been reminded of leaving the little clinic in Pasadena with your mother. Now, as you walk alone down the hall to the Jessie room, you are reminded of the two of you, you and your mother, going down the hall with a nurse to where the procedure would be performed. Now, years later, you would still not let yourself remember being in that room, although you recognize the fact that from time to time in your life you will still remember that walk with your mom and the nurse. Maybe you don't remember the room because your eyes had been clenched shut most of the time you were there, closing that particular box tightly shut. You tell yourself that you will come out on the other side; that you have come out on the other side.

For the longest time, even most of the way through college, you didn't realize that you were reliving that walk, but now you see it clearly and you have learned to recognize it each time it thrusts itself up to your consciousness. Usually, you can leave that hallway by focusing on the Jaybird and whatever he is doing or by asking your husband to explain the significance of some inane event that just happened in the world of sports.

Jaybird, of course, has no idea how he is helping you. He is just exploring his little world, playing with his toys on the floor, coloring in a book, or singing along with Barney on the television. Your husband seems to know, however, that you don't really care whom the Cowboys drafted or what position so-and-so plays, that you are really asking him to take your mind off of whatever it is that is haunting you. And he tries.

You are jealous of the fact that he can have such passion for something other than work. You laugh at his explanation that everyone in the stands wishes that they were out on the field and everyone on the field is trying to earn for themselves a "normal" life that will permit them to sit in the stands and enjoy a game.

You stop at the door to the patient's room and sit down in the plastic and metal chair outside to wait for the male nurse to join you. When you sit down, a man's jacket that has been hung over the back of the chair falls to the floor, and some hand written pages spill out of the breast pocket. You pick up the pages and try to put them back in order. As you do so, you start to read the pages. You have some difficulty making out the handwriting.

La Aguada

"I enjoy the shooting, but the killing is a bit much." She shouted loudly enough that she thought he could hear her.

She rested the slim, double-barreled 28-gauge on her hip. He removed his earplugs and looked at the dead, blue-grey "eared" dove littering the barren field around the water tank in front of them. They were each standing thirty yards from a fence corner which formed a right angle between them. Behind them were giant trees, which looked to her like eucalyptus, that followed the fence line in both directions.

He was shooting a rented, semi-automatic Beretta 20-gauge that held four shells, including the one in the chamber. He was firing rounds more than twice as fast as she was, but he doubted that he had killed as many doves as she had. She fired two more shots. She broke open the side-by-side. Two thin shells ejected. Her "bird boy" dropped two new shells into the barrels.

It had been a bureaucratic and costly ordeal to bring the 28-gauge with the straight English stock and splinter fore-arm into Argentina, but Angela had insisted upon it when she agreed to the trip. He had pointed out to her that the number of rounds they would be firing might add considerable wear to the weapon, but he didn't say anything about the costs of bringing the gun into the country or the increased costs of the 28-gauge shells. The purpose of the trip was diversion, and he did not want to upset Angela more than she already was. She pointed out that the practice with the gun would be worth whatever was involved in getting to use it. He had bought the gun, a Parker reproduction in a fitted leather case, as a baby gift, when they had first learned the sex of the baby and discussed "Parker," (Harry's mother's maiden name,) as a Christian name for the child. Angela and Harry had both laughed at Harry's baby gift, and Angela had commented that the boy would probably never grow up to like hunting because it was important to Harry. That seemed like a lifetime ago.

Another flight of birds streamed towards the tank across the dry field. Gracefully, Angela shouldered the gun and fired at a bird to her right and then to her left as if she were standing at the six spot on a skeet range. Two doves fell, one spinning in the helicopter fashion that indicated a head shot. She opened the gun for the bird boy to reload. "Bird boy" was not an appropriate title. Harry had been on dove hunting trips to Mexico where local boys did pick up the dead birds for the hunters to take home. Here the young men only picked up a few of the birds, some as appetizers for the asado lunch that the outfitter prepared in the field, and some for the fellow to take home to his family. "Reload boy" would be a better title Harry thought to himself.

Harry admired the coordinated ease with which his wife handled the little gun. His own arms were tired from raising and lowering the gun the outfitter had provided, though it had not seemed at all heavy three days earlier when they had started shooting. Now it felt like a heavy crossbeam. Despite the fact that the gas ejection of the spent shells absorbed much of the recoil, Harry's right shoulder was hurting enough that he caught himself firing the gun without actually bringing it all the way to his shoulder.

She was wearing a pair of slim, oatmeal-colored riding pants tucked into her green rubber boots; a blue chambray shirt with the sleeves rolled up to the elbows; a green bandana around her neck; and a wide-brimmed, western-style straw hat. It was the same outfit she wore whenever they went dove hunting in Texas. He, of course, had on two or three different forms of camouflage, none of which seemed to make any difference in the flight patterns of the dove.

She was still a beautiful woman, thin and athletic (she had lost most of the weight in the last ninety days), and he was proud of her and glad that she had taken up bird hunting when they had married so that they could do it together.

"You've got to admit," he responded, "you are pretty good at it." He put his earplugs back in and went back to firing four rounds in succession as fast as his bird boy could reload the gun.

She started to ask him if he was referring to the shooting or the killing, wondered if he had even heard what she said, and realized that he had already returned his attention to the birds. She watched as one of the half-dozen, large brown eagles that had perched in the towering trees behind her swooped down into the field, picked up a dove, and returned to the trees. There the eagle devoured the small bird sending feathers down like snowflakes.

After shooting into a few more waves of birds, she broke the little gun open, took the two live shells out of the barrels, rolled them around in her left hand, and then stuffed them into her pants pocket. She rested the gun over her left shoulder. To nobody in particular she said aloud, "Oh that I had wings like a dove! For then I would fly away, and be at rest."

"Madam?" her bird boy asked.

"Nothing Gustavo. Just a fragment of a psalm. That is all I remember. Just fragments. Are you religious?" It was probably the most she had said to him in three days and certainly the most personal thing she had asked.

"No *Senora*. I am not religious, *pero yo creo*."

She thought for a moment about how much more poetic "*pero yo creo*" sounded than "but I believe." The internal rhyme of the Spanish seemed to her more cultured than the jack-in-the-box alliteration of the English.

Trying to be conversational, Gustavo asked, "Have you memorized many passages from the Bible, *Senora*?"

"No, not many," she said, "The only other one I can remember right now is part of another psalm. 'As a snail which melteth, let every one of them pass away: like the untimely

birth of a woman, that they may not see the sun.' Not a very
happy thought that one."

"It is significant that you have committed so much to
memory, *Senora*," Gustavo said and smiled.

She smiled back at him and patted him on the back. "I
think that is enough for this evening," she said. Gustavo took
the shotgun from her, put it into a soft sleeve, and handed it
back to her. He began to clean up the area where they had
been standing, boxing up the unused shells, sheathing his ma-
chete, and picking up the spent hulls with a device made from
a sawed-off broom handle with a large round magnet on one
end.

"Will I see you tomorrow morning?" she asked.

Yes, *Senora*" he said. "Tomorrow is your last day to shoot?"

"I am afraid so. Just a half-day tomorrow," She said. "I
have certainly enjoyed the trip. You have been a great help
Gustavo."

"Do you want me to take your gun back to the van?" Gustavo asked. "It is no problem."

Usually the hunters, her husband included, left the shot-
guns with the bird boys, but she took hers in with her each
evening to the lodge. "No. I'll get it. Thank you," she said.
"That was a wonderful day."

"Can I get you something cold to drink, a beer perhaps?"
Gustavo asked, still picking up spent shells and putting
them in a nylon feed sack.

"No thank you. I will get a glass of wine when I get back
to the van," she said. She cradled the sleeved gun in her left
arm as she walked around the fence corner to where Harry
was positioned. She sat down on the stool behind where his
bird boy Daniel was standing. Harry continued to shoot,
and his bird boy continued to re-load Harry's shotgun.

After missing badly at a couple of birds that flew right
at him, Harry turned to his left and shot a high-flying bird

that was a considerable distance away. The bird folded and fell.

"What a shot," Angela said, and smiled.

"I wonder why I can't hit the ones coming directly to me," Harry said, also smiling.

"Too much time to think about them," she said. She watched Harry shoot at several more groups of birds and then stood. "I suppose you are going to shoot until dark?" she asked.

"Maybe another box or two," he said.

"I think I'll find my way back to the van. I'm pretty tired, but don't let me stop you. We came all the way to Argentina to do this."

When she had walked the few hundred yards to the van, the outfitter hopped out, came around to the passenger side, and opened the sliding door for her. "How was your afternoon?" he asked.

"Very nice, thank you. *Muchas palomas.*"

"*Si Senora. Muchas palomas en Jesus Maria.* You shoot very well with the little gun. Do you want me to take it for you?"

"No. I'll just keep it in the van here with me."

"Very good. Would you like something to drink?"

"If it is not too much trouble, I would like a glass of the Malbec we had at lunch."

"Of course, *Senora*," the outfitter said. He went to the small trailer behind the van, and after shuffling the contents around, returned with a wine glass and a corked bottle of Malbec. He handed her the glass, poured the Malbec, put the cork back in the bottle, and set the bottle on the floor of the van.

"Thank you very much," she said. "*Salud.*" She took a sip of the wine, put the shotgun on the middle seat of the van, and sat on the running board looking back to where she could see her husband continuing to shoot, reload, and shoot again. The outfitter went back to the driver's seat and turned the radio to a music station.

After a while, the outfitter climbed out of the van again and walked towards where Harry was standing. She had finished the glass and most of another before the shooting party returned to the van. The bird boys were carrying sacks of spent hulls, cases of unused shells, and stools. The outfitter carried the cased 20-gauge. Harry walked along behind them, drinking beer from a can. "Cheers," Harry said as he climbed into the front passenger seat of the van. Angela raised her wine glass and then climbed into the middle seat of the van. The bird boys loaded their materials into the trailer, and then got into the backseat of the van.

"How was it?" she asked.

"The birds just kept coming. I shot a case and a half. My right arm is about to fall off," Harry said. The outfitter took his place in the driver's seat, started the van, and drove out of the field and onto the two-lane country road. The outfitter sang along with the music from the radio on the thirty-kilometer trip back to the lodge.

At La Aguada, the proprietor's adult son, Oscar, greeted the van, opened the sliding passenger door, and offered to assist Angela out. He walked with Harry and Angela across the manicured courtyard divided by a small stream to the couple's room in one of the white, stucco buildings with a red-tiled roof. At the door to the room, Harry asked the proprietor's son what they would be having for dinner.

"Steaks, *senor*. Beautiful filets." Oscar said.

"Great," said Harry. "With chimichurri?"

"Of course."

"And Malbec?" Angela asked.

"Of course, *Senora*. Would you like for me to clean your shotgun? I will be very careful with it and put it back in your room when I am finished."

"Excellent. Thank you, Oscar," Angela said and handed him the sleeved shotgun. It was a ritual they had practiced each evening of the trip.

"Will eight o'clock be okay for dinner?" the proprietor's son asked.

"See you then," Harry said, and he and his wife went into their room.

Harry sat on the corner of the large bed and began taking off his boots.

"I'm going to take a hot shower," Angela said as she began taking off her clothes and folding them over a chair in the corner of the room. She took the two live shells out of the front pocket of her pants and put them on the nightstand next to her side of the bed.

"Sounds good," Harry said and laid back across the foot of the bed. He stared at the pitched ceiling made of paver-like tiles set on wooden beams. He closed his eyes and was almost asleep when Angela came out of the bathroom wearing a towel.

"That felt good," she said.

Harry groaned as he got up from the bed and started to strip off his clothes. He leaned over to kiss Angela as she walked by him toward the heavy armoire where her clean clothes were stored. She pulled away from him. "You need a shower," she said. He finished underdressing, leaving his clothes in a pile on the floor, and went into the bathroom.

At dinner they sat across from each other at the long, wooden dining table in the dining room in the main house. They were the only hunters at the lodge, but La Aguada had a full staff of white-jacketed, white-gloved waiters and a captain hurried about with wine and water to fill the couple's glasses. The food came in courses: a simple salad with lettuce and tomatoes dressed with olive oil and vinegar, a grilled steak marinated in chimichurri, boiled potatoes, and a flan with thick caramel for dessert. With each course, the waiters removed the plates and disappeared into the kitchen through a swinging door at the end of the dining room.

"Have you ever thought about a place having a particular flavor?" she asked.

"What do you mean?" he responded, recognizing that it was about the only thing she had said during dinner and that she was trying to make conversation. He assumed that this was some parlor game she had read about on how to get a conversation started.

"Well," she said, "when you think of Texas what flavor do you think of?"

He dabbed at the corners of his mouth with the cloth napkin and placed it on the table. "You mean like jalapenos?"

"Sure," she said, glad that he had at least tried to join her attempt at conversation. "But a lot of places serve jalapenos. I think Texas tastes like that smoky bark on the edge of a brisket."

"Yeah," he said. "Sometimes it's almost like creosote, but sometimes it's just right. So that is what you think Texas tastes like? I'm not sure you can minimize each region or state to just one food. How would you say France or Italy or Louisiana tastes? You know, some place that is famous for food?"

"Different places may be famous for multiple dishes, but there is usually one signature flavor that you find in most of the authentic dishes."

He laughed, curious at how her mind worked and almost proud of how much more observant she was than he. True, he did like the ends of a brisket that many people just threw away, but he had never thought about that being the ideal flavor of his native state.

"France tastes like French butter," she said. "It's the kind you find on every table in every restaurant, whether it has Michelin stars or is just the local brasserie. Italy tastes like tomatoes. Not like the ones we get back home at the grocery store. I mean real tomatoes."

"Louisiana is something spicy, I guess?"

"No, Louisiana is soft and rich like rainwater." When he paused and did not respond, she took her spoon and dipped it into the top of her flan. "This is what Argentina tastes like."

"Not the grass-fed beef or the Malbec?" he asked.

"It's the caramel." She reached over to the small, white pot that contained caramel. It sat as a condiment next to the salt and pepper shakers. She took the top off the porcelain container and held it to her nose. "Argentina may be famous for its beef and Malbec, but it's the taste of caramel found in both that makes them distinctive. Smooth. Not too sweet. Almost creamy."

The captain smiled and made sure that the couples' wine glasses were full.

After the dessert, the captain took a crumber from the chest pocket of his jacket, swept the tablecloth of any crumbs, and asked the couple if they would like an after-dinner drink. Harry ordered a brandy and Angela had another glass of Malbec. When the drinks were served, the staff left the room, and the captain stood off to one side.

"Let's take these into the other room," Harry said, and picked up his drink. Angela followed him with her glass of wine into the den off the dining room. A small fire was burning the in the fireplace. They sat down beside each other on the brown leather couch.

Other than commenting on regional foods and complimenting the captain, they had hardly spoken before sitting on the couch.

"Can you believe we leave tomorrow afternoon? Harry asked.

"No," Angela responded. "The week has flown by. This was a good idea. I'm dreading the long flight back. I guess we could stay a few more days. They don't seem to be booked up."

"We could, if you like," he said.

She sipped her wine and thought about it for a moment. "I guess we have to go back eventually." She said. "I'd just be putting off going back. Let's just shoot in the morning like we'd planned and then start back tomorrow afternoon. We still need to get from Córdoba to Buenos Aires. We can sleep on the plane out of Buenos Aires."

"Whatever you want." He said.

"I think I'm ready," she said. "As ready as I'm going to be. This was a good idea. Thank you for putting it together on such short notice." She leaned over and kissed him on the cheek.

"I didn't have to do much. My secretary did all the planning and reservations once I told her where we were going. It was all laid out on the website. I'd certainly come back. The hunting is incredible. There are a lot more birds in Argentina than I have ever seen in Mexico. And imagine shooting twenty or thirty boxes of shells in an afternoon back in Texas?"

"There would not be anything to shoot twenty boxes at," she said. "We will have to come back."

"Yes," he said. "For different reasons though. But we will have to come back."

"There will not be that reason again. I don't think I can go through that again."

He recognized that now was the first time that Angela seemed willing to talk about what she had been through. He recognized that now would be a good time to talk about it.

"Some time I want to take that train trip out of Pretoria where you get off and shoot different kinds of birds. It's supposed to be a first-class deal. The train cars look really nice in the pictures."

She sighed and set her empty wine glass down on the coffee table. She put her hands behind her head and leaned back against the couch.

Harry didn't say anything for a moment. "We don't have to go to Africa any time soon. It's just an idea. We'll do whatever you want. We could go shoot driven grouse in Scotland or red-legged partridge in Spain. You may need to take a little more gun."

She stood up from the couch. "Africa would be nice." She said flatly. "I would love to see Africa someday."

"We'll go someday," he said. "I think the shooting would be fun."

"We don't have to go right away, Harry. Let's see. I'm tired. I think I'm going to go to bed now. Finish your brandy. I'll see you in the room." She combed her fingers through his hair as she walked behind the couch. After she left the room, he rested his head on the arm of the couch and his glass on his chest. He sipped his drink, then lightly set the glass back on his chest.

In the room, Angela got her nightgown out of the bureau, placed it on the bed, and began taking off her clothes which she then hung neatly in the armoire. She checked to see that the sleeved shotgun was propped in the corner of the room. She slipped the nightgown over her head, turned the overhead light off at the wall, and walked over to get into bed. But before doing so, she stopped, turned on the bedside light, pulled the nightgown off over her head, folded it, and put it back in the bureau.

Naked, she crawled into bed, leaving on the dim, bedside light. She picked up the two shotgun shells form the bedside table, rolled the shells in her left hand, and stared at the heavy ceiling.

Back in the lodge, with his brandy and the fire, Harry closed his eyes, and, though he intended to rest them only for a moment, he drifted off to sleep.

When he was sure the young man was asleep, the captain took the wool throw from the upholstered chair across from the couch and draped the blanket over the young man's legs. Delicately, so as not to disturb the young man's slumber, the captain took the brandy glass from the young man's hands. The captain paused at the wall to turn off the chandelier in the den, walked across the dining room (smoothing the tablecloth with his free hand and putting the lid back on the little caramel pot), and went through the swinging door into the kitchen.

You close your eyes and lean back in the chair after you read the story, gripping the pages in both hands at your lap. You question whether you should have read the pages. You recognize the sadness and hopelessness of the two main characters in the story. You wonder about their loss of the ability to enjoy the things they obviously once enjoyed, their isolation, their feelings of worthlessness, and their inability to communicate with each other. You wonder what the mention of the two live shotgun shells was all about. Was the story finished? You think about how you would finish it.

You wonder about the author, whom you assume was the young man you left in the hospital room with his wife and baby. Was he recognizing that he and his wife were unable to discuss the things in life that mattered and was trying to capture that loss in his story? One thing was clear. The author was not as innocent as the young lawyer in the room with his wife and their dying child appeared to be. In a way, his story (which you decide had to have been written before tonight) seemed to presage the events that had unfolded here. You fold the pages up and return them to the breast pocket of the jacket that you hang over the back of the chair.

The male nurse walks up and pauses. You stand and you loop your arm in the nurse's arm just as you had looped your arm into your mother's back when. The male nurse seems grateful for the gesture and you feel him sigh and lean his shoulder against yours. You wonder for a moment what experience he has had in his life that he relives at times like this. Maybe he has been to a room like this one to see a family member of his that wasn't going to make it. Maybe he just remembers similar occasions with other patients. You tell yourself that it's a sign of your improving mental health that you can consider what others around you are going through and not just think about your own life experiences.

The two of you pause at the door to the room, each of you taking a deep breath. He looks at you and you nod, and you wait for the nurse to knock gently on the door and go inside. You follow him over to the bed.

28

MICHELLE'S ROOM, LIKE THE HOSPITAL lobby, reminded me more of a hotel than a hospital. There were dark wooden cabinets, upholstered wingback chairs, and an Impressionistic painting of a field of flowers above the bed. Early morning light was coming through the window, and a standing lamp illuminated one corner of the room. There was no noise at all in the room.

Michelle was in the bed. If the family in front of the glass in the hallway I had just left had most of the life drained out of them, it seemed Michelle had been wrung like a washrag until every ounce of life had been wrenched from her. Exhausted but beautiful, she was reclining against a stack of clean, white pillows.

For the first time since I had met her, I couldn't tell what Michelle was thinking by just looking at her face. In the past her expression told you exactly what was going on with her, and how she felt about what was happening around her. She had been incapable of artifice or guile. But beyond the physical depletion of the last few hours and the grogginess she still felt from the surgery, Michelle's affect had changed. I had known, though I had never articulated the thought even to myself, that my deception would have a profound effect on how Michelle would see the world. I could tell just by looking at her as she lay in the hospital bed that she was now less able to trust, less inclined to love.

I didn't know where to stand or sit, and I couldn't force myself to speak. I wanted to rush to her and to bury my head next to her in the pillows until this all went away, but I just stood there by her hospital bed waiting numbly to see what was going to happen next.

The door opened and the attendant who had been standing over our child in the NICU incubator walked in carrying our baby. His concealed running shoes squeaked on the tile floor as he walked in. He held the baby in his left arm as he caught the door with his right hand so that it closed gently behind Dr. Godsman who came into the room behind him.

Paul was tightly wrapped in a cocoon of blankets, and his head was now covered by the smallest stocking cap I had ever seen. The man walked directly across the room to Michelle, without hesitating or speaking, and placed the infant in the crook of her arm. As Michelle made sure that she had a comfortable hold on the baby, the man adjusted the pillows behind Michelle, and said in the most gentle voice that I had ever heard, "He's breathing on his own right now. I don't know how long he'll be with us. Dr. Godsman and I will be available by this button here, if . . . when . . . you need us." He turned to look at me and then the doctor, and then the two of them started to leave the room.

"Doctor, there is one thing," Michelle said.

"What is that?" Dr. Godsman asked softly and walked back over to the bed.

"It's my breasts. I know I'm probably on some kind of pain medicine, but my breasts are really starting to hurt."

"After a while, I can give you something to help you stop lactating. But for now we should massage the breasts gently and then let you try to nurse the baby," Dr. Godsman said.

"Would you do that?" Michelle asked.

"Actually, Luke here is the best at the massage. All our new mothers think so." Dr. Godsman took the baby from Michelle, and the male nurse walked back over to the bed. He pulled back the covers, untied Michelle's gown from around her neck, and with his fingers tried to release delicately the knots that were developing in Michelle's breasts. At first the massaging appeared to be painful, but after a moment a soothed, relaxed look came over Michelle's face.

"Would you like to try nursing the baby now?" Dr. Godsman asked.

Michelle nodded and Dr. Godsman nestled baby Paul to her right breast. "A little lower fellow," Michelle said and adjusted her breast with her left hand. For a brief instant, he tried to nurse but then stopped.

"He is probably just too tired," Dr. Godsman said. "He has had a long night also." She helped Michelle with her gown and repositioned the baby. The doctor and nurse then looked at each other and left the room.

I walked over and sat down on the bed next to Michelle and Paul. The dimly lit room was perfectly still. I touched his face with my hand. Both Michelle and I smiled at each other before tears began to flow down each of our faces. "I'm so sorry," I whispered between tears.

"I know, Davy. I know," she said and nodded. Her voice told me that she was too tired for apologies or long explanations about what had happened. She kissed Paul gently on the top of his little stocking cap and shut her eyes tightly to stop the flow of tears.

"I don't know how I ever let things get this messed up," I said. "I never meant to hurt you or the baby. I've ruined everything. I'm sorry, I'm sorry, I'm sorry."

"I know, Davy. I know."

And then, it just came flooding out of me. The words, pressed down inside of me by the weight of my guilt, escaped like they had a life of their own and needed to be in the open air to breathe.

"I just couldn't tell you. I couldn't admit it to myself. I had an affair. I got a venereal disease. I was afraid that I gave it to you, to the baby. I didn't want you to see me like that kind of person, like the kind of person that would cheat on his wife or lie to her about what he was doing. I know it sounds unbelievable now, but I just couldn't talk to you about it. I was afraid. I was afraid to tell you. I was afraid of what might happen. I'm so tired of carrying around all these secrets. I've got to get rid of them, get them off of me, out of me. I can't carry them anymore. I feel so guilty and horrible. I just want to feel good. I need this all out of me and over. I wish I could save him, Michelle. I'd do anything to save him for you, Michelle. I'd trade my life for his, Michelle, but I can't. I can't fix this. I can't fix this. I've destroyed us and ruined our lives, and our baby's life, and I can't fix this. I've practiced and practiced at controlling everything and every situation, and making sure it all comes out the way I want it to come out every time, but I can't this time. I don't know what to do. I don't know what to say. There is nothing I can do. There is nothing the doctors can do. There is nothing I can say that is going to make this any better. I'm sorry, Michelle. I am so sorry. I wanted everything to be perfect for us: the perfect house, the perfect cars, the perfect baby, the perfect life. And now, I've fucked it all up so badly, it can never be straightened out."

I took a deep breath and let it out before beginning again. "I got so caught up in the success part, the money, the power, and the prestige, the trappings of success that I lost sight of us, of what was important, of what it was I really wanted or needed. Trappings of success. It is a trap. It is all a trap. I'm so sorry, Michelle. I wish I could—we could—go back to law school. I wish we were back in law school, sitting on that gold couch in your apartment, pretending to be studying, worried about tests, thinking we were under a lot of pressure. There was no pressure. That was just pretend. Our lives stretched out before us, and we could do anything. I felt like I could do anything. I felt like you thought I could do anything.

"It was all so clean and perfect, and there was no guilt and no shame, and it was all about us and what good things we were going to do. Not about what money we were going to make, or making partner, or moving into West University so that we could move into River Oaks. It was about doing something that might actually help somebody. At least, I thought it was. Somewhere, that focus shifted to helping me. Me helping me. My home, my wife, my law practice. Mine. Mine. Mine. I deserve this. I work hard. This is good for me. Look at me. Watch me. I can win this case. I can make these facts. I can control this situation to my advantage. I can take what I want when I want, as long as it's good for me in the end. But, it's just a trap, Michelle. I can't control anything. I can't fix anything. I'm so sorry, Michelle. I am so sorry."

With her free hand, Michelle wiped the tears from her eyes. "Davy, I knew everything wasn't right. We haven't had sex in months. We never talk. We rarely sleep together in the same bed. You rarely sleep, period. Usually, just until the scotch wears off, and then you're up and showered and off to work or God knows where. I could see you becoming just like my dad. I guess you thought that was what I wanted. But that isn't what I wanted. I may not have been perfect, but I didn't deserve this, Davy."

She was right, of course. Nobody deserved this—alone, with a dying baby, in an eerily still tomb of a hospital room, trying to sort out what had gone wrong before the child passes away, because after he's gone, you know that you will never be able to talk to each other again in a meaningful way. Neither of us had said it, but I didn't see how there would ever be any life for us, for Michelle and me together, after Paul was gone.

That was the very moment I saw God.

"Oh, sure," you're saying, "God appeared and raised the baby from the dead, like Lazarus, another first born son if I'm remembering my Bible stories correctly."

No, God didn't appear as a beam of light streaming through the morning window or as an angelic doctor that rushed into the room with a miracle cure for an incurable disease or as a gossamer apparition induced by an alcohol haze.

Our baby was dying, indeed did die in the few minutes that we got to hold him there in Michelle's bed in the Dunn Tower at Methodist Hospital in Houston, Texas. And truthfully, I didn't really *see* God. I just got a glimpse of Him.

At the time I didn't even know I had seen Him. It was like when you're quail hunting with your dad and little brother and you're walking with the sun at your back. You're watching the field in front of you and trying to keep up with where the dog is and looking for quail at the same time because you don't really have any confidence in the dog who for ten months out of the year is just a family pet.

The rolling, late-autumn hillside is covered in a low, coarse, Harris tweed of greens (celadon clump grasses, hunter cedar bushes, grey prickly pear, and olive mesquite trees); flecks of burgundies (red clays, cordovan post oaks, flame leaf sumac, and wine-colored cactus apples); streaks of gold (patches of yellow broom weed, outcroppings of egg-shell caliche, and bronze sandstone washed in amber, afternoon sun-light); and purples (no longer blue but not yet black shadows of cactus, yucca, live oak motts, and mesquite thickets). And you see another shadow move silently across the field. A hawk is flying somewhere be-hind you. You don't look back at the hawk, but you know he is there. Or you hear the call of sandhill cranes that are flying so high and so far out of sight that you can't see them, but you know they are there.

As I reflect on what transpired in that hospital room, I am sure that I saw a shadow or heard an echo of Him.

I keep saying Him with a capital "H." I don't know if It's a Him or a Her, if It's Catholic or Protestant, or Jew or Gentile, or Muslim or Bud-dhist. I don't know if He or She or It or Whatever prefers Abilene over Lubbock or Austin over Houston. He may like Kentucky, for all I know (though I saw little evidence of His presence there).

But when Michelle turned to Paul and said, "Paul, your dad and that gold couch with the acanthus leaves . . . the stories we could tell you," I laughed out loud from somewhere so deep within me that I knew something miraculous was possible. It wasn't that Michelle had for-given me. She hadn't. I didn't know if she ever would, and I didn't know that I could her ever expect her to forgive me. But I saw for the first time, in Michelle's attempt at humor with our dying son, that the ca-pacity for forgiveness exists in the world. And forgiveness, even the opportunity for forgiveness, if you haven't already figured it out on your own, is an expression of love. And God is love.

That is what I always say, Podzy.

We talked to Paul about who we were and how we had gotten to this horrible point in our lives; and we told him in hushed tones things that we loved about each other, and that we disliked about each other; and we told him how we had such great plans for him as he grew up, and that now we knew we weren't going to get that chance, and that we were grateful to have the chance to talk to him at all. He lay there, lis-tening quietly. When he stopped breathing, I couldn't say. Then when we noticed it, Michelle looked at the button above the bed, and I pressed it to signal to the doctor to come back into the room.

The attendant and Dr. Godsman both came in quickly after I pressed the button, as if they had been waiting outside the door. The attendant took Paul from Michelle and left the room. The doctor paused by the bed, and asked Michelle if she would like something to help her sleep for a little while.

"Yes, I'd like that," Michelle said. She squeezed my hand as I got up from the bed to leave the room. "What are you going to do now, Davy?" she asked, sincerely concerned about where I was headed.

"I don't know," I said, and shrugged my shoulders. "I think I need to get something to eat. I don't think that I've eaten in days." I knew that it sounded odd to think about eating at a time like that, but I knew there was nothing that I could say or do that would bring our son back. I guessed that if I ever saw Paul again, it was just another thing I would have to try to explain.

Michelle nodded.

The doctor filled a syringe from a vial, swabbed alcohol on Michelle's arm with a cotton ball, and gave her an injection. I waited by the bedside until Michelle fell asleep.

When I went through the double doors into the lobby in front of the NICU, only my parents were still standing there. I wondered what had become of the other babies that had been behind the window in NICU and whether their families were now with them in private rooms playing out the quiet, final scenes of brief lives or whether the infants had improved and been moved to the general maternity rooms. Apparently the doctor had already come out and told my family that the baby, our baby, had passed away.

Dad told me what was happening with the others while Mom gave me a hug. Tim had left to go see about making funeral arrangements. Jonathan had taken his mom and William home to the house in River Oaks. Rod and his wife had left, and Rod had said that he would take care of notifying the office about what had transpired that night. I thought to myself for a moment that I was glad Rod had taken the job because he would be as sympathetic as possible, and whatever was told to the office would be told to the entire Harris County legal community in a matter of hours.

Of course, with each retelling of the story, it would change. By the time it got to Kentucky, some people would hear that it was Beth in the delivery room. At the same time, I thought to myself, I didn't really care what Rod told the office or anyone else. I didn't see how things could get any worse than they were. Dad told me what was happening with the others while Mom gave me a hug.

"What are y'all going to do now?" I asked. We stood there looking at each other for a moment while Dad thought about what he should do next.

"I don't know," he finally said shrugging his shoulders and looking at Mom for suggestions. "I guess we need to get a hotel room."

Mom nodded her agreement.

"Why don't you just come to the house?" I said. "That's where I'm headed. Michelle is sleeping. I'll come back and check on her in a little while. I might try to take a nap myself."

My dad nodded, and we headed off down the hall toward the elevator. On the way we passed by the series of rooms where 624 was located. For the first time, I noticed that different rooms had pink or blue balloons floating from the door handles. I imagined the happy scenes inside each room as we walked by. There was no balloon on the door handle of room 624.

"Was it like this when I was born?" I asked. "Balloons on the doors?"

"No," Mom said softly. "Your dad had to wait in a waiting room until you were delivered, and you and I were back in a regular hospital room. Now the deliveries take place in the room with the father there. There also have been many changes in hospitals since you were born. This place looks more like a hotel than a hospital to me." I thought to myself that hanging Impressionist paintings, setting plush leather wingbacks around, and piping in Beatles' music might change the sterile appearance of a place, even though it's still a hospital where life, disease, and death converge on a daily basis. The elevator door opened, and we stepped inside.

"I almost forgot," Dad said, as I tried to figure out which elevator button to push. "This came to you at our house in Abilene." He handed me the crumpled envelope he had been carrying since I had first seen him in the chapel. "It looks like it has something to do with medicine."

The envelope was addressed to me at my parents' home in Abilene. The return address was from Dr. Mock in Lexington, Kentucky.

"Thanks, Dad," I said. "I'll open it later."

We were standing in front of the hospital under a porte cochère, and the valet brought my parents' pickup around first after Dad and I gave him both of our tickets. Mercifully, Mom had put on her sunglasses that fit over her eyeglasses so that we couldn't see her eyes. I gave Dad a door key and an automatic opener to the wrought iron gate that enclosed the driveway at the house in West University. "I'd ask you what you're going to do now, but I imagine that you're asking yourself that same question." Dad said.

"In fact, it had occurred to me to ask you what I should do." I said.

He smiled. "I'm happy to talk to you about it, though, honestly, I don't know what you should do next. You'll figure it out. You've always been good at figuring things out on your own. You probably don't believe that right now. But you have been." He handed a dollar he found in his pants pocket to the valet who rejected it with a wave of his hand, opened the passenger door for Mom, and we slowly walked around to the driver's side of the car.

"You know that your mom and I have always been proud of you and we always will be. I think trying to get a little sleep sounds like a good start. I'll bet that you'll want to be back up here before too long." He paused for a second before getting into the truck. I was standing beside his open door. "I know this isn't a baseball game. It isn't a game at all," Dad said calmly shaking his head from side to side.

"What if it was a baseball game? What would you tell me to do next?" I asked.

"I'd tell you to do the next right thing as correctly as you know how. If you're at the plate and the count is '3 and 0,' you take the next pitch. If it is '0 and 2,' the next pitch is probably not going to be anywhere near the plate so you better make sure it's good before you swing. Doing the right thing only improves your chances. It's not a guarantee of success. The trouble is that I can't tell you what the next right thing to do is," he said slowly shaking his head again. "That's what you have to figure out."

I nodded and he shrugged his shoulders and started the engine. I closed his door and Dad eased the pickup away from the hospital.

I watched as they drove off, and then I opened the envelope. Dr. Mock addressed his letter to me, and referenced the *Henderson* case. I scanned it quickly searching for the salient points. After discussing his education, work history, and the materials he had reviewed in the case, he wrote the following:

> Based on this report and findings of carcinoma, bilateral simple mastectomy was performed on 9-11-04. No cancer was found in either breast. On 10-14-04, the 8-22-04 biopsy slides that had originally been read by Dr. Valdez were submitted to the University of Texas MD Anderson Cancer Center in Houston, Texas . . . those pathologists reported atypical cells and fibrous reactive tissues, no carcinoma. I independently examined the slides from the 8-22-04 biopsy, and I found . . . no carcinoma.
>
> In my opinion, Dr. Valdez failed to use the ordinary care required of a reasonable and prudent pathologist in reading the pathology slides . . . and that such professional negligence resulted in improper diagnosis and the resulting unwarranted double mastectomy . . .
>
> Such negligence caused great harm to Ms. Henderson, including unnecessary surgery of double mastectomy . . . pain and suffering . . . disfigurement . . . unnecessary medical expenses . . . including reconstructive surgery.
>
> Thank you for the privilege of consulting with me in this very interesting case.
>
> Very truly yours,
> Larry Mock, MD

I finished reading the report, and stuffed it back into the FedEx envelope. When my car arrived, I opened the passenger door and threw the envelope onto the front seat. Then I got the box with the infant car seat out of the back and set it on the curb. I walked around the car. Before I got into the driver's seat, I asked the valet to see that somebody that needed a car seat got the one in the box, and he said that he would. I pressed the button to put the top down and waited for it to retract automatically before I pulled away.

It was a damp morning and it would be a few hours before the sun became too hot to leave the top down. When I looked back in my rearview mirror, the box with the little blue bow on top was still sitting on the curb, and the valet had gone off to get somebody else's car.

After I had shifted through the gears, I picked up the cell phone. I dialed information, and asked for the number for Dr. and Mrs. Jean Henderson on River Oaks Boulevard. The cellular phone service connected me to the number. After several rings, Mrs. Henderson answered the phone.

"Hello," she said. Her voice sounded like I might have woken her.

"Hello Mrs. Henderson. This is David Jessie."

"Yes, Mr. Jessie. How are you?" She asked, her voice warming as she recognized who it was that was calling.

"I'm . . . I'm okay I guess. How are you?"

"Fine I suppose. I haven't had my first cup of coffee yet so it's too early to tell."

"I apologize for calling you from the car and for calling so early in the morning. I wanted to tell you I just read the report that our pathologist has prepared in your case. You remember that this is the report I explained to you we would need in order to go forward with a medical malpractice case on your behalf?"

"Yes, I understand," she said. "What does it say?"

"Honestly, it's both good news and bad news, Mrs. Henderson. The good news is that you appear to have a very good case. The cellular changes that the defendant pathologist observed on the biopsy were the result of the previous radiation therapy you underwent. Obviously, that is also good news, as the cancer did not reoccur. The bad news is that there was no medical reason for removing your breasts."

I could hear Mrs. Henderson start to cry softly on the other end of the call. I waited for a moment to see if she was going to say anything.

"Are you okay, Mrs. Henderson?"

"Yes," she said, as she tried to cover up her voice cracking.

"I'm sorry that you also had to go through this second cancer scare, Mrs. Henderson."

"It's not that," she said and paused again. "I've personally already come to terms with that. Dr. Valdez and his pathology group are pretty well known in this town. I didn't know if anybody would be willing to help me stand up to them."

"I understand," I said. And maybe, for the first time since I had been practicing personal injury trial law, I did understand. She needed to know that someone, anyone, was on her side, whatever the odds and whatever the outcome. It doesn't matter whether you live on River Oaks Boulevard or deep in the Fifth Ward, sometimes you just need to know that somebody is on your side.

I had not given much thought about Dr. Valdez' reputation or how highly respected his pathology group might have been in Houston. His was just a name on what I anticipated would be a large insurance policy. Despite the fact that tort reform (Sullivan always called it "tort de-form") legislation had made it virtually impossible for a plaintiff to win a medical malpractice case in Texas, I had a clean plaintiff, an injury with which a jury could sympathize, and a qualified expert. I liked our chances. I didn't know if the case was good enough to stake a career upon, but I didn't have any alternatives.

"Mrs. Henderson?" I asked. "If you need to reach me in the next few weeks, you should probably call this number. I'm going to take off a few days. And then, I'm going to look for office space in Austin. I'm going to be setting up my own law office there."

"Oh, Dr. Henderson and I love Austin. We were there as undergraduates. We've always talked about moving back there. I'm jealous. Why is it that we all want to move back to the town where we went to college?"

"I don't know," I said. I started to tell her that I thought it had something to do with how we perceived God at different stages in our lives, and then thought better of it.

"You will be able to continue to work on my case, won't you?"

"Yes, of course. In fact, it may seem to you that the only case I'm working on will be yours. Because, it will be."

"That's fine with me. We make a pretty good team, don't you think? You're a good, young lawyer. You'll do just fine. I'm sure there will be other cases eventually, Mr. Jessie."

I hoped that she was right. Not only would I need the income, but I looked forward to getting back into the courtroom and watching trials unfold. I told myself that I was in my element in the courtroom where I had some chance at controlling what might happen. It was out in the real world where I was lost.

I drove down Fannin, and turned west on University, passing under the crossover between the Dunn Tower and the Smith Tower. Though it was mid-September, the morning was already turning hot and humid, but University was shaded by the ancient oaks that lined the boulevard on both sides. Just past Rice University and the Rice Village shopping center, I crossed Kirby and entered West University.

When I pulled up to my house, I parked on the street rather than in the driveway. My dad's car was pulled far enough up the driveway for me to park inside the automatic wrought-iron gate, but I wanted to go up the steps to the front door. It really was a nice little house, though, admittedly, we had paid too much for it. I figured there would be somebody else, some other young professional couple, who would be willing to make the same mistake.

When the builder sold us the house, he had done some minimal landscaping in the front and planted a small patch of St. Augustine grass in the back. There was not much yard to work with, really. The house took up almost the entire lot.

Michelle had hired some workers to enlarge the flowerbeds that symmetrically framed the front of the house by pulling the beds out toward the street. She had planted small, ornamental trees at the corners of the house, and filled the beds with alternating red and white begonias that complemented the painted brick on the house and continued to bloom this late in the year. Two large, terra-cotta pots of red and white impatiens framed the front door, and a purple blooming wisteria vine had been trained along a wire hidden over the arched entryway.

Each spring, white narcissus bloomed in the beds along each side of the sidewalk that went from the front porch down to the street, while at this time of year only their olive-colored leaves sprouted in bunches along the walkway. Except for the small, climbing jasmine plants that Michelle had planted along the back fence, we had left the backyard alone until kids came along.

As I put the key in the door, I thought to myself that it felt like I was going into somebody else's house and not my own. To my right would be the formal dining room where we hardly ever ate unless Michelle's parents were there for dinner. To my left there would be a formal living room where nobody ever sat, much less "lived." In front of me would be the oak stairs with the painted, white risers that led to the bedrooms, including the master bedroom and a small room next to that with a custom-made, ark-shaped baby bed for Paul.

The house didn't have the familiar feel to me that it had even the day before when I had picked up Michelle to take her to the hospital. I wondered how long it would be before I would go into a place and feel like it was not some place new and unknown to me, and instead was my home and a place where I felt like I belonged.

ACKNOWLEDGMENTS

Thank you to my family and friends who provided support and suggestions through the writing process. I have frequently turned to the following works for insight and guidance: Kenneth C. Davis, *Don't Know Much About the Bible* (1998); Brian Greene, *The Elegant Universe* (2003); Norman Mailer with Michael Lennon, *On God* (2007); David Plotz, *Good Book* (2009); and Alan Light, *The Holy or The Broken* (2012).

ABOUT THE AUTHOR

PRICE AINSWORTH is a trial lawyer in Austin, Texas. A graduate of Texas Tech University (summa cum laude 1981) and The University of Texas School of Law (1984), he has been practicing law for more than thirty years. He primarily represents personal injury clients and has been Board Certified in personal injury trial law by the Texas Board of Legal Specialization since 1991. He has been consistently recognized as a "Super Lawyer" by *Texas Monthly Magazine* beginning in 2003, and Mr. Ainsworth is an Advocate in the American Board of Trial Advocates.

While he has coauthored numerous law journal articles and frequently presents papers at continuing legal education conferences, *A Minor Fall* is his first foray into published fiction. He and his wife of twenty-seven years have two handsome, intelligent adult sons that visit them on occasion and an old bird dog whose eyesight is fading but whose nose is still strong enough to find her food bowl.